VOLUME FOUR: HIGH FANTASIES

Shadowline®

image

FIRST PRINTING: OCTOBER 2017

ISBN: 978-1-63215-89

4

KURTIS J. WIEBE
story

OWEN GIENI
art, colors,
covers (unless
otherwise noted)

RYAN FERRIER
letters

TIM DANIEL
cover design

COLLEEN DORAN

JIM VALENTINO and
CHANCE WOLF

JONATHAN HICKMAN

KERRIE FULKER and
LEIGH HYLAND
alternative covers

IMAGE COMICS, INC.
Robert Kirkman—Chief Operating Officer
Erik Larsen—Chief Financial Officer
Todd McFarlane—President
Marc Silvestri—Chief Executive Officer
Jim Valentino—Vice President

Eric Stephenson—Publisher
Corey Murphy—Director of Sales
Jeff Boison—Director of Publishing Planning & Book Trade Sales
Chris Ross—Director of Digital Sales
Jeff Stang—Director of Specialty Sales
Kat Salazar—Director of PR & Marketing
Branwyn Bigglestone—Controller
Kat Salazar—Director of PR & Marketing
Sue Korpela—Accounting & HR Manager
Drew Gill—Art Director
Heather Doornink—Production Director
Leigh Thomas—Print Manager
Tricia Ramos—Traffic Manager
Briah Skelly—Publicist
Aly Hoffman—Events & Conventions Coordinator
Sasha Head—Sales & Marketing Production Designer
David Brothers—Branding Manager
Melissa Gifford—Content Manager
Drew Fitzgerald—Publicity Assistant
Vincent Kukua—Production Artist
Erika Schnatz—Production Artist
Ryan Brewer—Production Artist
Shanna Matuszak—Production Artist
Carey Hall—Production Artist
Esther Kim—Direct Market Sales Representative
Emilio Bautista—Digital Sales Representative
Leanna Caunter—Accounting Analyst
Chloe Ramos-Peterson—Library Market Sales Representative
Marla Eizik—Administrative Assistant
IMAGECOMICS.COM

LAURA TAVISHATI
edits

MARC LOMBARDI
communications

JIM VALENTINO
publisher/book design

RAT QUEENS created by KURTIS J. WIEBE and ROC UPCHURCH

A
Shadowline®
PRODUCTION

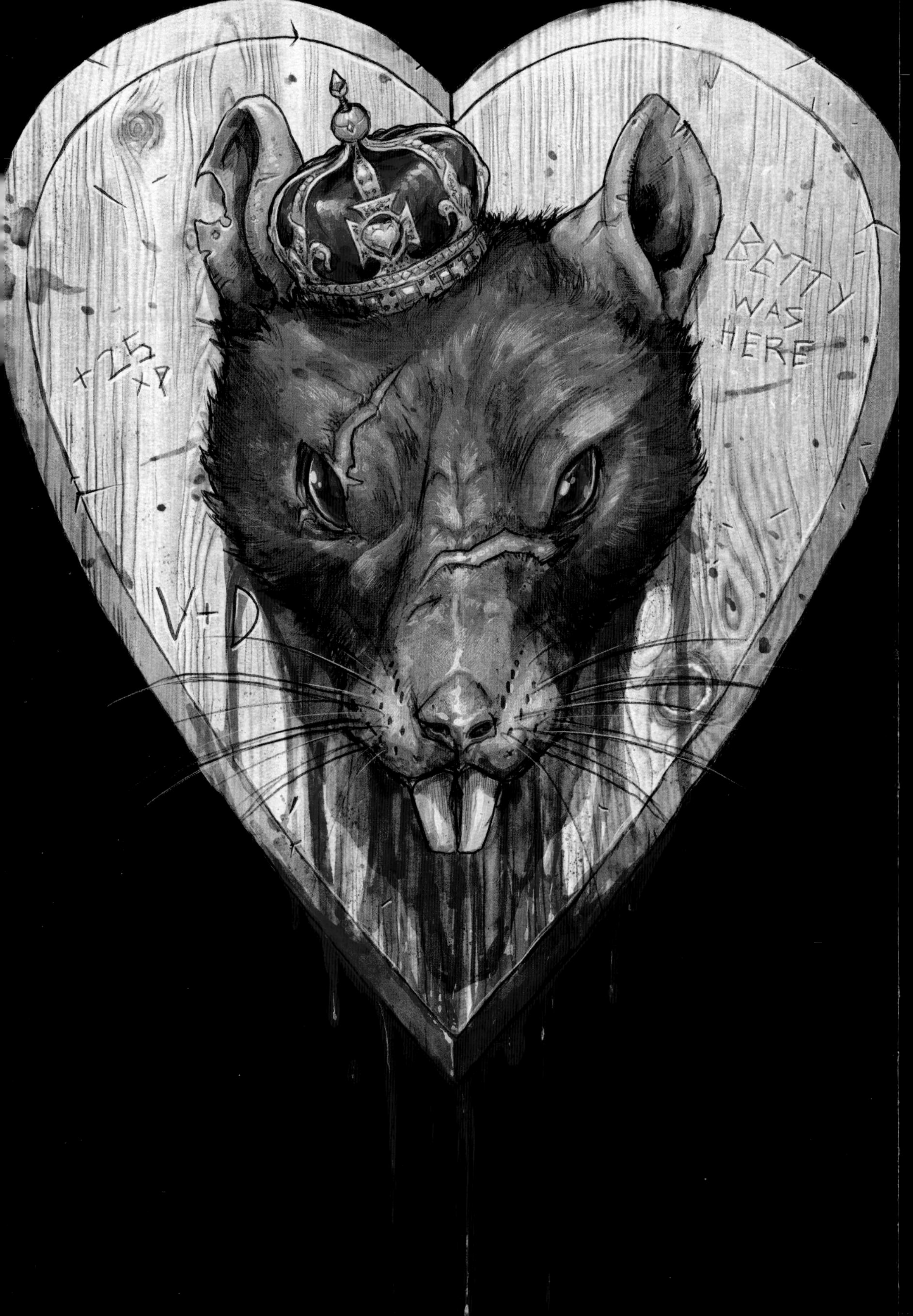
+25 XP
BETTY WAS HERE
V+D

Issue #1 second printing cover

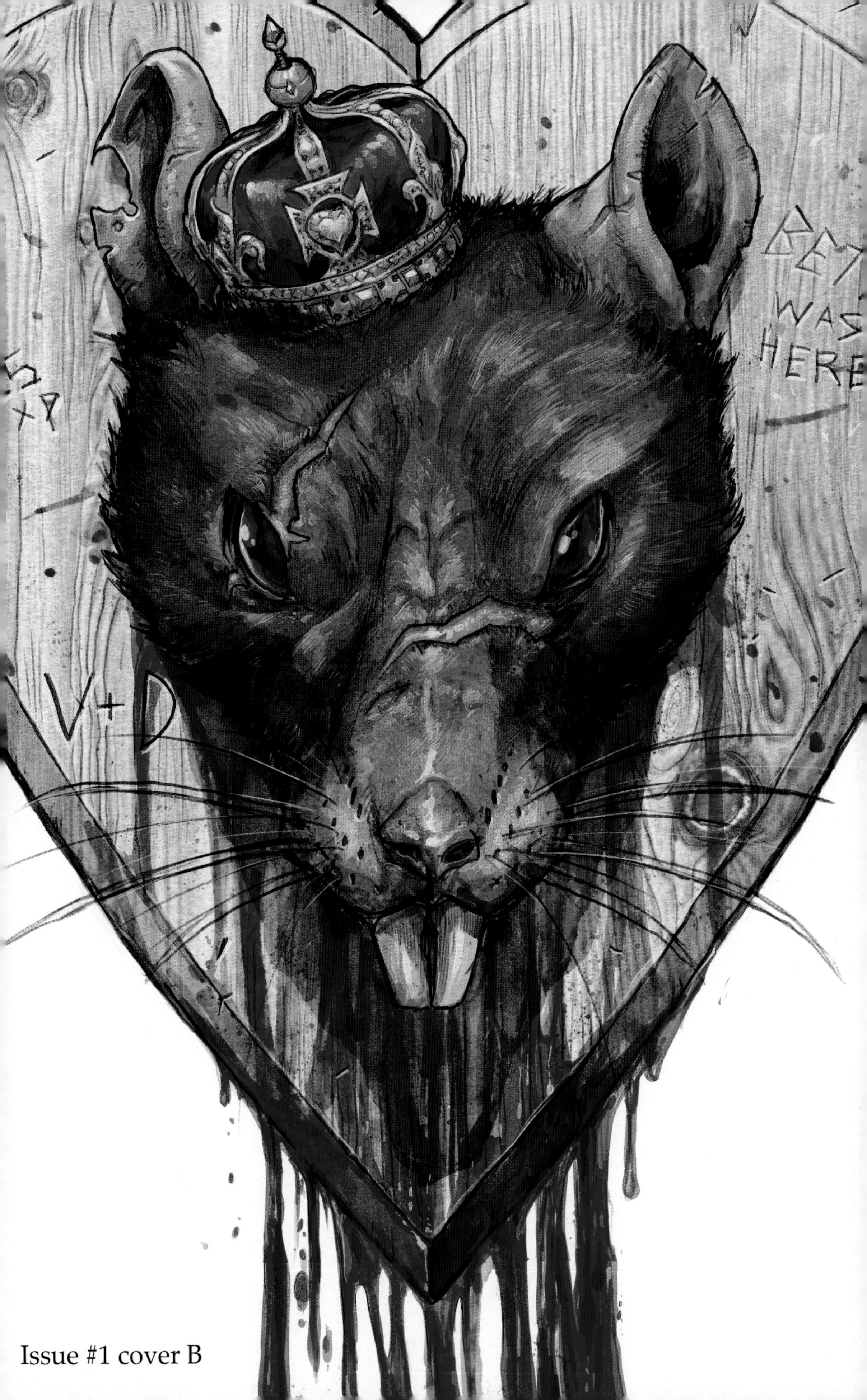
WAS HERE
V+D

Issue #1 cover B

CHAPTER ONE

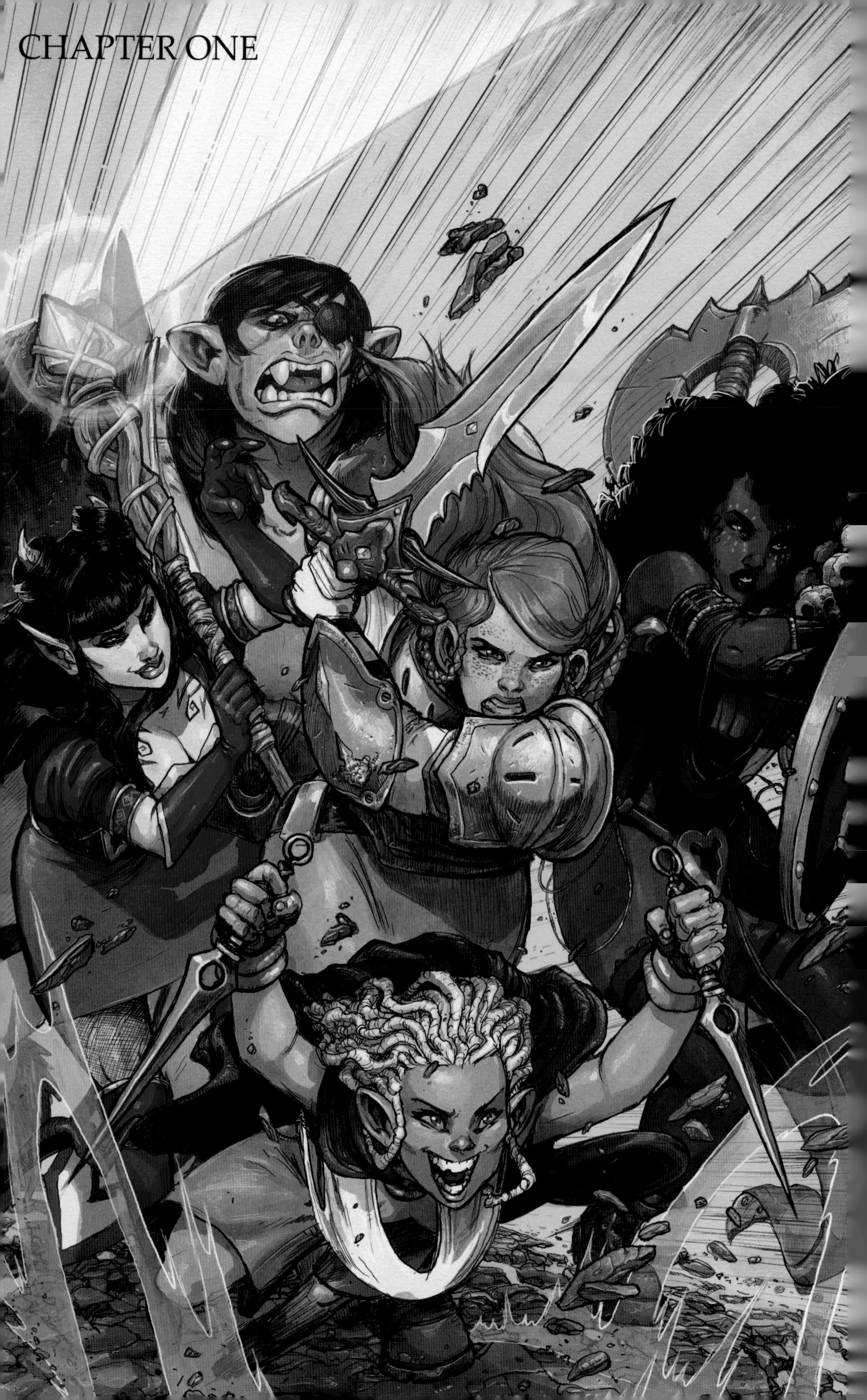

UGHHH...

OWWW.

WHAT DID
YOU--

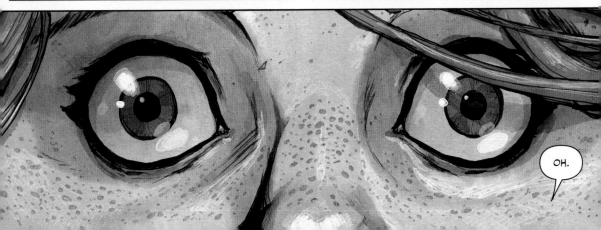

OH.

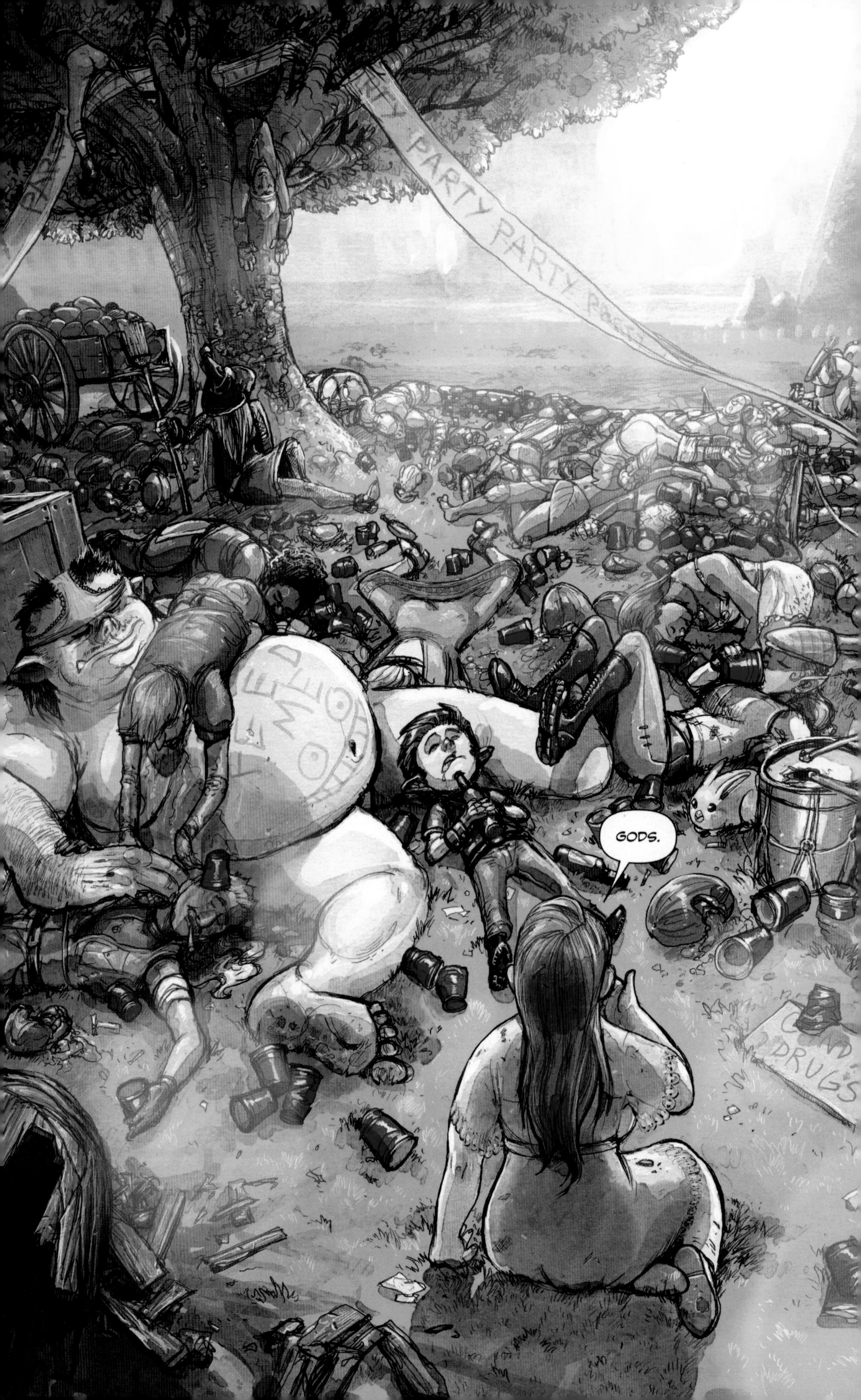
PARTY PARTY
GODS.
DRUGS

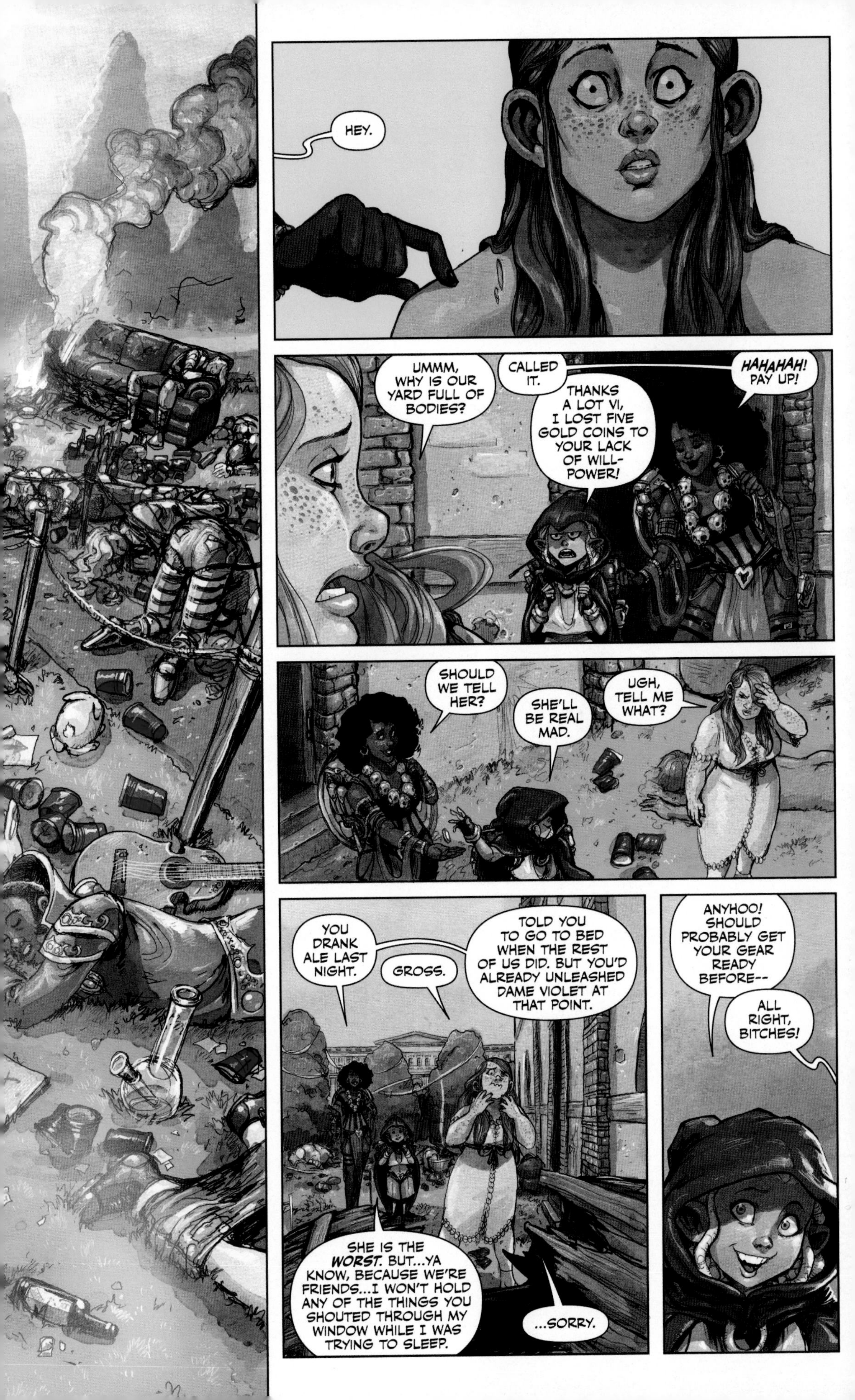
HEY.
UMMM, WHY IS OUR YARD FULL OF BODIES?
CALLED IT.
THANKS A LOT VI, I LOST FIVE GOLD COINS TO YOUR LACK OF WILL-POWER!
HAHAHAH! PAY UP!
SHOULD WE TELL HER?
SHE'LL BE REAL MAD.
UGH, TELL ME WHAT?
YOU DRANK ALE LAST NIGHT.
GROSS.
TOLD YOU TO GO TO BED WHEN THE REST OF US DID. BUT YOU'D ALREADY UNLEASHED DAME VIOLET AT THAT POINT.
SHE IS THE WORST. BUT...YA KNOW, BECAUSE WE'RE FRIENDS...I WON'T HOLD ANY OF THE THINGS YOU SHOUTED THROUGH MY WINDOW WHILE I WAS TRYING TO SLEEP.
...SORRY.
ANYHOO! SHOULD PROBABLY GET YOUR GEAR READY BEFORE--
ALL RIGHT, BITCHES!

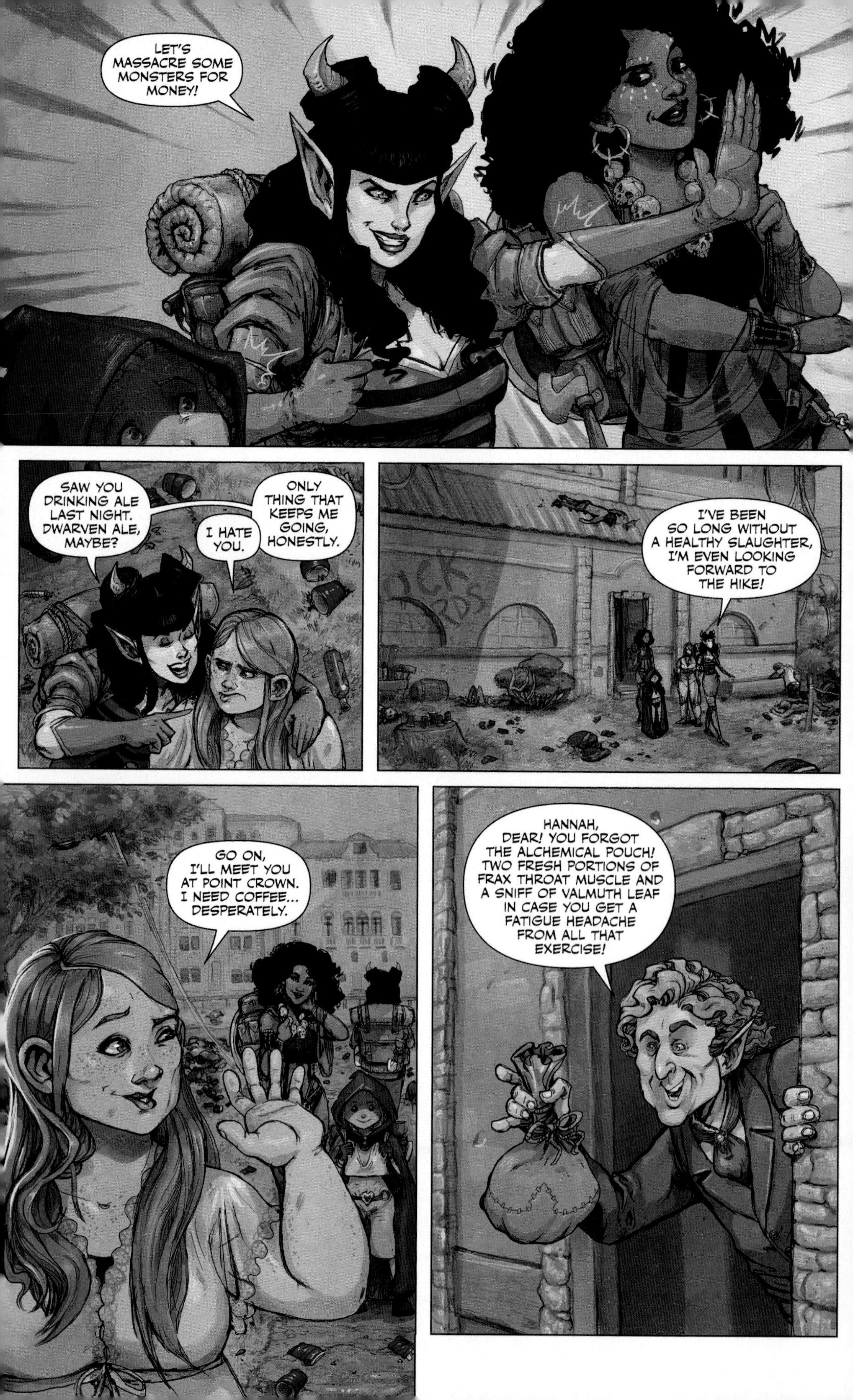
LET'S MASSACRE SOME MONSTERS FOR MONEY!
SAW YOU DRINKING ALE LAST NIGHT. DWARVEN ALE, MAYBE?
I HATE YOU.
ONLY THING THAT KEEPS ME GOING, HONESTLY.
I'VE BEEN SO LONG WITHOUT A HEALTHY SLAUGHTER, I'M EVEN LOOKING FORWARD TO THE HIKE!
GO ON, I'LL MEET YOU AT POINT CROWN. I NEED COFFEE... DESPERATELY.
HANNAH, DEAR! YOU FORGOT THE ALCHEMICAL POUCH! TWO FRESH PORTIONS OF FRAX THROAT MUSCLE AND A SNIFF OF VALMUTH LEAF IN CASE YOU GET A FATIGUE HEADACHE FROM ALL THAT EXERCISE!

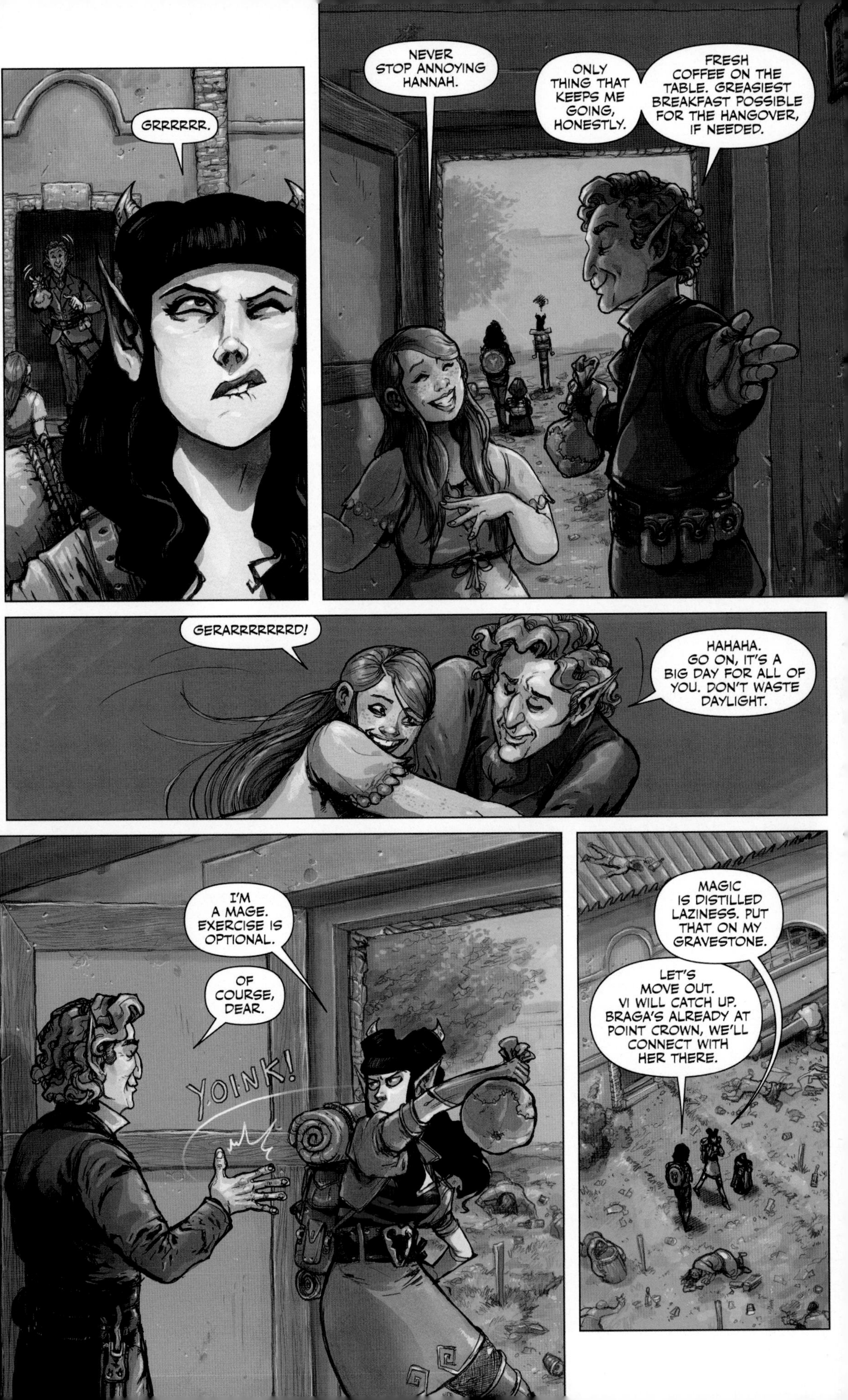
GRRRRRR.
NEVER STOP ANNOYING HANNAH.
ONLY THING THAT KEEPS ME GOING, HONESTLY.
FRESH COFFEE ON THE TABLE. GREASIEST BREAKFAST POSSIBLE FOR THE HANGOVER, IF NEEDED.
GERARRRRRRRD!
HAHAHA. GO ON, IT'S A BIG DAY FOR ALL OF YOU. DON'T WASTE DAYLIGHT.
I'M A MAGE. EXERCISE IS OPTIONAL.
OF COURSE, DEAR.
YOINK!
MAGIC IS DISTILLED LAZINESS. PUT THAT ON MY GRAVESTONE.
LET'S MOVE OUT. VI WILL CATCH UP. BRAGA'S ALREADY AT POINT CROWN, WE'LL CONNECT WITH HER THERE.

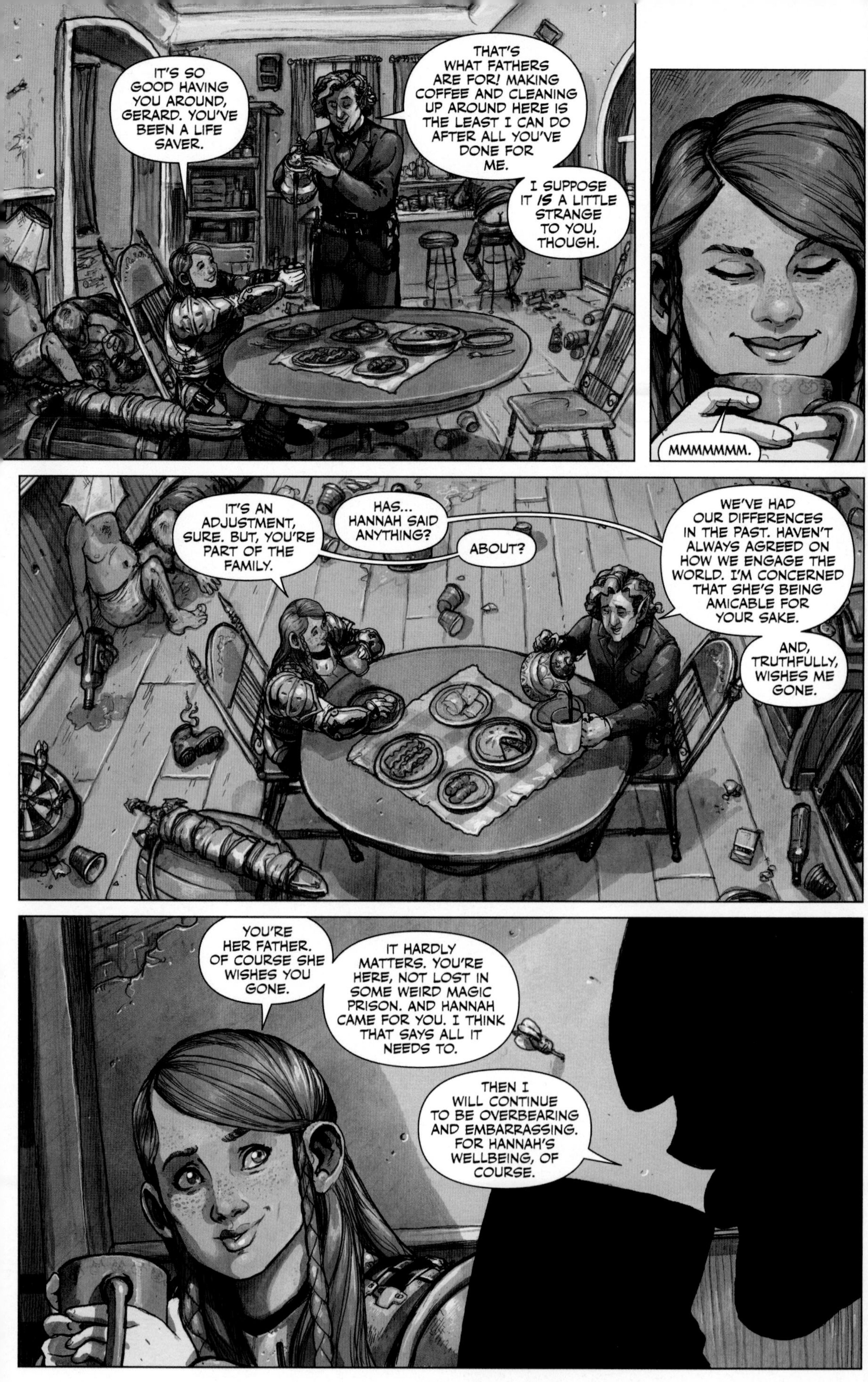
IT'S SO GOOD HAVING YOU AROUND, GERARD. YOU'VE BEEN A LIFE SAVER.
THAT'S WHAT FATHERS ARE FOR! MAKING COFFEE AND CLEANING UP AROUND HERE IS THE LEAST I CAN DO AFTER ALL YOU'VE DONE FOR ME.
I SUPPOSE IT *IS* A LITTLE STRANGE TO YOU, THOUGH.
MMMMMMM.
IT'S AN ADJUSTMENT, SURE. BUT, YOU'RE PART OF THE FAMILY.
HAS... HANNAH SAID ANYTHING?
ABOUT?
WE'VE HAD OUR DIFFERENCES IN THE PAST. HAVEN'T ALWAYS AGREED ON HOW WE ENGAGE THE WORLD. I'M CONCERNED THAT SHE'S BEING AMICABLE FOR YOUR SAKE.
AND, TRUTHFULLY, WISHES ME GONE.
YOU'RE HER FATHER. OF COURSE SHE WISHES YOU GONE.
IT HARDLY MATTERS. YOU'RE HERE, NOT LOST IN SOME WEIRD MAGIC PRISON. AND HANNAH CAME FOR YOU. I THINK THAT SAYS ALL IT NEEDS TO.
THEN I WILL CONTINUE TO BE OVERBEARING AND EMBARRASSING. FOR HANNAH'S WELLBEING, OF COURSE.

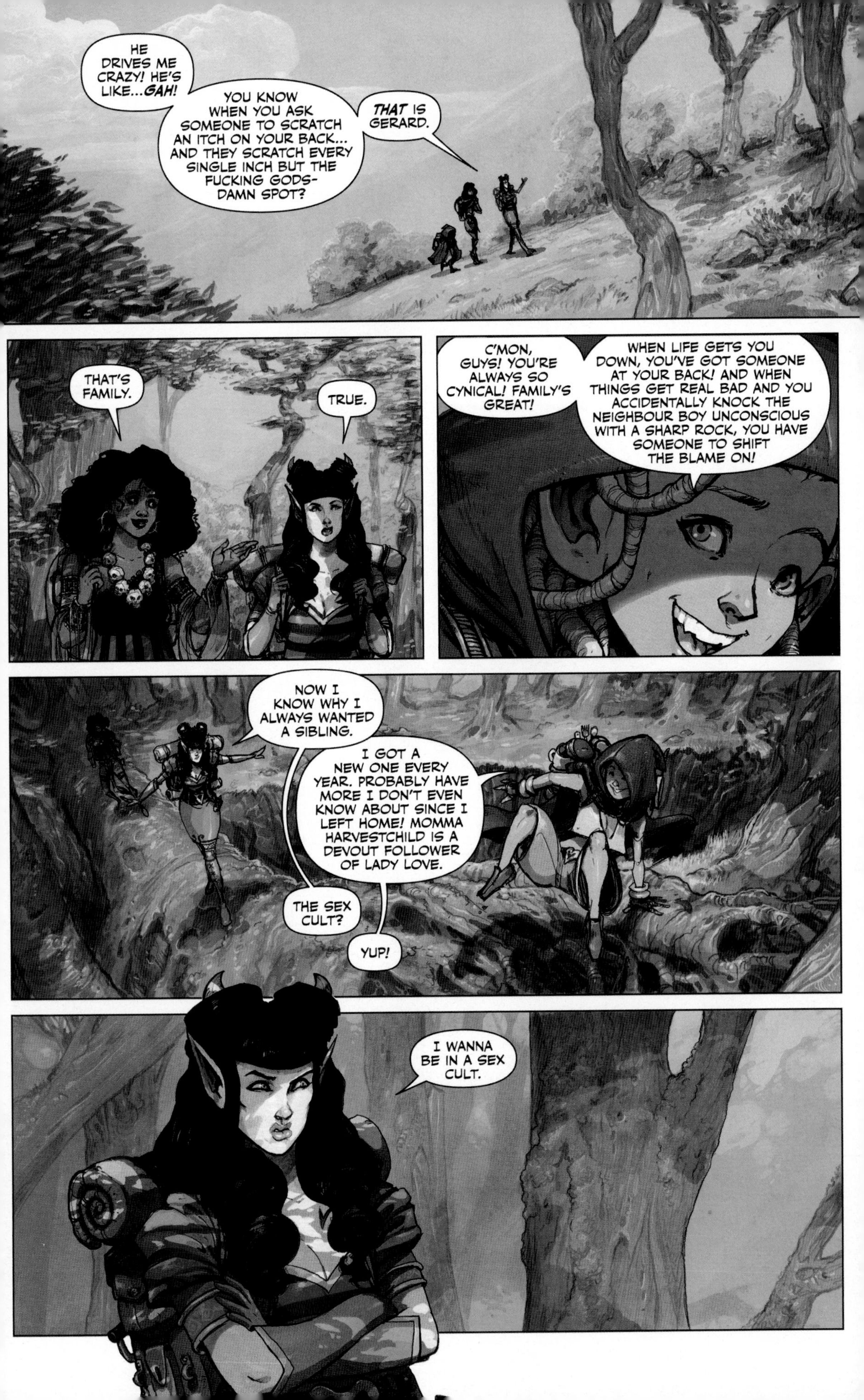
HE DRIVES ME CRAZY! HE'S LIKE...**GAH!**
YOU KNOW WHEN YOU ASK SOMEONE TO SCRATCH AN ITCH ON YOUR BACK... AND THEY SCRATCH EVERY SINGLE INCH BUT THE FUCKING GODS-DAMN SPOT?
THAT IS GERARD.
THAT'S FAMILY.
TRUE.
C'MON, GUYS! YOU'RE ALWAYS SO CYNICAL! FAMILY'S GREAT!
WHEN LIFE GETS YOU DOWN, YOU'VE GOT SOMEONE AT YOUR BACK! AND WHEN THINGS GET REAL BAD AND YOU ACCIDENTALLY KNOCK THE NEIGHBOUR BOY UNCONSCIOUS WITH A SHARP ROCK, YOU HAVE SOMEONE TO SHIFT THE BLAME ON!
NOW I KNOW WHY I ALWAYS WANTED A SIBLING.
I GOT A NEW ONE EVERY YEAR. PROBABLY HAVE MORE I DON'T EVEN KNOW ABOUT SINCE I LEFT HOME! MOMMA HARVESTCHILD IS A DEVOUT FOLLOWER OF LADY LOVE.
THE SEX CULT?
YUP!
I WANNA BE IN A SEX CULT.

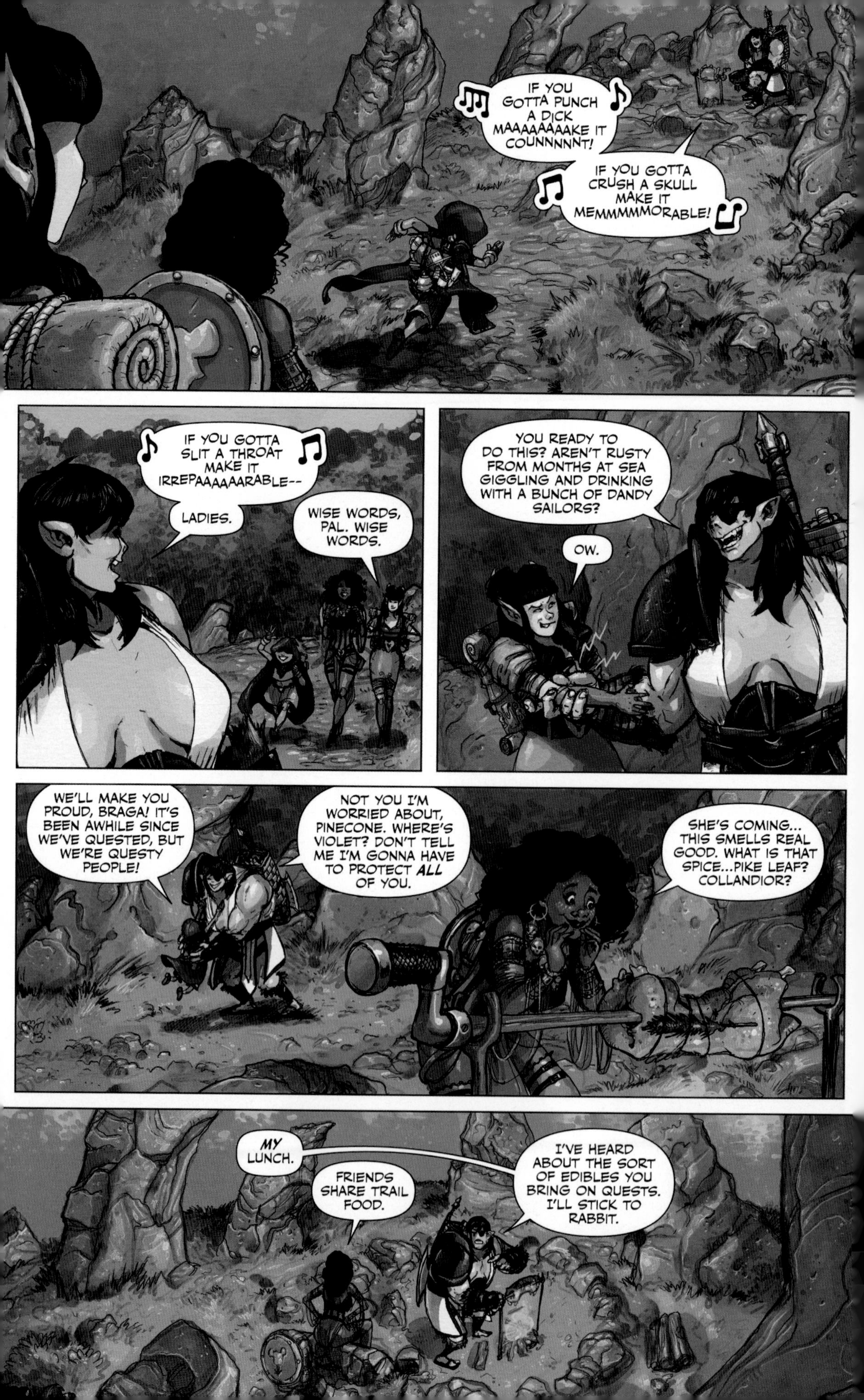
IF YOU GOTTA PUNCH A DICK MAAAAAAAAKE IT COUNNNNNT!
IF YOU GOTTA CRUSH A SKULL MAKE IT MEMMMMMORABLE!
IF YOU GOTTA SLIT A THROAT MAKE IT IRREPAAAAAARABLE--
LADIES.
WISE WORDS, PAL. WISE WORDS.
YOU READY TO DO THIS? AREN'T RUSTY FROM MONTHS AT SEA GIGGLING AND DRINKING WITH A BUNCH OF DANDY SAILORS?
OW.
WE'LL MAKE YOU PROUD, BRAGA! IT'S BEEN AWHILE SINCE WE'VE QUESTED, BUT WE'RE QUESTY PEOPLE!
NOT YOU I'M WORRIED ABOUT, PINECONE. WHERE'S VIOLET? DON'T TELL ME I'M GONNA HAVE TO PROTECT ALL OF YOU.
SHE'S COMING... THIS SMELLS REAL GOOD. WHAT IS THAT SPICE...PIKE LEAF? COLLANDIOR?
MY LUNCH.
FRIENDS SHARE TRAIL FOOD.
I'VE HEARD ABOUT THE SORT OF EDIBLES YOU BRING ON QUESTS. I'LL STICK TO RABBIT.

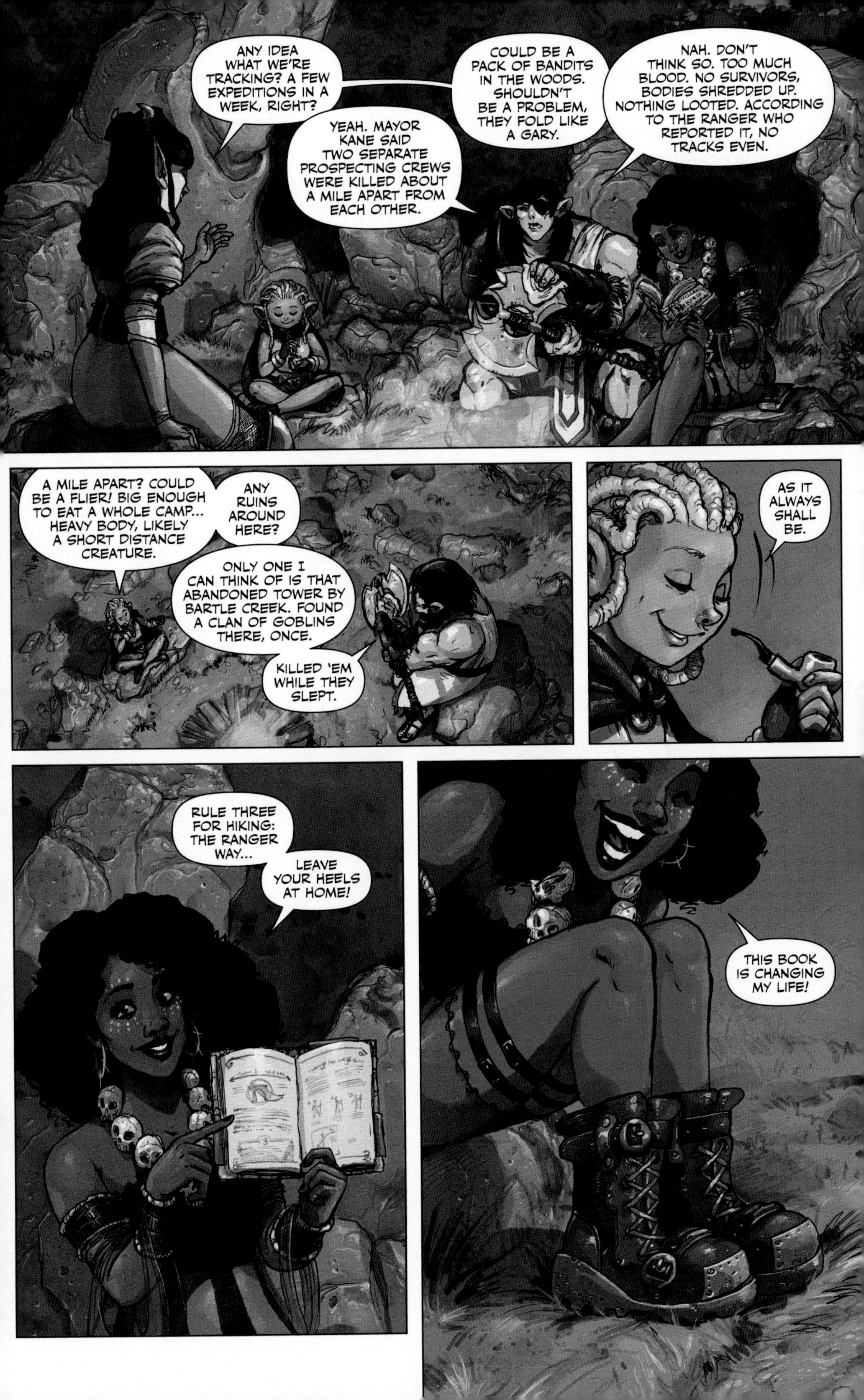
ANY IDEA WHAT WE'RE TRACKING? A FEW EXPEDITIONS IN A WEEK, RIGHT?
YEAH. MAYOR KANE SAID TWO SEPARATE PROSPECTING CREWS WERE KILLED ABOUT A MILE APART FROM EACH OTHER.
COULD BE A PACK OF BANDITS IN THE WOODS. SHOULDN'T BE A PROBLEM, THEY FOLD LIKE A GARY.
NAH. DON'T THINK SO. TOO MUCH BLOOD. NO SURVIVORS, BODIES SHREDDED UP. NOTHING LOOTED. ACCORDING TO THE RANGER WHO REPORTED IT, NO TRACKS EVEN.
A MILE APART? COULD BE A FLIER! BIG ENOUGH TO EAT A WHOLE CAMP... HEAVY BODY, LIKELY A SHORT DISTANCE CREATURE.
ANY RUINS AROUND HERE?
ONLY ONE I CAN THINK OF IS THAT ABANDONED TOWER BY BARTLE CREEK. FOUND A CLAN OF GOBLINS THERE, ONCE.
KILLED 'EM WHILE THEY SLEPT.
AS IT ALWAYS SHALL BE.
RULE THREE FOR HIKING: THE RANGER WAY...
LEAVE YOUR HEELS AT HOME!
THIS BOOK IS CHANGING MY LIFE!

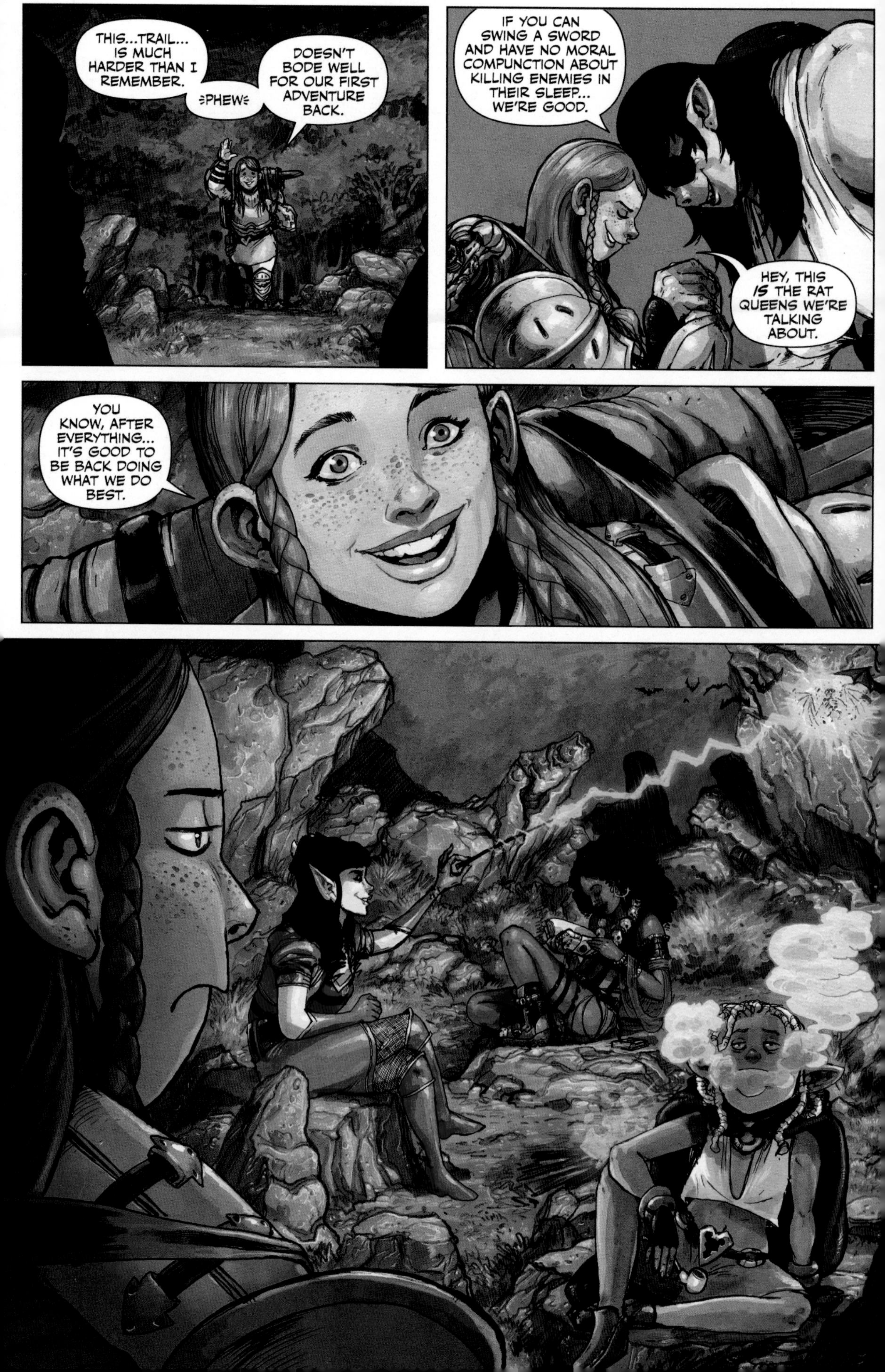

THIS...TRAIL... IS MUCH HARDER THAN I REMEMBER.
PHEW
DOESN'T BODE WELL FOR OUR FIRST ADVENTURE BACK.
IF YOU CAN SWING A SWORD AND HAVE NO MORAL COMPUNCTION ABOUT KILLING ENEMIES IN THEIR SLEEP... WE'RE GOOD.
HEY, THIS *IS* THE RAT QUEENS WE'RE TALKING ABOUT.
YOU KNOW, AFTER EVERYTHING... IT'S GOOD TO BE BACK DOING WHAT WE DO BEST.

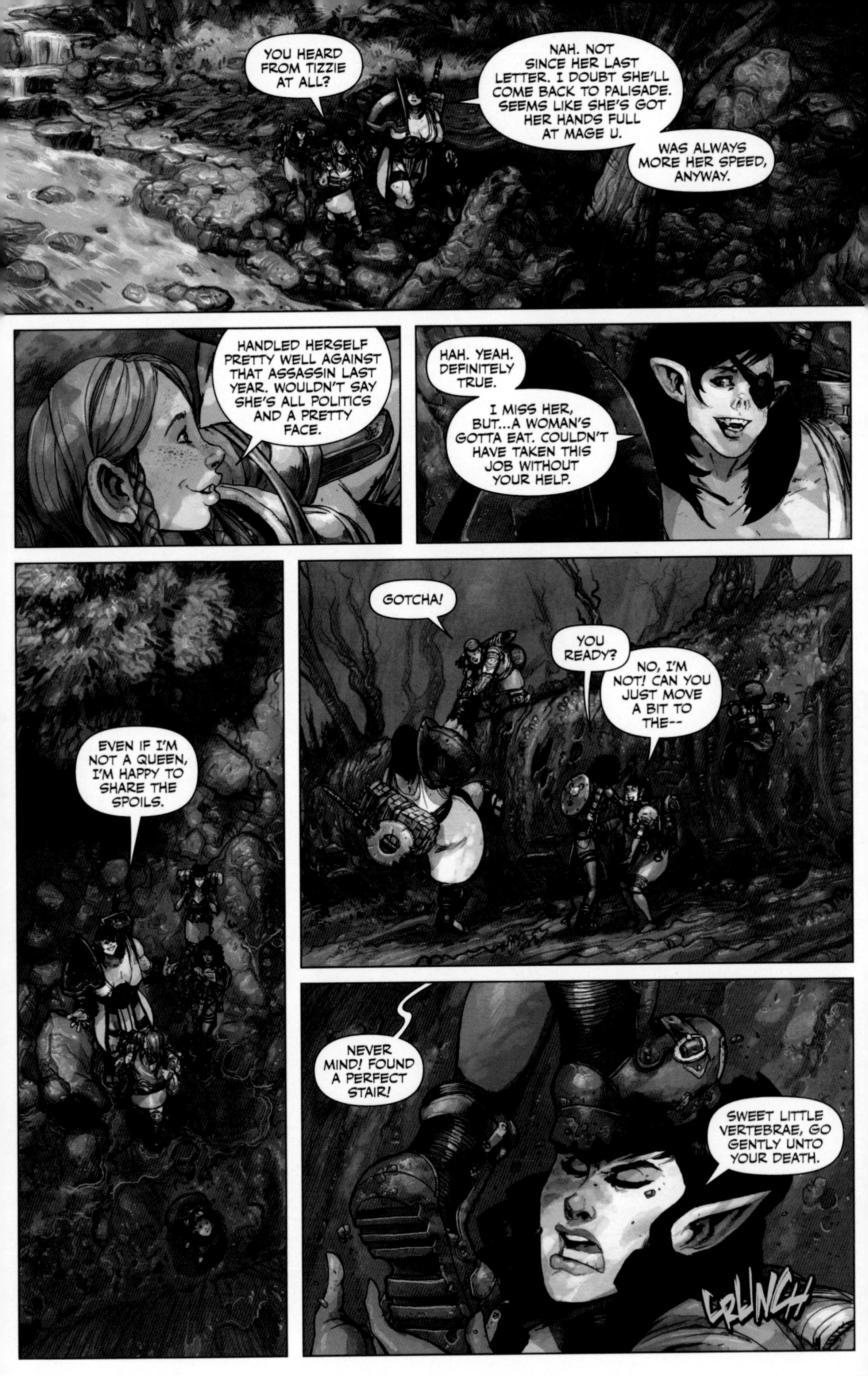
YOU HEARD FROM TIZZIE AT ALL?
NAH. NOT SINCE HER LAST LETTER. I DOUBT SHE'LL COME BACK TO PALISADE. SEEMS LIKE SHE'S GOT HER HANDS FULL AT MAGE U.
WAS ALWAYS MORE HER SPEED, ANYWAY.
HANDLED HERSELF PRETTY WELL AGAINST THAT ASSASSIN LAST YEAR. WOULDN'T SAY SHE'S ALL POLITICS AND A PRETTY FACE.
HAH. YEAH. DEFINITELY TRUE.
I MISS HER, BUT...A WOMAN'S GOTTA EAT. COULDN'T HAVE TAKEN THIS JOB WITHOUT YOUR HELP.
EVEN IF I'M NOT A QUEEN, I'M HAPPY TO SHARE THE SPOILS.
GOTCHA!
YOU READY?
NO, I'M NOT! CAN YOU JUST MOVE A BIT TO THE--
NEVER MIND! FOUND A PERFECT STAIR!
SWEET LITTLE VERTEBRAE, GO GENTLY UNTO YOUR DEATH.
CRUNCH

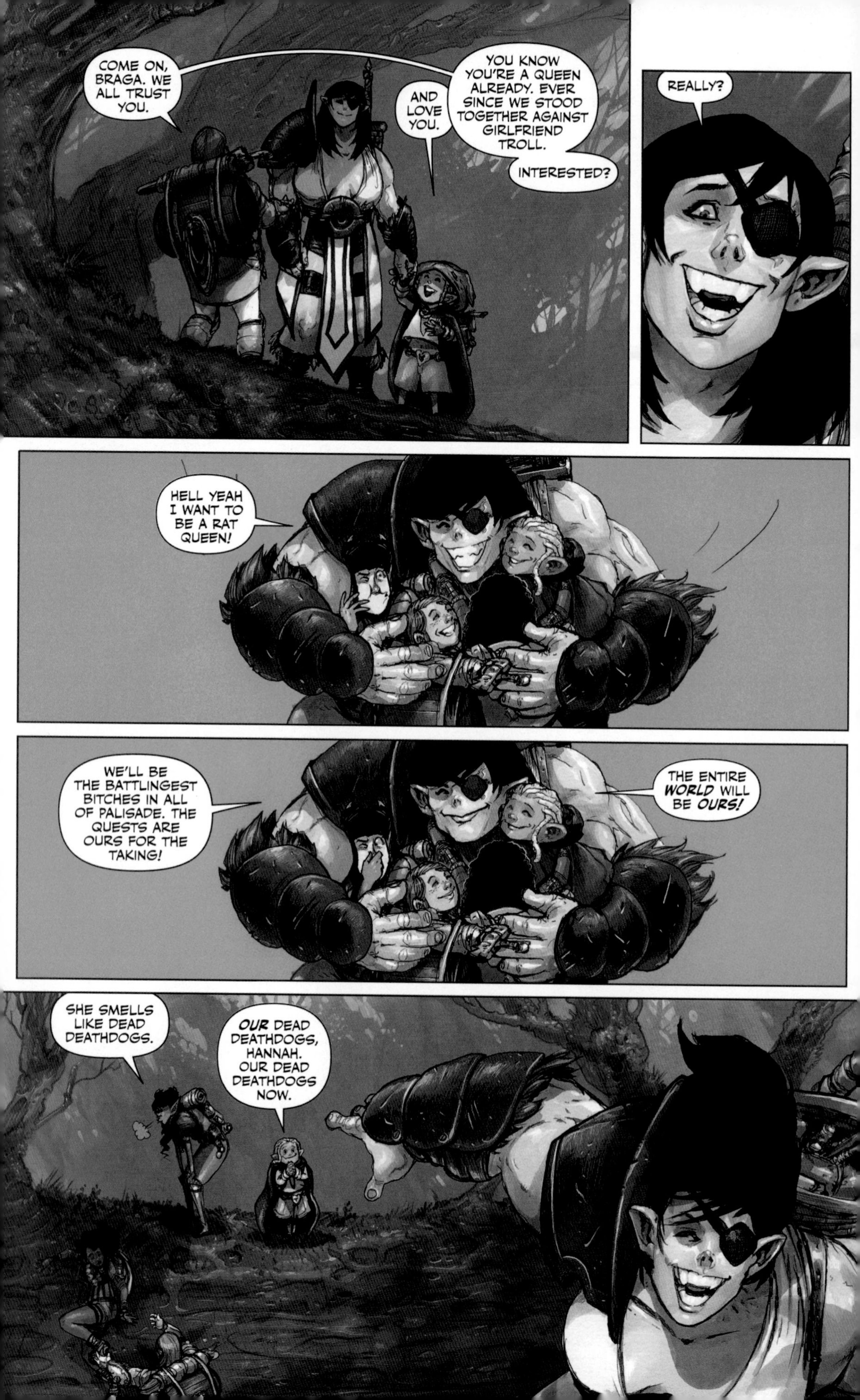
COME ON, BRAGA. WE ALL TRUST YOU.
AND LOVE YOU.
YOU KNOW YOU'RE A QUEEN ALREADY. EVER SINCE WE STOOD TOGETHER AGAINST GIRLFRIEND TROLL.
INTERESTED?
REALLY?
HELL YEAH I WANT TO BE A RAT QUEEN!
WE'LL BE THE BATTLINGEST BITCHES IN ALL OF PALISADE. THE QUESTS ARE OURS FOR THE TAKING!
THE ENTIRE *WORLD* WILL BE *OURS!*
SHE SMELLS LIKE DEAD DEATHDOGS.
OUR DEAD DEATHDOGS, HANNAH. OUR DEAD DEATHDOGS NOW.

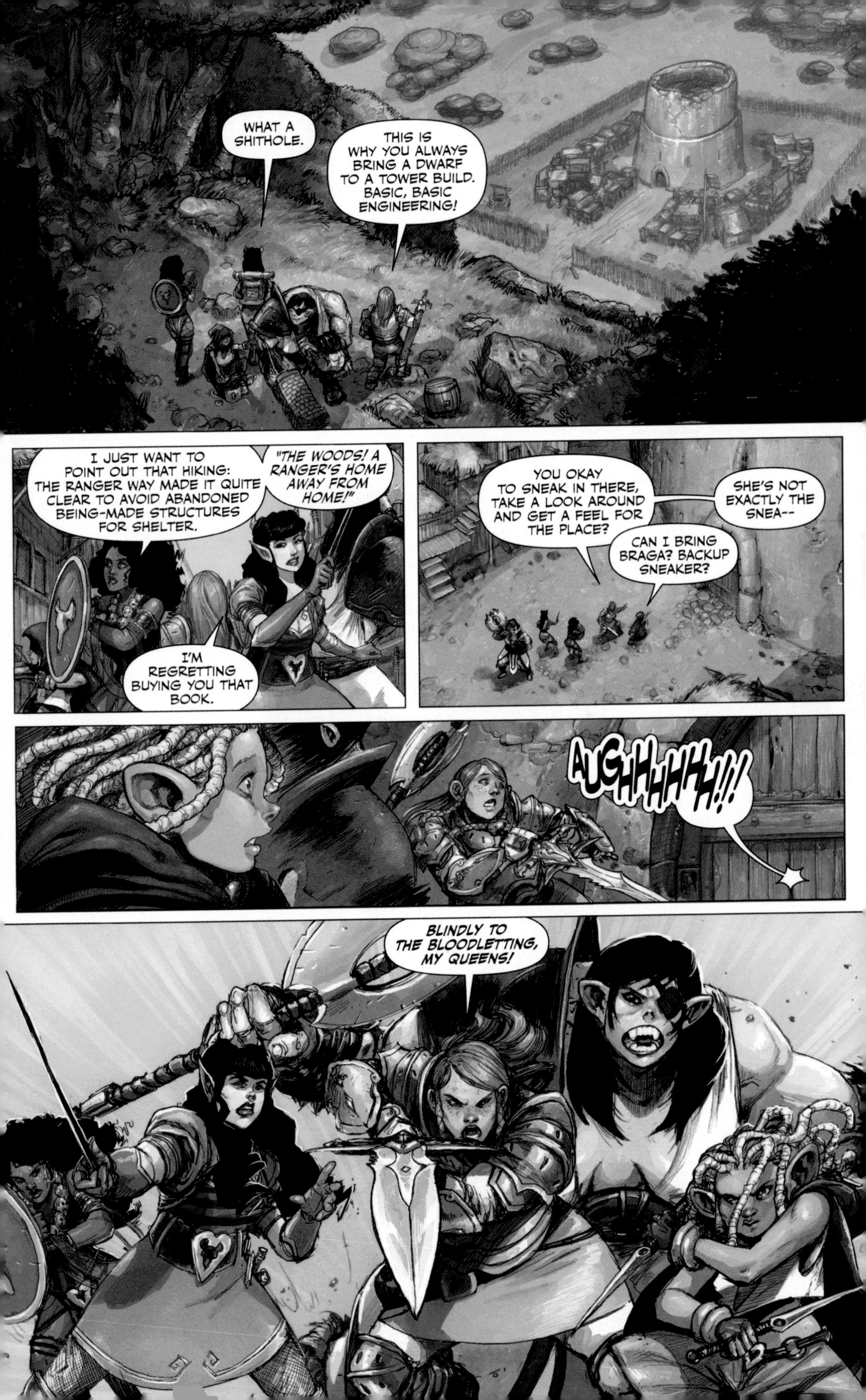
WHAT A SHITHOLE.
THIS IS WHY YOU ALWAYS BRING A DWARF TO A TOWER BUILD. BASIC, BASIC ENGINEERING!
I JUST WANT TO POINT OUT THAT HIKING: THE RANGER WAY MADE IT QUITE CLEAR TO AVOID ABANDONED BEING-MADE STRUCTURES FOR SHELTER.
"THE WOODS! A RANGER'S HOME AWAY FROM HOME!"
I'M REGRETTING BUYING YOU THAT BOOK.
YOU OKAY TO SNEAK IN THERE, TAKE A LOOK AROUND AND GET A FEEL FOR THE PLACE?
SHE'S NOT EXACTLY THE SNEA--
CAN I BRING BRAGA? BACKUP SNEAKER?
AUGHHHHHH!!!
BLINDLY TO THE BLOODLETTING, MY QUEENS!

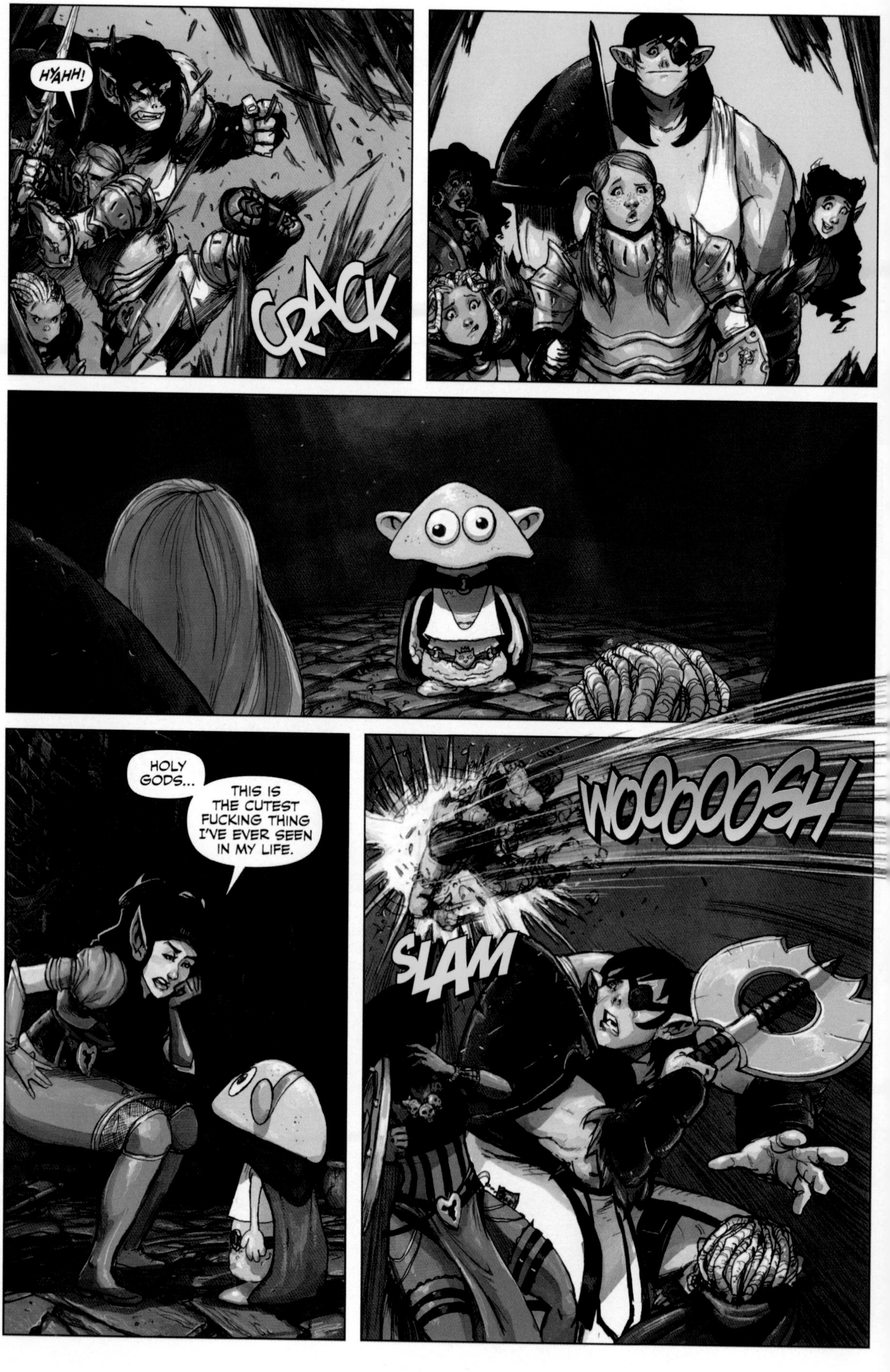
HYAHH!
CRACK
HOLY GODS...
THIS IS THE CUTEST FUCKING THING I'VE EVER SEEN IN MY LIFE.
WOOOOOOSH
SLAM

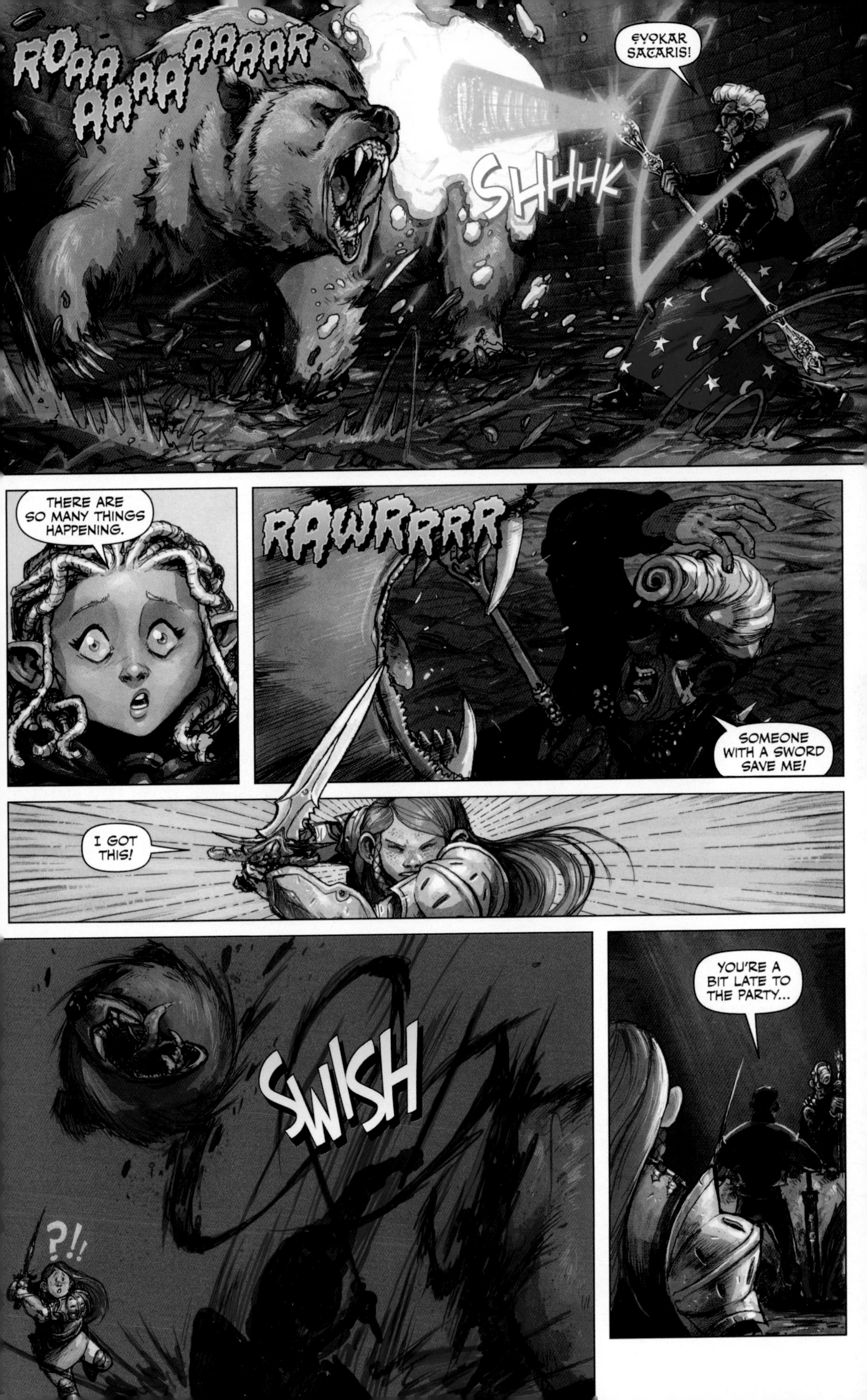
ROAAAAAAAAAR
EVOKAR SATARIS!
SHHHK
THERE ARE SO MANY THINGS HAPPENING.
RAWRRRRR
SOMEONE WITH A SWORD SAVE ME!
I GOT THIS!
SWISH
?!!
YOU'RE A BIT LATE TO THE PARTY...

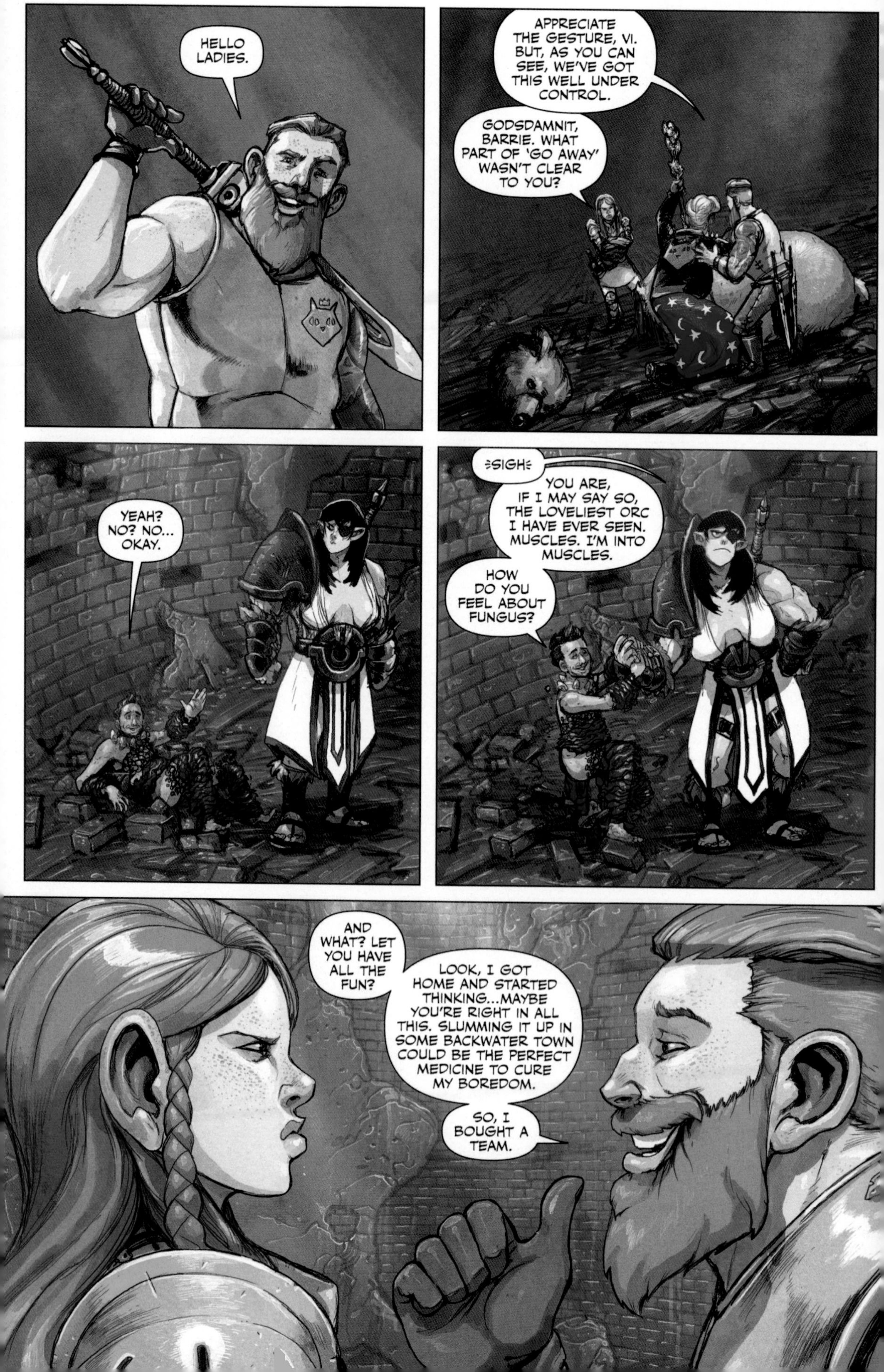
HELLO LADIES.
APPRECIATE THE GESTURE, VI. BUT, AS YOU CAN SEE, WE'VE GOT THIS WELL UNDER CONTROL.
GODSDAMNIT, BARRIE. WHAT PART OF 'GO AWAY' WASN'T CLEAR TO YOU?
YEAH? NO? NO... OKAY.
SIGH
YOU ARE, IF I MAY SAY SO, THE LOVELIEST ORC I HAVE EVER SEEN. MUSCLES. I'M INTO MUSCLES.
HOW DO YOU FEEL ABOUT FUNGUS?
AND WHAT? LET YOU HAVE ALL THE FUN?
LOOK, I GOT HOME AND STARTED THINKING...MAYBE YOU'RE RIGHT IN ALL THIS. SLUMMING IT UP IN SOME BACKWATER TOWN COULD BE THE PERFECT MEDICINE TO CURE MY BOREDOM.
SO, I BOUGHT A TEAM.

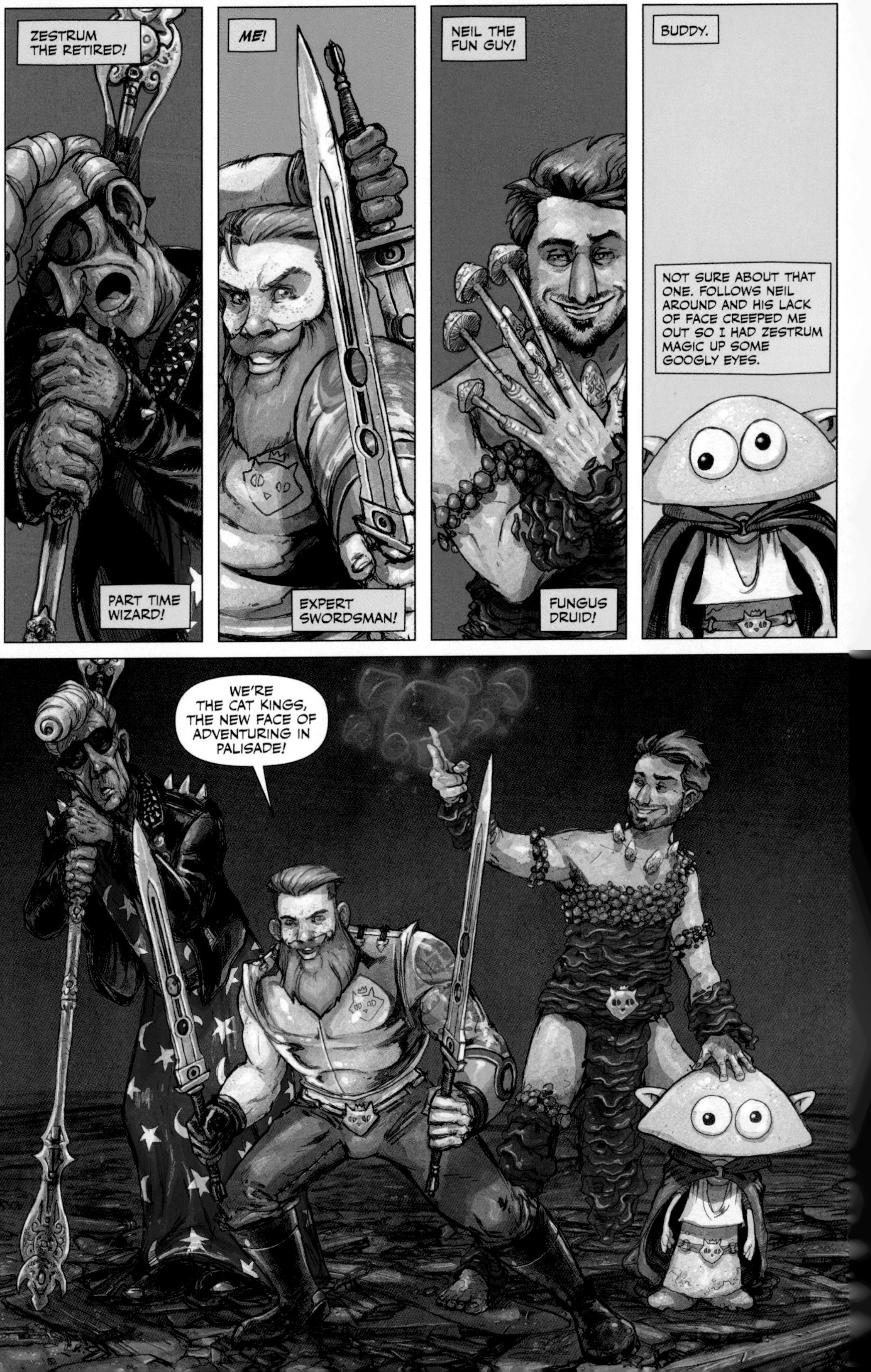
ZESTRUM THE RETIRED!
PART TIME WIZARD!
ME!
EXPERT SWORDSMAN!
NEIL THE FUN GUY!
FUNGUS DRUID!
BUDDY.
NOT SURE ABOUT THAT ONE. FOLLOWS NEIL AROUND AND HIS LACK OF FACE CREEPED ME OUT SO I HAD ZESTRUM MAGIC UP SOME GOOGLY EYES.
WE'RE THE CAT KINGS, THE NEW FACE OF ADVENTURING IN PALISADE!

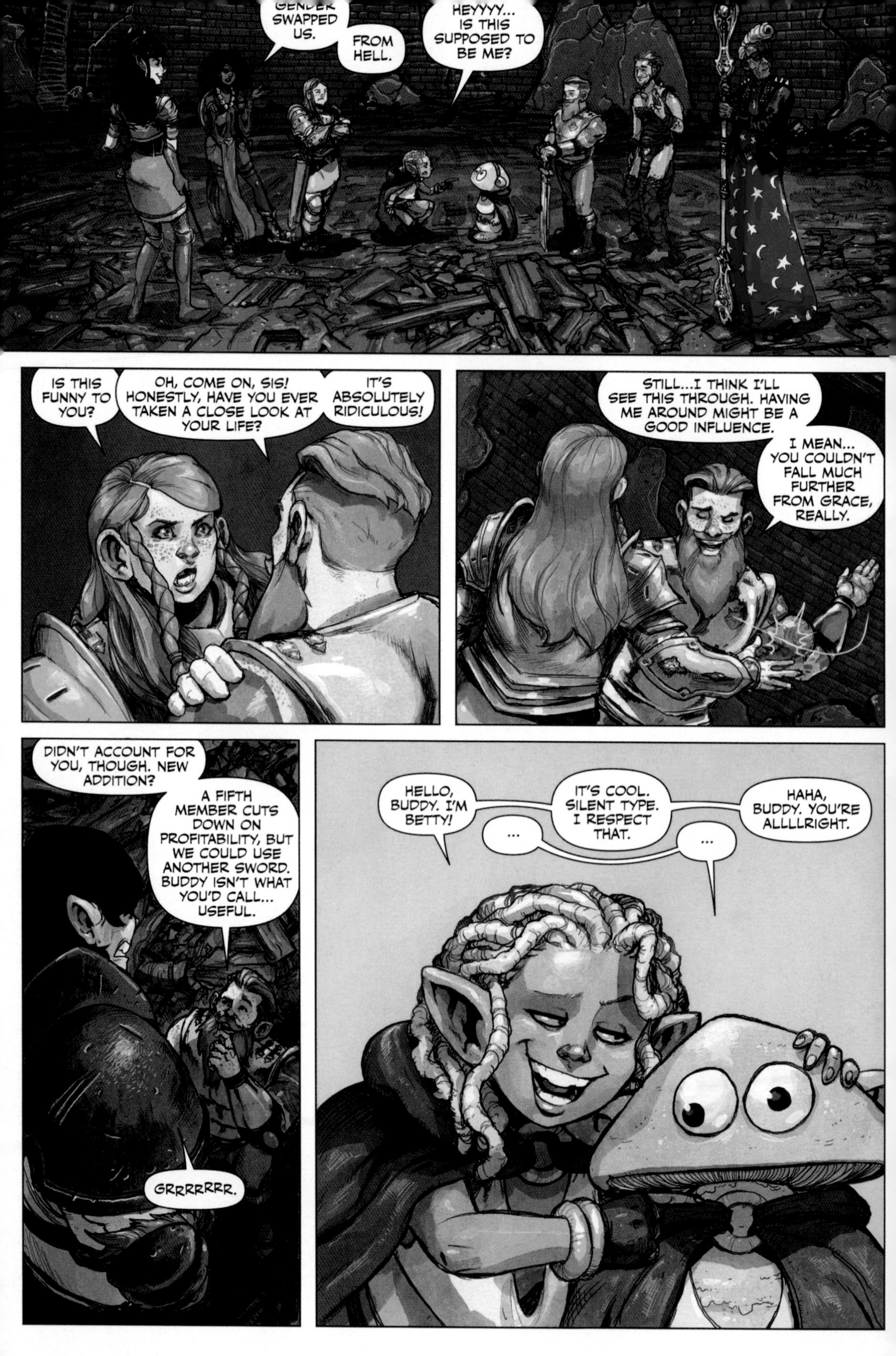
GENDER SWAPPED US.
FROM HELL.
HEYYYY... IS THIS SUPPOSED TO BE ME?
IS THIS FUNNY TO YOU?
OH, COME ON, SIS! HONESTLY, HAVE YOU EVER TAKEN A CLOSE LOOK AT YOUR LIFE?
IT'S ABSOLUTELY RIDICULOUS!
STILL...I THINK I'LL SEE THIS THROUGH. HAVING ME AROUND MIGHT BE A GOOD INFLUENCE.
I MEAN... YOU COULDN'T FALL MUCH FURTHER FROM GRACE, REALLY.
DIDN'T ACCOUNT FOR YOU, THOUGH. NEW ADDITION?
A FIFTH MEMBER CUTS DOWN ON PROFITABILITY, BUT WE COULD USE ANOTHER SWORD. BUDDY ISN'T WHAT YOU'D CALL... USEFUL.
GRRRRRRR.
HELLO, BUDDY. I'M BETTY!
...
IT'S COOL. SILENT TYPE. I RESPECT THAT.
...
HAHA, BUDDY. YOU'RE ALLLLRIGHT.

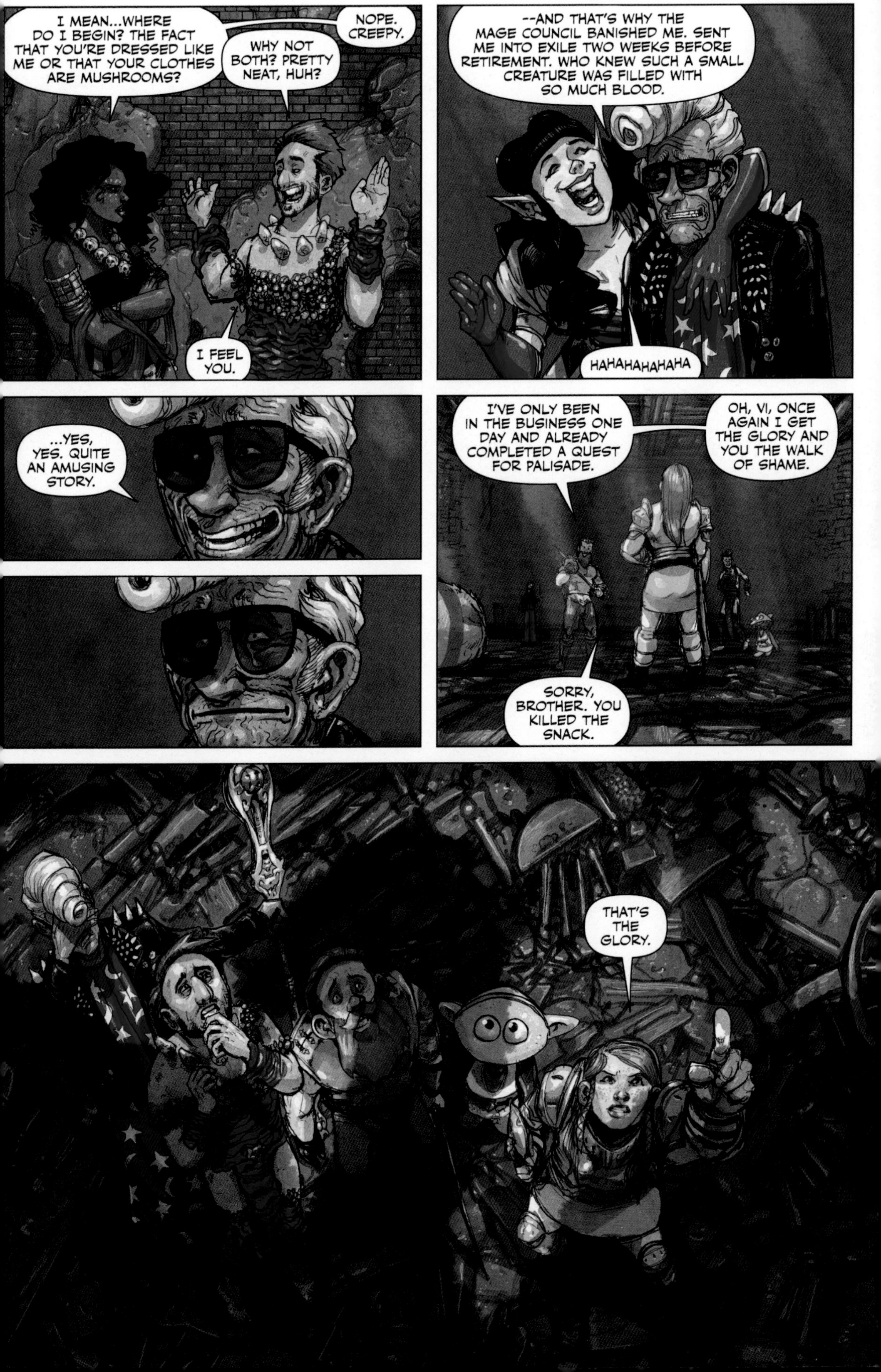
I MEAN...WHERE DO I BEGIN? THE FACT THAT YOU'RE DRESSED LIKE ME OR THAT YOUR CLOTHES ARE MUSHROOMS?
WHY NOT BOTH? PRETTY NEAT, HUH?
NOPE. CREEPY.
I FEEL YOU.
--AND THAT'S WHY THE MAGE COUNCIL BANISHED ME. SENT ME INTO EXILE TWO WEEKS BEFORE RETIREMENT. WHO KNEW SUCH A SMALL CREATURE WAS FILLED WITH SO MUCH BLOOD.
HAHAHAHAHAHA
...YES, YES. QUITE AN AMUSING STORY.
I'VE ONLY BEEN IN THE BUSINESS ONE DAY AND ALREADY COMPLETED A QUEST FOR PALISADE.
OH, VI, ONCE AGAIN I GET THE GLORY AND YOU THE WALK OF SHAME.
SORRY, BROTHER. YOU KILLED THE SNACK.
THAT'S THE GLORY.

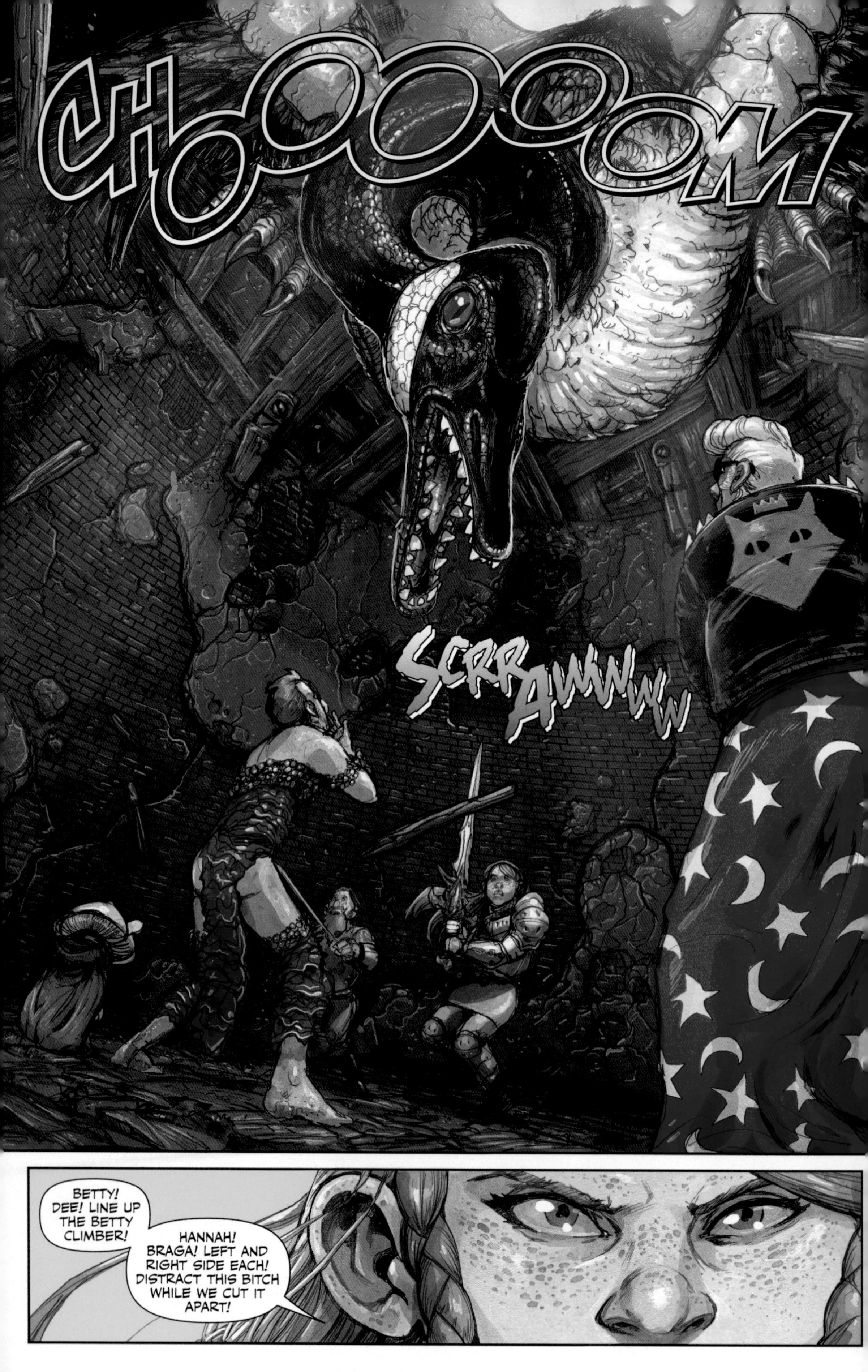
CHOOOOOOM
SCRRAWWWW
BETTY! DEE! LINE UP THE BETTY CLIMBER!
HANNAH! BRAGA! LEFT AND RIGHT SIDE EACH! DISTRACT THIS BITCH WHILE WE CUT IT APART!

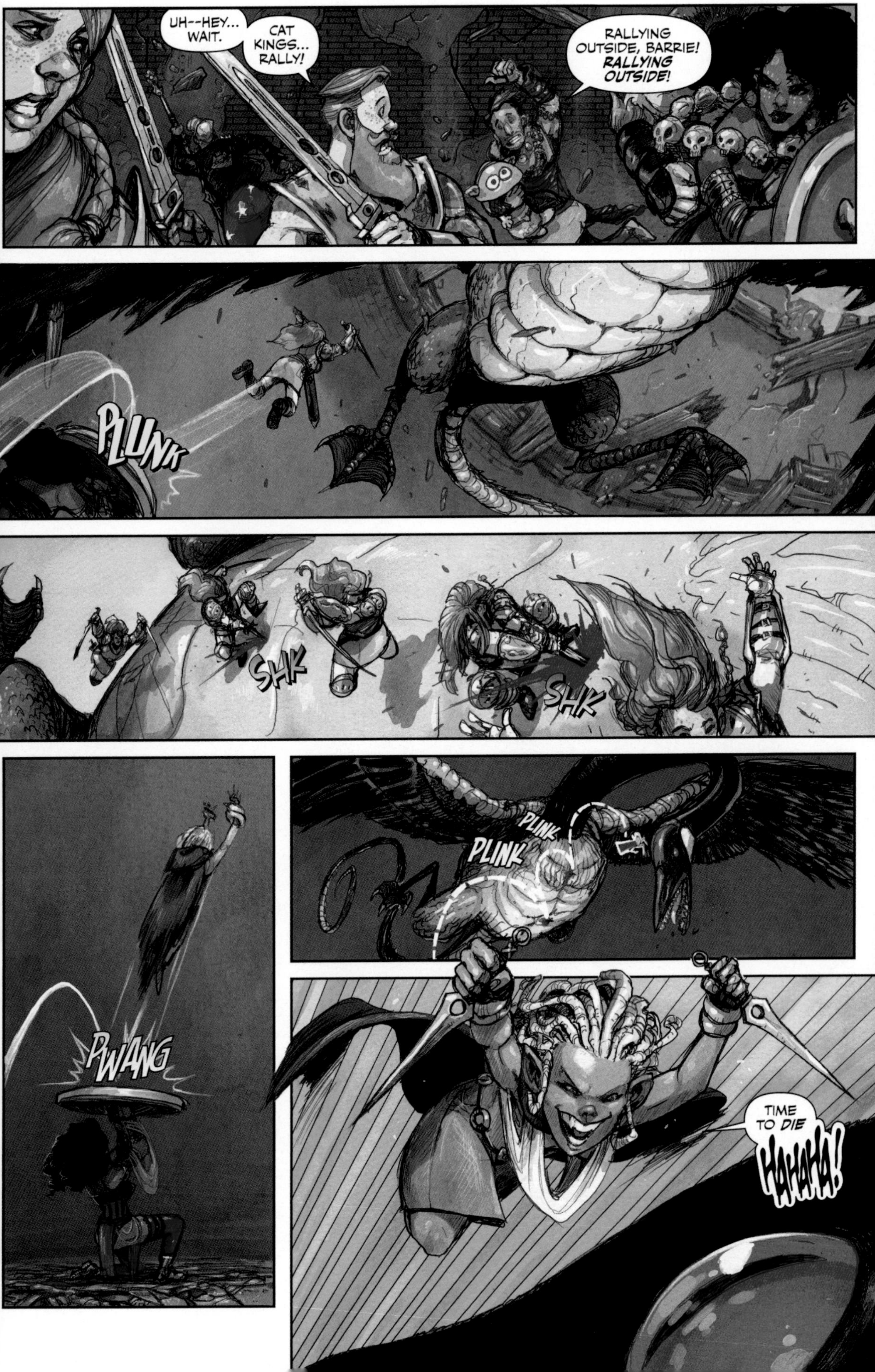
UH--HEY... WAIT.
CAT KINGS... RALLY!
RALLYING OUTSIDE, BARRIE! *RALLYING OUTSIDE!*
PLUNK
SHK
SHK
PWANG
PLINK
PLINK
TIME TO *DIE*
HAHAHA!

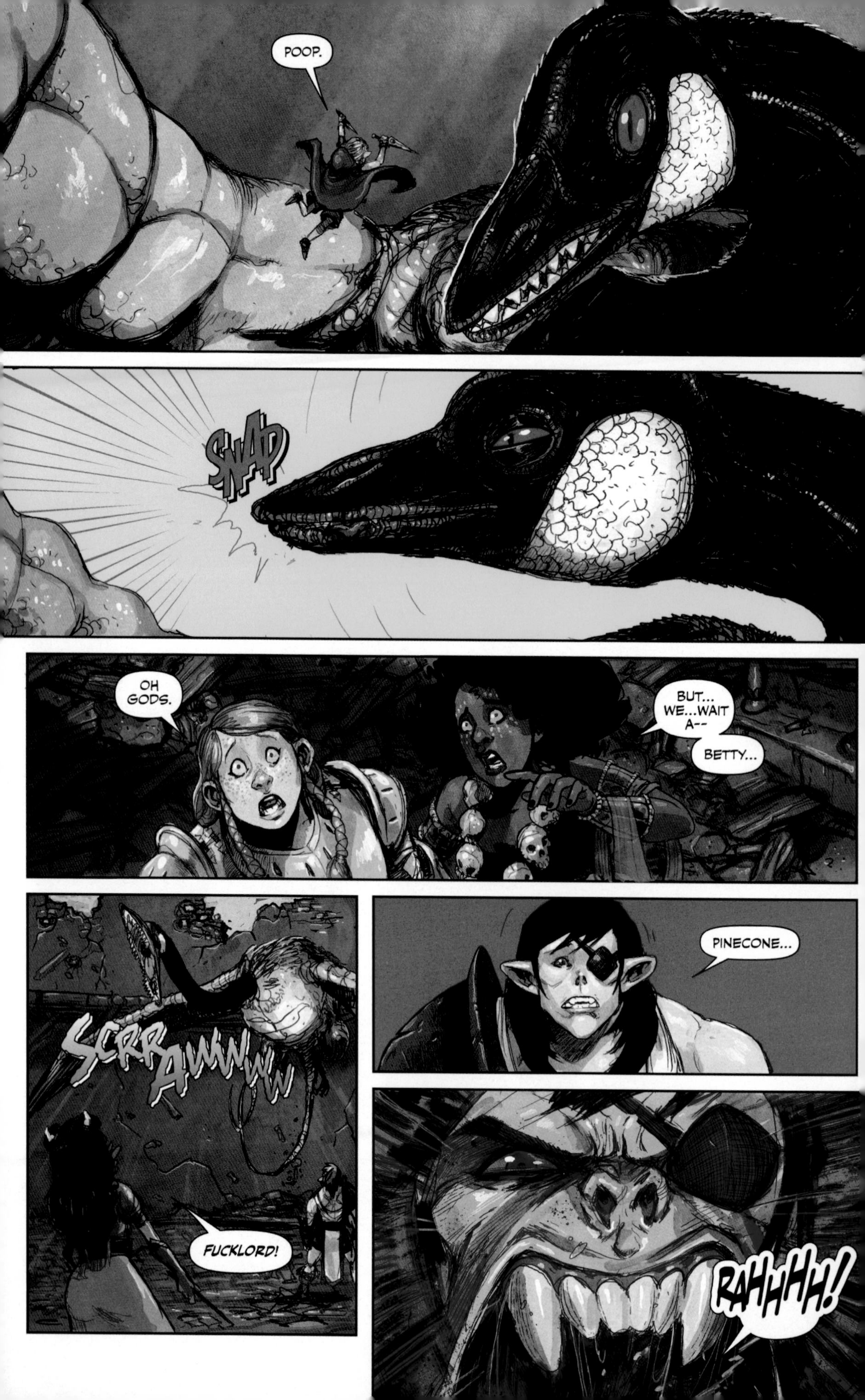
POOP.
SNAP
OH GODS.
BUT... WE...WAIT A--
BETTY...
SCRRAWWW
FUCKLORD!
PINECONE...
RAHHHH!

TIK TIK TIK

≈WHEEZE≈

BOQF WOOOOOM

≈COUGH≈

KARAMMM

CCCCCCCCC

KRAK

FWISSHHHHHH

≈BLECH≈

IT'S OVER...

WE'RE FUCKED AND DOOMED! DOOM FUCKED!

NO. IT'S NEVER OVER--

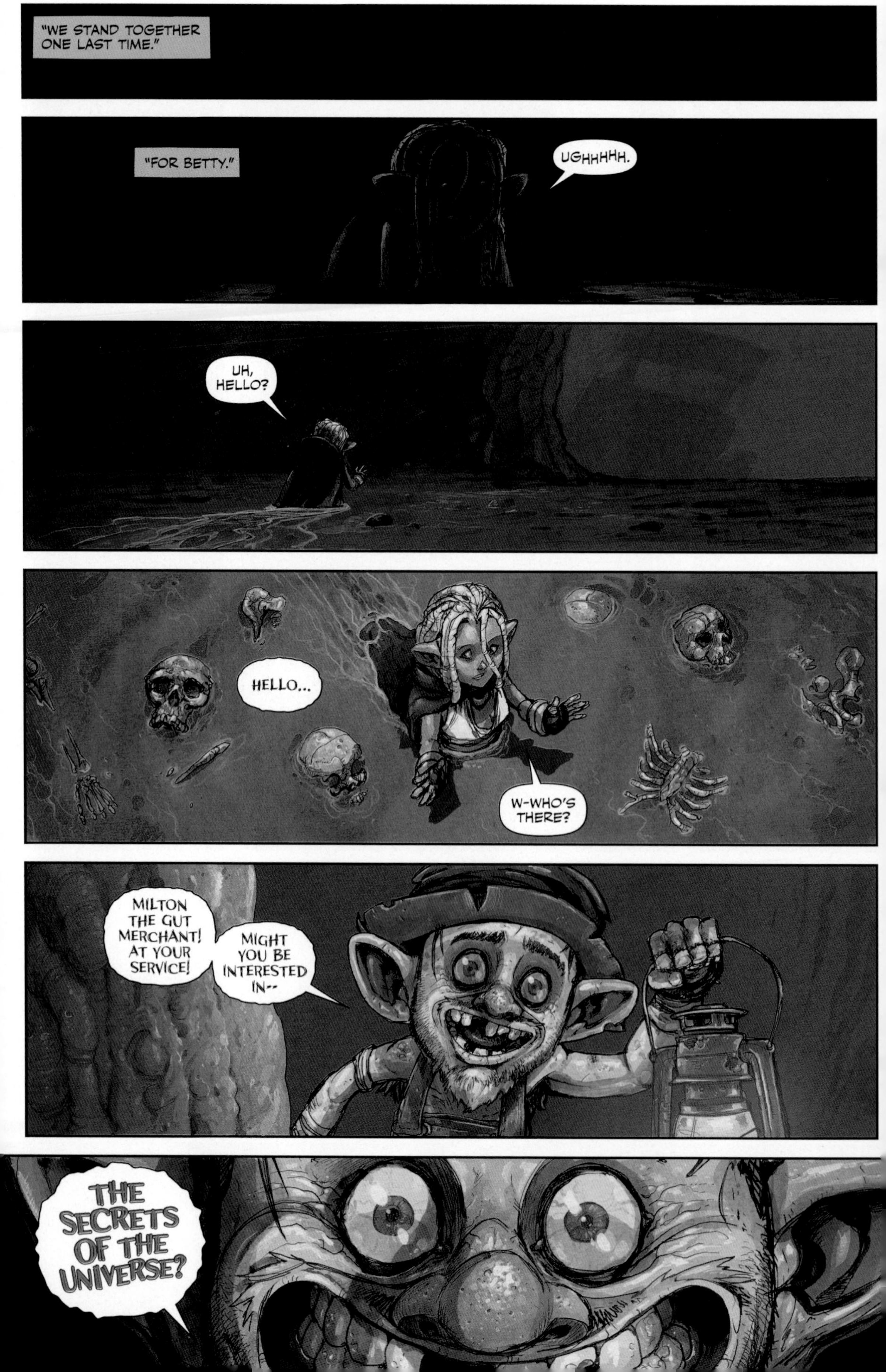
"WE STAND TOGETHER ONE LAST TIME."
"FOR BETTY."
UGHHHHH.
UH, HELLO?
HELLO...
W-WHO'S THERE?
MILTON THE GUT MERCHANT! AT YOUR SERVICE!
MIGHT YOU BE INTERESTED IN--
THE SECRETS OF THE UNIVERSE?

CHAPTER TWO

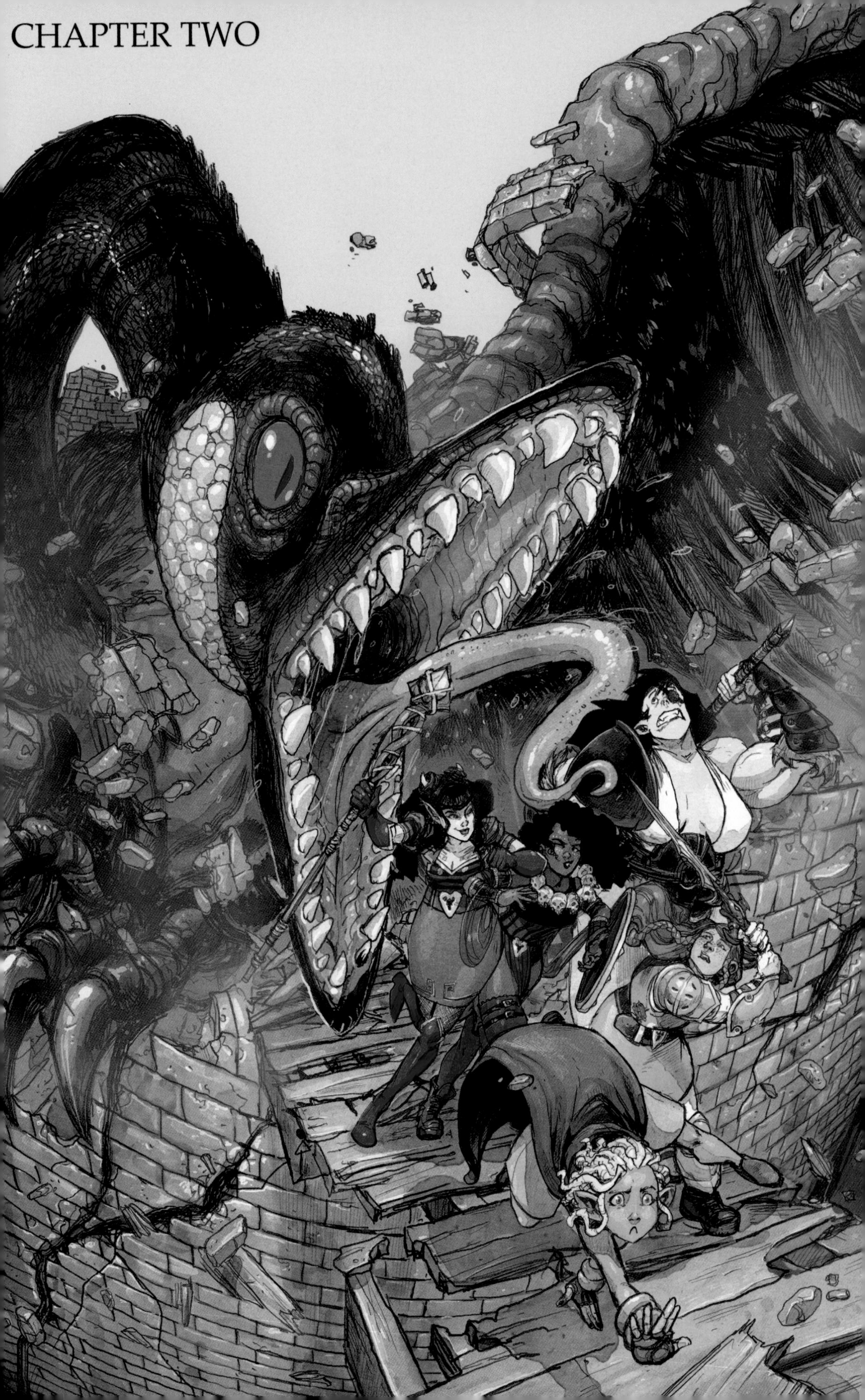

Issue #2 cover B

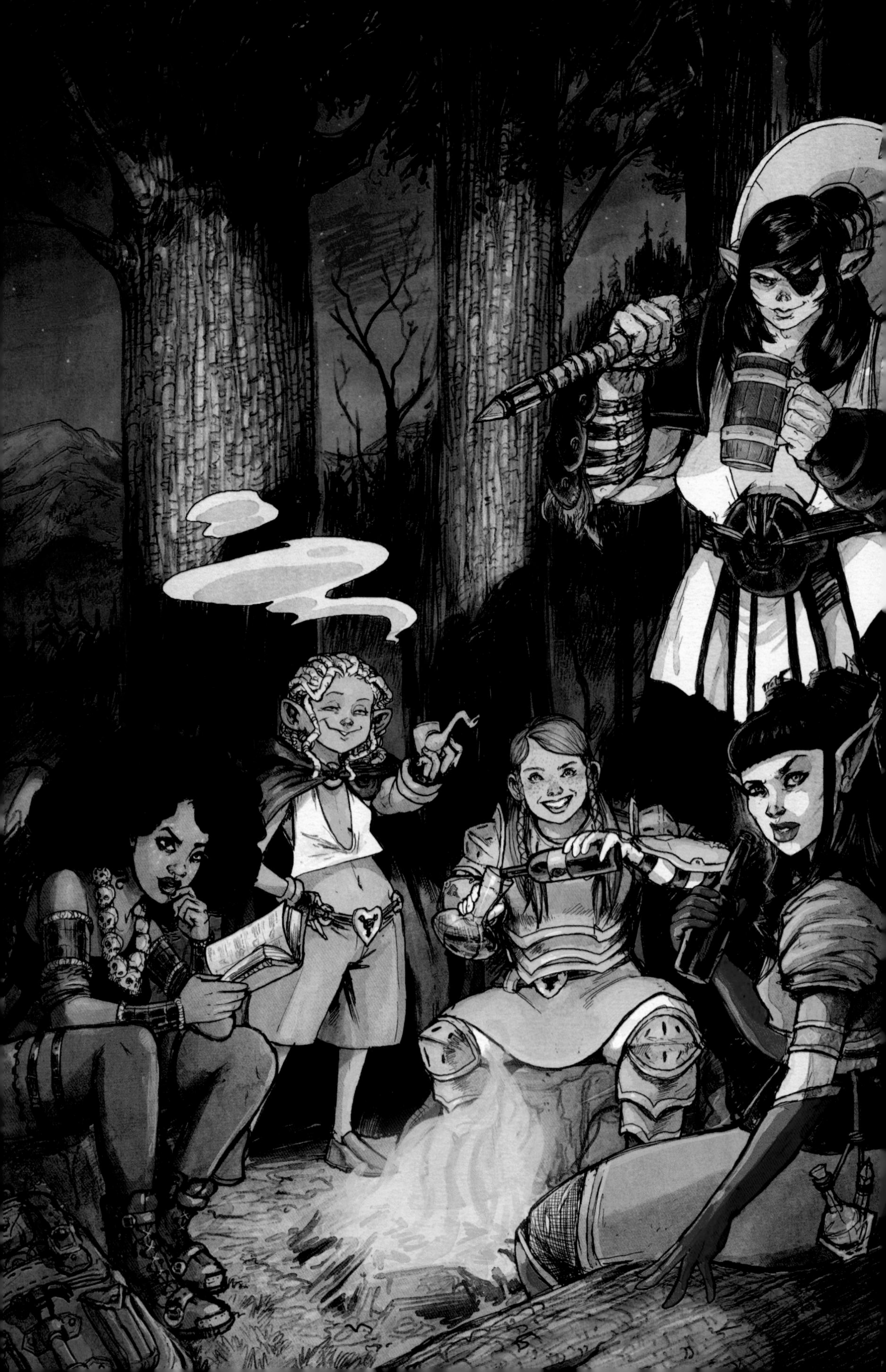

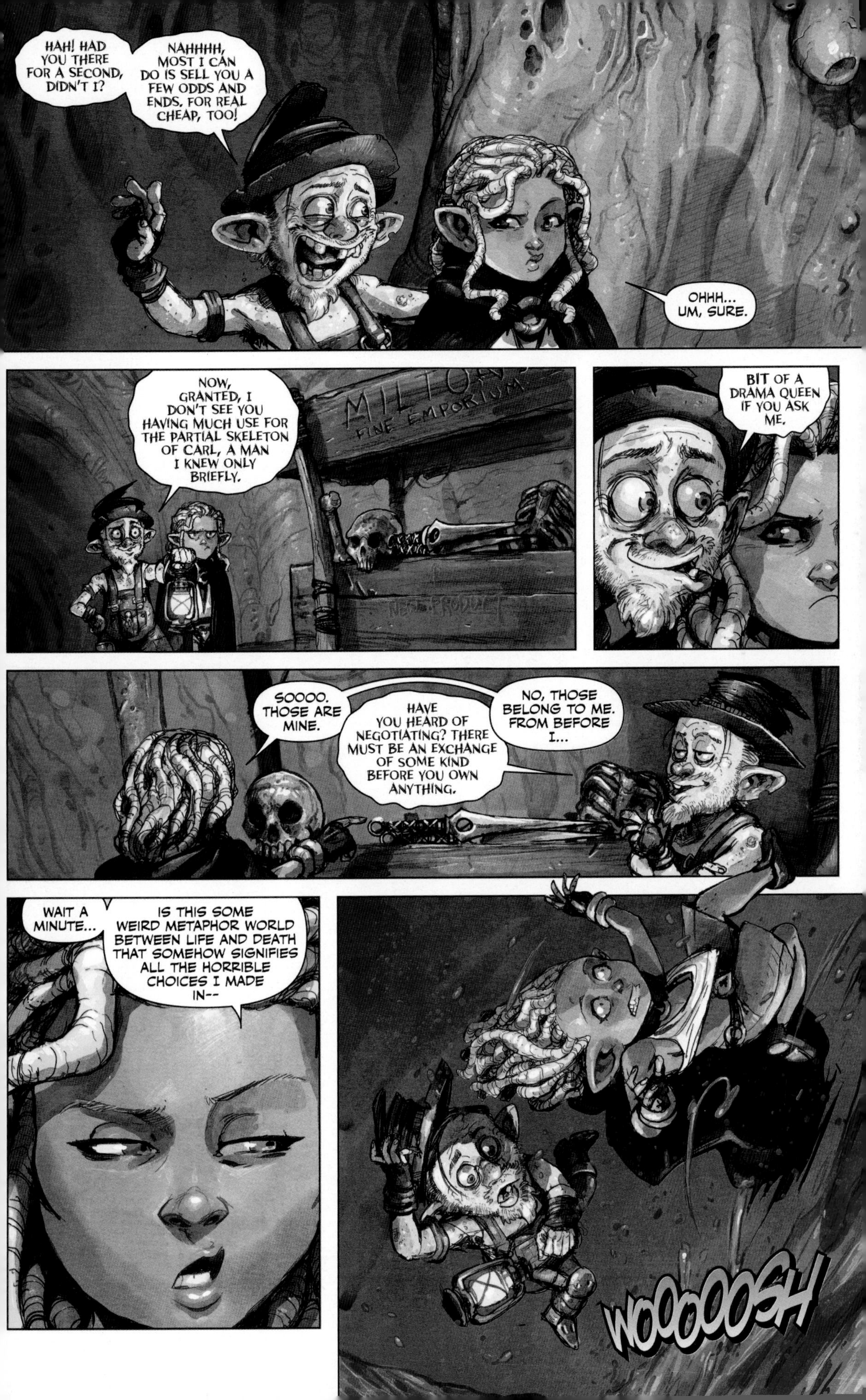
HAH! HAD YOU THERE FOR A SECOND, DIDN'T I?
NAHHHH, MOST I CAN DO IS SELL YOU A FEW ODDS AND ENDS. FOR REAL CHEAP, TOO!
OHHH... UM, SURE.
NOW, GRANTED, I DON'T SEE YOU HAVING MUCH USE FOR THE PARTIAL SKELETON OF CARL, A MAN I KNEW ONLY BRIEFLY.
BIT OF A DRAMA QUEEN IF YOU ASK ME.
SOOOO. THOSE ARE MINE.
NO, THOSE BELONG TO ME. FROM BEFORE I...
HAVE YOU HEARD OF NEGOTIATING? THERE MUST BE AN EXCHANGE OF SOME KIND BEFORE YOU OWN ANYTHING.
WAIT A MINUTE...
IS THIS SOME WEIRD METAPHOR WORLD BETWEEN LIFE AND DEATH THAT SOMEHOW SIGNIFIES ALL THE HORRIBLE CHOICES I MADE IN--
WOOOOOSH

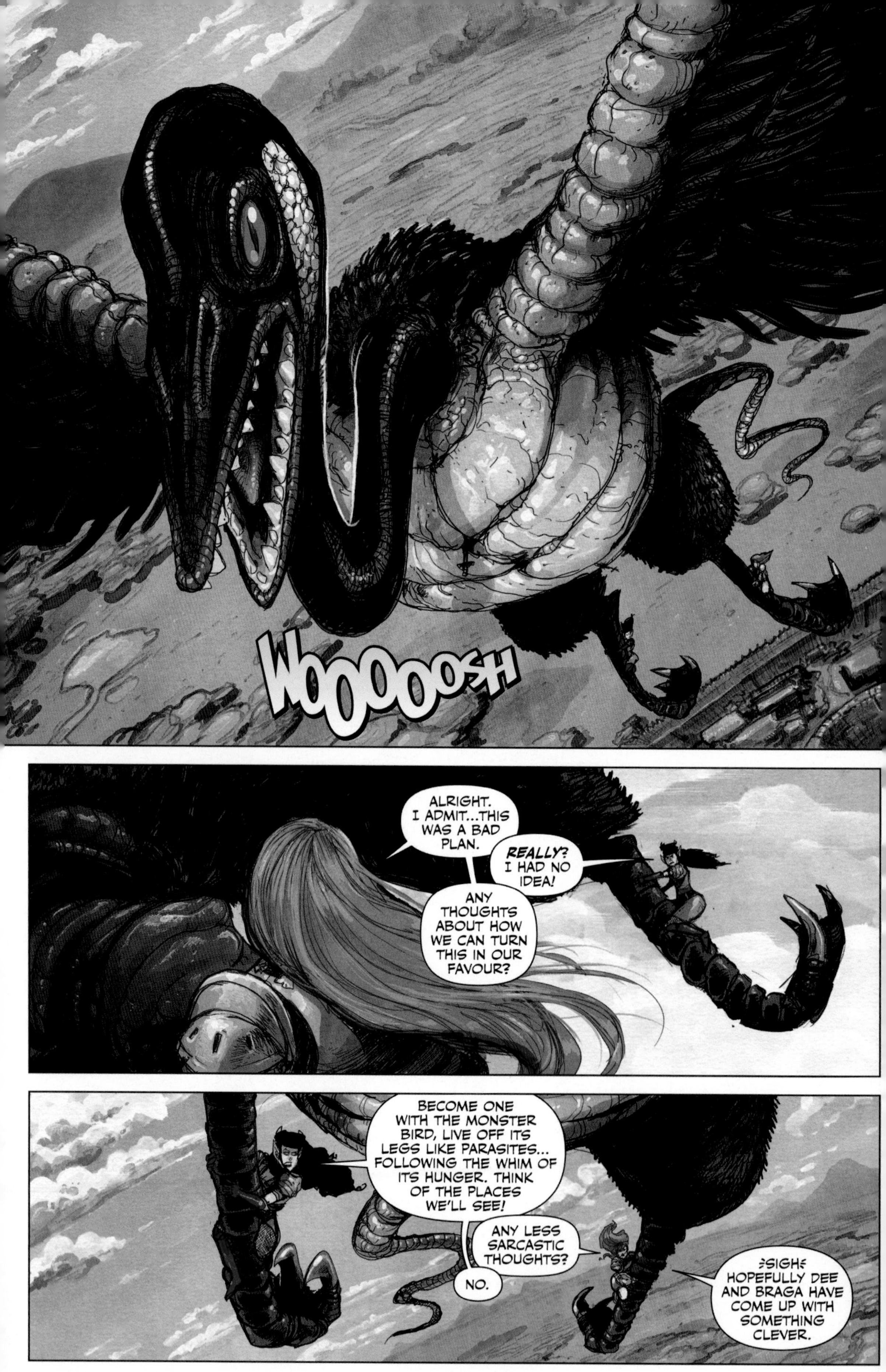
WOOOOOSH
ALRIGHT. I ADMIT...THIS WAS A BAD PLAN.
REALLY? I HAD NO IDEA!
ANY THOUGHTS ABOUT HOW WE CAN TURN THIS IN OUR FAVOUR?
BECOME ONE WITH THE MONSTER BIRD, LIVE OFF ITS LEGS LIKE PARASITES... FOLLOWING THE WHIM OF ITS HUNGER. THINK OF THE PLACES WE'LL SEE!
ANY LESS SARCASTIC THOUGHTS?
NO.
SIGH
HOPEFULLY DEE AND BRAGA HAVE COME UP WITH SOMETHING CLEVER.

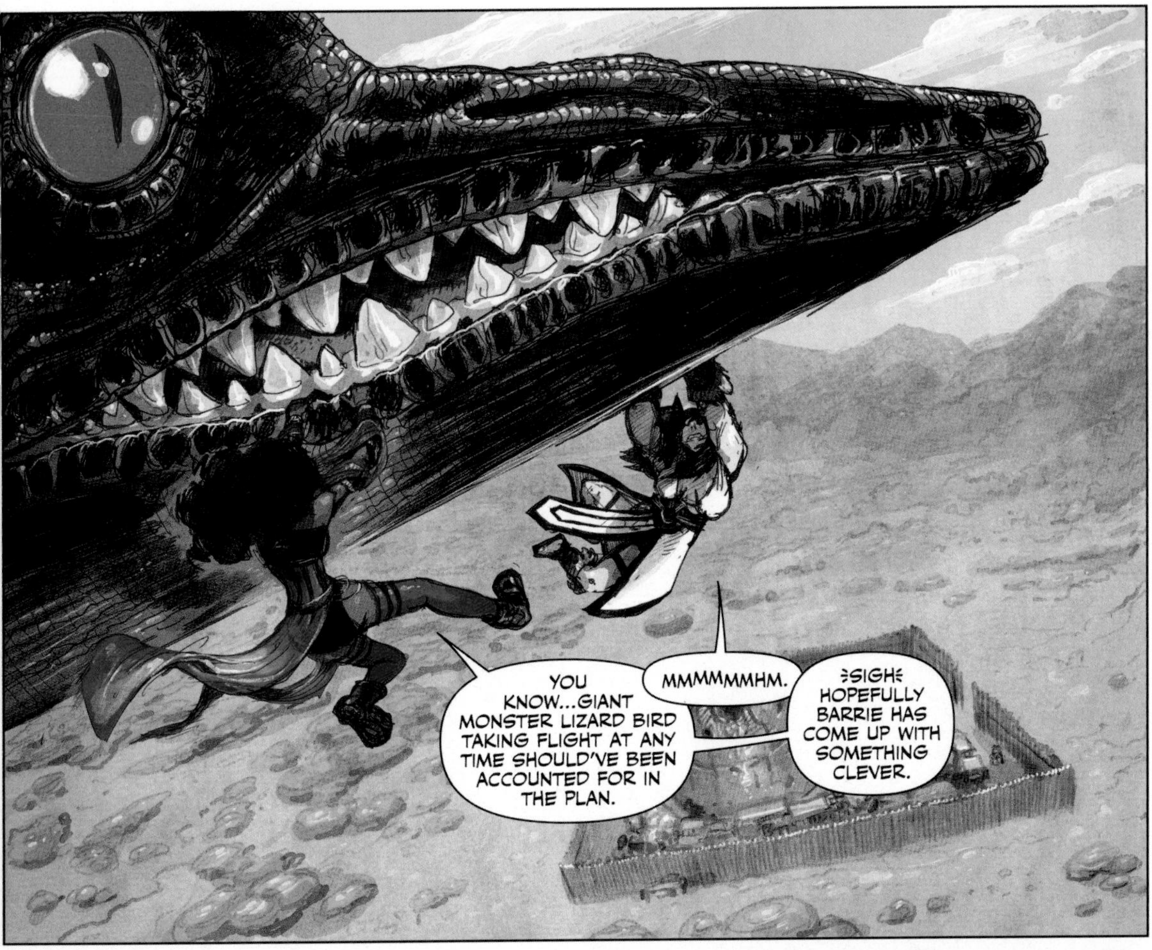
YOU KNOW...GIANT MONSTER LIZARD BIRD TAKING FLIGHT AT ANY TIME SHOULD'VE BEEN ACCOUNTED FOR IN THE PLAN.
MMMMMMHM.
≶SIGH≷ HOPEFULLY BARRIE HAS COME UP WITH SOMETHING CLEVER.

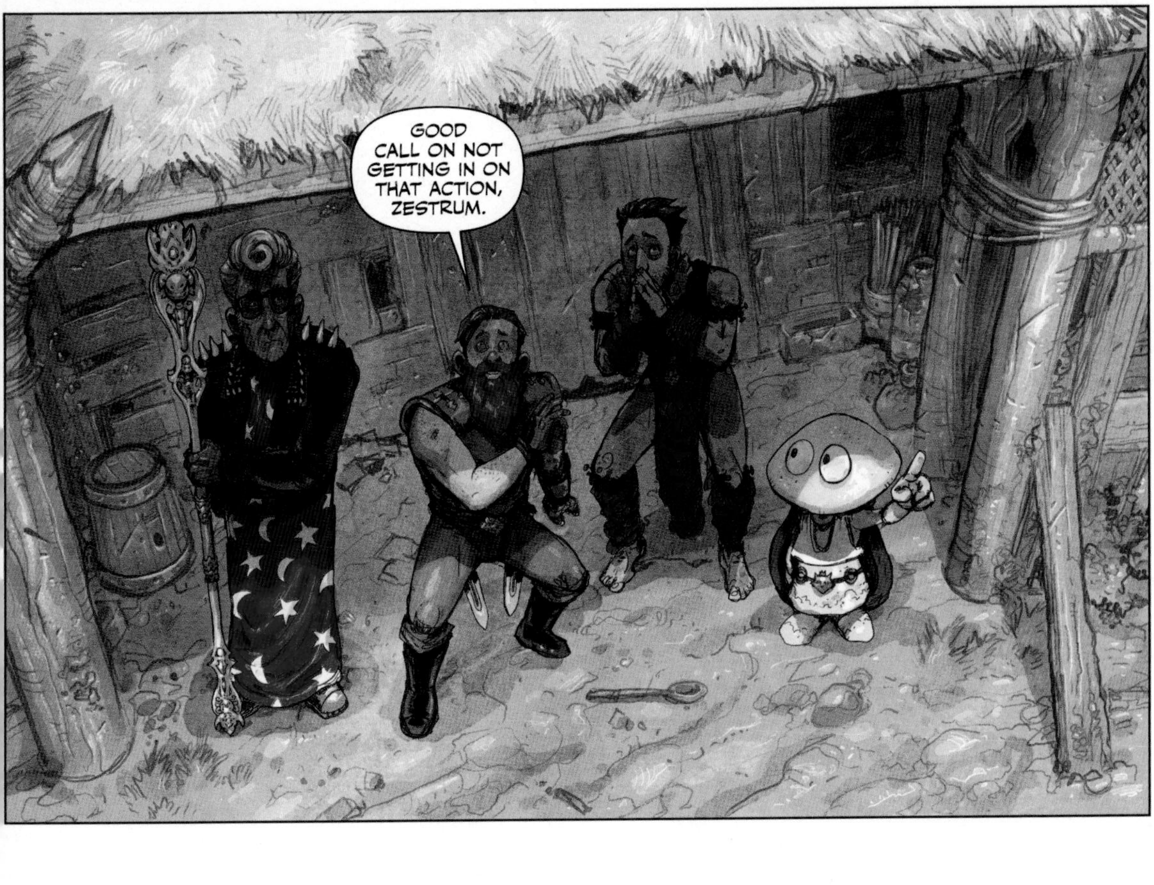
GOOD CALL ON NOT GETTING IN ON THAT ACTION, ZESTRUM.

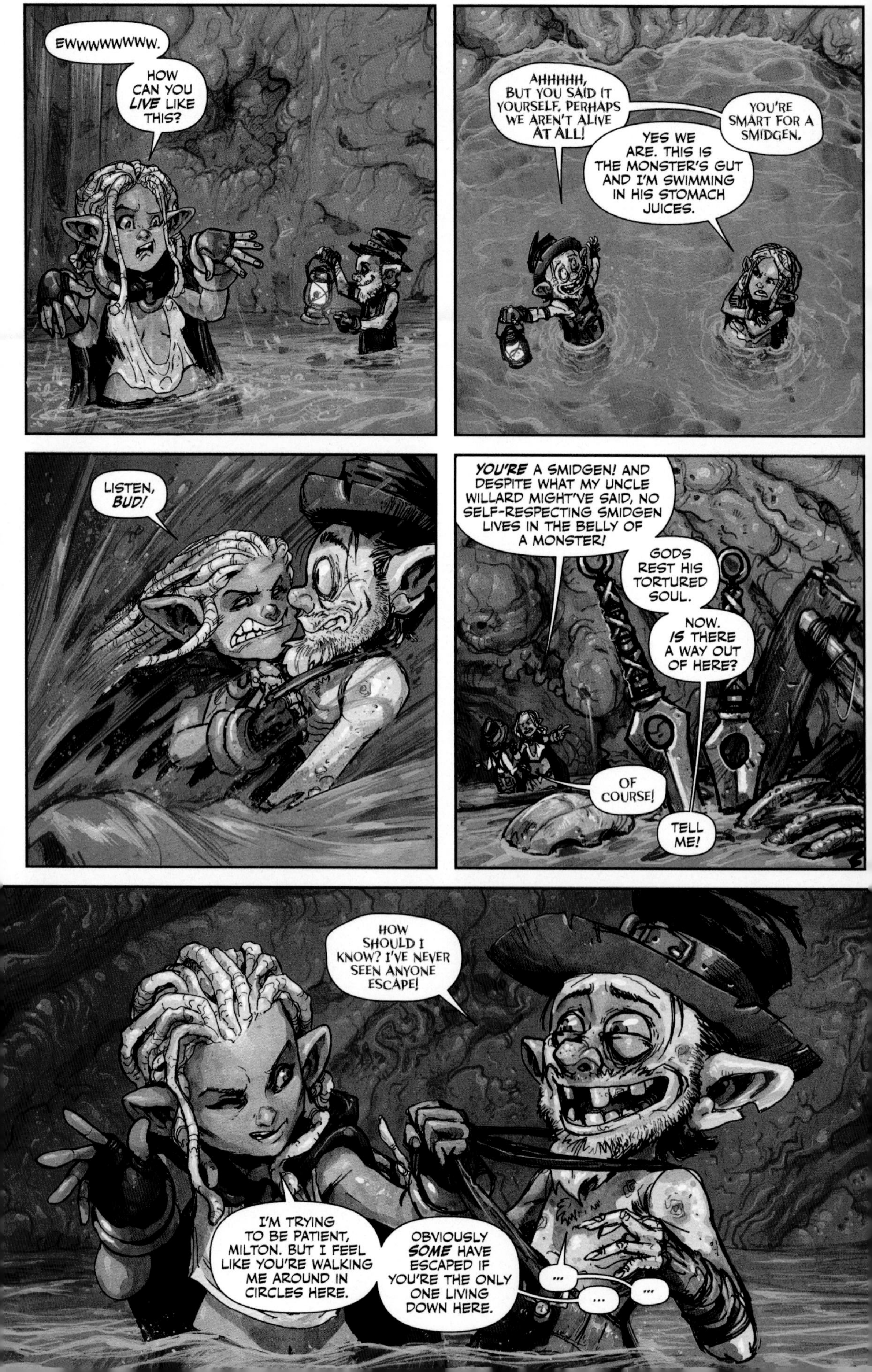
EWWWWWWWW.
HOW CAN YOU LIVE LIKE THIS?
AHHHHH, BUT YOU SAID IT YOURSELF, PERHAPS WE AREN'T ALIVE AT ALL!
YOU'RE SMART FOR A SMIDGEN.
YES WE ARE. THIS IS THE MONSTER'S GUT AND I'M SWIMMING IN HIS STOMACH JUICES.
LISTEN, BUD!
YOU'RE A SMIDGEN! AND DESPITE WHAT MY UNCLE WILLARD MIGHT'VE SAID, NO SELF-RESPECTING SMIDGEN LIVES IN THE BELLY OF A MONSTER!
GODS REST HIS TORTURED SOUL.
NOW. IS THERE A WAY OUT OF HERE?
OF COURSE!
TELL ME!
HOW SHOULD I KNOW? I'VE NEVER SEEN ANYONE ESCAPE!
I'M TRYING TO BE PATIENT, MILTON. BUT I FEEL LIKE YOU'RE WALKING ME AROUND IN CIRCLES HERE.
OBVIOUSLY SOME HAVE ESCAPED IF YOU'RE THE ONLY ONE LIVING DOWN HERE.
...
...
...

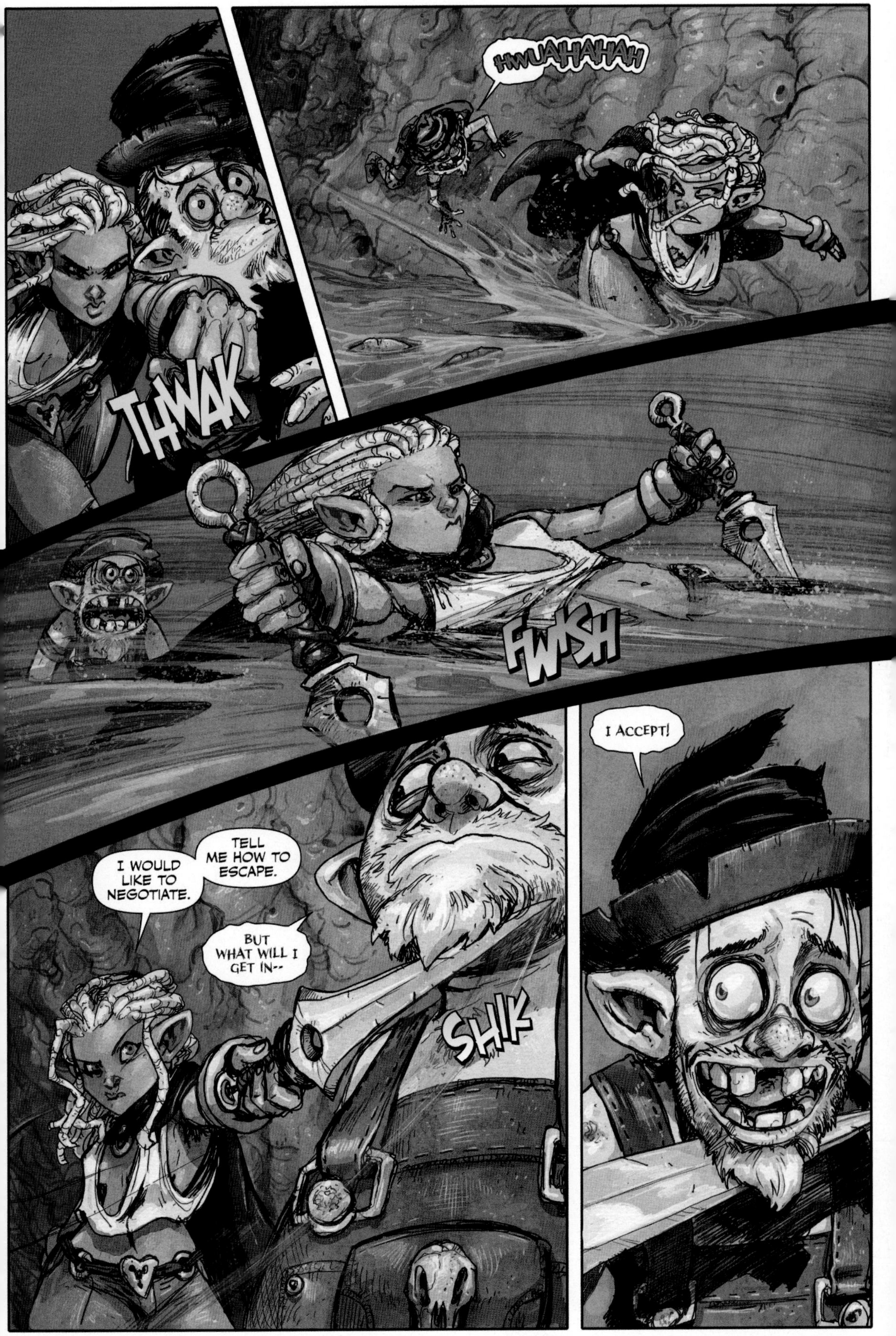
THWAK
HWUAHAHAH
FWISH
I WOULD LIKE TO NEGOTIATE.
TELL ME HOW TO ESCAPE.
BUT WHAT WILL I GET IN--
SHIK
I ACCEPT!

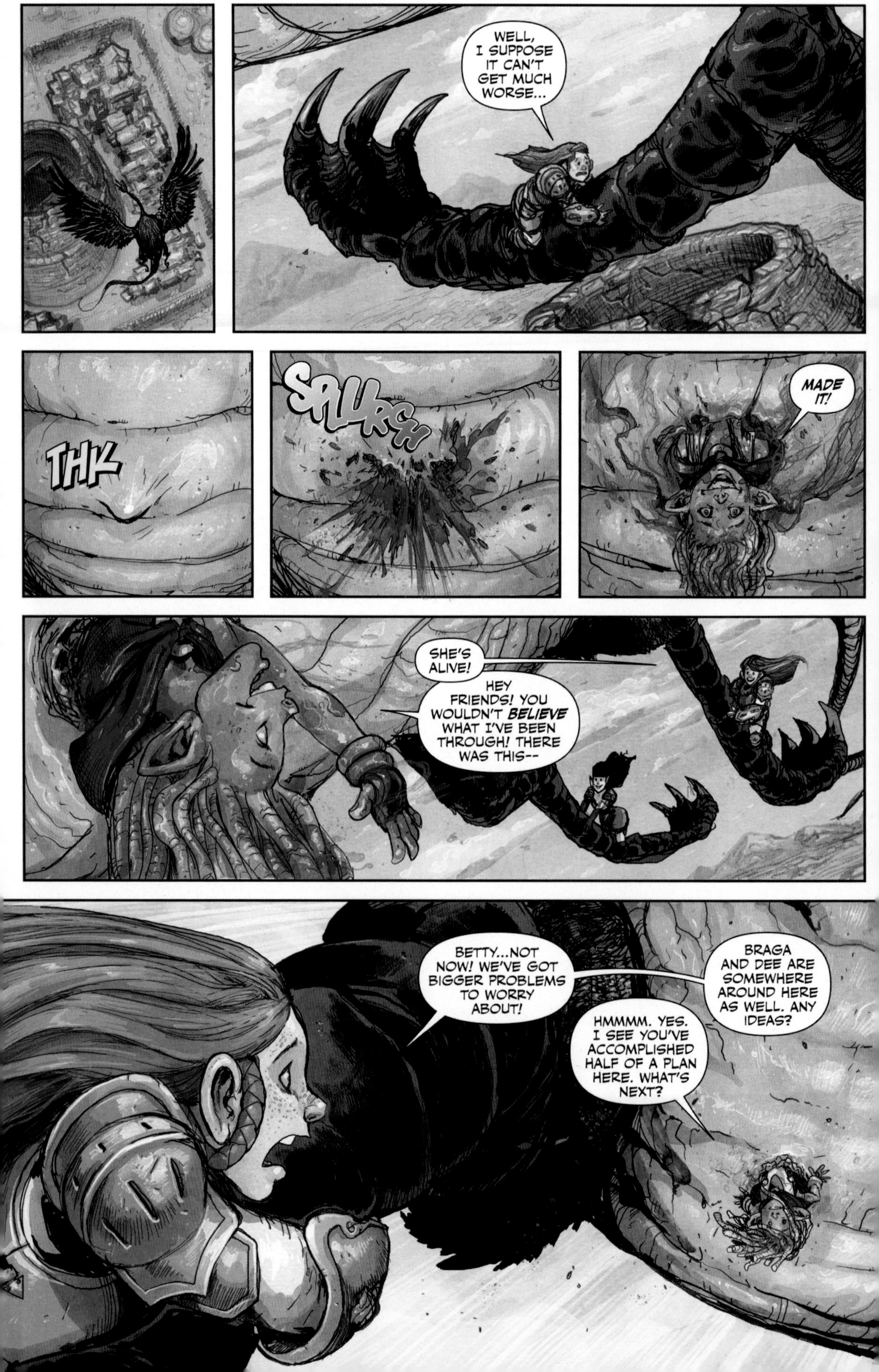
WELL, I SUPPOSE IT CAN'T GET MUCH WORSE...
THK
SPLURCH
MADE IT!
SHE'S ALIVE!
HEY FRIENDS! YOU WOULDN'T BELIEVE WHAT I'VE BEEN THROUGH! THERE WAS THIS--
BETTY...NOT NOW! WE'VE GOT BIGGER PROBLEMS TO WORRY ABOUT!
BRAGA AND DEE ARE SOMEWHERE AROUND HERE AS WELL. ANY IDEAS?
HMMMM. YES. I SEE YOU'VE ACCOMPLISHED HALF OF A PLAN HERE. WHAT'S NEXT?

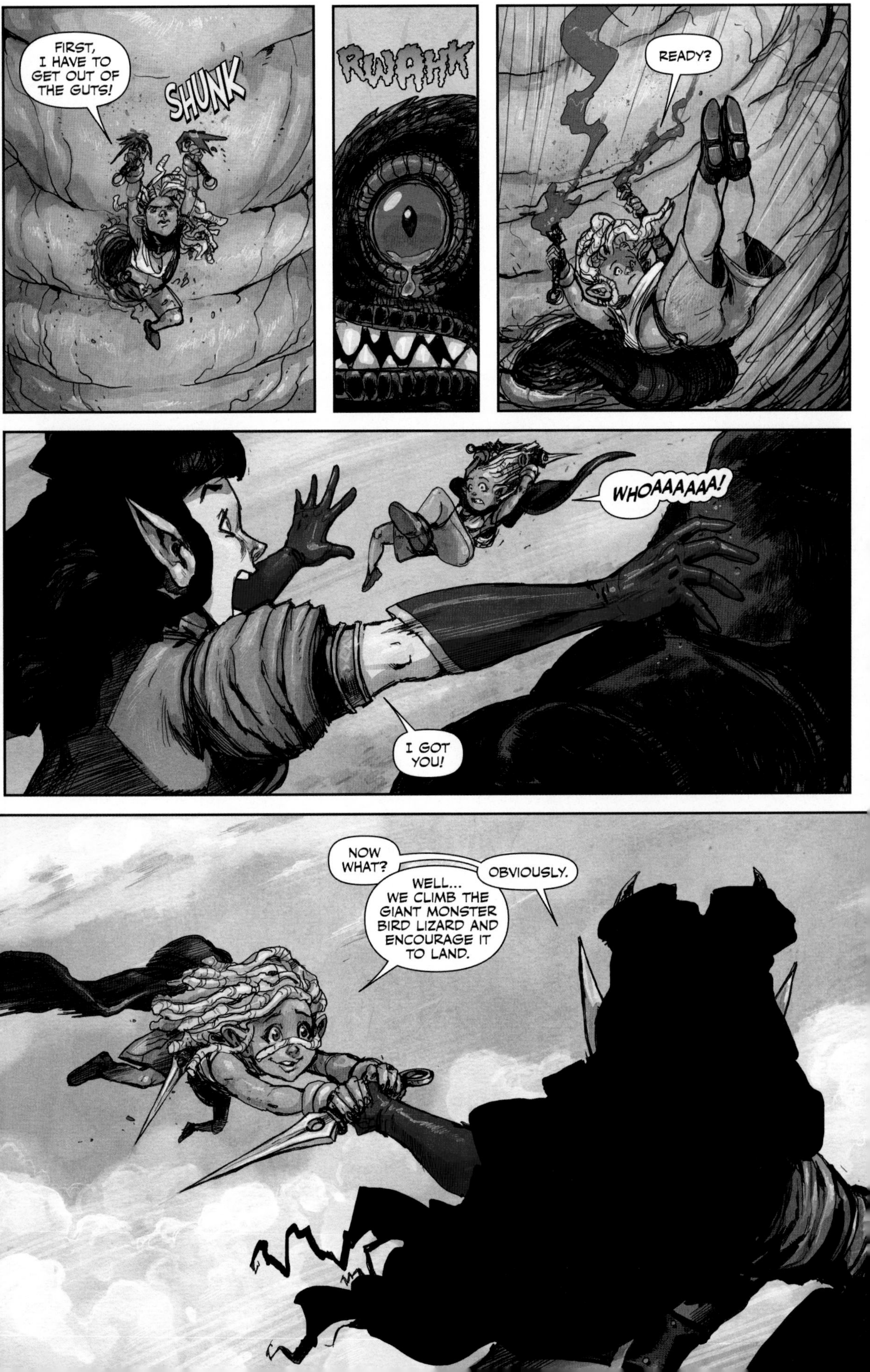
FIRST, I HAVE TO GET OUT OF THE GUTS!
SHUNK
RWAHK
READY?
WHOAAAAAA!
I GOT YOU!
NOW WHAT?
WELL... WE CLIMB THE GIANT MONSTER BIRD LIZARD AND ENCOURAGE IT TO LAND.
OBVIOUSLY.

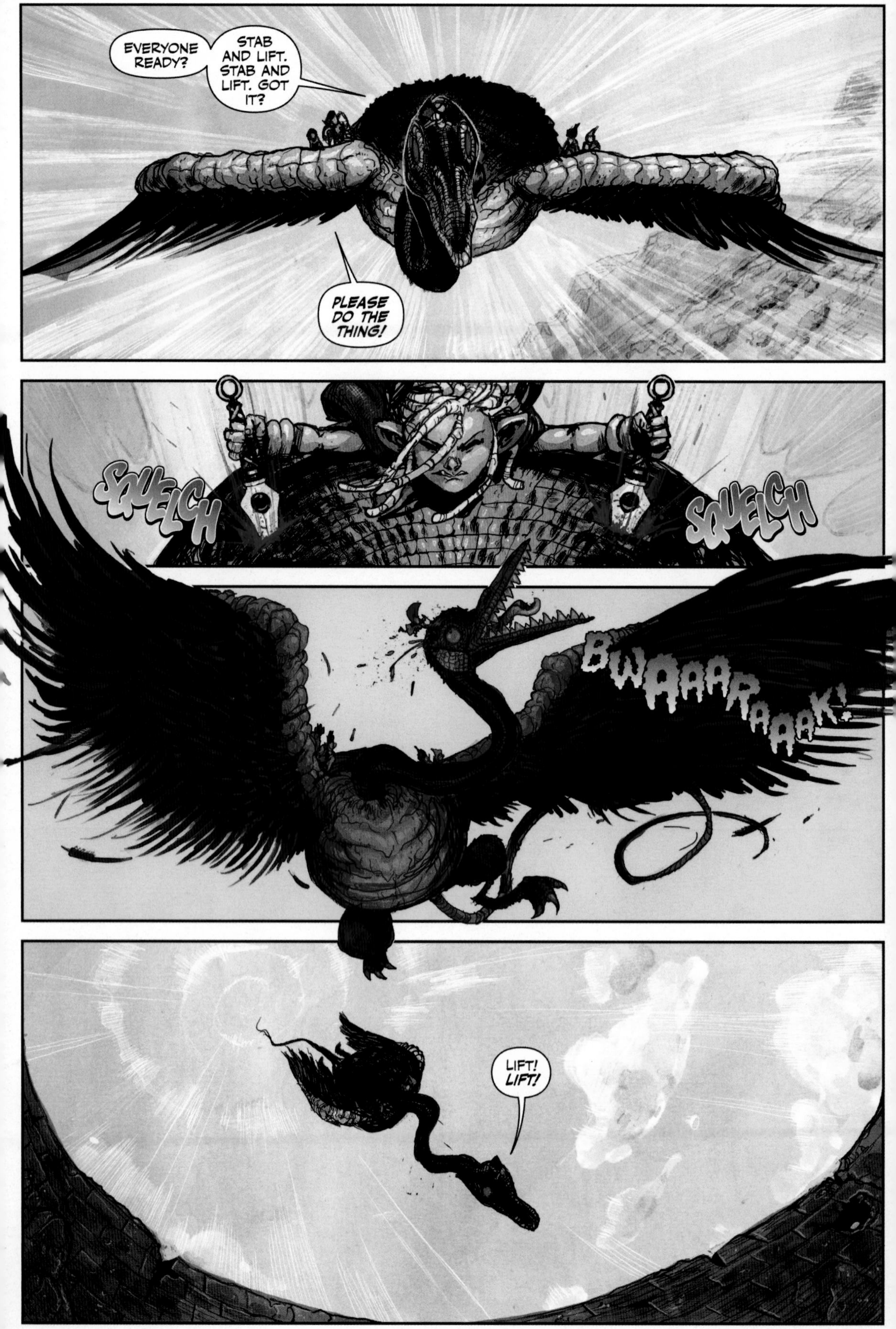
EVERYONE READY?
STAB AND LIFT. STAB AND LIFT. GOT IT?
PLEASE DO THE THING!
SQUELCH
SQUELCH
BWAAAARAAAK!
LIFT! LIFT!

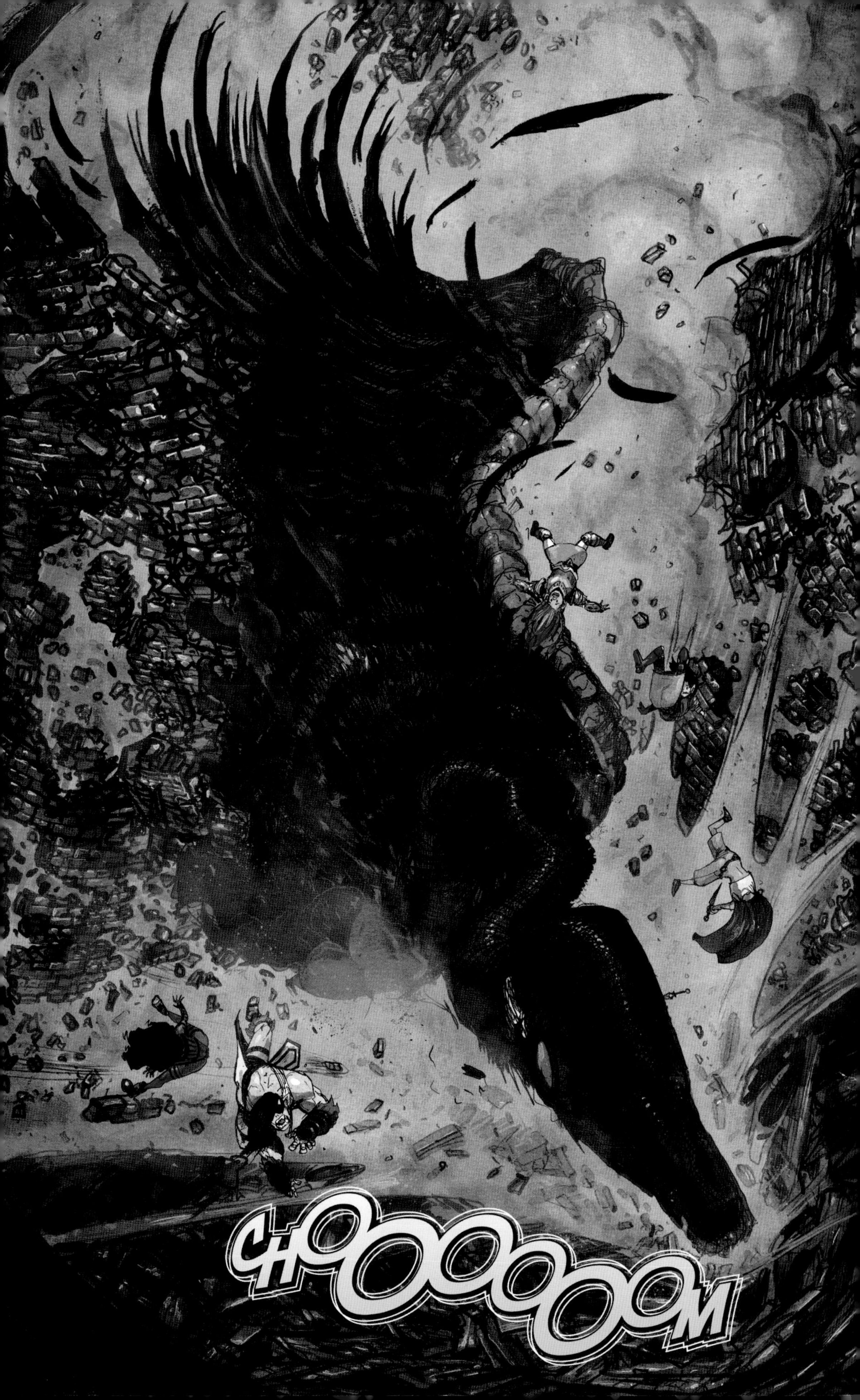
CHOOOOOOOM

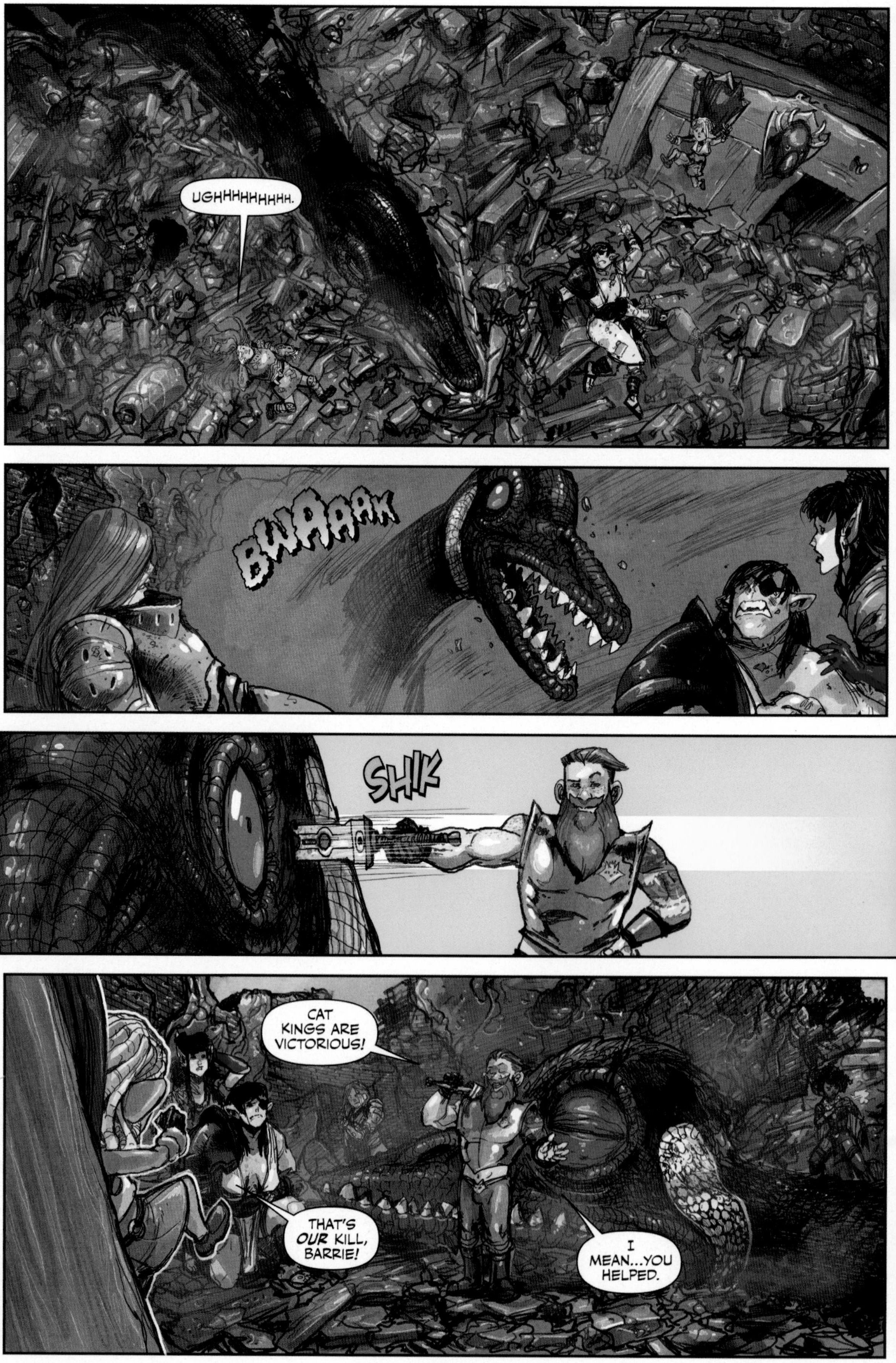
UGHHHHHHHH.
BWAAAK
SHIK
CAT KINGS ARE VICTORIOUS!
THAT'S *OUR* KILL, BARRIE!
I MEAN...YOU HELPED.

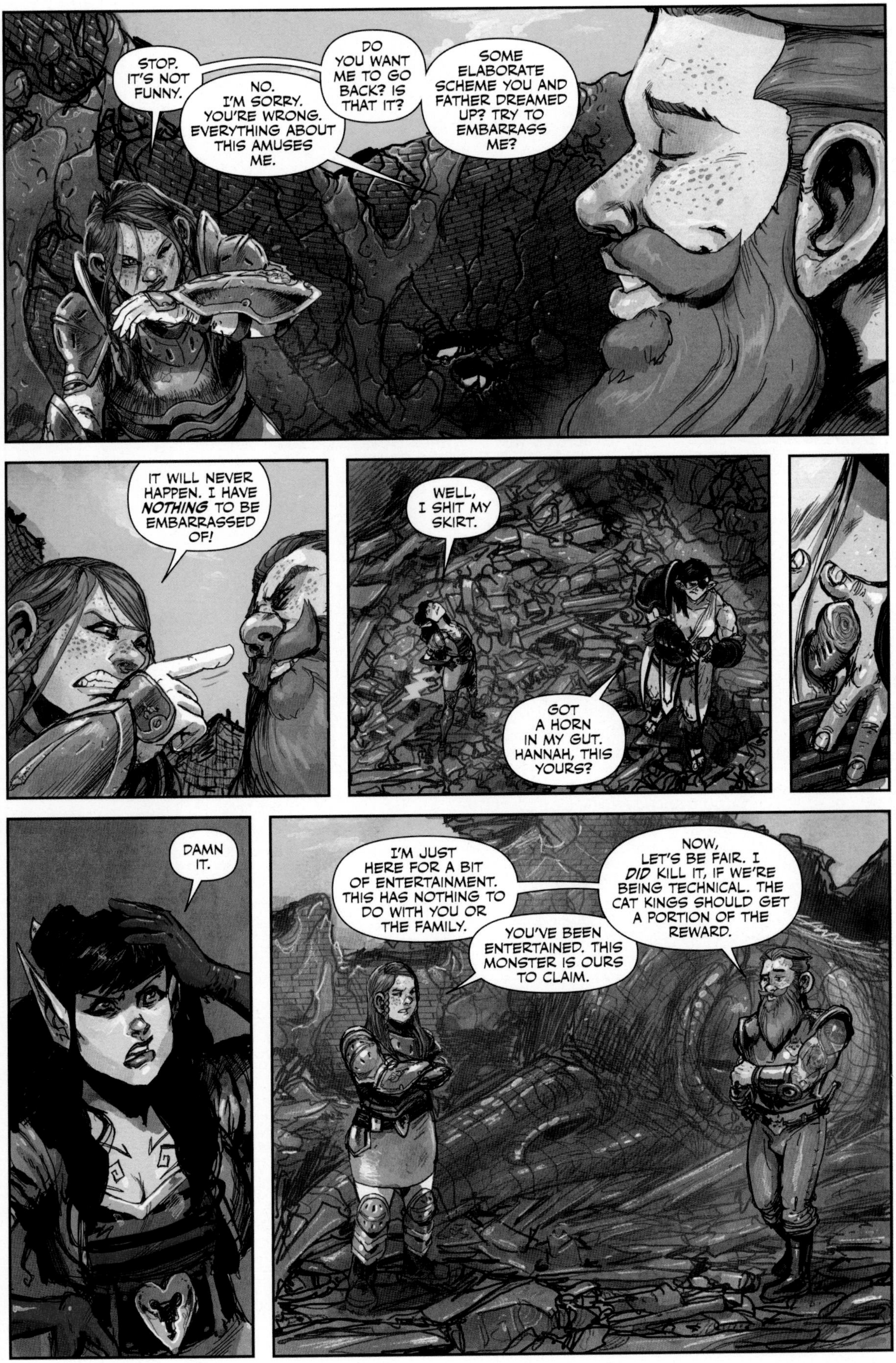

STOP. IT'S NOT FUNNY.
NO. I'M SORRY. YOU'RE WRONG. EVERYTHING ABOUT THIS AMUSES ME.
DO YOU WANT ME TO GO BACK? IS THAT IT?
SOME ELABORATE SCHEME YOU AND FATHER DREAMED UP? TRY TO EMBARRASS ME?
IT WILL NEVER HAPPEN. I HAVE *NOTHING* TO BE EMBARRASSED OF!
WELL, I SHIT MY SKIRT.
GOT A HORN IN MY GUT. HANNAH, THIS YOURS?
DAMN IT.
I'M JUST HERE FOR A BIT OF ENTERTAINMENT. THIS HAS NOTHING TO DO WITH YOU OR THE FAMILY.
NOW, LET'S BE FAIR. I *DID* KILL IT, IF WE'RE BEING TECHNICAL. THE CAT KINGS SHOULD GET A PORTION OF THE REWARD.
YOU'VE BEEN ENTERTAINED. THIS MONSTER IS OURS TO CLAIM.

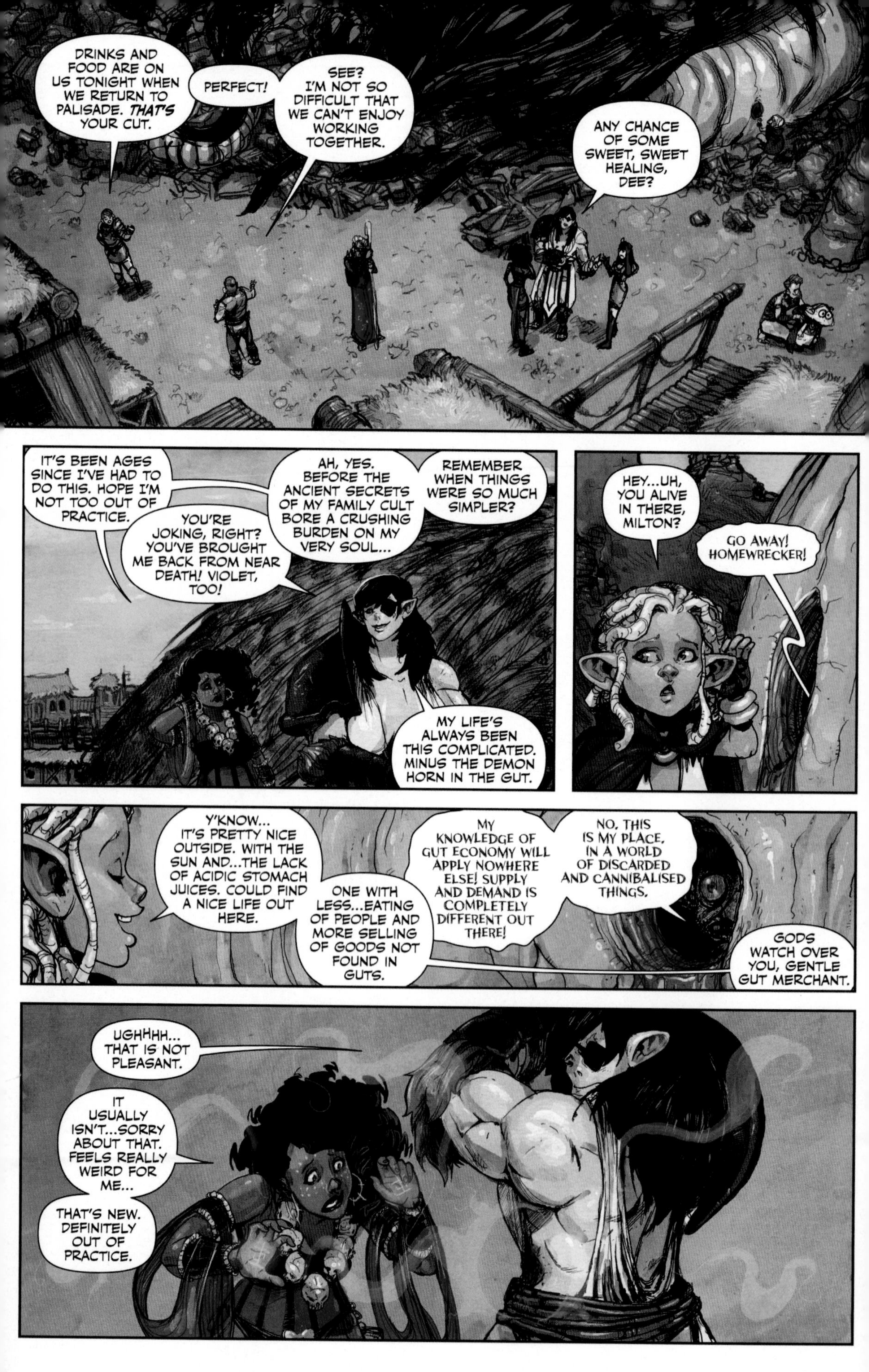
DRINKS AND FOOD ARE ON US TONIGHT WHEN WE RETURN TO PALISADE. *THAT'S* YOUR CUT.
PERFECT!
SEE? I'M NOT SO DIFFICULT THAT WE CAN'T ENJOY WORKING TOGETHER.
ANY CHANCE OF SOME SWEET, SWEET HEALING, DEE?
IT'S BEEN AGES SINCE I'VE HAD TO DO THIS. HOPE I'M NOT TOO OUT OF PRACTICE.
YOU'RE JOKING, RIGHT? YOU'VE BROUGHT ME BACK FROM NEAR DEATH! VIOLET, TOO!
AH, YES. BEFORE THE ANCIENT SECRETS OF MY FAMILY CULT BORE A CRUSHING BURDEN ON MY VERY SOUL...
REMEMBER WHEN THINGS WERE SO MUCH SIMPLER?
MY LIFE'S ALWAYS BEEN THIS COMPLICATED. MINUS THE DEMON HORN IN THE GUT.
HEY...UH, YOU ALIVE IN THERE, MILTON?
GO AWAY! HOMEWRECKER!
Y'KNOW... IT'S PRETTY NICE OUTSIDE. WITH THE SUN AND...THE LACK OF ACIDIC STOMACH JUICES. COULD FIND A NICE LIFE OUT HERE.
ONE WITH LESS...EATING OF PEOPLE AND MORE SELLING OF GOODS NOT FOUND IN GUTS.
MY KNOWLEDGE OF GUT ECONOMY WILL APPLY NOWHERE ELSE! SUPPLY AND DEMAND IS COMPLETELY DIFFERENT OUT THERE!
NO, THIS IS MY PLACE, IN A WORLD OF DISCARDED AND CANNIBALISED THINGS.
GODS WATCH OVER YOU, GENTLE GUT MERCHANT.
UGHHHH... THAT IS NOT PLEASANT.
IT USUALLY ISN'T...SORRY ABOUT THAT. FEELS REALLY WEIRD FOR ME...
THAT'S NEW. DEFINITELY OUT OF PRACTICE.

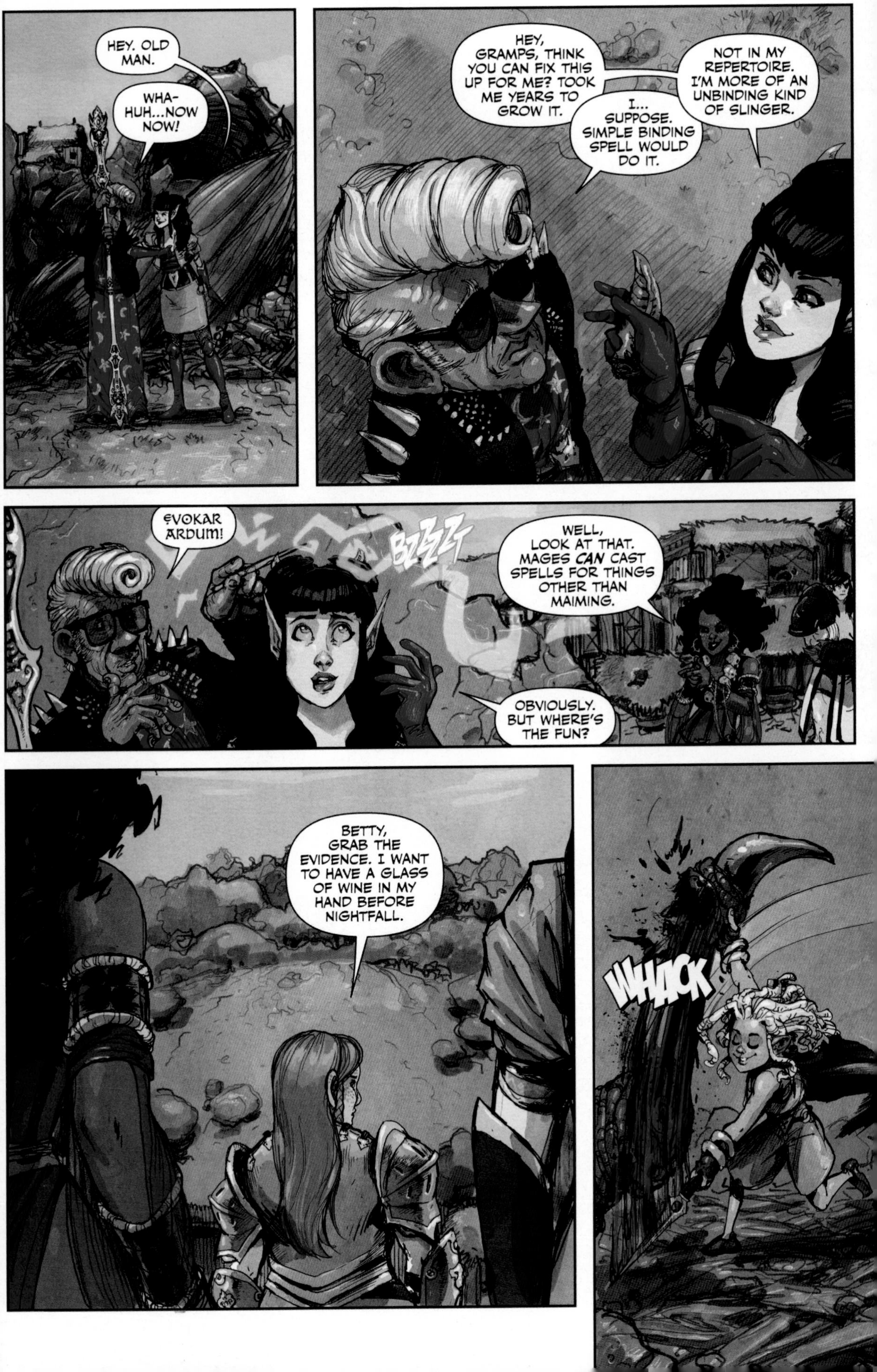
HEY. OLD MAN.
WHA-HUH...NOW NOW!
HEY, GRAMPS, THINK YOU CAN FIX THIS UP FOR ME? TOOK ME YEARS TO GROW IT.
I... SUPPOSE. SIMPLE BINDING SPELL WOULD DO IT.
NOT IN MY REPERTOIRE. I'M MORE OF AN UNBINDING KIND OF SLINGER.
EVOKAR ARDUM!
BZZZZT
WELL, LOOK AT THAT. MAGES CAN CAST SPELLS FOR THINGS OTHER THAN MAIMING.
OBVIOUSLY. BUT WHERE'S THE FUN?
BETTY, GRAB THE EVIDENCE. I WANT TO HAVE A GLASS OF WINE IN MY HAND BEFORE NIGHTFALL.
WHACK

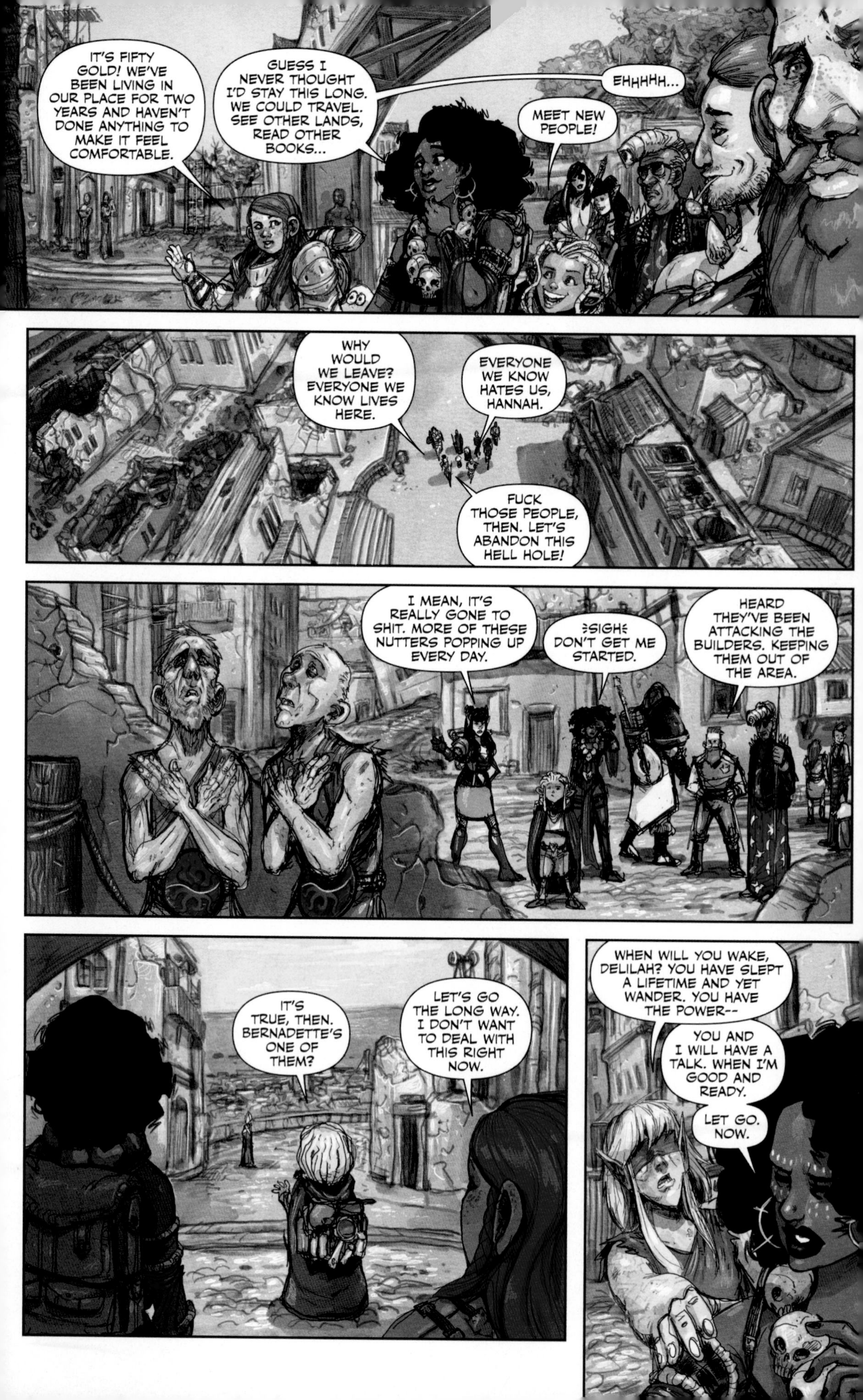
IT'S FIFTY GOLD! WE'VE BEEN LIVING IN OUR PLACE FOR TWO YEARS AND HAVEN'T DONE ANYTHING TO MAKE IT FEEL COMFORTABLE.
GUESS I NEVER THOUGHT I'D STAY THIS LONG. WE COULD TRAVEL. SEE OTHER LANDS, READ OTHER BOOKS...
EHHHHH...
MEET NEW PEOPLE!
WHY WOULD WE LEAVE? EVERYONE WE KNOW LIVES HERE.
EVERYONE WE KNOW HATES US, HANNAH.
FUCK THOSE PEOPLE, THEN. LET'S ABANDON THIS HELL HOLE!
I MEAN, IT'S REALLY GONE TO SHIT. MORE OF THESE NUTTERS POPPING UP EVERY DAY.
SIGH DON'T GET ME STARTED.
HEARD THEY'VE BEEN ATTACKING THE BUILDERS. KEEPING THEM OUT OF THE AREA.
IT'S TRUE, THEN. BERNADETTE'S ONE OF THEM?
LET'S GO THE LONG WAY. I DON'T WANT TO DEAL WITH THIS RIGHT NOW.
WHEN WILL YOU WAKE, DELILAH? YOU HAVE SLEPT A LIFETIME AND YET WANDER. YOU HAVE THE POWER--
YOU AND I WILL HAVE A TALK. WHEN I'M GOOD AND READY.
LET GO. NOW.

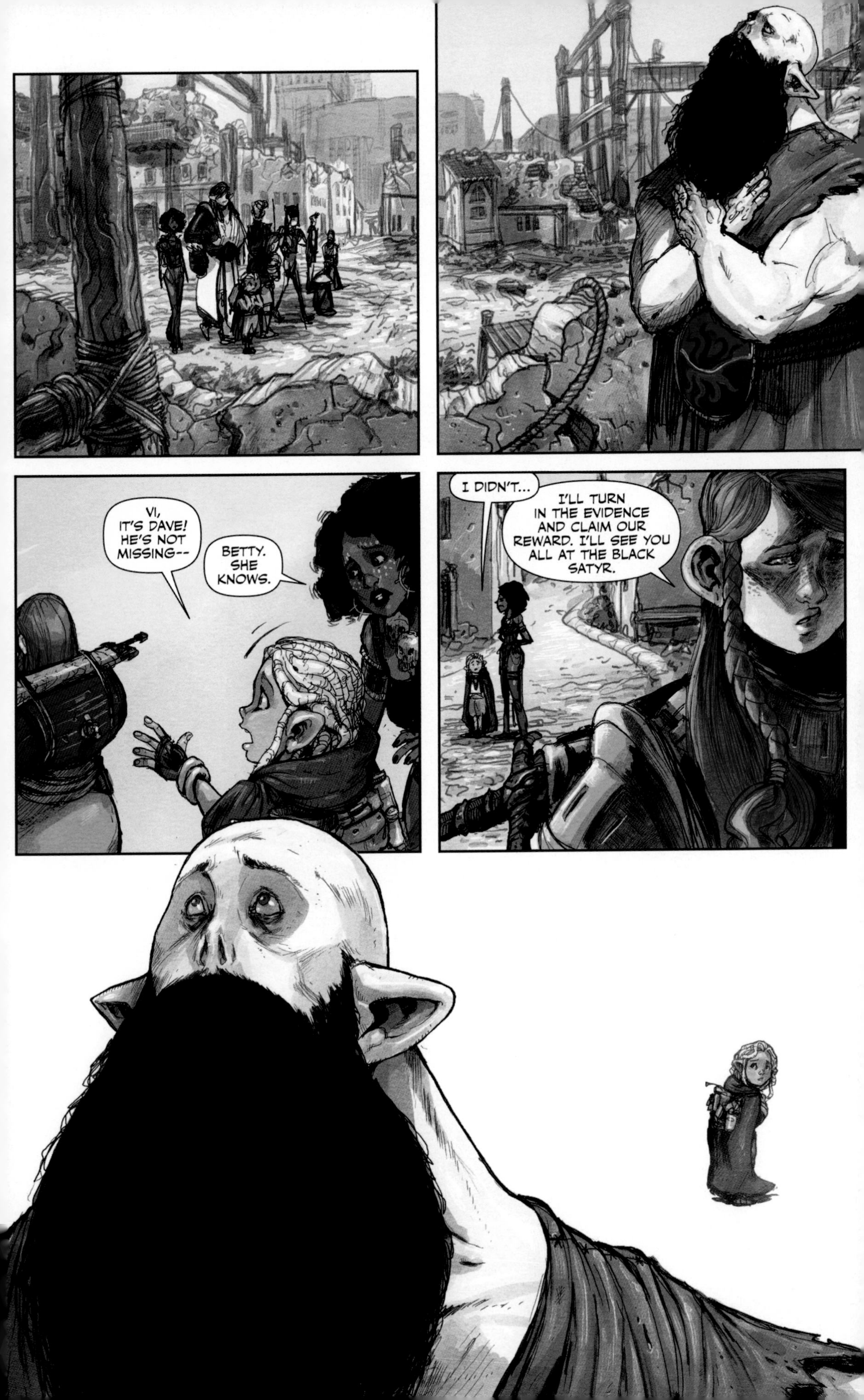
VI, IT'S DAVE! HE'S NOT MISSING--
BETTY. SHE KNOWS.
I DIDN'T...
I'LL TURN IN THE EVIDENCE AND CLAIM OUR REWARD. I'LL SEE YOU ALL AT THE BLACK SATYR.

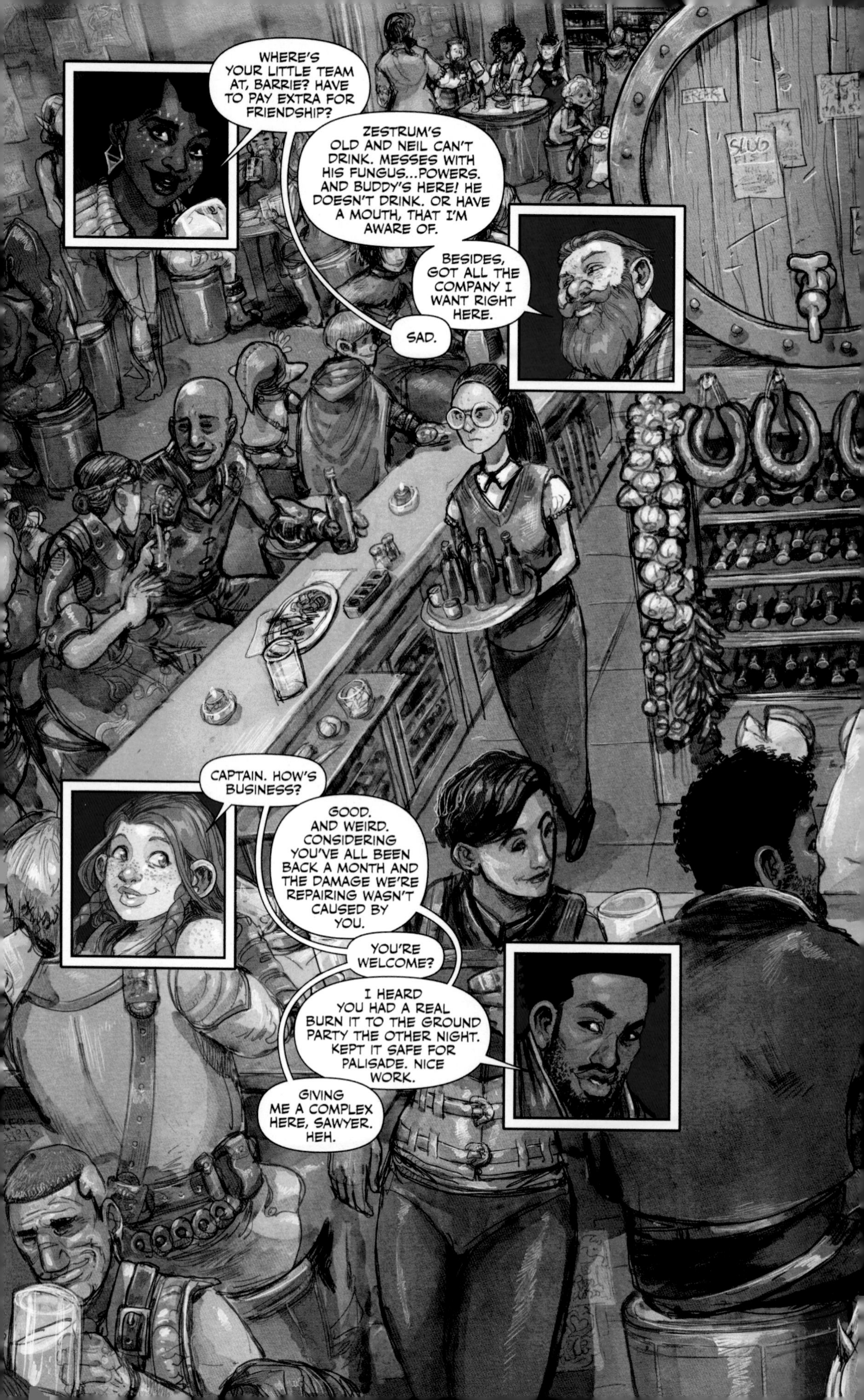
WHERE'S YOUR LITTLE TEAM AT, BARRIE? HAVE TO PAY EXTRA FOR FRIENDSHIP?
ZESTRUM'S OLD AND NEIL CAN'T DRINK. MESSES WITH HIS FUNGUS...POWERS. AND BUDDY'S HERE! HE DOESN'T DRINK. OR HAVE A MOUTH, THAT I'M AWARE OF.
BESIDES, GOT ALL THE COMPANY I WANT RIGHT HERE.
SAD.
CAPTAIN. HOW'S BUSINESS?
GOOD. AND WEIRD. CONSIDERING YOU'VE ALL BEEN BACK A MONTH AND THE DAMAGE WE'RE REPAIRING WASN'T CAUSED BY YOU.
YOU'RE WELCOME?
I HEARD YOU HAD A REAL BURN IT TO THE GROUND PARTY THE OTHER NIGHT. KEPT IT SAFE FOR PALISADE. NICE WORK.
GIVING ME A COMPLEX HERE, SAWYER. HEH.

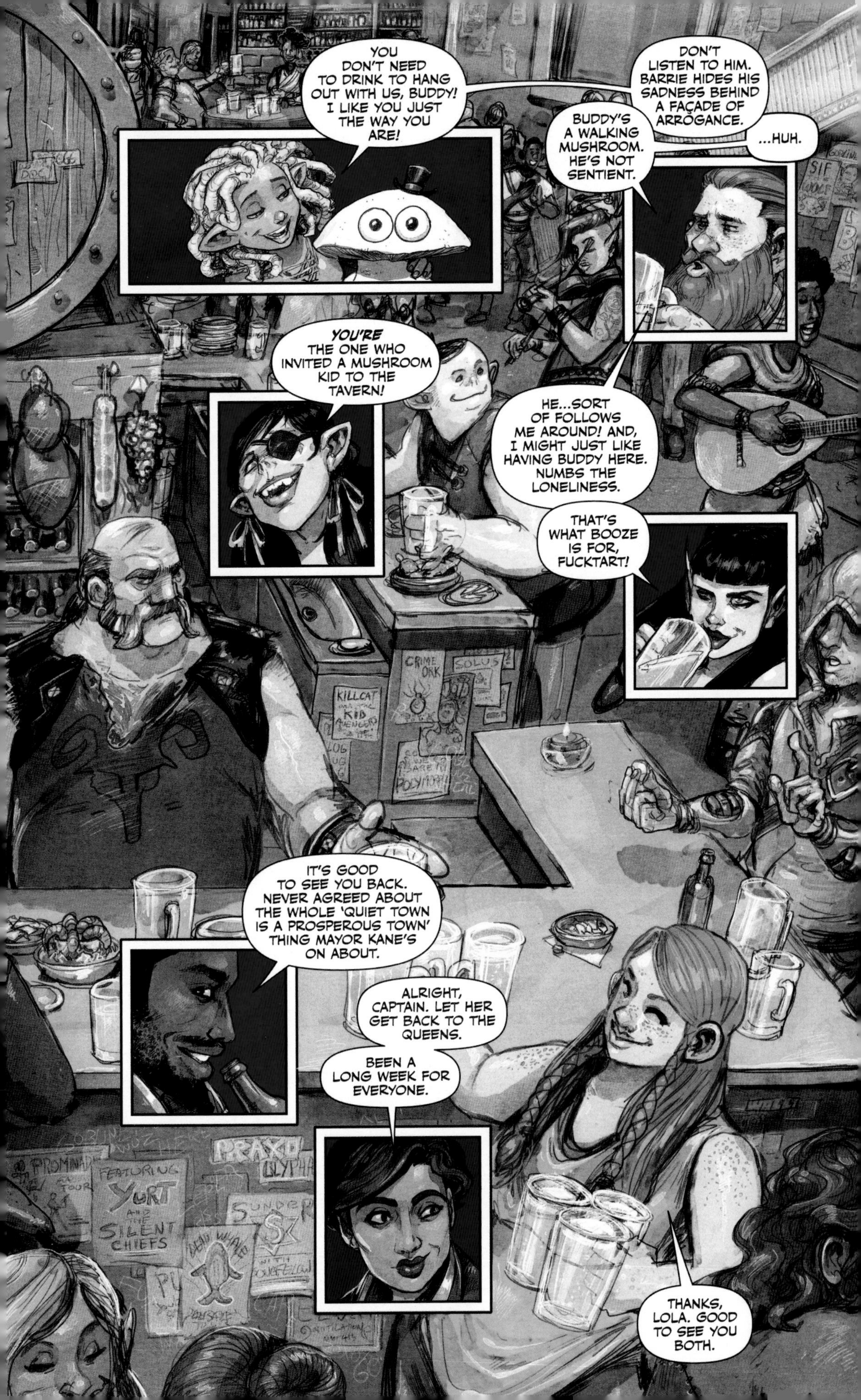
YOU DON'T NEED TO DRINK TO HANG OUT WITH US, BUDDY! I LIKE YOU JUST THE WAY YOU ARE!
DON'T LISTEN TO HIM. BARRIE HIDES HIS SADNESS BEHIND A FAÇADE OF ARROGANCE.
BUDDY'S A WALKING MUSHROOM. HE'S NOT SENTIENT.
...HUH.
YOU'RE THE ONE WHO INVITED A MUSHROOM KID TO THE TAVERN!
HE...SORT OF FOLLOWS ME AROUND! AND, I MIGHT JUST LIKE HAVING BUDDY HERE. NUMBS THE LONELINESS.
THAT'S WHAT BOOZE IS FOR, FUCKTART!
IT'S GOOD TO SEE YOU BACK. NEVER AGREED ABOUT THE WHOLE 'QUIET TOWN IS A PROSPEROUS TOWN' THING MAYOR KANE'S ON ABOUT.
ALRIGHT, CAPTAIN. LET HER GET BACK TO THE QUEENS.
BEEN A LONG WEEK FOR EVERYONE.
THANKS, LOLA. GOOD TO SEE YOU BOTH.

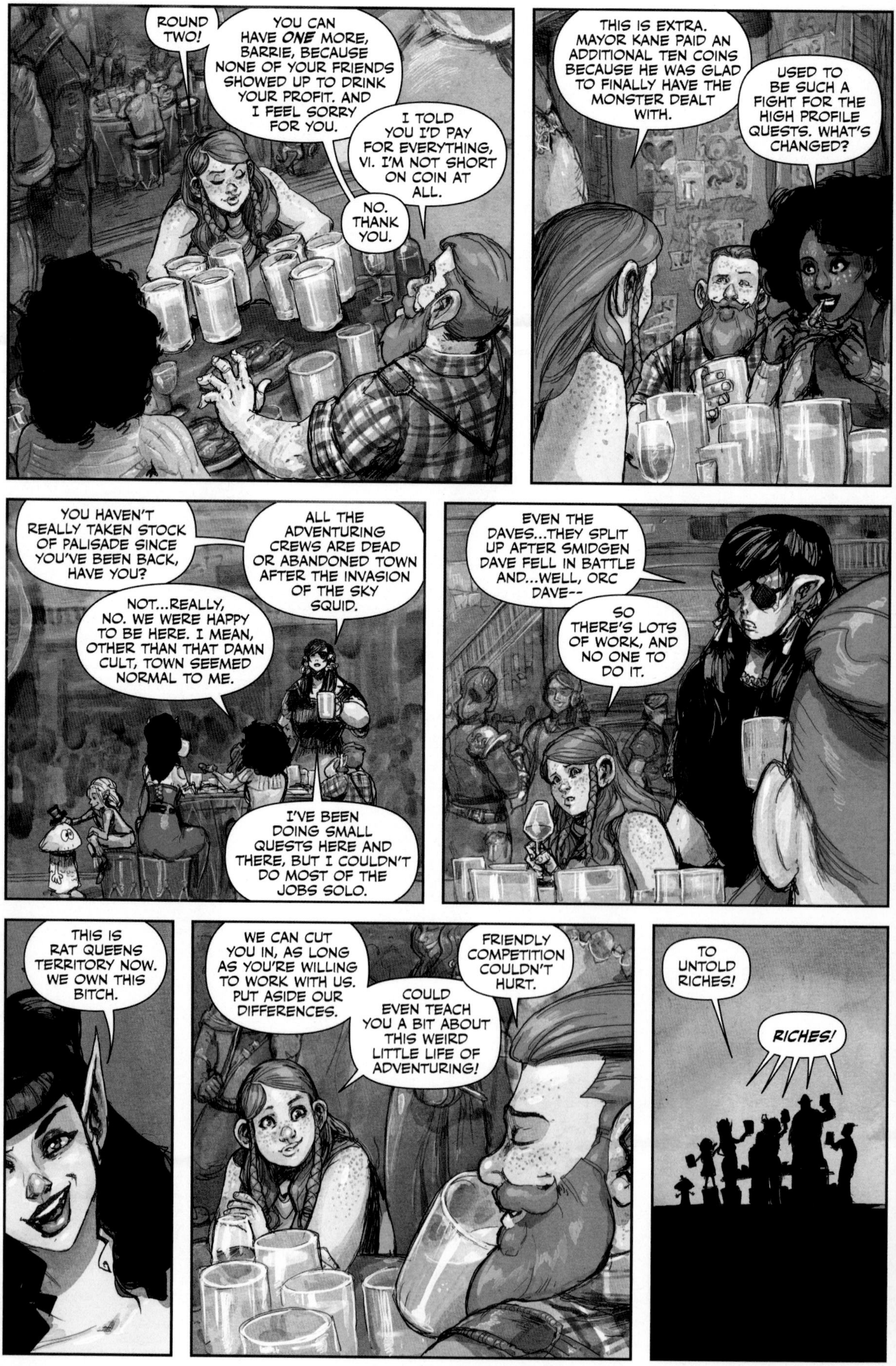
ROUND TWO!
YOU CAN HAVE ONE MORE, BARRIE, BECAUSE NONE OF YOUR FRIENDS SHOWED UP TO DRINK YOUR PROFIT. AND I FEEL SORRY FOR YOU.
I TOLD YOU I'D PAY FOR EVERYTHING, VI. I'M NOT SHORT ON COIN AT ALL.
NO. THANK YOU.
THIS IS EXTRA. MAYOR KANE PAID AN ADDITIONAL TEN COINS BECAUSE HE WAS GLAD TO FINALLY HAVE THE MONSTER DEALT WITH.
USED TO BE SUCH A FIGHT FOR THE HIGH PROFILE QUESTS. WHAT'S CHANGED?
YOU HAVEN'T REALLY TAKEN STOCK OF PALISADE SINCE YOU'VE BEEN BACK, HAVE YOU?
ALL THE ADVENTURING CREWS ARE DEAD OR ABANDONED TOWN AFTER THE INVASION OF THE SKY SQUID.
NOT...REALLY, NO. WE WERE HAPPY TO BE HERE. I MEAN, OTHER THAN THAT DAMN CULT, TOWN SEEMED NORMAL TO ME.
I'VE BEEN DOING SMALL QUESTS HERE AND THERE, BUT I COULDN'T DO MOST OF THE JOBS SOLO.
EVEN THE DAVES...THEY SPLIT UP AFTER SMIDGEN DAVE FELL IN BATTLE AND...WELL, ORC DAVE--
SO THERE'S LOTS OF WORK, AND NO ONE TO DO IT.
THIS IS RAT QUEENS TERRITORY NOW. WE OWN THIS BITCH.
WE CAN CUT YOU IN, AS LONG AS YOU'RE WILLING TO WORK WITH US. PUT ASIDE OUR DIFFERENCES.
COULD EVEN TEACH YOU A BIT ABOUT THIS WEIRD LITTLE LIFE OF ADVENTURING!
FRIENDLY COMPETITION COULDN'T HURT.
TO UNTOLD RICHES!
RICHES!

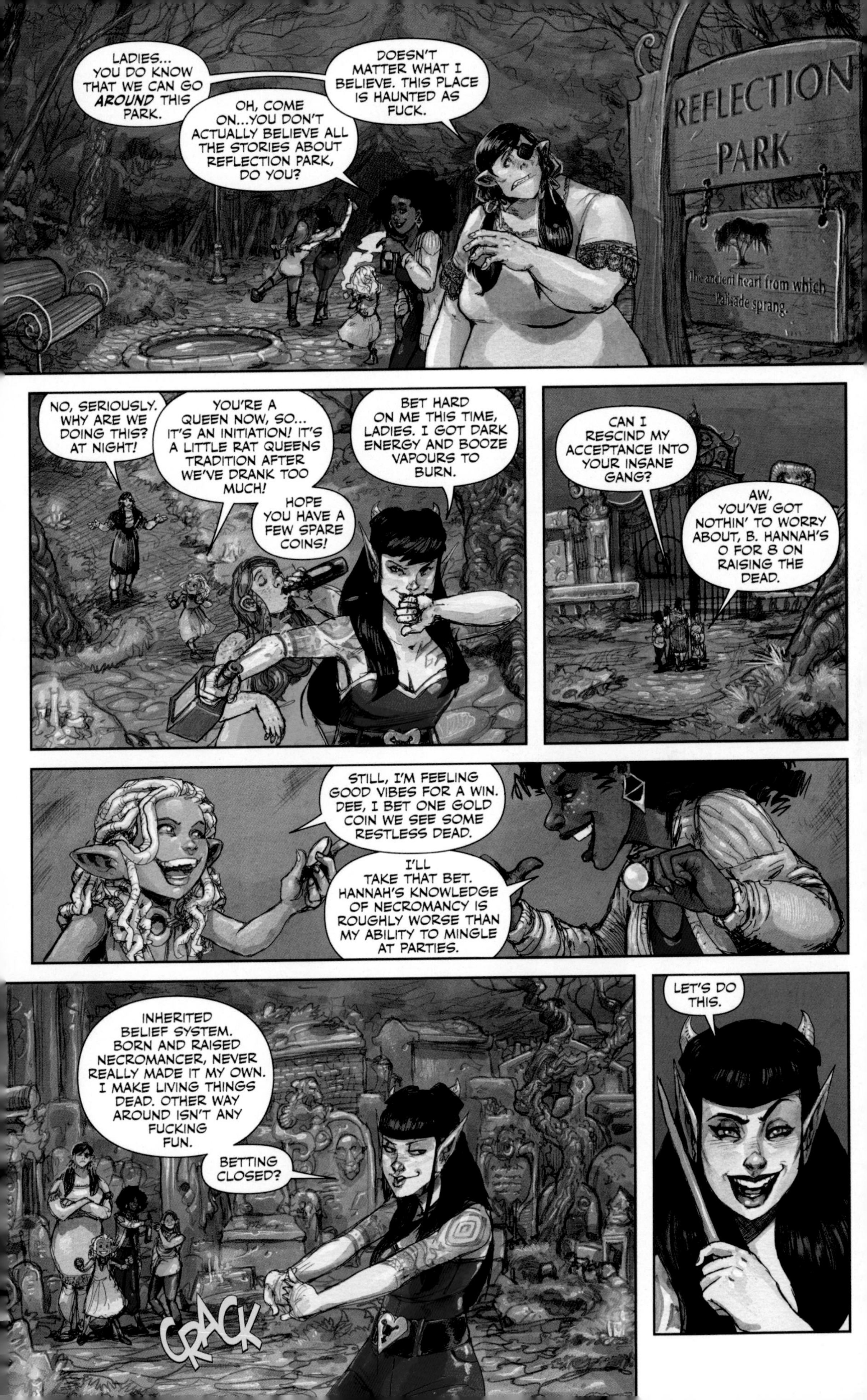
LADIES... YOU DO KNOW THAT WE CAN GO *AROUND* THIS PARK.
OH, COME ON...YOU DON'T ACTUALLY BELIEVE ALL THE STORIES ABOUT REFLECTION PARK, DO YOU?
DOESN'T MATTER WHAT I BELIEVE. THIS PLACE IS HAUNTED AS FUCK.
REFLECTION PARK
The ancient heart from which Palisade sprang.
NO, SERIOUSLY. WHY ARE WE DOING THIS? AT NIGHT!
YOU'RE A QUEEN NOW, SO... IT'S AN INITIATION! IT'S A LITTLE RAT QUEENS TRADITION AFTER WE'VE DRANK TOO MUCH!
HOPE YOU HAVE A FEW SPARE COINS!
BET HARD ON ME THIS TIME, LADIES. I GOT DARK ENERGY AND BOOZE VAPOURS TO BURN.
CAN I RESCIND MY ACCEPTANCE INTO YOUR INSANE GANG?
AW, YOU'VE GOT NOTHIN' TO WORRY ABOUT, B. HANNAH'S 0 FOR 8 ON RAISING THE DEAD.
STILL, I'M FEELING GOOD VIBES FOR A WIN. DEE, I BET ONE GOLD COIN WE SEE SOME RESTLESS DEAD.
I'LL TAKE THAT BET. HANNAH'S KNOWLEDGE OF NECROMANCY IS ROUGHLY WORSE THAN MY ABILITY TO MINGLE AT PARTIES.
INHERITED BELIEF SYSTEM. BORN AND RAISED NECROMANCER, NEVER REALLY MADE IT MY OWN. I MAKE LIVING THINGS DEAD. OTHER WAY AROUND ISN'T ANY FUCKING FUN.
BETTING CLOSED?
CRACK
LET'S DO THIS.

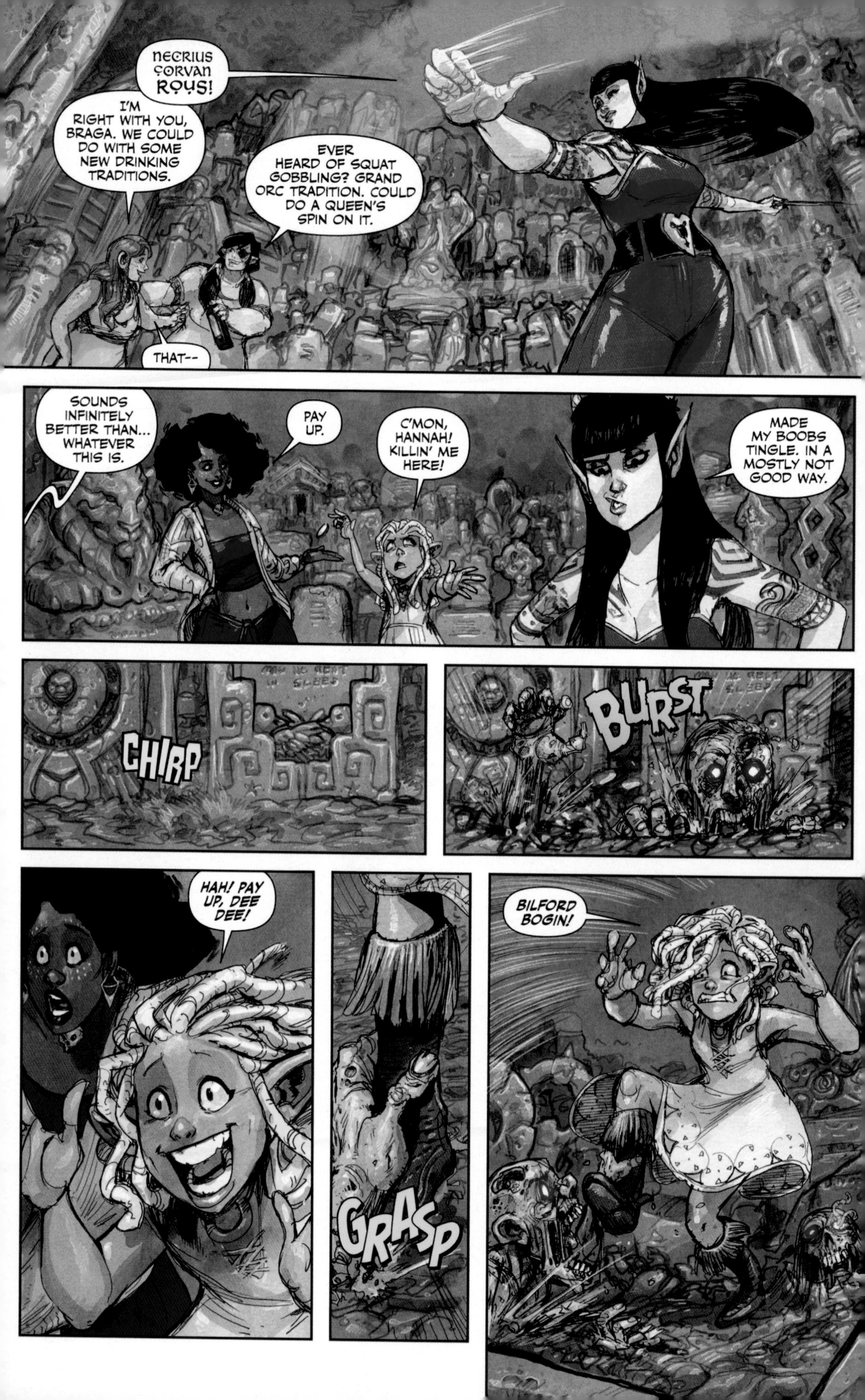
NECRIUS CORVAN ROUS!
I'M RIGHT WITH YOU, BRAGA. WE COULD DO WITH SOME NEW DRINKING TRADITIONS.
EVER HEARD OF SQUAT GOBBLING? GRAND ORC TRADITION. COULD DO A QUEEN'S SPIN ON IT.
THAT--
SOUNDS INFINITELY BETTER THAN... WHATEVER THIS IS.
PAY UP.
C'MON, HANNAH! KILLIN' ME HERE!
MADE MY BOOBS TINGLE. IN A MOSTLY NOT GOOD WAY.
CHIRP
BURST
HAH! PAY UP, DEE DEE!
GRASP
BILFORD BOGIN!

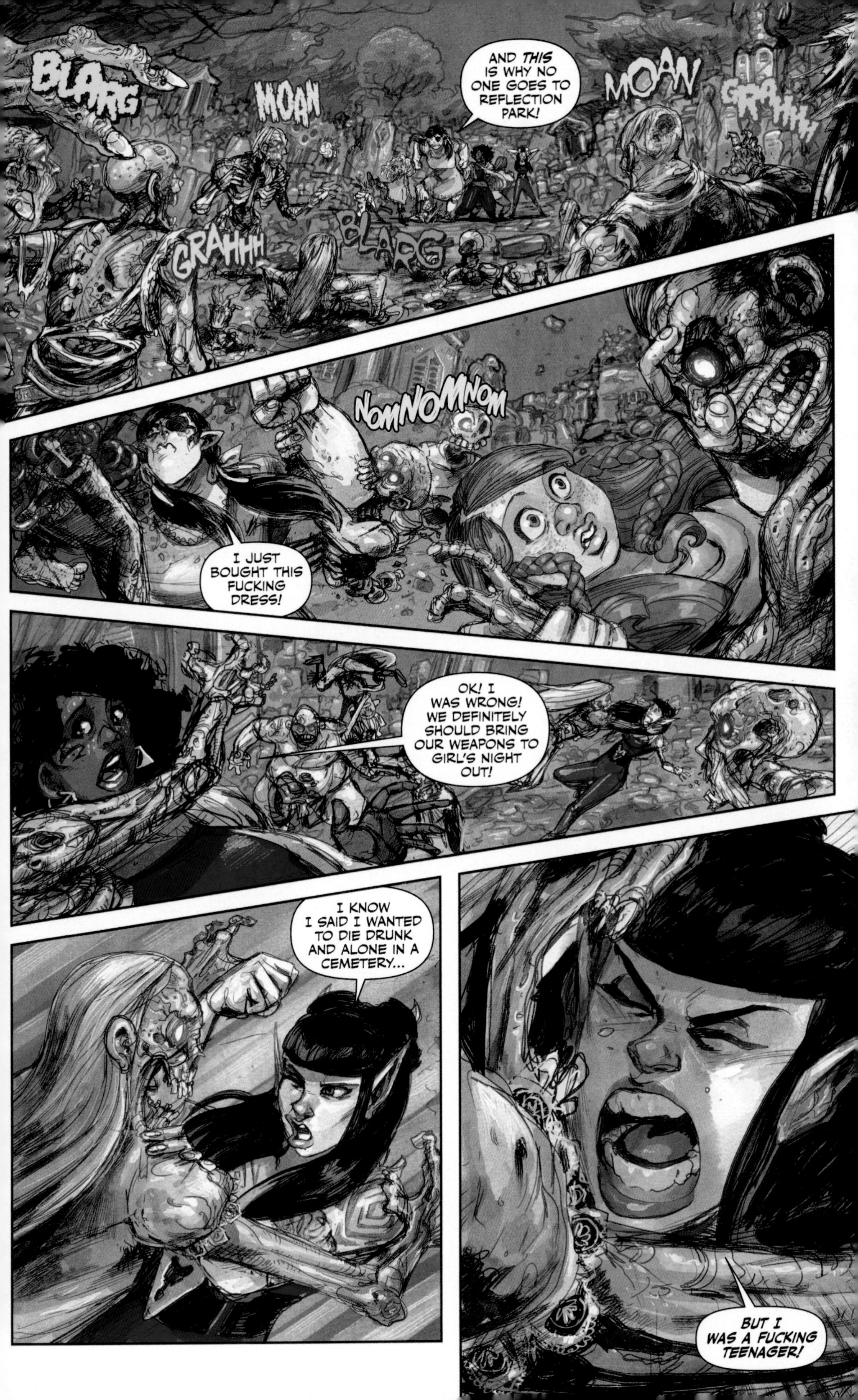
BLARG
MOAN
AND THIS IS WHY NO ONE GOES TO REFLECTION PARK!
MOAN
GRAHHH
GRAHHH
BLARG
NOMNOMNOM
I JUST BOUGHT THIS FUCKING DRESS!
OK! I WAS WRONG! WE DEFINITELY SHOULD BRING OUR WEAPONS TO GIRL'S NIGHT OUT!
I KNOW I SAID I WANTED TO DIE DRUNK AND ALONE IN A CEMETERY...
BUT I WAS A FUCKING TEENAGER!

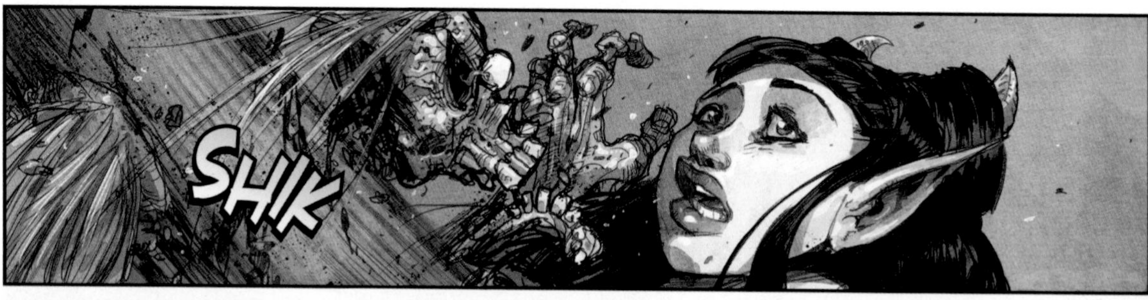
SHIK

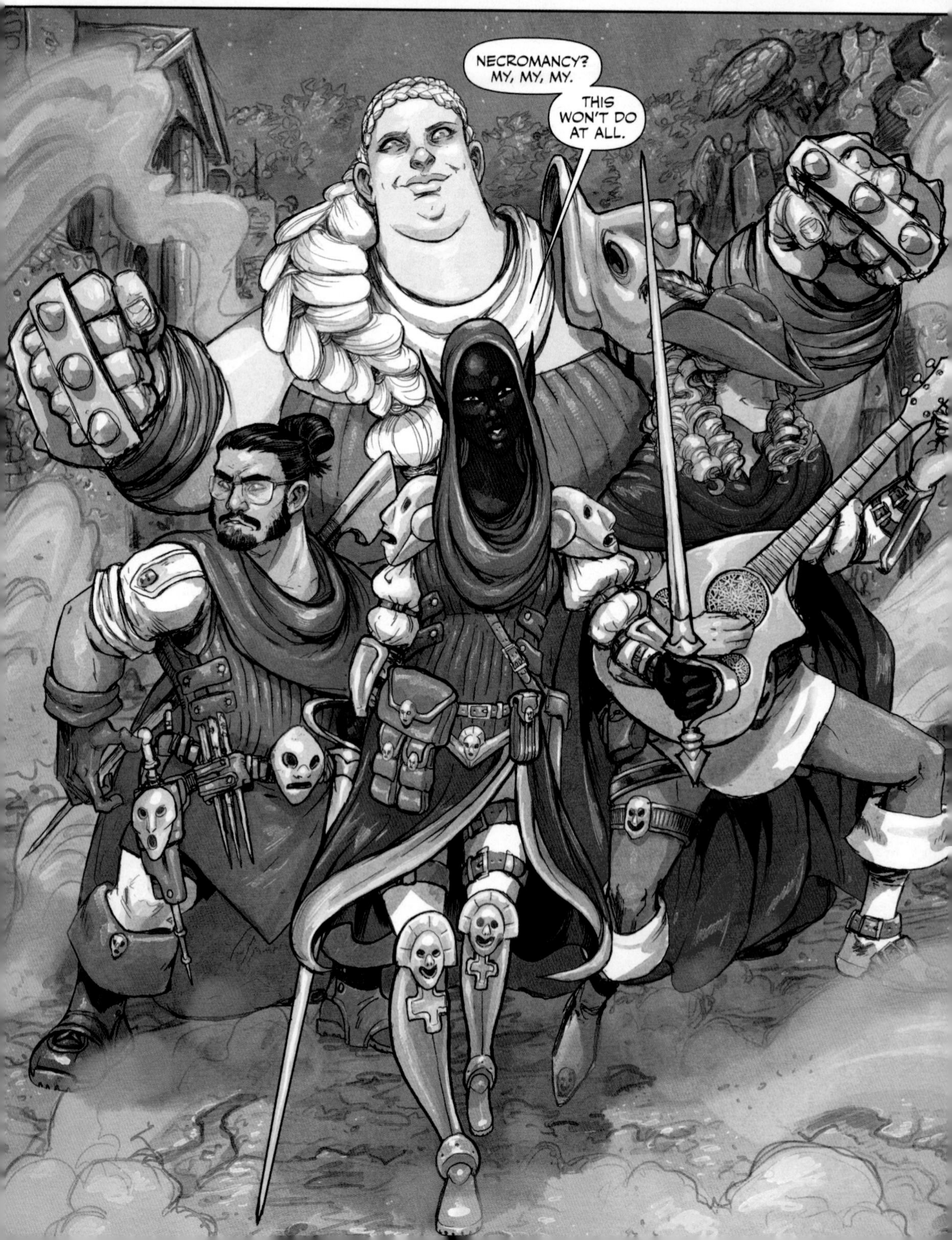
NECROMANCY? MY, MY, MY.
THIS WON'T DO AT ALL.

CHAPTER THREE

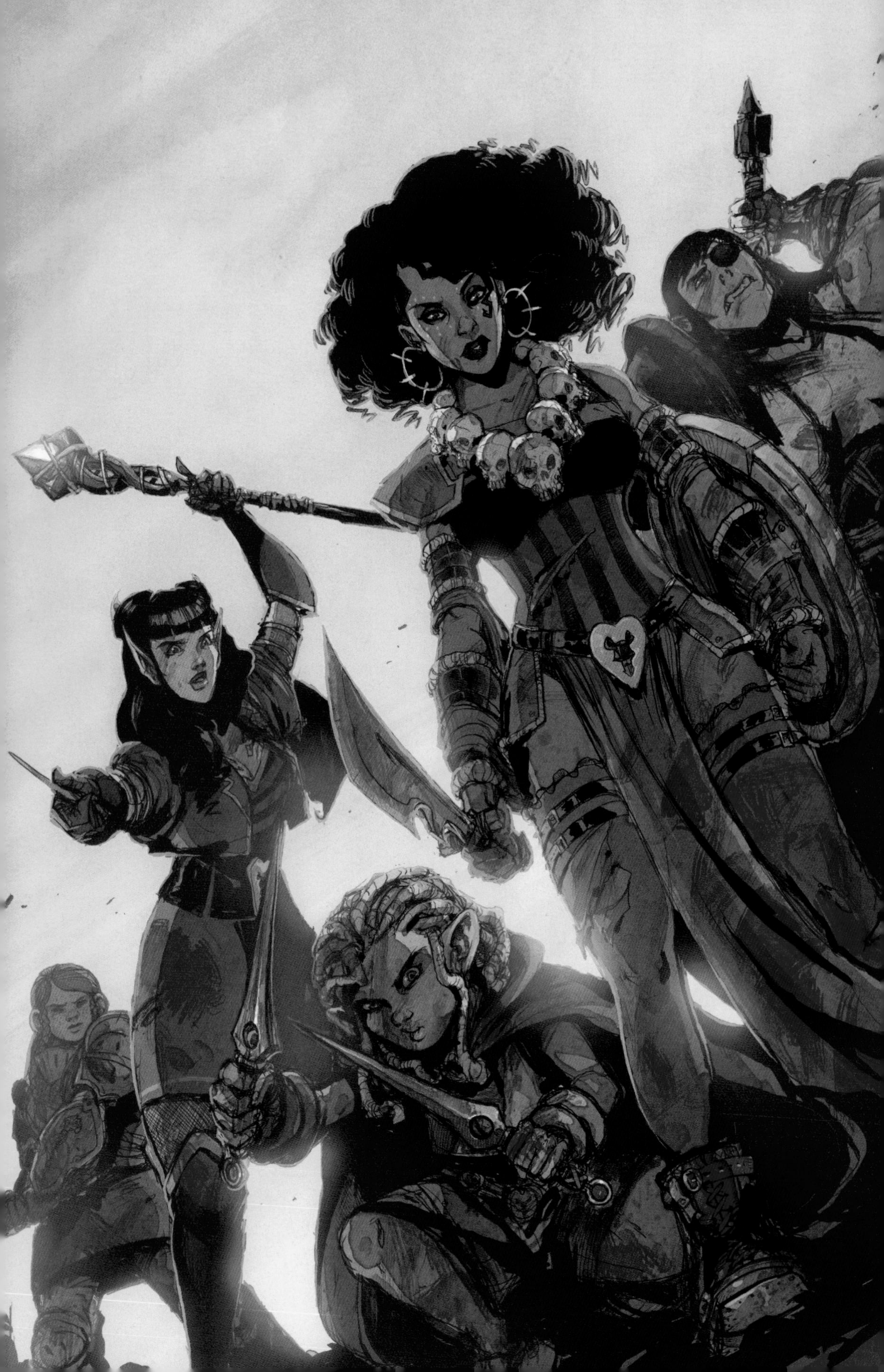

Virgin cover for this volume

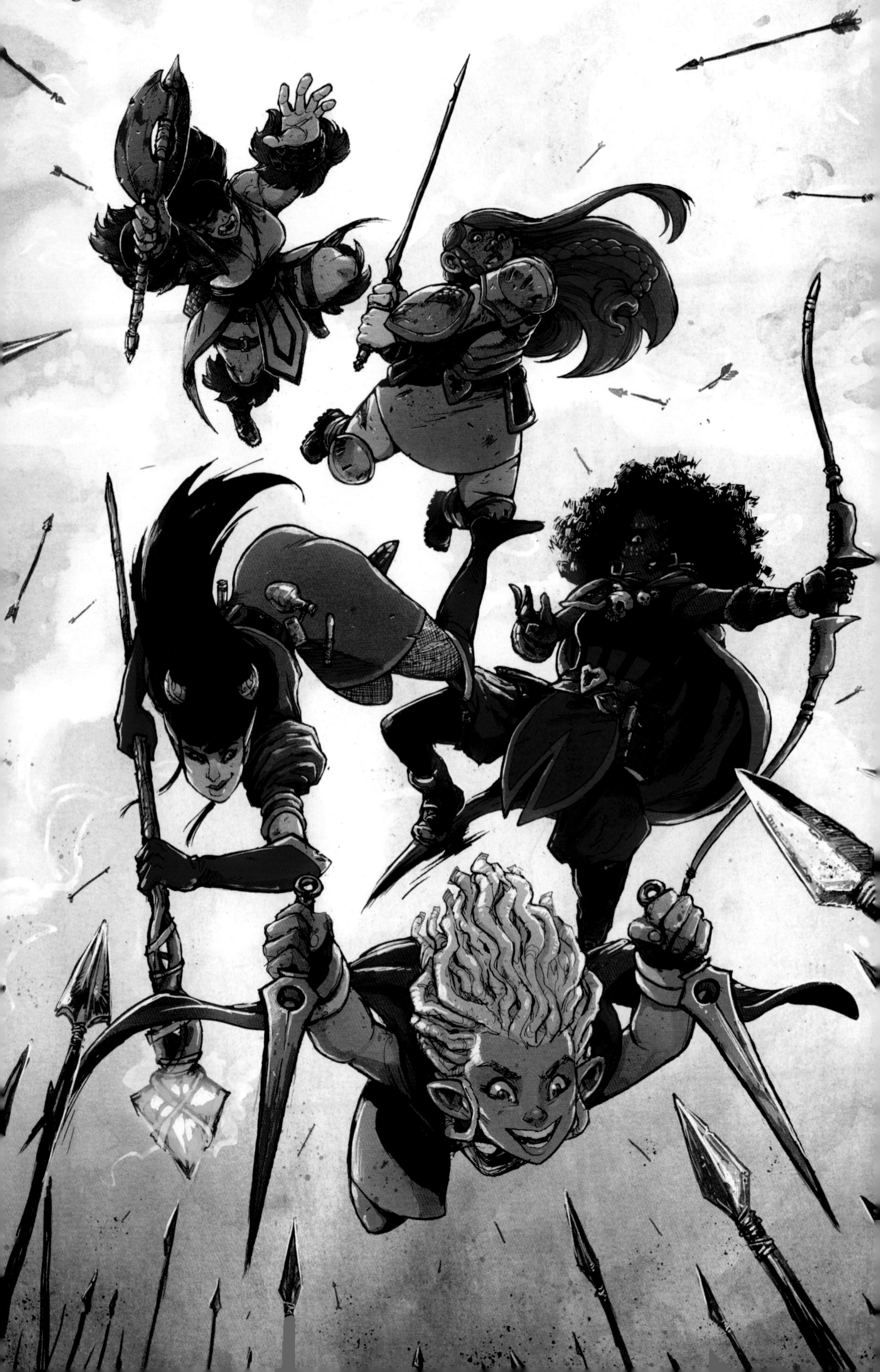

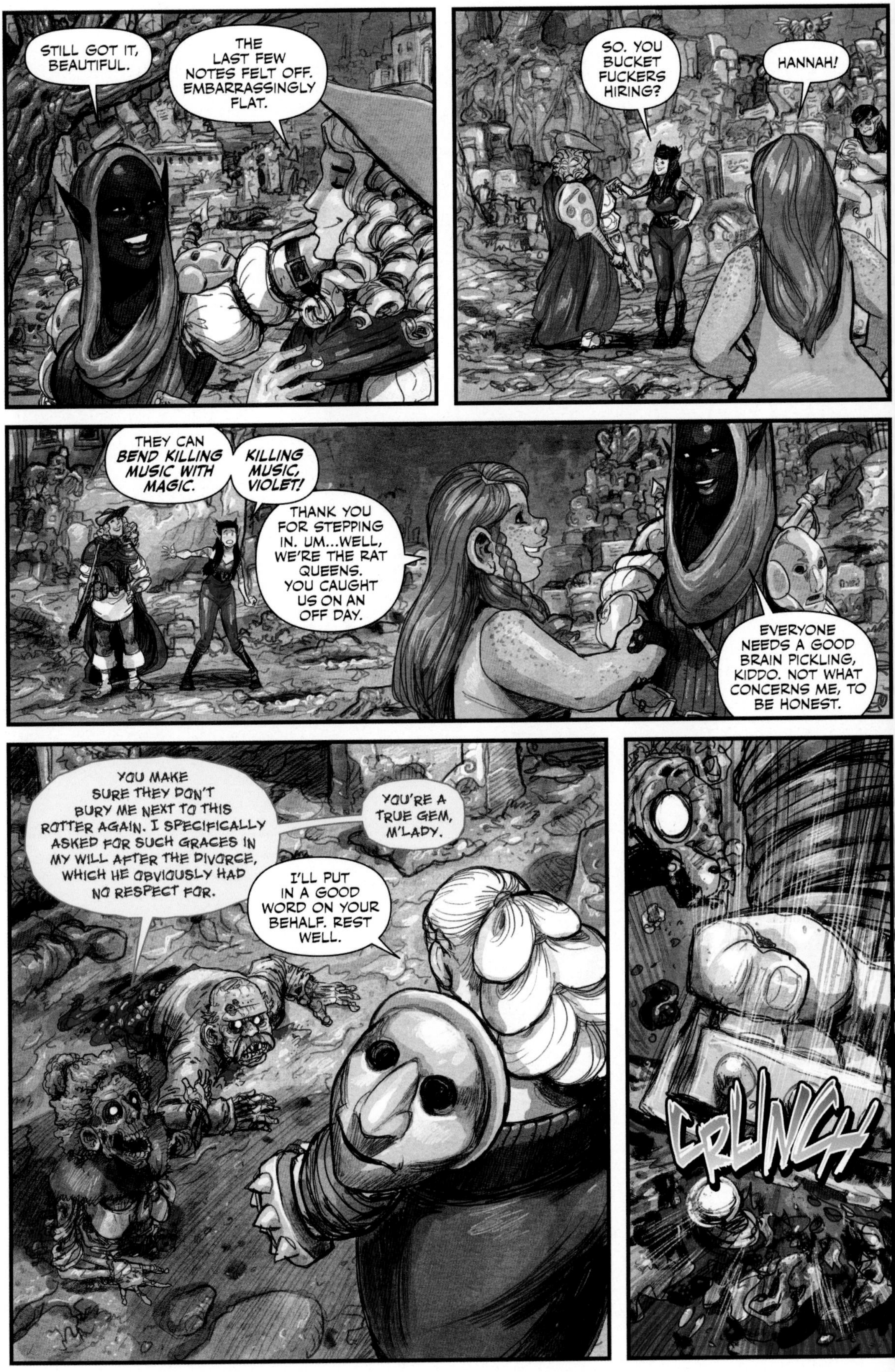
STILL GOT IT, BEAUTIFUL.
THE LAST FEW NOTES FELT OFF. EMBARRASSINGLY FLAT.
SO. YOU BUCKET FUCKERS HIRING?
HANNAH!
THEY CAN *BEND KILLING MUSIC WITH MAGIC.*
KILLING MUSIC, VIOLET!
THANK YOU FOR STEPPING IN. UM...WELL, WE'RE THE RAT QUEENS. YOU CAUGHT US ON AN OFF DAY.
EVERYONE NEEDS A GOOD BRAIN PICKLING, KIDDO. NOT WHAT CONCERNS ME, TO BE HONEST.
YOU MAKE SURE THEY DON'T BURY ME NEXT TO THIS ROTTER AGAIN. I SPECIFICALLY ASKED FOR SUCH GRACES IN MY WILL AFTER THE DIVORCE, WHICH HE OBVIOUSLY HAD NO RESPECT FOR.
YOU'RE A TRUE GEM, M'LADY.
I'LL PUT IN A GOOD WORD ON YOUR BEHALF. REST WELL.
CRUNCH

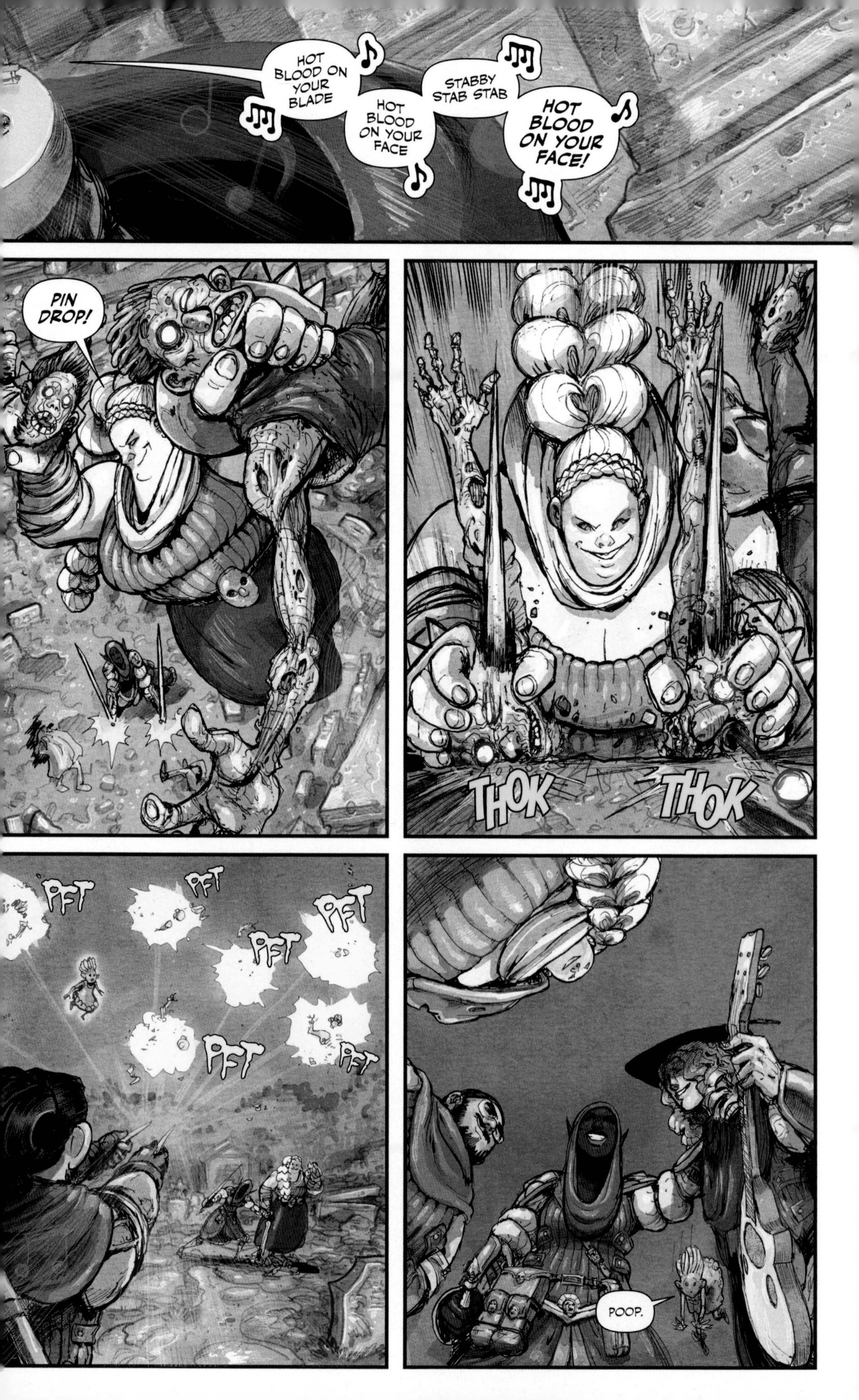
HOT BLOOD ON YOUR BLADE
HOT BLOOD ON YOUR FACE
STABBY STAB STAB
HOT BLOOD ON YOUR FACE!
PIN DROP!
THOK
THOK
PFT
PFT
PFT
PFT
PFT
PFT
POOP.

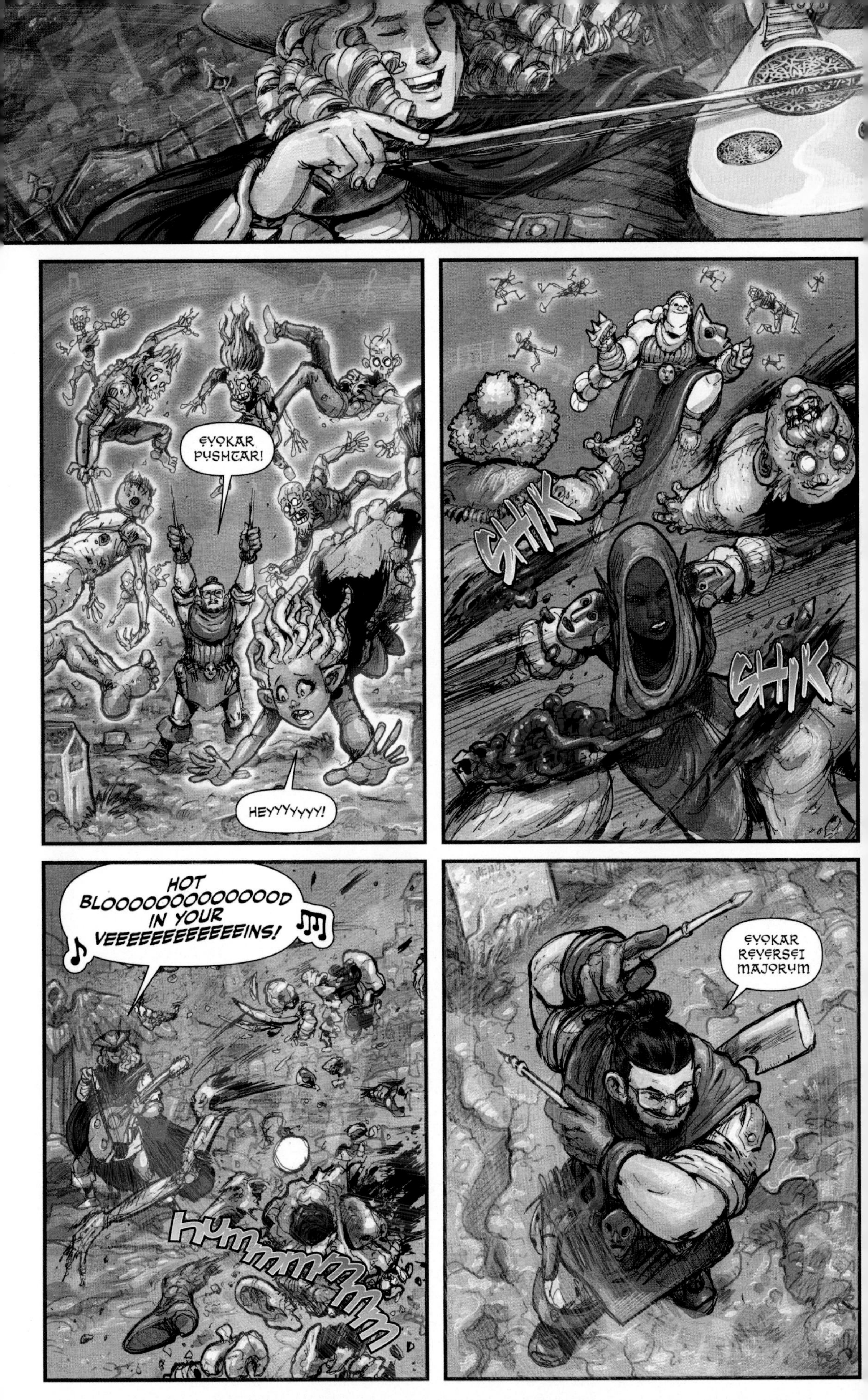

EVOKAR PUSHTAR!
HEYYYYYYY!
SHIK
SHIK
HOT BLOOOOOOOOOOOOOD IN YOUR VEEEEEEEEEEEEINS!
HUMMMMMM
EVOKAR REVERSEI MAJORUM

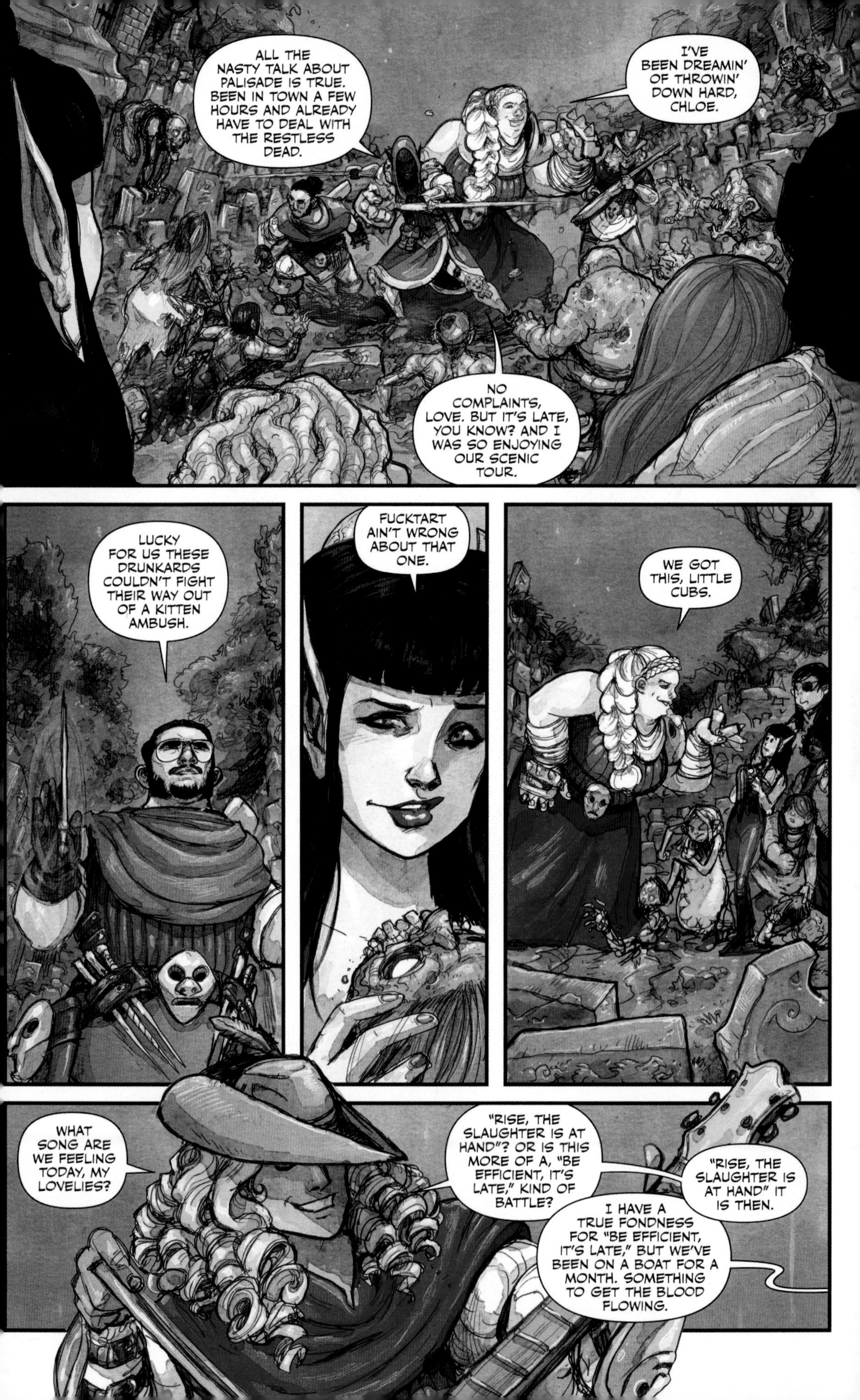
ALL THE NASTY TALK ABOUT PALISADE IS TRUE. BEEN IN TOWN A FEW HOURS AND ALREADY HAVE TO DEAL WITH THE RESTLESS DEAD.
I'VE BEEN DREAMIN' OF THROWIN' DOWN HARD, CHLOE.
NO COMPLAINTS, LOVE. BUT IT'S LATE, YOU KNOW? AND I WAS SO ENJOYING OUR SCENIC TOUR.
LUCKY FOR US THESE DRUNKARDS COULDN'T FIGHT THEIR WAY OUT OF A KITTEN AMBUSH.
FUCKTART AIN'T WRONG ABOUT THAT ONE.
WE GOT THIS, LITTLE CUBS.
WHAT SONG ARE WE FEELING TODAY, MY LOVELIES?
"RISE, THE SLAUGHTER IS AT HAND"? OR IS THIS MORE OF A, "BE EFFICIENT, IT'S LATE," KIND OF BATTLE?
"RISE, THE SLAUGHTER IS AT HAND" IT IS THEN.
I HAVE A TRUE FONDNESS FOR "BE EFFICIENT, IT'S LATE," BUT WE'VE BEEN ON A BOAT FOR A MONTH. SOMETHING TO GET THE BLOOD FLOWING.

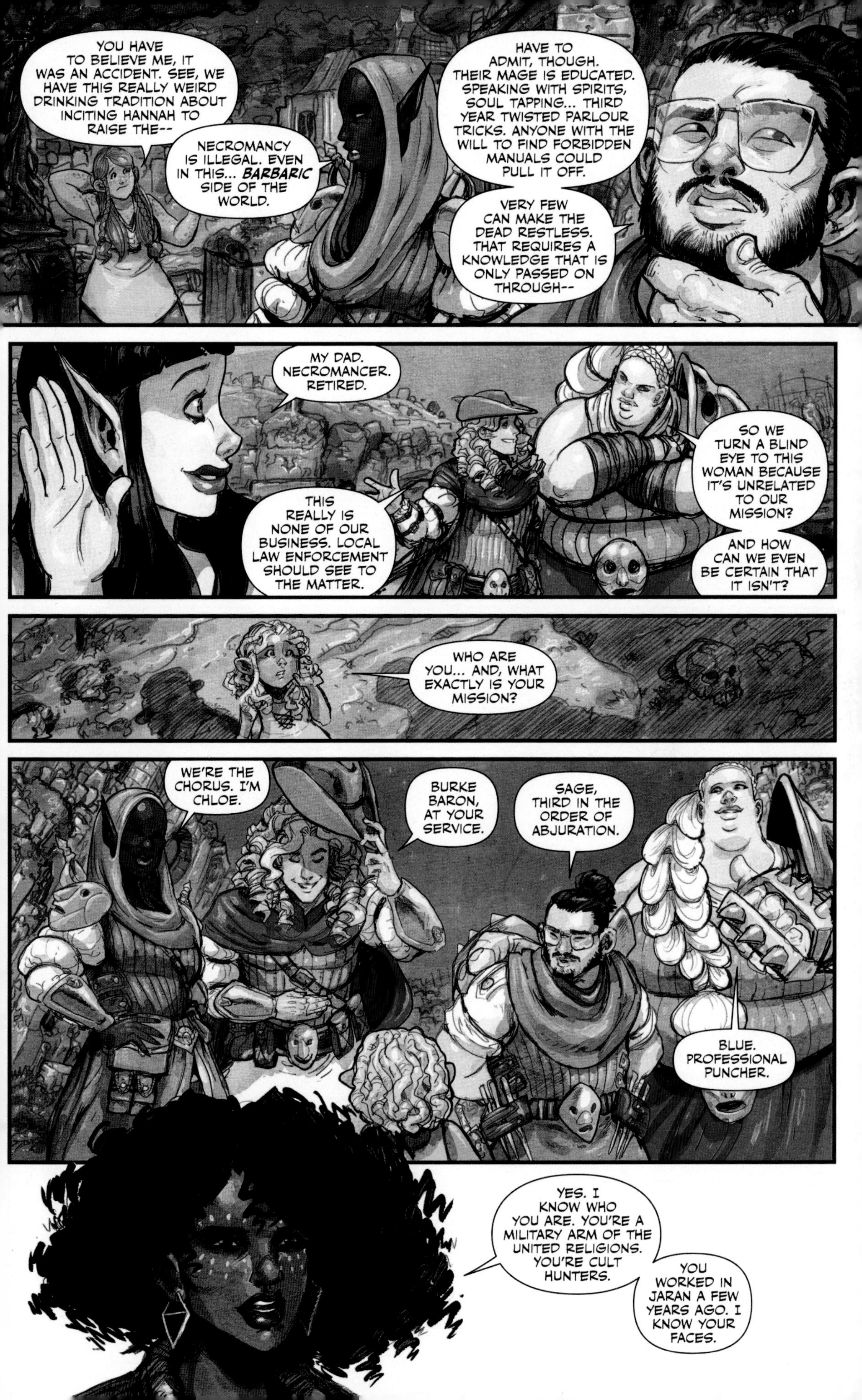
YOU HAVE TO BELIEVE ME, IT WAS AN ACCIDENT. SEE, WE HAVE THIS REALLY WEIRD DRINKING TRADITION ABOUT INCITING HANNAH TO RAISE THE--
NECROMANCY IS ILLEGAL. EVEN IN THIS... BARBARIC SIDE OF THE WORLD.
HAVE TO ADMIT, THOUGH. THEIR MAGE IS EDUCATED. SPEAKING WITH SPIRITS, SOUL TAPPING... THIRD YEAR TWISTED PARLOUR TRICKS. ANYONE WITH THE WILL TO FIND FORBIDDEN MANUALS COULD PULL IT OFF.
VERY FEW CAN MAKE THE DEAD RESTLESS. THAT REQUIRES A KNOWLEDGE THAT IS ONLY PASSED ON THROUGH--
MY DAD. NECROMANCER. RETIRED.
THIS REALLY IS NONE OF OUR BUSINESS. LOCAL LAW ENFORCEMENT SHOULD SEE TO THE MATTER.
SO WE TURN A BLIND EYE TO THIS WOMAN BECAUSE IT'S UNRELATED TO OUR MISSION?
AND HOW CAN WE EVEN BE CERTAIN THAT IT ISN'T?
WHO ARE YOU... AND, WHAT EXACTLY IS YOUR MISSION?
WE'RE THE CHORUS. I'M CHLOE.
BURKE BARON, AT YOUR SERVICE.
SAGE, THIRD IN THE ORDER OF ABJURATION.
BLUE. PROFESSIONAL PUNCHER.
YES. I KNOW WHO YOU ARE. YOU'RE A MILITARY ARM OF THE UNITED RELIGIONS. YOU'RE CULT HUNTERS.
YOU WORKED IN JARAN A FEW YEARS AGO. I KNOW YOUR FACES.

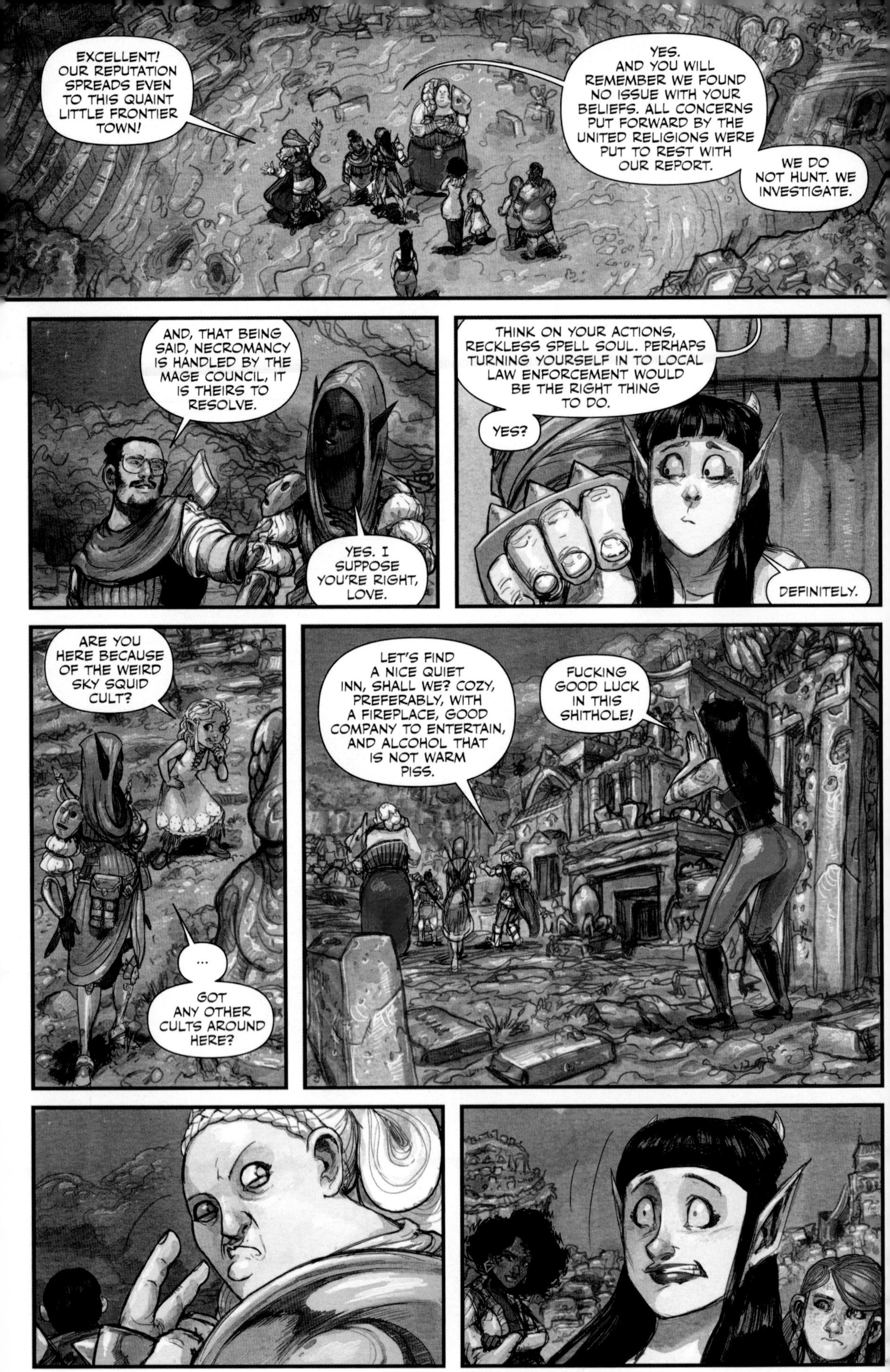
EXCELLENT! OUR REPUTATION SPREADS EVEN TO THIS QUAINT LITTLE FRONTIER TOWN!
YES. AND YOU WILL REMEMBER WE FOUND NO ISSUE WITH YOUR BELIEFS. ALL CONCERNS PUT FORWARD BY THE UNITED RELIGIONS WERE PUT TO REST WITH OUR REPORT.
WE DO NOT HUNT. WE INVESTIGATE.
AND, THAT BEING SAID, NECROMANCY IS HANDLED BY THE MAGE COUNCIL, IT IS THEIRS TO RESOLVE.
YES. I SUPPOSE YOU'RE RIGHT, LOVE.
THINK ON YOUR ACTIONS, RECKLESS SPELL SOUL. PERHAPS TURNING YOURSELF IN TO LOCAL LAW ENFORCEMENT WOULD BE THE RIGHT THING TO DO.
YES?
DEFINITELY.
ARE YOU HERE BECAUSE OF THE WEIRD SKY SQUID CULT?
...
GOT ANY OTHER CULTS AROUND HERE?
LET'S FIND A NICE QUIET INN, SHALL WE? COZY, PREFERABLY, WITH A FIREPLACE, GOOD COMPANY TO ENTERTAIN, AND ALCOHOL THAT IS NOT WARM PISS.
FUCKING GOOD LUCK IN THIS SHITHOLE!

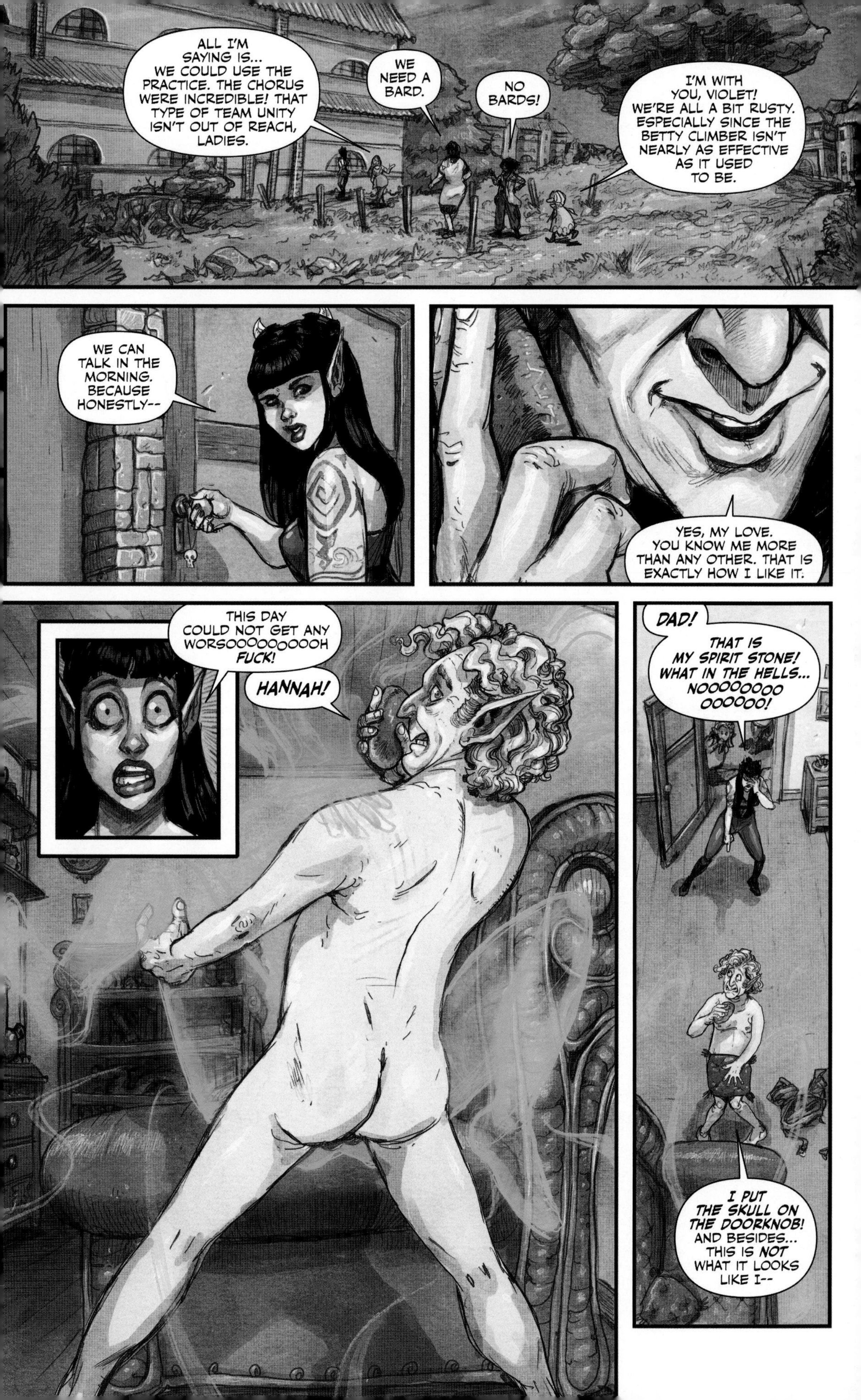
ALL I'M SAYING IS... WE COULD USE THE PRACTICE. THE CHORUS WERE INCREDIBLE! THAT TYPE OF TEAM UNITY ISN'T OUT OF REACH, LADIES.
WE NEED A BARD.
NO BARDS!
I'M WITH YOU, VIOLET! WE'RE ALL A BIT RUSTY. ESPECIALLY SINCE THE BETTY CLIMBER ISN'T NEARLY AS EFFECTIVE AS IT USED TO BE.
WE CAN TALK IN THE MORNING. BECAUSE HONESTLY--
YES, MY LOVE. YOU KNOW ME MORE THAN ANY OTHER. THAT IS EXACTLY HOW I LIKE IT.
THIS DAY COULD NOT GET ANY WORSOOOOOOOOOOH *FUCK!*
HANNAH!
DAD!
THAT IS MY SPIRIT STONE! WHAT IN THE HELLS... NOOOOOOOO OOOOOO!
I PUT THE SKULL ON THE DOORKNOB! AND BESIDES... THIS IS *NOT* WHAT IT LOOKS LIKE I--

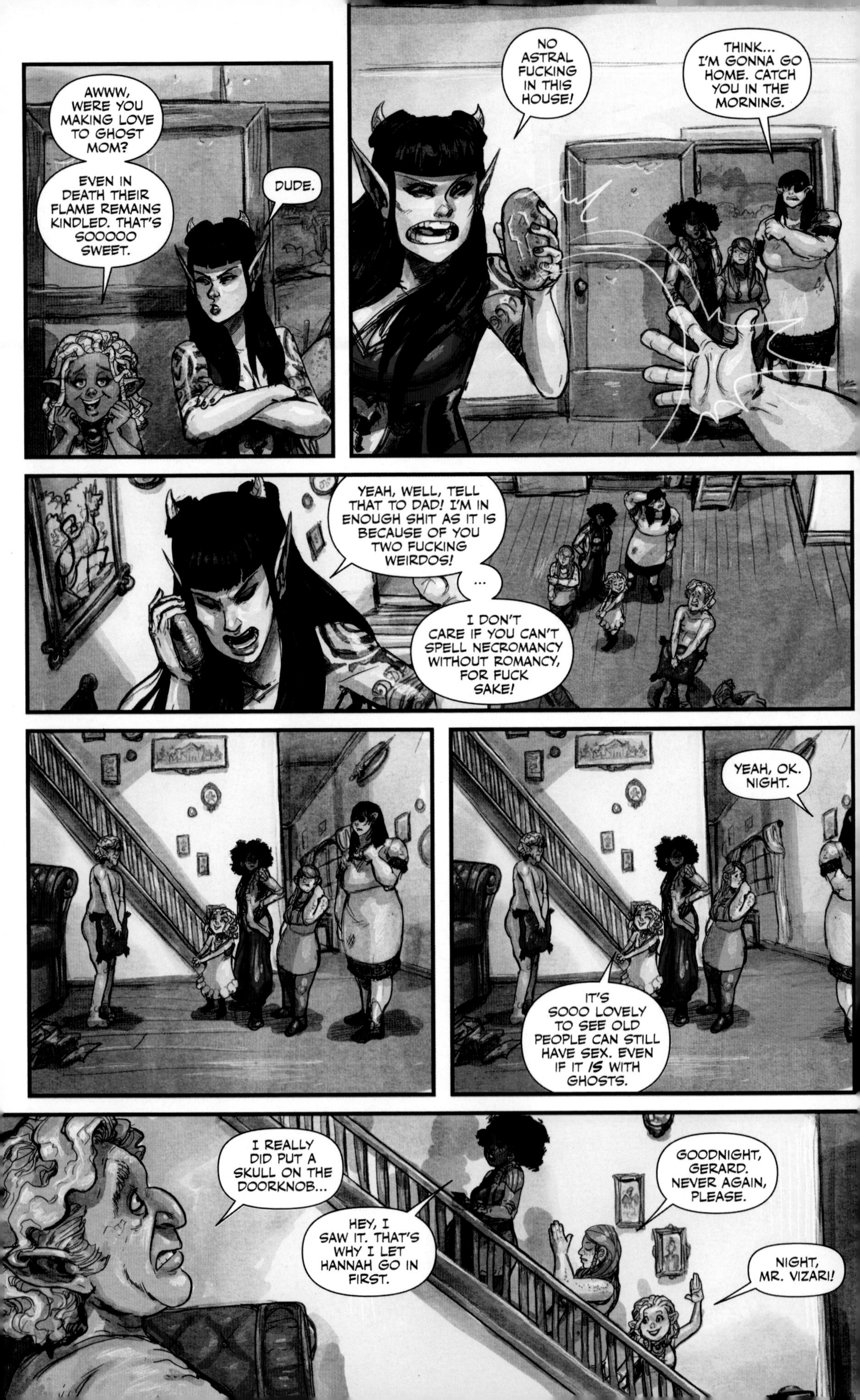
AWWW, WERE YOU MAKING LOVE TO GHOST MOM?
EVEN IN DEATH THEIR FLAME REMAINS KINDLED. THAT'S SOOOOO SWEET.
DUDE.
NO ASTRAL FUCKING IN THIS HOUSE!
THINK... I'M GONNA GO HOME. CATCH YOU IN THE MORNING.
YEAH, WELL, TELL THAT TO DAD! I'M IN ENOUGH SHIT AS IT IS BECAUSE OF YOU TWO FUCKING WEIRDOS!
...
I DON'T CARE IF YOU CAN'T SPELL NECROMANCY WITHOUT ROMANCY, FOR FUCK SAKE!
YEAH, OK. NIGHT.
IT'S SOOO LOVELY TO SEE OLD PEOPLE CAN STILL HAVE SEX. EVEN IF IT *IS* WITH GHOSTS.
I REALLY DID PUT A SKULL ON THE DOORKNOB...
HEY, I SAW IT. THAT'S WHY I LET HANNAH GO IN FIRST.
GOODNIGHT, GERARD. NEVER AGAIN, PLEASE.
NIGHT, MR. VIZARI!

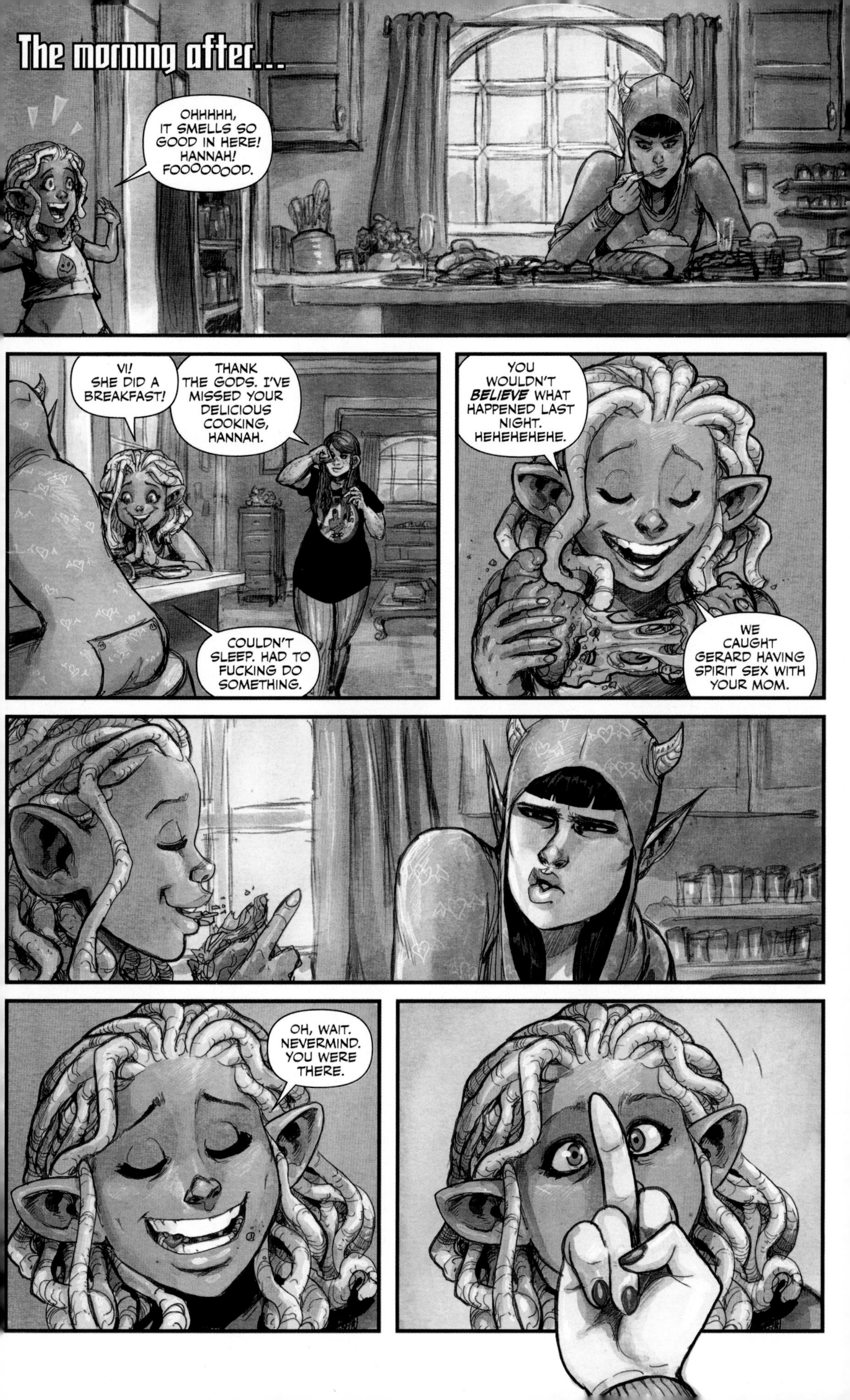
The morning after...
OHHHHH, IT SMELLS SO GOOD IN HERE! HANNAH! FOOOOOOOD.
VI! SHE DID A BREAKFAST!
THANK THE GODS. I'VE MISSED YOUR DELICIOUS COOKING, HANNAH.
COULDN'T SLEEP. HAD TO FUCKING DO SOMETHING.
YOU WOULDN'T *BELIEVE* WHAT HAPPENED LAST NIGHT. HEHEHEHEHE.
WE CAUGHT GERARD HAVING SPIRIT SEX WITH YOUR MOM.
OH, WAIT. NEVERMIND. YOU WERE THERE.

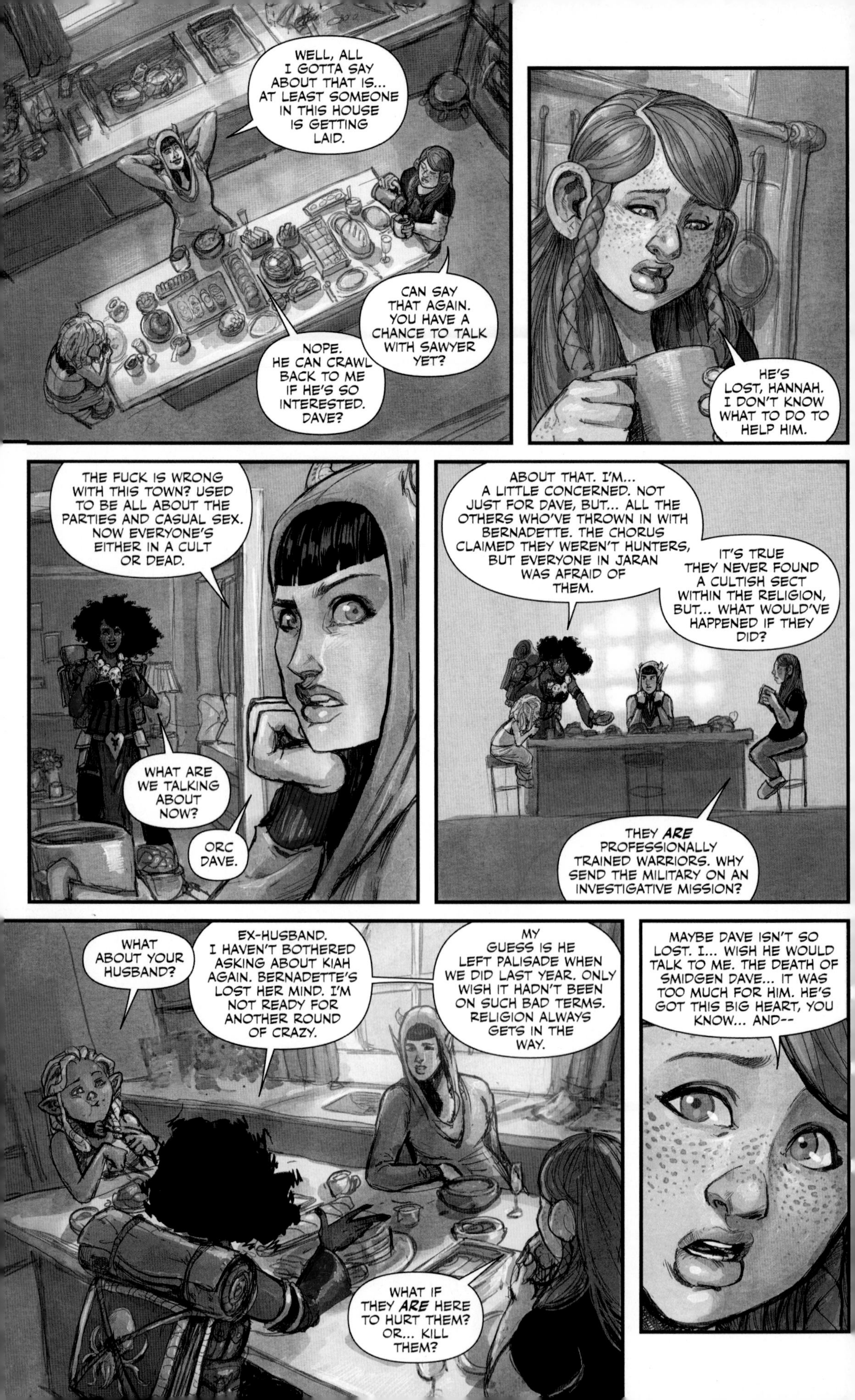
WELL, ALL I GOTTA SAY ABOUT THAT IS... AT LEAST SOMEONE IN THIS HOUSE IS GETTING LAID.
CAN SAY THAT AGAIN. YOU HAVE A CHANCE TO TALK WITH SAWYER YET?
NOPE. HE CAN CRAWL BACK TO ME IF HE'S SO INTERESTED. DAVE?
HE'S LOST, HANNAH. I DON'T KNOW WHAT TO DO TO HELP HIM.
THE FUCK IS WRONG WITH THIS TOWN? USED TO BE ALL ABOUT THE PARTIES AND CASUAL SEX. NOW EVERYONE'S EITHER IN A CULT OR DEAD.
WHAT ARE WE TALKING ABOUT NOW?
ORC DAVE.
ABOUT THAT. I'M... A LITTLE CONCERNED. NOT JUST FOR DAVE, BUT... ALL THE OTHERS WHO'VE THROWN IN WITH BERNADETTE. THE CHORUS CLAIMED THEY WEREN'T HUNTERS, BUT EVERYONE IN JARAN WAS AFRAID OF THEM.
IT'S TRUE THEY NEVER FOUND A CULTISH SECT WITHIN THE RELIGION, BUT... WHAT WOULD'VE HAPPENED IF THEY DID?
THEY *ARE* PROFESSIONALLY TRAINED WARRIORS. WHY SEND THE MILITARY ON AN INVESTIGATIVE MISSION?
WHAT ABOUT YOUR HUSBAND?
EX-HUSBAND. I HAVEN'T BOTHERED ASKING ABOUT KIAH AGAIN. BERNADETTE'S LOST HER MIND. I'M NOT READY FOR ANOTHER ROUND OF CRAZY.
MY GUESS IS HE LEFT PALISADE WHEN WE DID LAST YEAR. ONLY WISH IT HADN'T BEEN ON SUCH BAD TERMS. RELIGION ALWAYS GETS IN THE WAY.
WHAT IF THEY *ARE* HERE TO HURT THEM? OR... KILL THEM?
MAYBE DAVE ISN'T SO LOST. I... WISH HE WOULD TALK TO ME. THE DEATH OF SMIDGEN DAVE... IT WAS TOO MUCH FOR HIM. HE'S GOT THIS BIG HEART, YOU KNOW... AND--

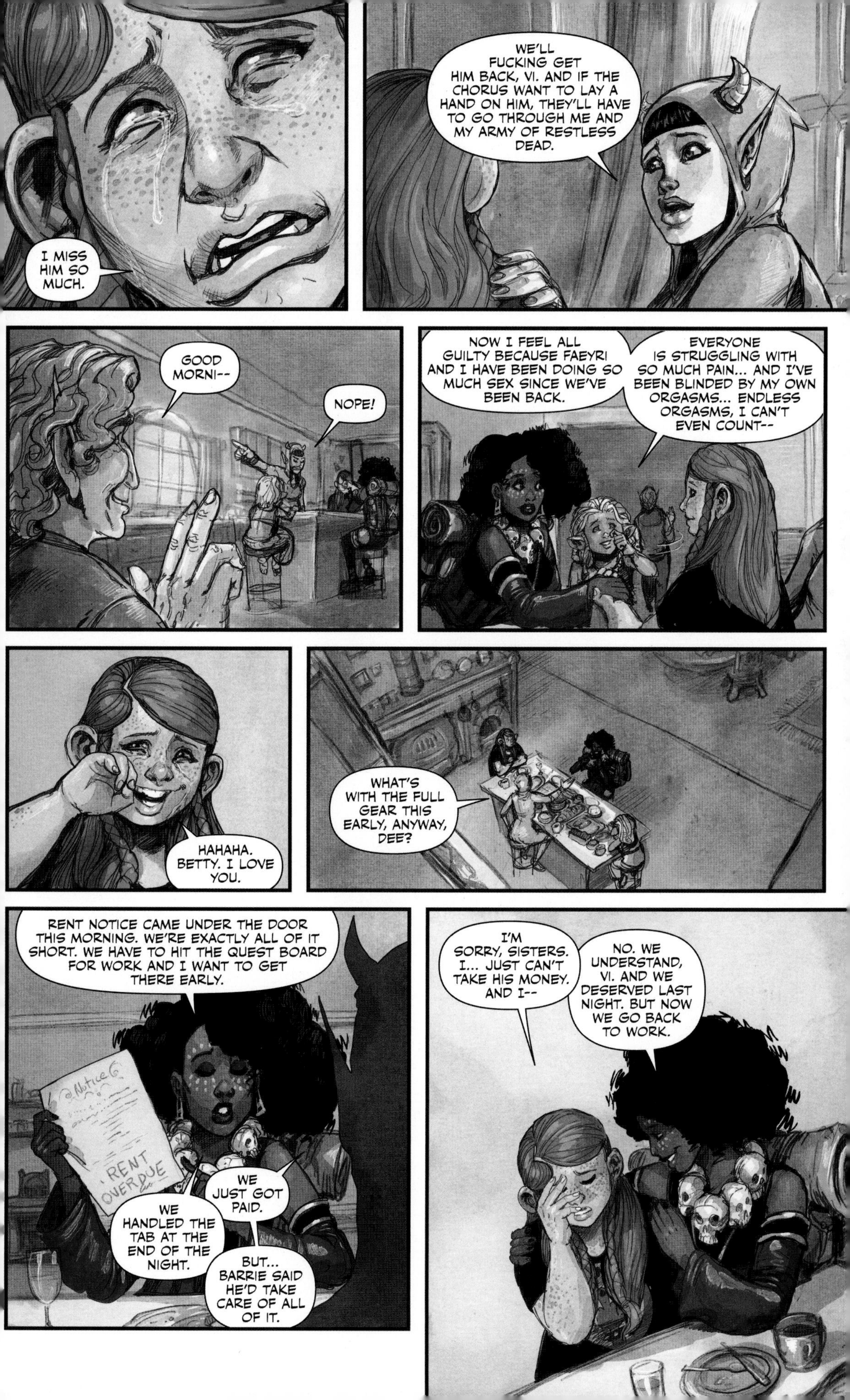
I MISS HIM SO MUCH.
WE'LL FUCKING GET HIM BACK, VI. AND IF THE CHORUS WANT TO LAY A HAND ON HIM, THEY'LL HAVE TO GO THROUGH ME AND MY ARMY OF RESTLESS DEAD.
GOOD MORNI--
NOPE!
NOW I FEEL ALL GUILTY BECAUSE FAEYRI AND I HAVE BEEN DOING SO MUCH SEX SINCE WE'VE BEEN BACK.
EVERYONE IS STRUGGLING WITH SO MUCH PAIN... AND I'VE BEEN BLINDED BY MY OWN ORGASMS... ENDLESS ORGASMS, I CAN'T EVEN COUNT--
HAHAHA. BETTY. I LOVE YOU.
WHAT'S WITH THE FULL GEAR THIS EARLY, ANYWAY, DEE?
RENT NOTICE CAME UNDER THE DOOR THIS MORNING. WE'RE EXACTLY ALL OF IT SHORT. WE HAVE TO HIT THE QUEST BOARD FOR WORK AND I WANT TO GET THERE EARLY.
RENT OVERDUE
WE HANDLED THE TAB AT THE END OF THE NIGHT.
WE JUST GOT PAID.
BUT... BARRIE SAID HE'D TAKE CARE OF ALL OF IT.
I'M SORRY, SISTERS. I... JUST CAN'T TAKE HIS MONEY. AND I--
NO. WE UNDERSTAND, VI. AND WE DESERVED LAST NIGHT. BUT NOW WE GO BACK TO WORK.

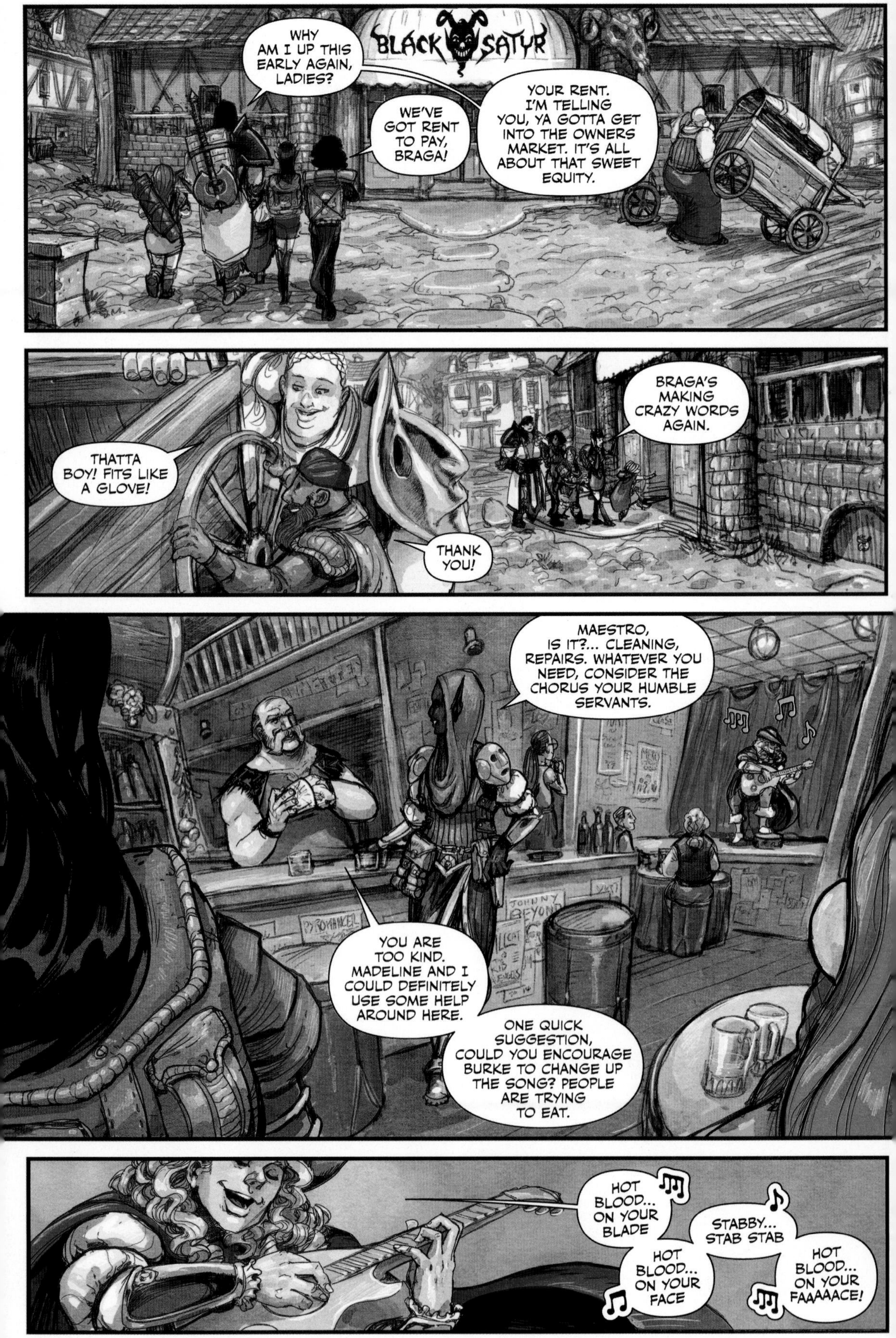
BLACK SATYR
WHY AM I UP THIS EARLY AGAIN, LADIES?
WE'VE GOT RENT TO PAY, BRAGA!
YOUR RENT. I'M TELLING YOU, YA GOTTA GET INTO THE OWNERS MARKET. IT'S ALL ABOUT THAT SWEET EQUITY.
THATTA BOY! FITS LIKE A GLOVE!
THANK YOU!
BRAGA'S MAKING CRAZY WORDS AGAIN.
MAESTRO, IS IT?... CLEANING, REPAIRS. WHATEVER YOU NEED, CONSIDER THE CHORUS YOUR HUMBLE SERVANTS.
YOU ARE TOO KIND. MADELINE AND I COULD DEFINITELY USE SOME HELP AROUND HERE.
ONE QUICK SUGGESTION, COULD YOU ENCOURAGE BURKE TO CHANGE UP THE SONG? PEOPLE ARE TRYING TO EAT.
HOT BLOOD... ON YOUR BLADE
HOT BLOOD... ON YOUR FACE
STABBY... STAB STAB
HOT BLOOD... ON YOUR FAAAAACE!

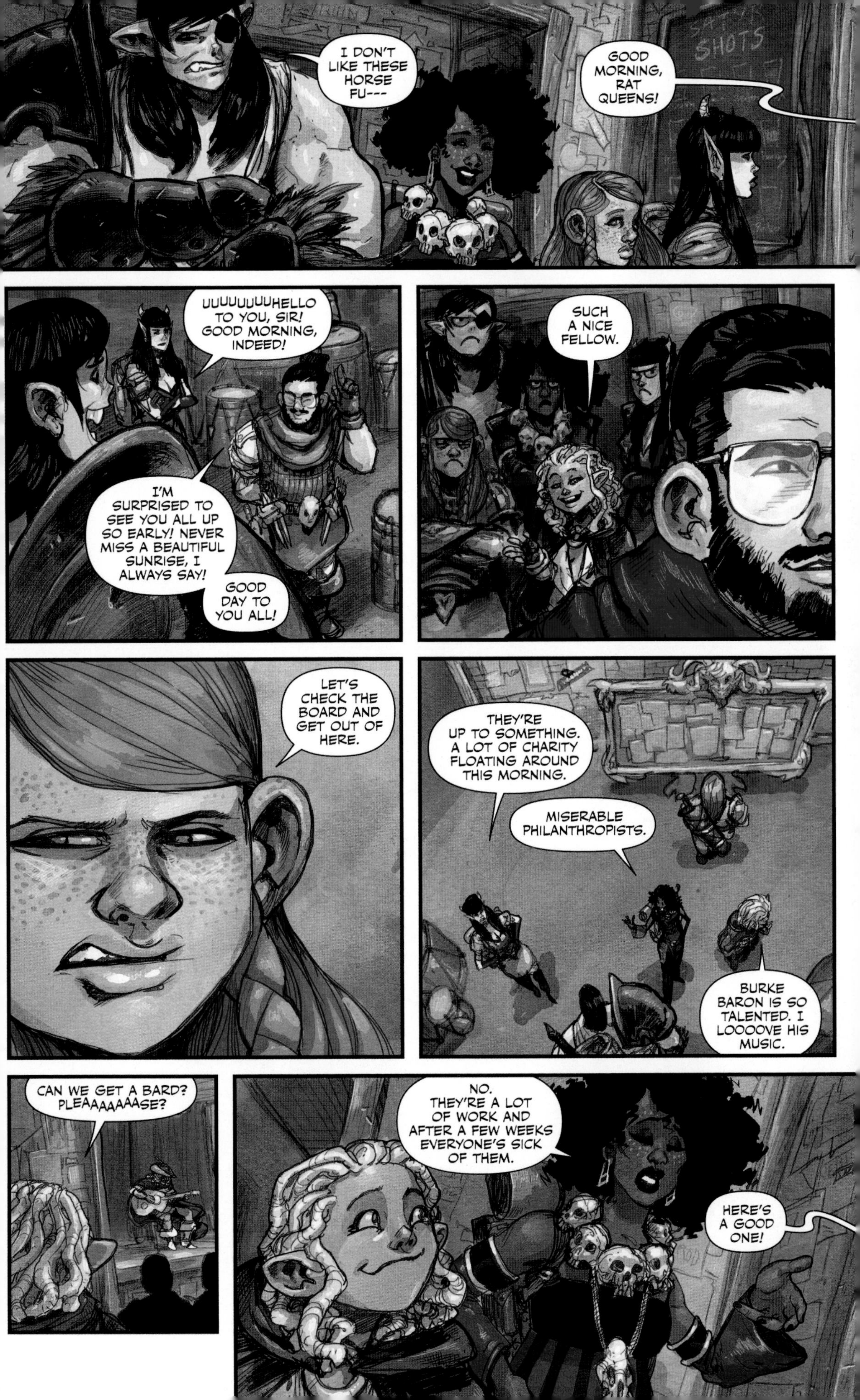
I DON'T LIKE THESE HORSE FU---
GOOD MORNING, RAT QUEENS!
SATYR SHOTS
UUUUUUUUHELLO TO YOU, SIR! GOOD MORNING, INDEED!
I'M SURPRISED TO SEE YOU ALL UP SO EARLY! NEVER MISS A BEAUTIFUL SUNRISE, I ALWAYS SAY!
GOOD DAY TO YOU ALL!
SUCH A NICE FELLOW.
LET'S CHECK THE BOARD AND GET OUT OF HERE.
THEY'RE UP TO SOMETHING. A LOT OF CHARITY FLOATING AROUND THIS MORNING.
MISERABLE PHILANTHROPISTS.
BURKE BARON IS SO TALENTED. I LOOOOVE HIS MUSIC.
CAN WE GET A BARD? PLEAAAAAAASE?
NO. THEY'RE A LOT OF WORK AND AFTER A FEW WEEKS EVERYONE'S SICK OF THEM.
HERE'S A GOOD ONE!

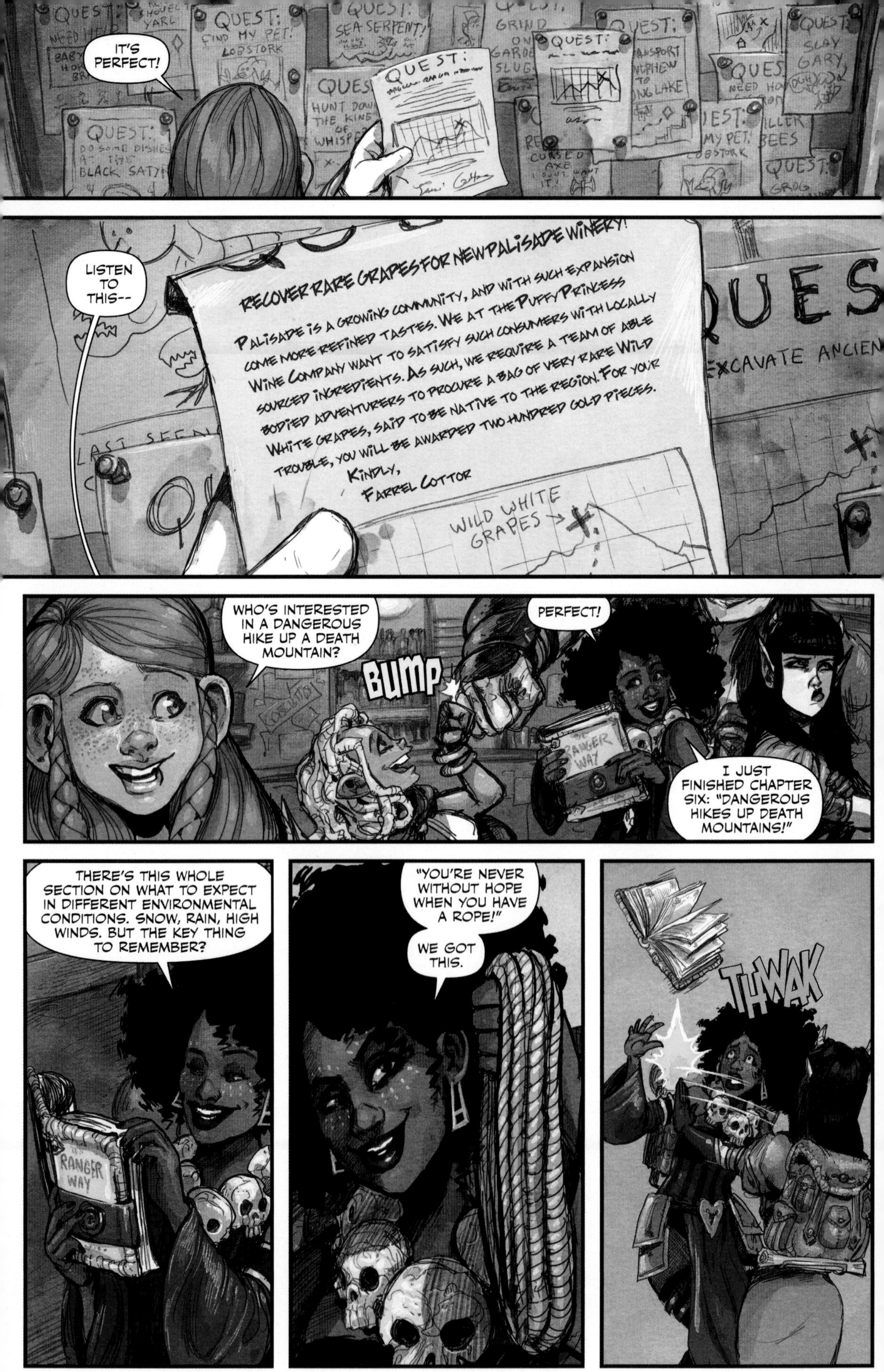
IT'S PERFECT!
LISTEN TO THIS--
RECOVER RARE GRAPES FOR NEW PALISADE WINERY!
PALISADE IS A GROWING COMMUNITY, AND WITH SUCH EXPANSION COME MORE REFINED TASTES. WE AT THE PUFFY PRINCESS WINE COMPANY WANT TO SATISFY SUCH CONSUMERS WITH LOCALLY SOURCED INGREDIENTS. AS SUCH, WE REQUIRE A TEAM OF ABLE BODIED ADVENTURERS TO PROCURE A BAG OF VERY RARE WILD WHITE GRAPES, SAID TO BE NATIVE TO THE REGION. FOR YOUR TROUBLE, YOU WILL BE AWARDED TWO HUNDRED GOLD PIECES.
KINDLY,
FARREL COTTOR
WILD WHITE GRAPES
WHO'S INTERESTED IN A DANGEROUS HIKE UP A DEATH MOUNTAIN?
BUMP
PERFECT!
RANGER WAY
I JUST FINISHED CHAPTER SIX: "DANGEROUS HIKES UP DEATH MOUNTAINS!"
THERE'S THIS WHOLE SECTION ON WHAT TO EXPECT IN DIFFERENT ENVIRONMENTAL CONDITIONS. SNOW, RAIN, HIGH WINDS. BUT THE KEY THING TO REMEMBER?
RANGER WAY
"YOU'RE NEVER WITHOUT HOPE WHEN YOU HAVE A ROPE!"
WE GOT THIS.
THWAK

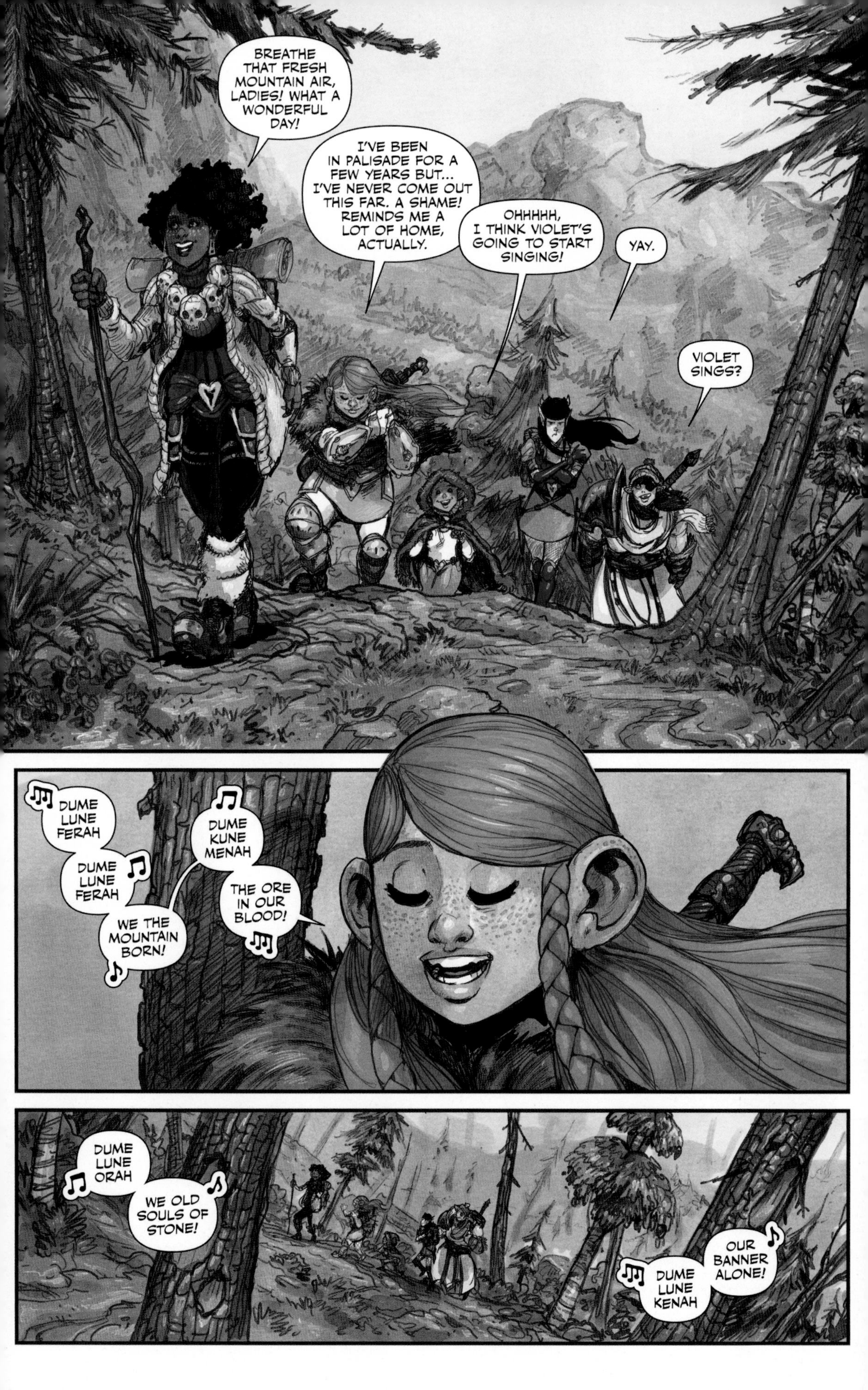
BREATHE THAT FRESH MOUNTAIN AIR, LADIES! WHAT A WONDERFUL DAY!
I'VE BEEN IN PALISADE FOR A FEW YEARS BUT... I'VE NEVER COME OUT THIS FAR. A SHAME! REMINDS ME A LOT OF HOME, ACTUALLY.
OHHHHH, I THINK VIOLET'S GOING TO START SINGING!
YAY.
VIOLET SINGS?
DUME LUNE FERAH
DUME LUNE FERAH
WE THE MOUNTAIN BORN!
DUME KUNE MENAH
THE ORE IN OUR BLOOD!
DUME LUNE ORAH
WE OLD SOULS OF STONE!
DUME LUNE KENAH
OUR BANNER ALONE!

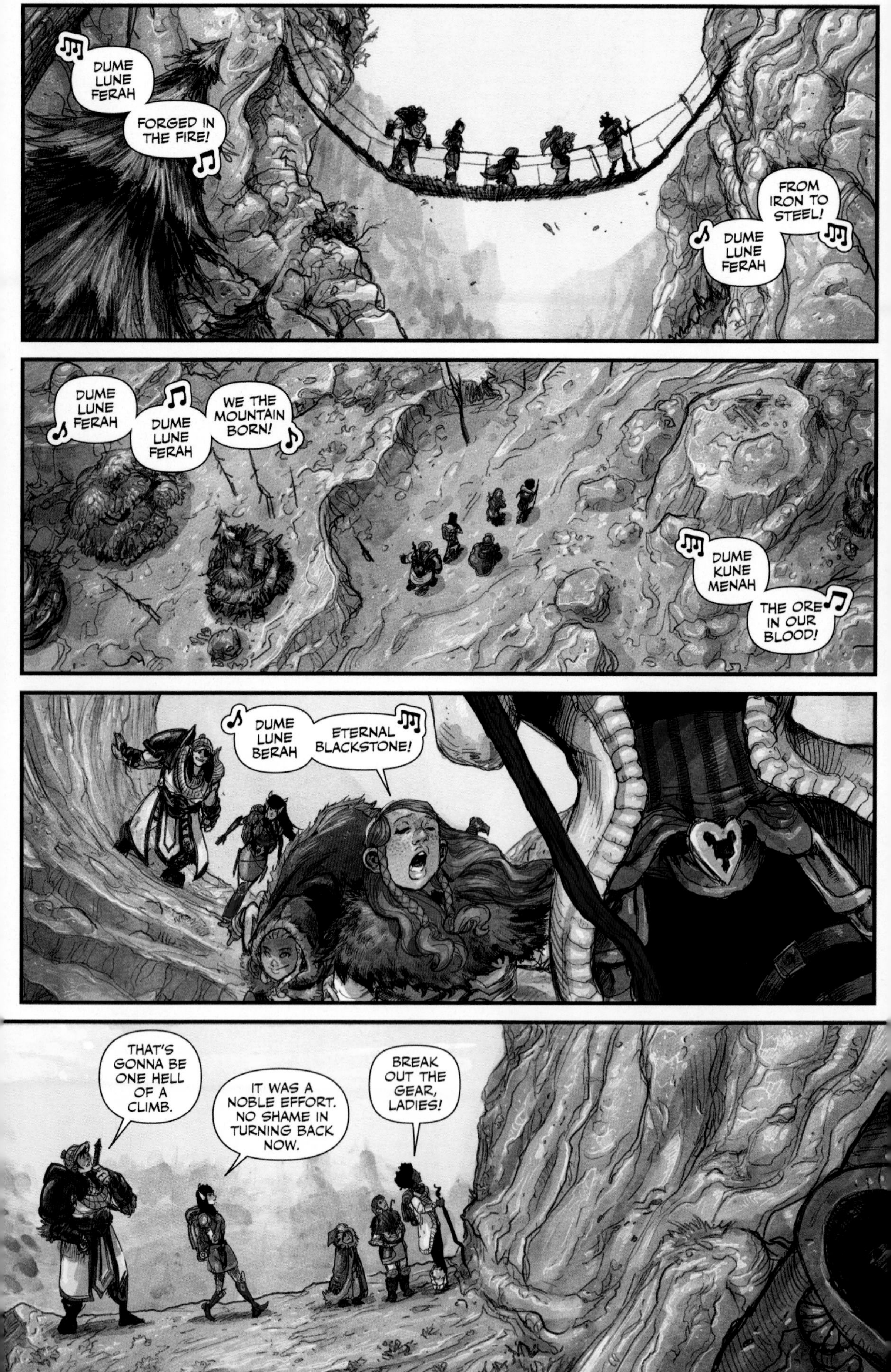
DUME LUNE FERAH
FORGED IN THE FIRE!
DUME LUNE FERAH
FROM IRON TO STEEL!
DUME LUNE FERAH
DUME LUNE FERAH
WE THE MOUNTAIN BORN!
DUME KUNE MENAH
THE ORE IN OUR BLOOD!
DUME LUNE BERAH
ETERNAL BLACKSTONE!
THAT'S GONNA BE ONE HELL OF A CLIMB.
IT WAS A NOBLE EFFORT. NO SHAME IN TURNING BACK NOW.
BREAK OUT THE GEAR, LADIES!

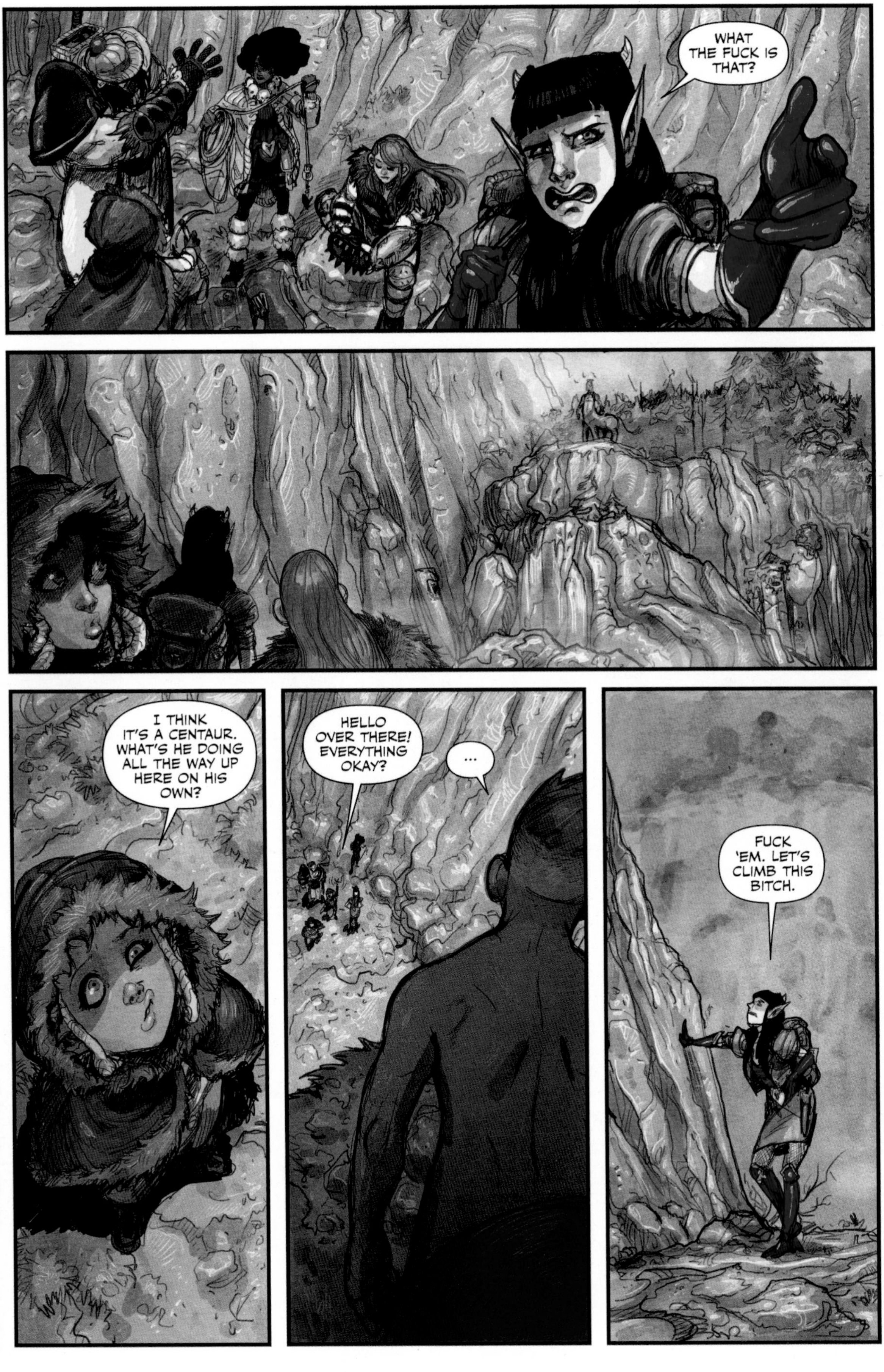
WHAT THE FUCK IS THAT?
I THINK IT'S A CENTAUR. WHAT'S HE DOING ALL THE WAY UP HERE ON HIS OWN?
HELLO OVER THERE! EVERYTHING OKAY?
...
FUCK 'EM. LET'S CLIMB THIS BITCH.

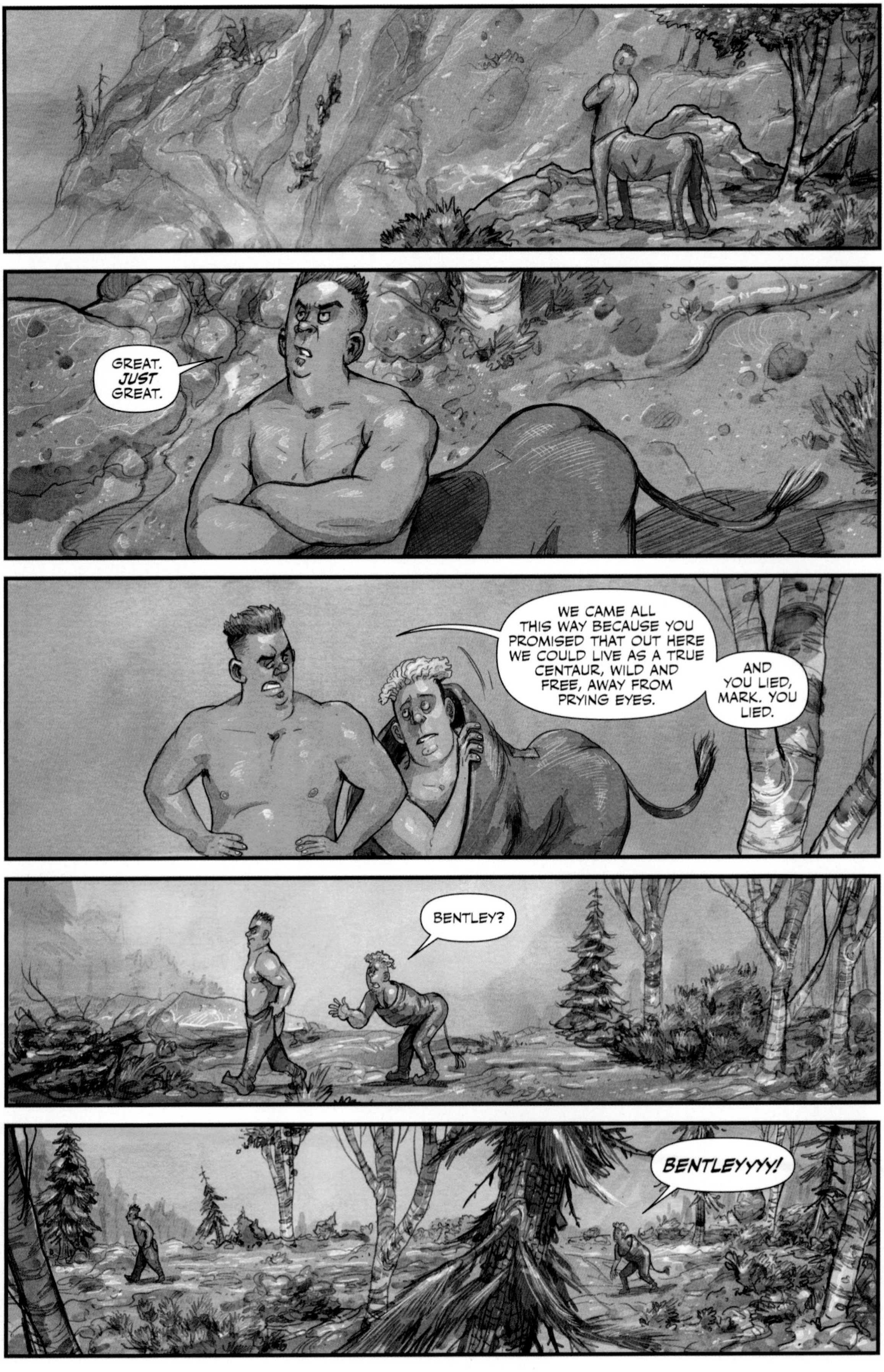
GREAT. JUST GREAT.
WE CAME ALL THIS WAY BECAUSE YOU PROMISED THAT OUT HERE WE COULD LIVE AS A TRUE CENTAUR, WILD AND FREE, AWAY FROM PRYING EYES.
AND YOU LIED, MARK. YOU LIED.
BENTLEY?
BENTLEYYYY!

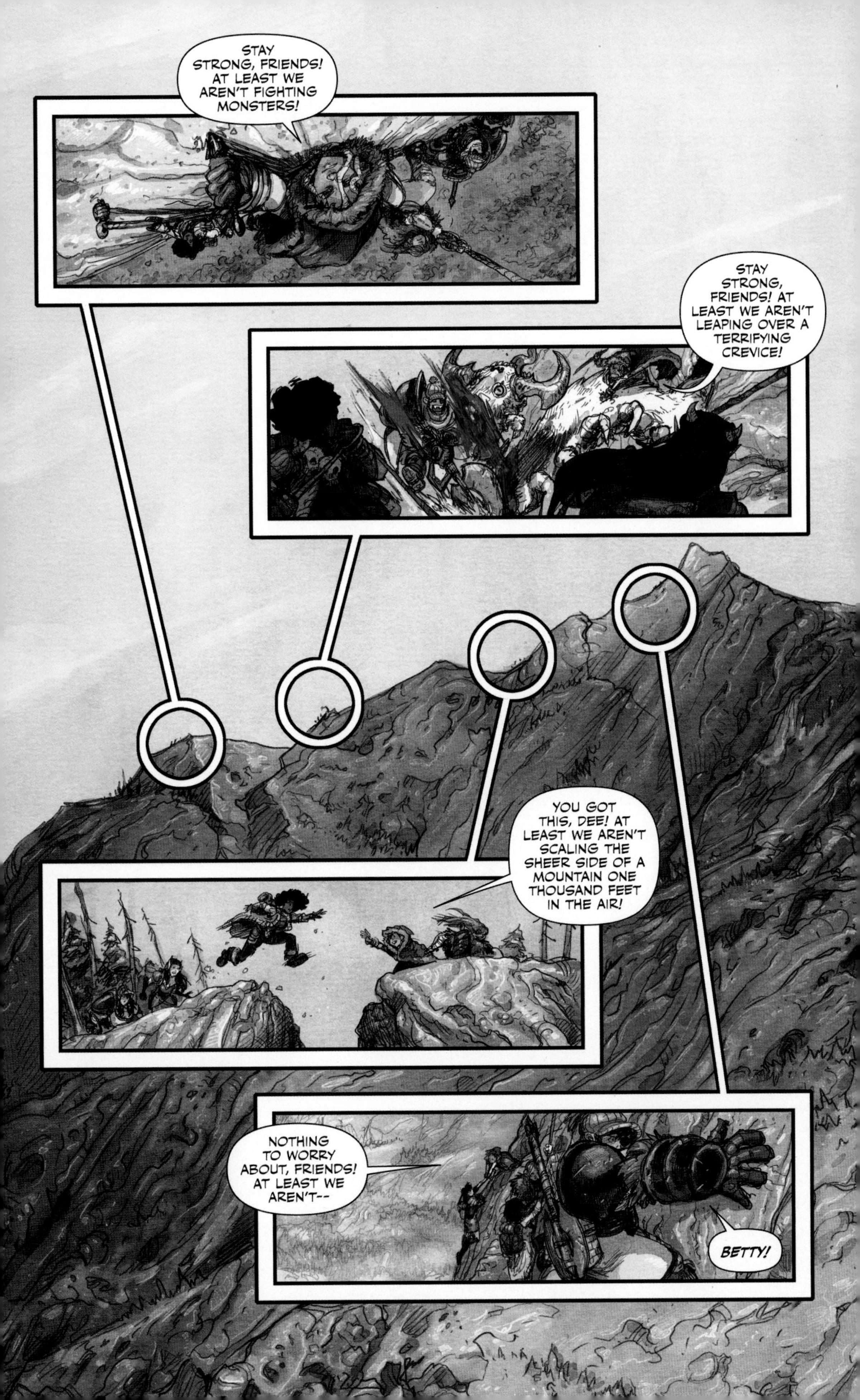
STAY STRONG, FRIENDS! AT LEAST WE AREN'T FIGHTING MONSTERS!
STAY STRONG, FRIENDS! AT LEAST WE AREN'T LEAPING OVER A TERRIFYING CREVICE!
YOU GOT THIS, DEE! AT LEAST WE AREN'T SCALING THE SHEER SIDE OF A MOUNTAIN ONE THOUSAND FEET IN THE AIR!
NOTHING TO WORRY ABOUT, FRIENDS! AT LEAST WE AREN'T--
BETTY!

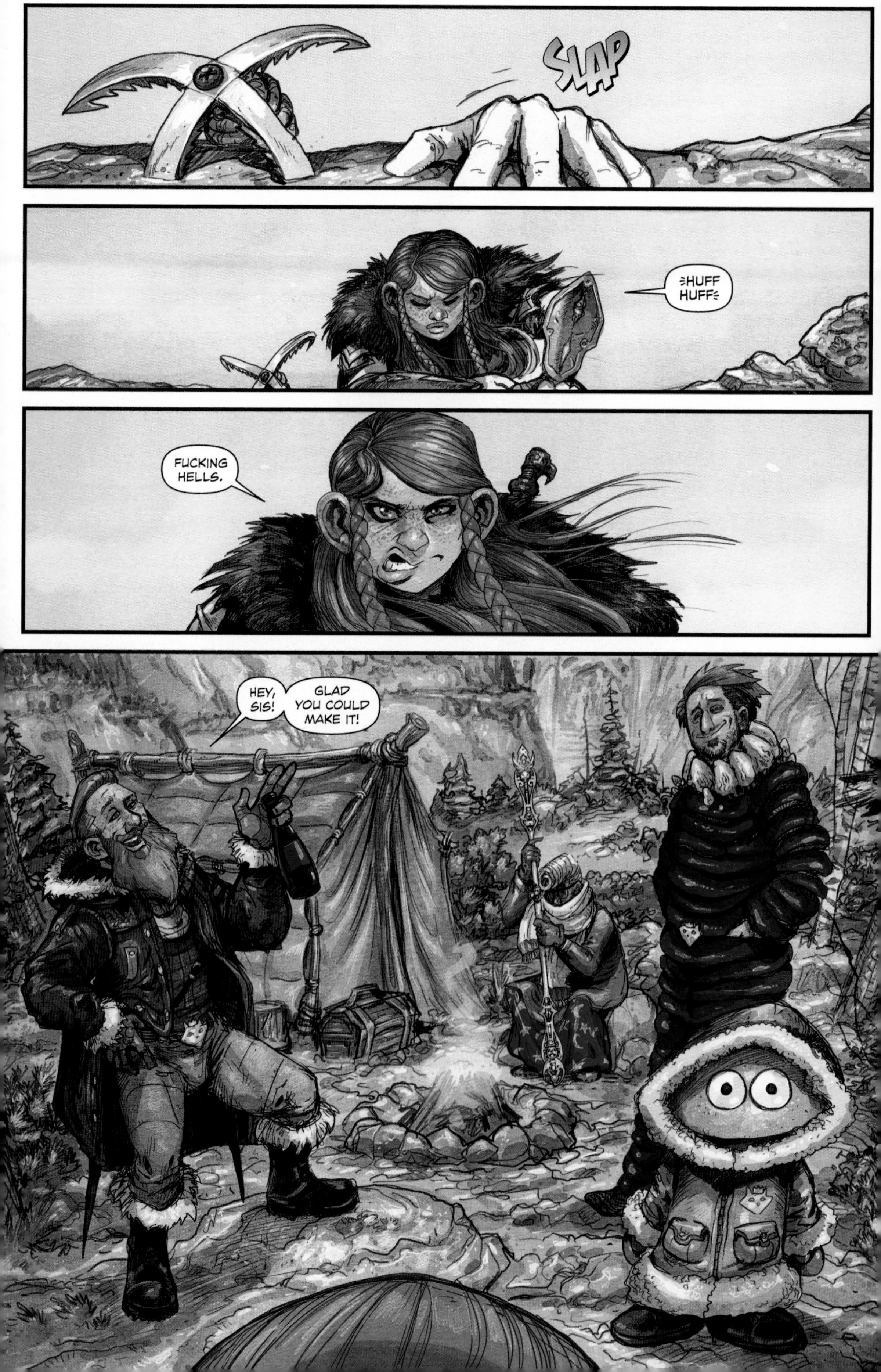
SLAP
HUFF HUFF
FUCKING HELLS.
HEY, SIS!
GLAD YOU COULD MAKE IT!

CHAPTER FOUR

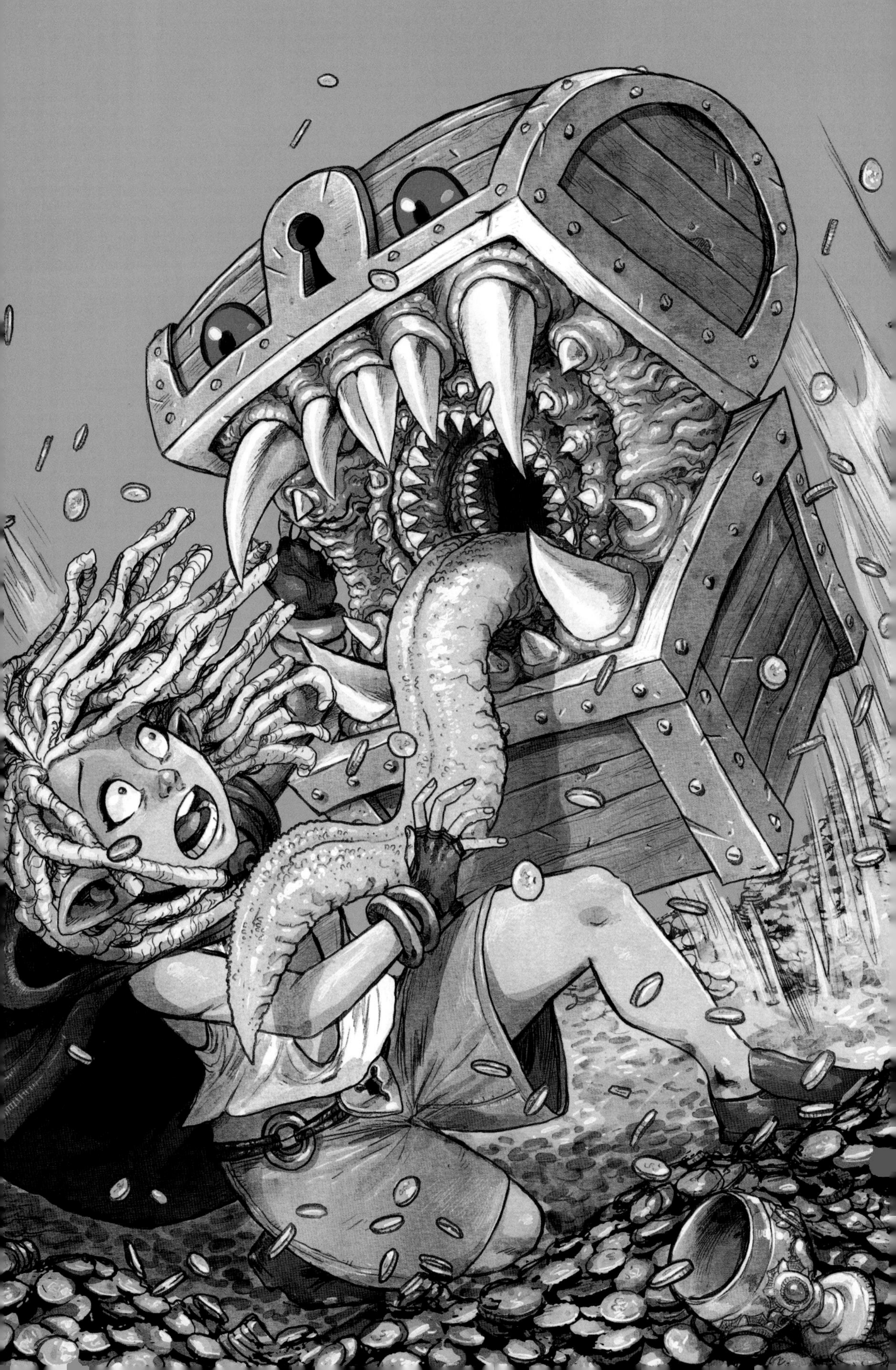

Issue #4 cover B

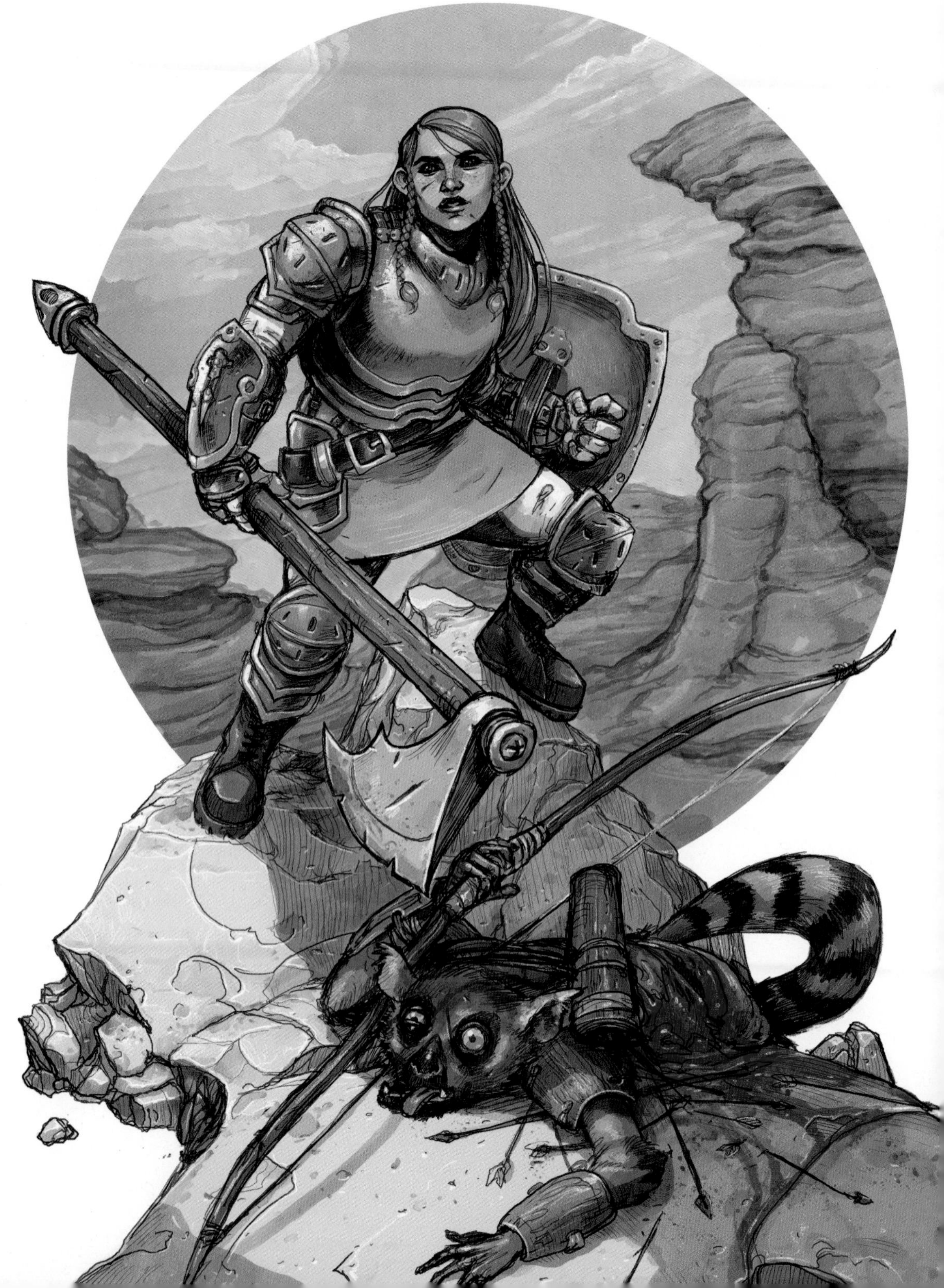

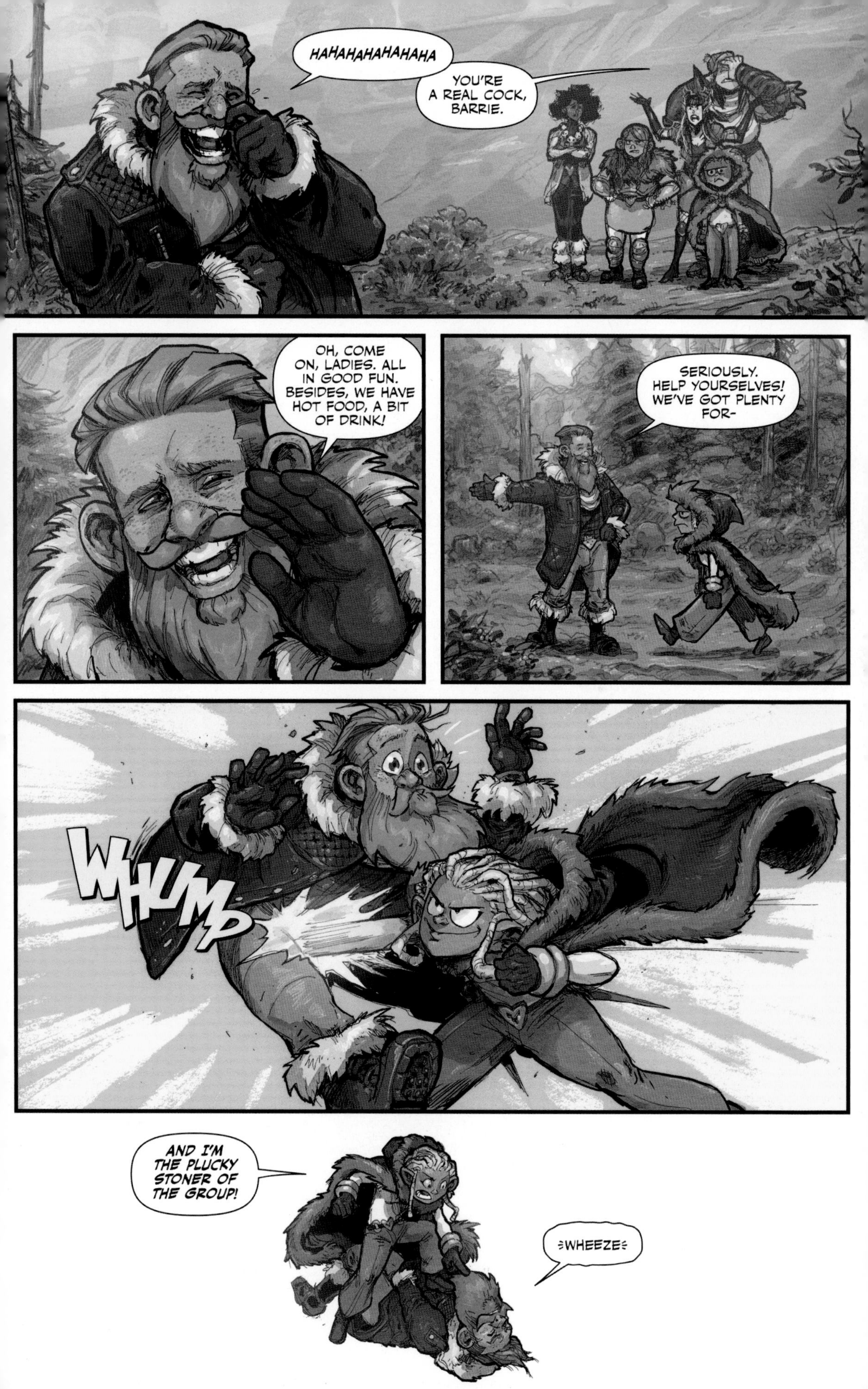
HAHAHAHAHAHAHA
YOU'RE A REAL COCK, BARRIE.
OH, COME ON, LADIES. ALL IN GOOD FUN. BESIDES, WE HAVE HOT FOOD, A BIT OF DRINK!
SERIOUSLY. HELP YOURSELVES! WE'VE GOT PLENTY FOR-
WHUMP
AND I'M THE PLUCKY STONER OF THE GROUP!
WHEEZE

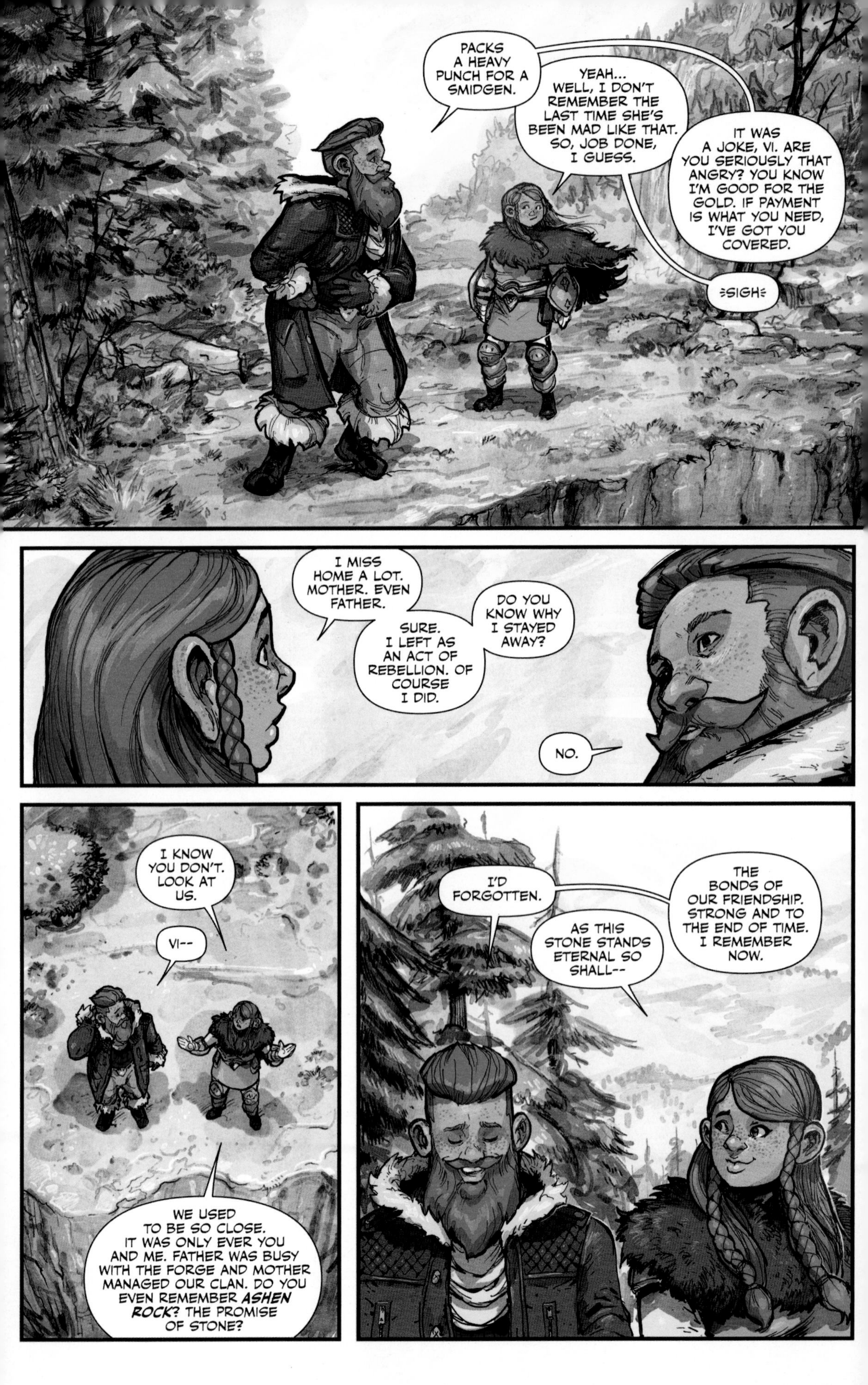

PACKS A HEAVY PUNCH FOR A SMIDGEN.
YEAH... WELL, I DON'T REMEMBER THE LAST TIME SHE'S BEEN MAD LIKE THAT. SO, JOB DONE, I GUESS.
IT WAS A JOKE, VI. ARE YOU SERIOUSLY THAT ANGRY? YOU KNOW I'M GOOD FOR THE GOLD. IF PAYMENT IS WHAT YOU NEED, I'VE GOT YOU COVERED.
SIGH
I MISS HOME A LOT. MOTHER. EVEN FATHER.
SURE. I LEFT AS AN ACT OF REBELLION. OF COURSE I DID.
DO YOU KNOW WHY I STAYED AWAY?
NO.
I KNOW YOU DON'T. LOOK AT US.
VI--
WE USED TO BE SO CLOSE. IT WAS ONLY EVER YOU AND ME. FATHER WAS BUSY WITH THE FORGE AND MOTHER MANAGED OUR CLAN. DO YOU EVEN REMEMBER *ASHEN ROCK*? THE PROMISE OF STONE?
I'D FORGOTTEN.
AS THIS STONE STANDS ETERNAL SO SHALL--
THE BONDS OF OUR FRIENDSHIP. STRONG AND TO THE END OF TIME. I REMEMBER NOW.

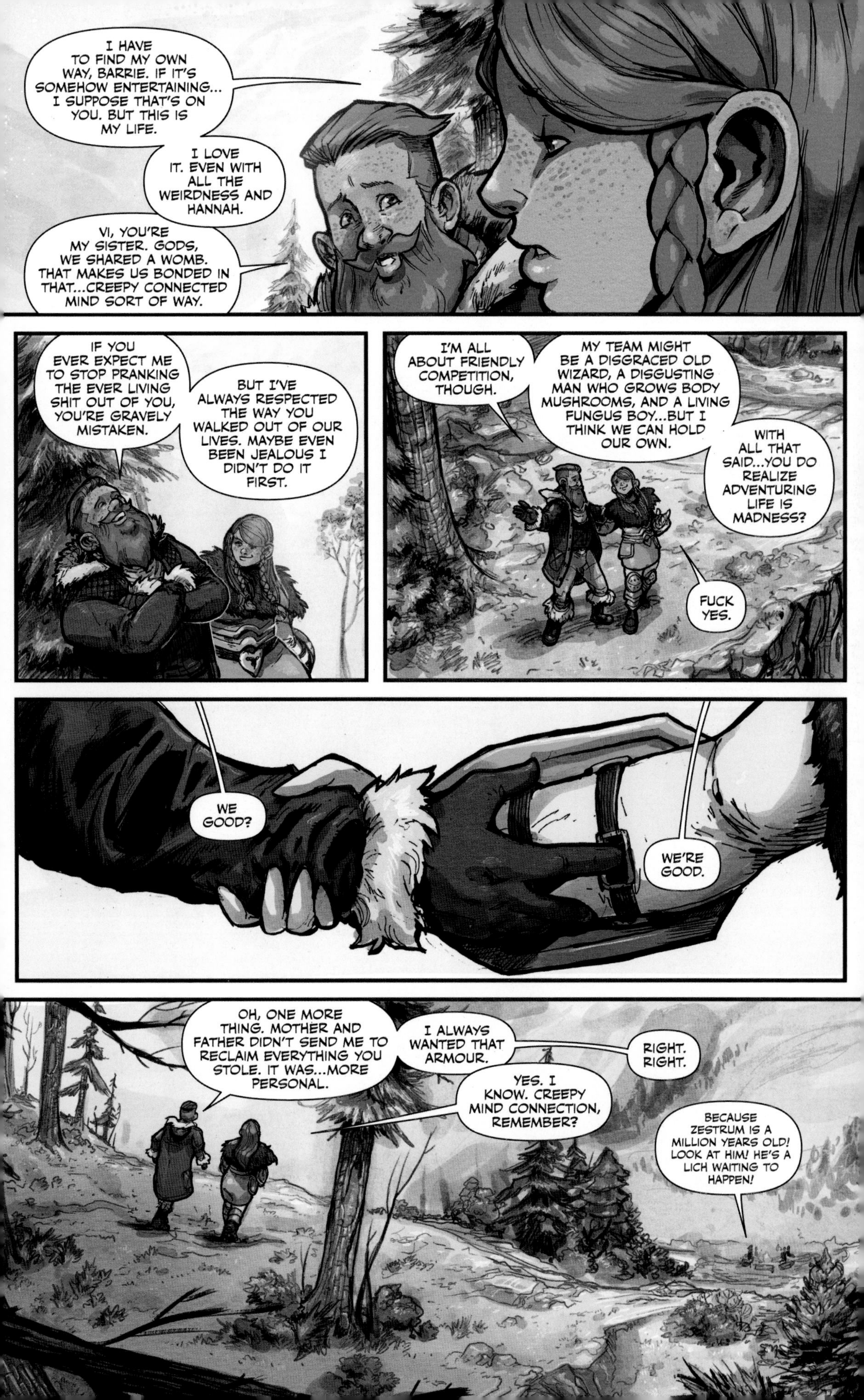
I HAVE TO FIND MY OWN WAY, BARRIE. IF IT'S SOMEHOW ENTERTAINING... I SUPPOSE THAT'S ON YOU. BUT THIS IS MY LIFE.
I LOVE IT. EVEN WITH ALL THE WEIRDNESS AND HANNAH.
VI, YOU'RE MY SISTER. GODS, WE SHARED A WOMB. THAT MAKES US BONDED IN THAT...CREEPY CONNECTED MIND SORT OF WAY.
IF YOU EVER EXPECT ME TO STOP PRANKING THE EVER LIVING SHIT OUT OF YOU, YOU'RE GRAVELY MISTAKEN.
BUT I'VE ALWAYS RESPECTED THE WAY YOU WALKED OUT OF OUR LIVES. MAYBE EVEN BEEN JEALOUS I DIDN'T DO IT FIRST.
I'M ALL ABOUT FRIENDLY COMPETITION, THOUGH.
MY TEAM MIGHT BE A DISGRACED OLD WIZARD, A DISGUSTING MAN WHO GROWS BODY MUSHROOMS, AND A LIVING FUNGUS BOY...BUT I THINK WE CAN HOLD OUR OWN.
WITH ALL THAT SAID...YOU DO REALIZE ADVENTURING LIFE IS MADNESS?
FUCK YES.
WE GOOD?
WE'RE GOOD.
OH, ONE MORE THING. MOTHER AND FATHER DIDN'T SEND ME TO RECLAIM EVERYTHING YOU STOLE. IT WAS...MORE PERSONAL.
YES. I KNOW. CREEPY MIND CONNECTION, REMEMBER?
I ALWAYS WANTED THAT ARMOUR.
RIGHT. RIGHT.
BECAUSE ZESTRUM IS A MILLION YEARS OLD! LOOK AT HIM! HE'S A LICH WAITING TO HAPPEN!

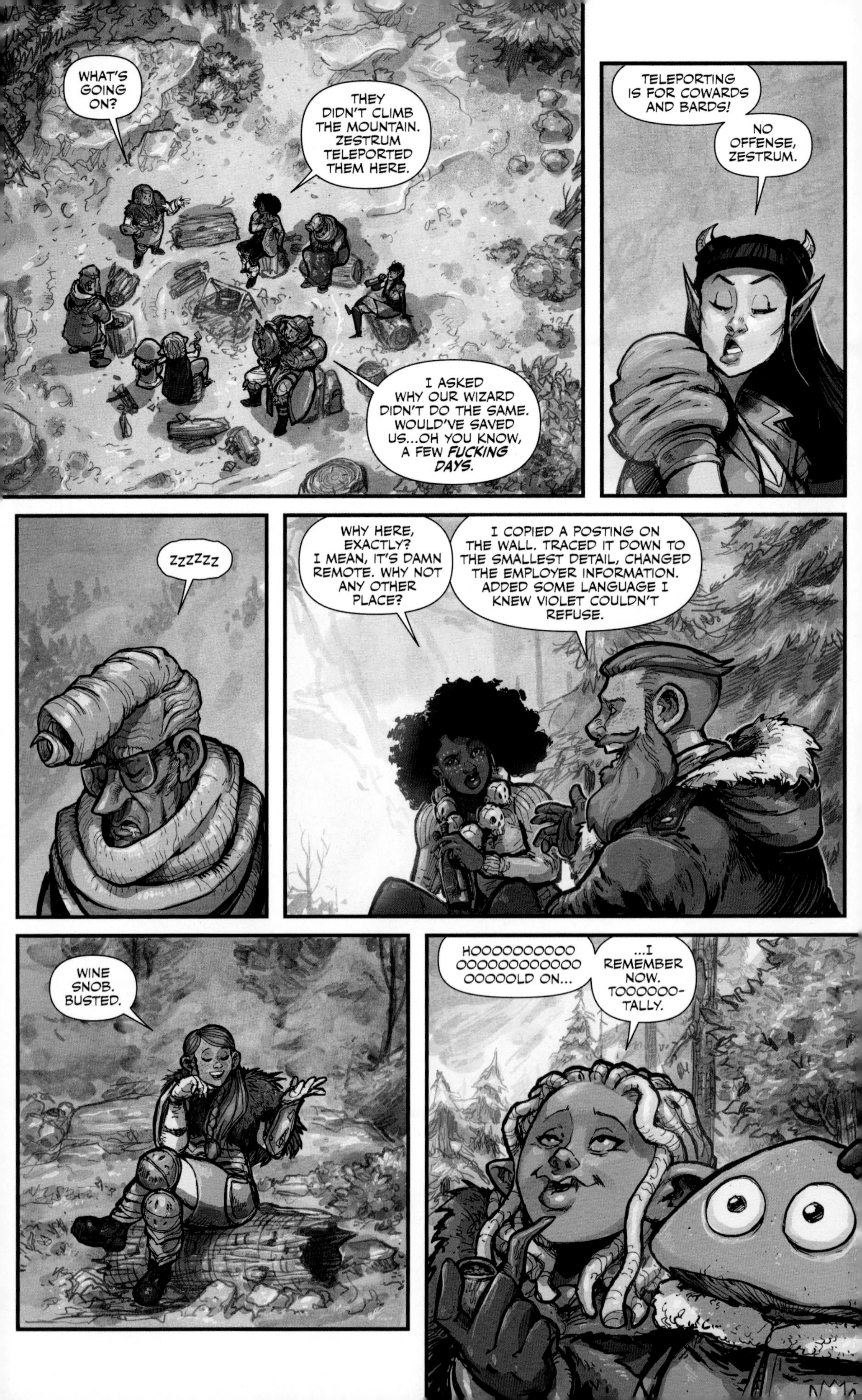
WHAT'S GOING ON?
THEY DIDN'T CLIMB THE MOUNTAIN. ZESTRUM TELEPORTED THEM HERE.
I ASKED WHY OUR WIZARD DIDN'T DO THE SAME. WOULD'VE SAVED US...OH YOU KNOW, A FEW *FUCKING DAYS.*
TELEPORTING IS FOR COWARDS AND BARDS!
NO OFFENSE, ZESTRUM.
ZZZZZZ
WHY HERE, EXACTLY? I MEAN, IT'S DAMN REMOTE. WHY NOT ANY OTHER PLACE?
I COPIED A POSTING ON THE WALL. TRACED IT DOWN TO THE SMALLEST DETAIL, CHANGED THE EMPLOYER INFORMATION. ADDED SOME LANGUAGE I KNEW VIOLET COULDN'T REFUSE.
WINE SNOB. BUSTED.
HOOOOOOOOOO OOOOOOOOOOO OOOOOLD ON...
...I REMEMBER NOW. TOOOOOO-TALLY.

I REMEMBER SEEING THE POSTING FOR A FEW SECONDS...

LET ME THINK.

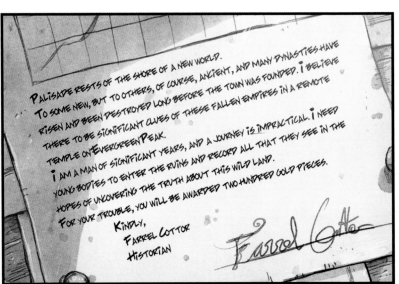

PALISADE RESTS OF THE SHORE OF A NEW WORLD.

TO SOME NEW, BUT TO OTHERS, OF COURSE, ANCIENT, AND MANY DYNASTIES HAVE RISEN AND BEEN DESTROYED LONG BEFORE THE TOWN WAS FOUNDED. I BELIEVE THERE TO BE SIGNIFICANT CLUES OF THESE FALLEN EMPIRES IN A REMOTE TEMPLE ON EVERGREEN PEAK.

I AM A MAN OF SIGNIFICANT YEARS, AND A JOURNEY IS IMPRACTICAL. I NEED YOUNG BODIES TO ENTER THE RUINS AND RECORD ALL THAT THEY SEE IN THE HOPES OF UNCOVERING THE TRUTH ABOUT THIS WILD LAND.

FOR YOUR TROUBLE, YOU WILL BE AWARDED TWO HUNDRED GOLD PIECES.

KINDLY,
FARREL COTTOR
HISTORIAN

I MEAN... THAT'S A PRETTY DETAILED RECOLLECTION.

THE MAP USED A DEVIL HORNED TREE AS A REFERENCE POINT. MAYBE IT'S REFERRING TO THAT?

COULD BE ONTO SOMETHING THERE, BETTY.

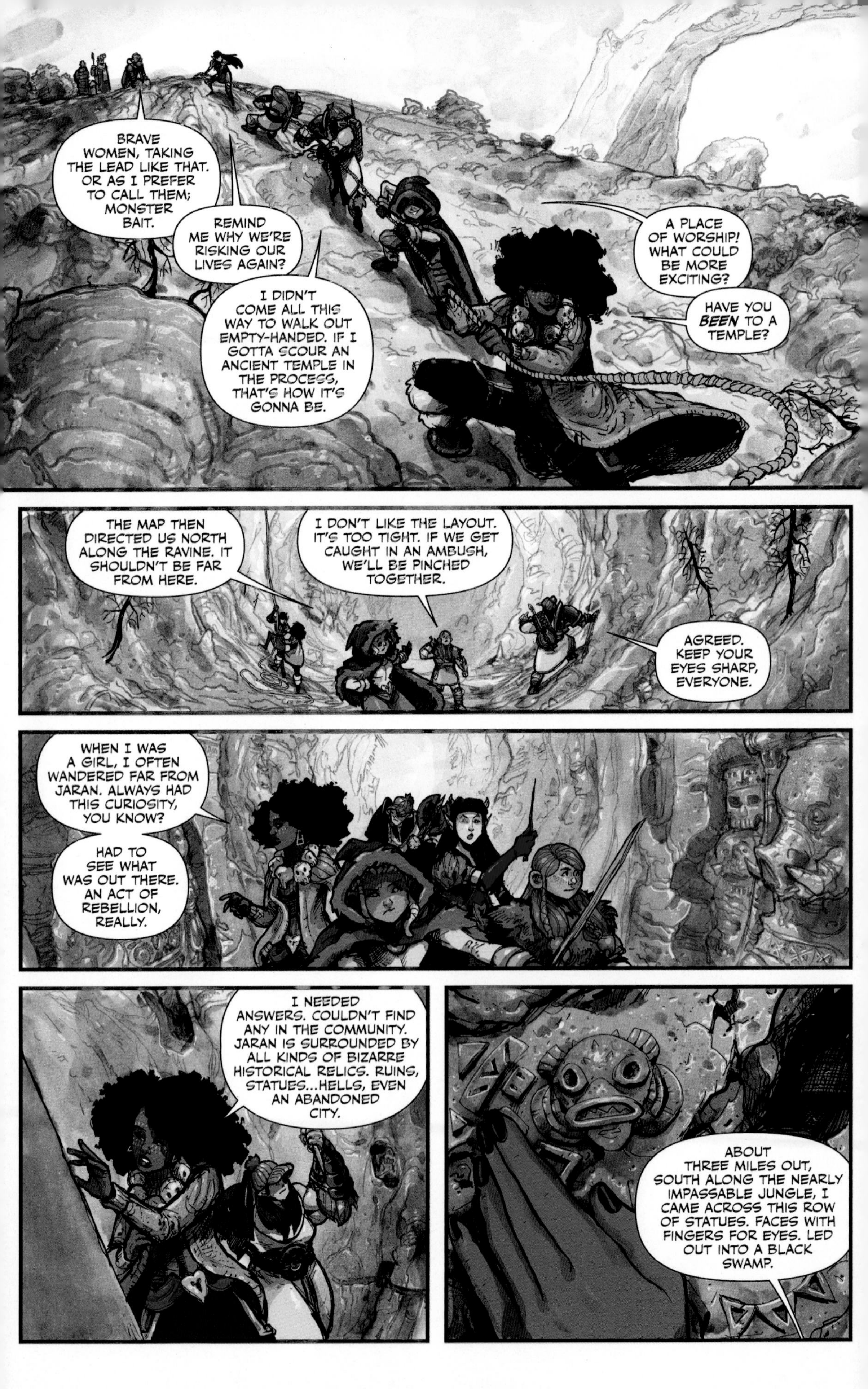
BRAVE WOMEN, TAKING THE LEAD LIKE THAT. OR AS I PREFER TO CALL THEM; MONSTER BAIT.
REMIND ME WHY WE'RE RISKING OUR LIVES AGAIN?
I DIDN'T COME ALL THIS WAY TO WALK OUT EMPTY-HANDED. IF I GOTTA SCOUR AN ANCIENT TEMPLE IN THE PROCESS, THAT'S HOW IT'S GONNA BE.
A PLACE OF WORSHIP! WHAT COULD BE MORE EXCITING?
HAVE YOU *BEEN* TO A TEMPLE?
THE MAP THEN DIRECTED US NORTH ALONG THE RAVINE. IT SHOULDN'T BE FAR FROM HERE.
I DON'T LIKE THE LAYOUT. IT'S TOO TIGHT. IF WE GET CAUGHT IN AN AMBUSH, WE'LL BE PINCHED TOGETHER.
AGREED. KEEP YOUR EYES SHARP, EVERYONE.
WHEN I WAS A GIRL, I OFTEN WANDERED FAR FROM JARAN. ALWAYS HAD THIS CURIOSITY, YOU KNOW?
HAD TO SEE WHAT WAS OUT THERE. AN ACT OF REBELLION, REALLY.
I NEEDED ANSWERS. COULDN'T FIND ANY IN THE COMMUNITY. JARAN IS SURROUNDED BY ALL KINDS OF BIZARRE HISTORICAL RELICS. RUINS, STATUES...HELLS, EVEN AN ABANDONED CITY.
ABOUT THREE MILES OUT, SOUTH ALONG THE NEARLY IMPASSABLE JUNGLE, I CAME ACROSS THIS ROW OF STATUES. FACES WITH FINGERS FOR EYES. LED OUT INTO A BLACK SWAMP.

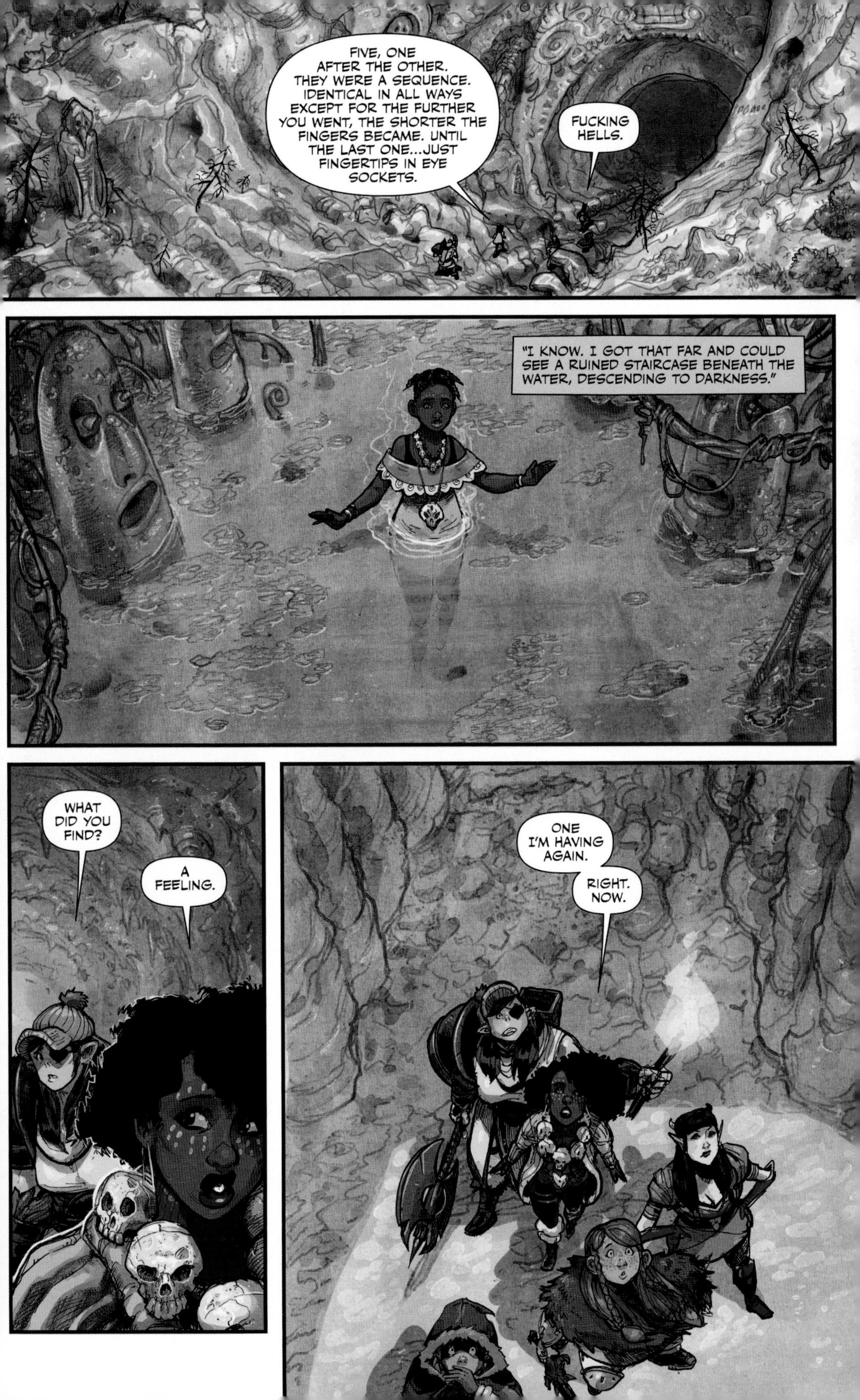
FIVE, ONE AFTER THE OTHER. THEY WERE A SEQUENCE. IDENTICAL IN ALL WAYS EXCEPT FOR THE FURTHER YOU WENT, THE SHORTER THE FINGERS BECAME. UNTIL THE LAST ONE...JUST FINGERTIPS IN EYE SOCKETS.
FUCKING HELLS.
"I KNOW. I GOT THAT FAR AND COULD SEE A RUINED STAIRCASE BENEATH THE WATER, DESCENDING TO DARKNESS."
WHAT DID YOU FIND?
A FEELING.
ONE I'M HAVING AGAIN.
RIGHT. NOW.

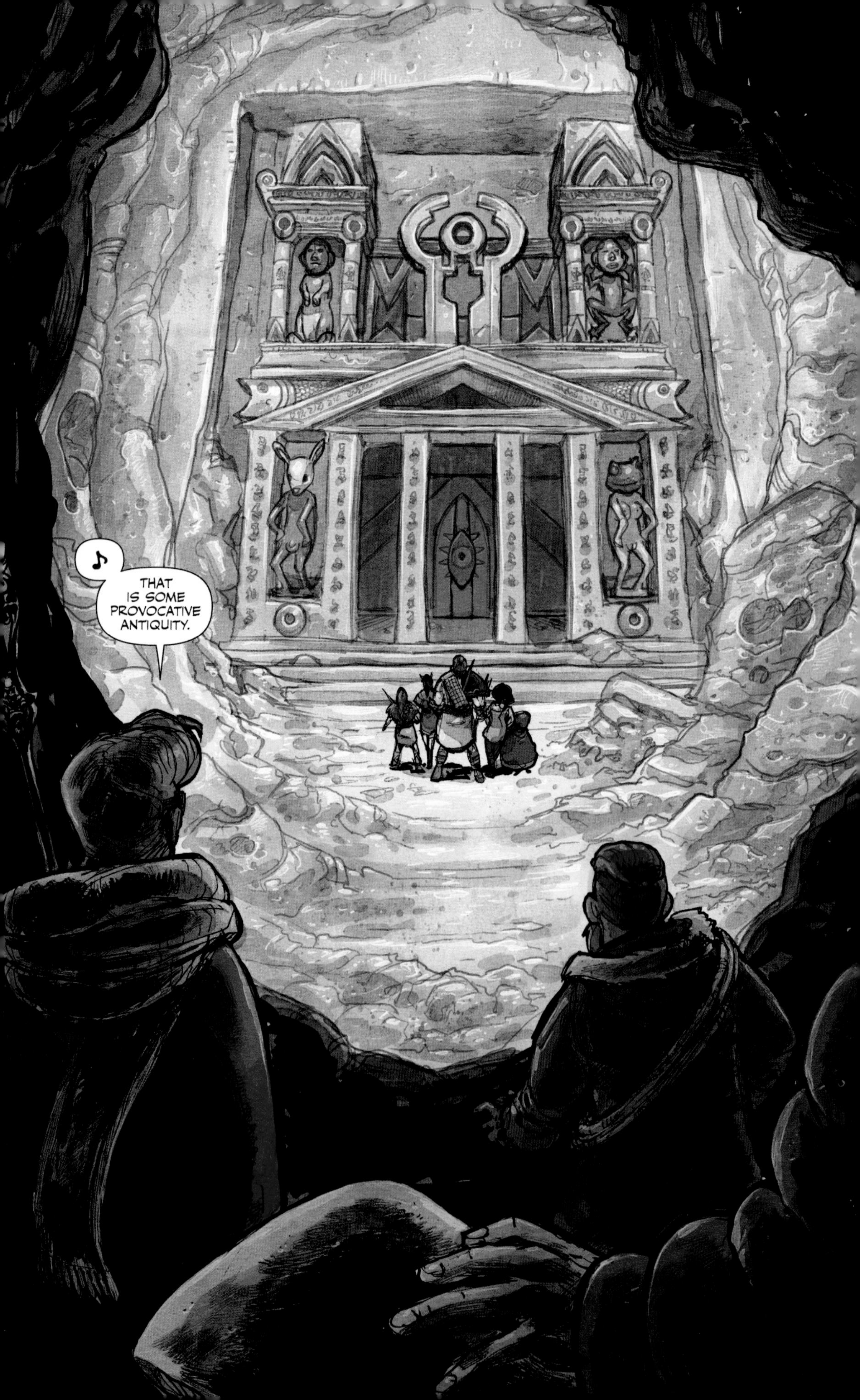
♪
THAT IS SOME PROVOCATIVE ANTIQUITY.

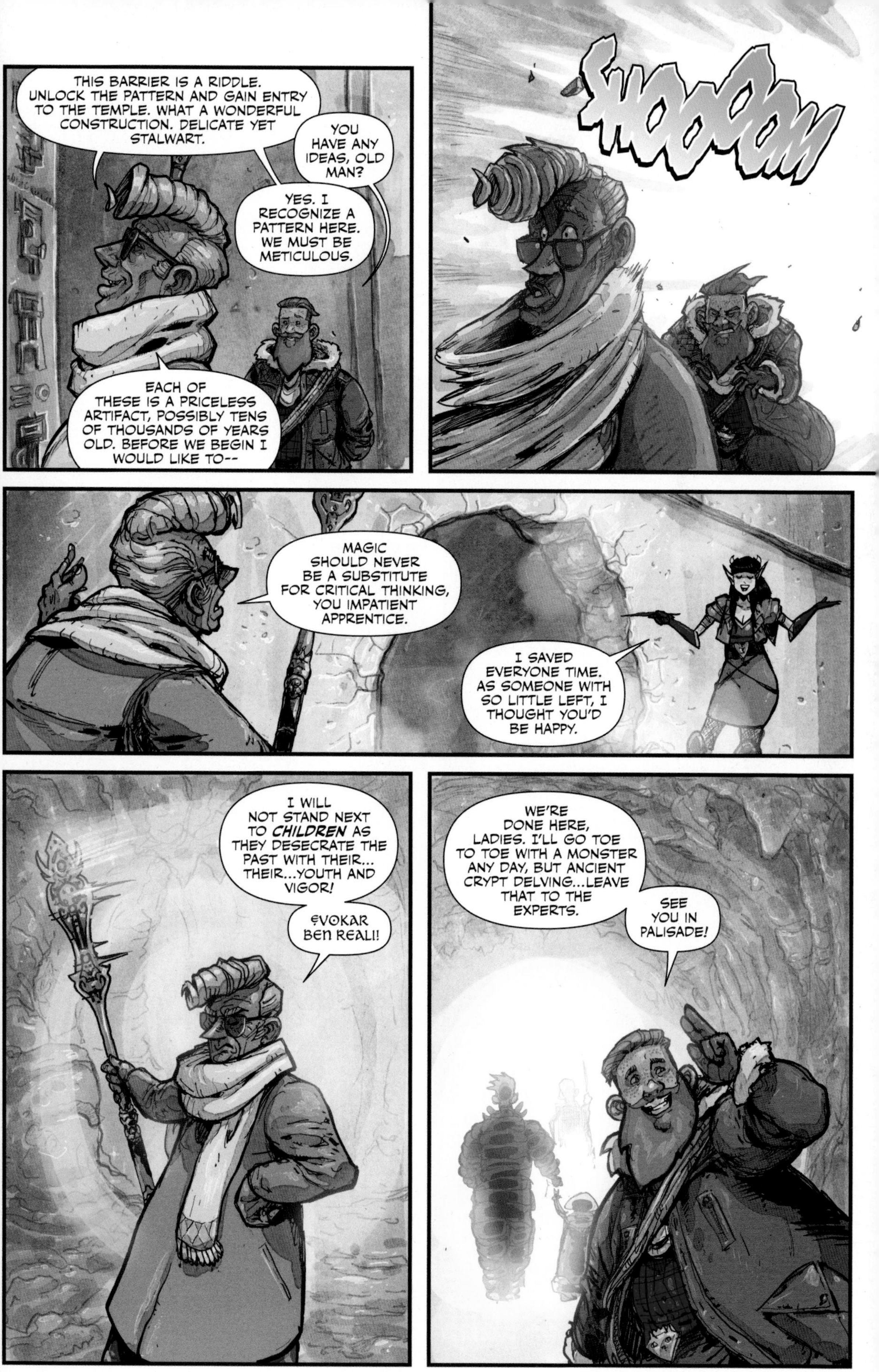
THIS BARRIER IS A RIDDLE. UNLOCK THE PATTERN AND GAIN ENTRY TO THE TEMPLE. WHAT A WONDERFUL CONSTRUCTION. DELICATE YET STALWART.
YOU HAVE ANY IDEAS, OLD MAN?
YES. I RECOGNIZE A PATTERN HERE. WE MUST BE METICULOUS.
EACH OF THESE IS A PRICELESS ARTIFACT, POSSIBLY TENS OF THOUSANDS OF YEARS OLD. BEFORE WE BEGIN I WOULD LIKE TO--
SHOOOOM
MAGIC SHOULD NEVER BE A SUBSTITUTE FOR CRITICAL THINKING, YOU IMPATIENT APPRENTICE.
I SAVED EVERYONE TIME. AS SOMEONE WITH SO LITTLE LEFT, I THOUGHT YOU'D BE HAPPY.
I WILL NOT STAND NEXT TO *CHILDREN* AS THEY DESECRATE THE PAST WITH THEIR... THEIR...YOUTH AND VIGOR!
EVOKAR BEN REALI!
WE'RE DONE HERE, LADIES. I'LL GO TOE TO TOE WITH A MONSTER ANY DAY, BUT ANCIENT CRYPT DELVING...LEAVE THAT TO THE EXPERTS.
SEE YOU IN PALISADE!

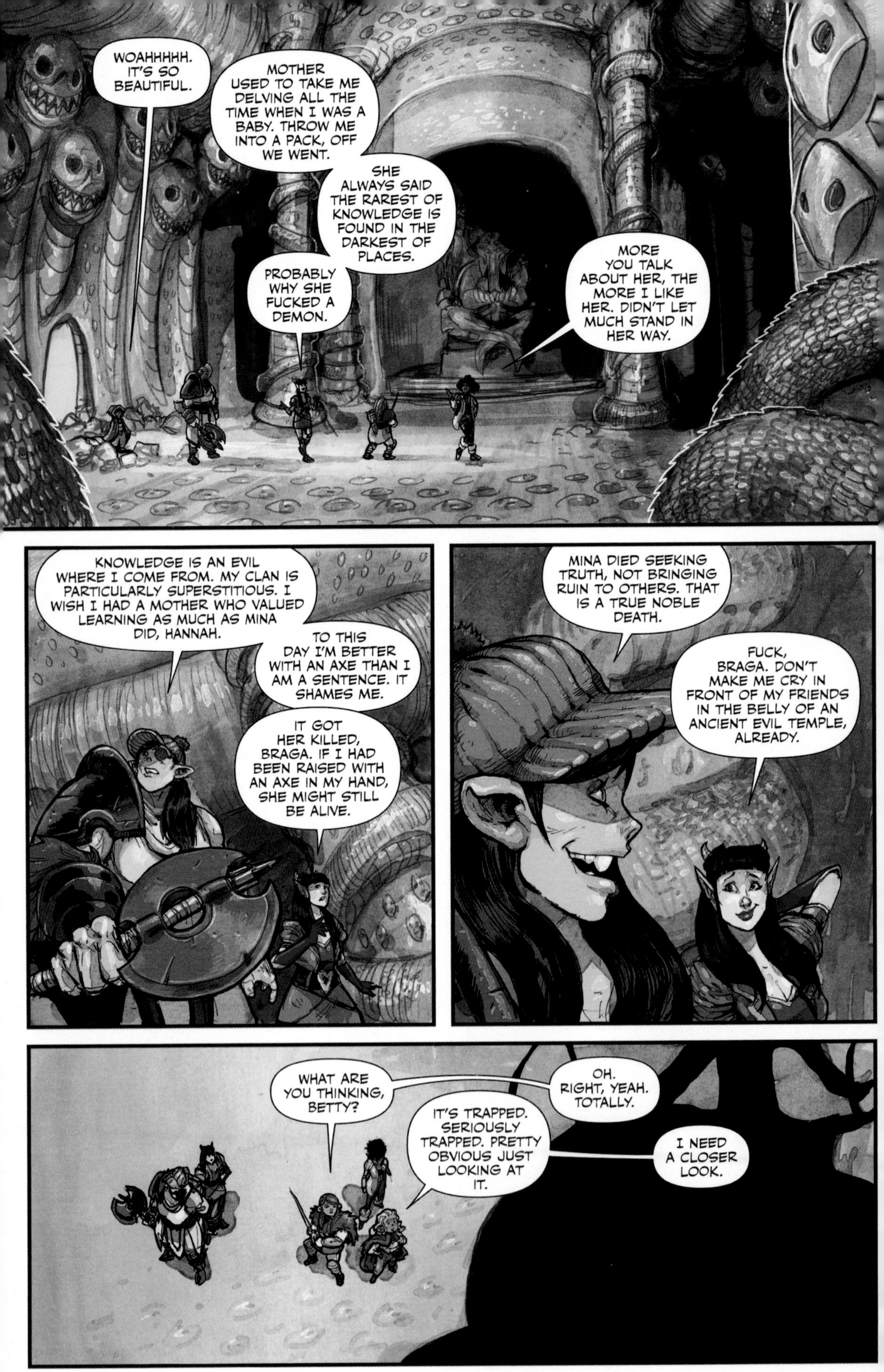
WOAHHHHH. IT'S SO BEAUTIFUL.
MOTHER USED TO TAKE ME DELVING ALL THE TIME WHEN I WAS A BABY. THROW ME INTO A PACK, OFF WE WENT.
SHE ALWAYS SAID THE RAREST OF KNOWLEDGE IS FOUND IN THE DARKEST OF PLACES.
PROBABLY WHY SHE FUCKED A DEMON.
MORE YOU TALK ABOUT HER, THE MORE I LIKE HER. DIDN'T LET MUCH STAND IN HER WAY.
KNOWLEDGE IS AN EVIL WHERE I COME FROM. MY CLAN IS PARTICULARLY SUPERSTITIOUS. I WISH I HAD A MOTHER WHO VALUED LEARNING AS MUCH AS MINA DID, HANNAH.
TO THIS DAY I'M BETTER WITH AN AXE THAN I AM A SENTENCE. IT SHAMES ME.
IT GOT HER KILLED, BRAGA. IF I HAD BEEN RAISED WITH AN AXE IN MY HAND, SHE MIGHT STILL BE ALIVE.
MINA DIED SEEKING TRUTH, NOT BRINGING RUIN TO OTHERS. THAT IS A TRUE NOBLE DEATH.
FUCK, BRAGA. DON'T MAKE ME CRY IN FRONT OF MY FRIENDS IN THE BELLY OF AN ANCIENT EVIL TEMPLE, ALREADY.
WHAT ARE YOU THINKING, BETTY?
OH. RIGHT, YEAH. TOTALLY.
IT'S TRAPPED. SERIOUSLY TRAPPED. PRETTY OBVIOUS JUST LOOKING AT IT.
I NEED A CLOSER LOOK.

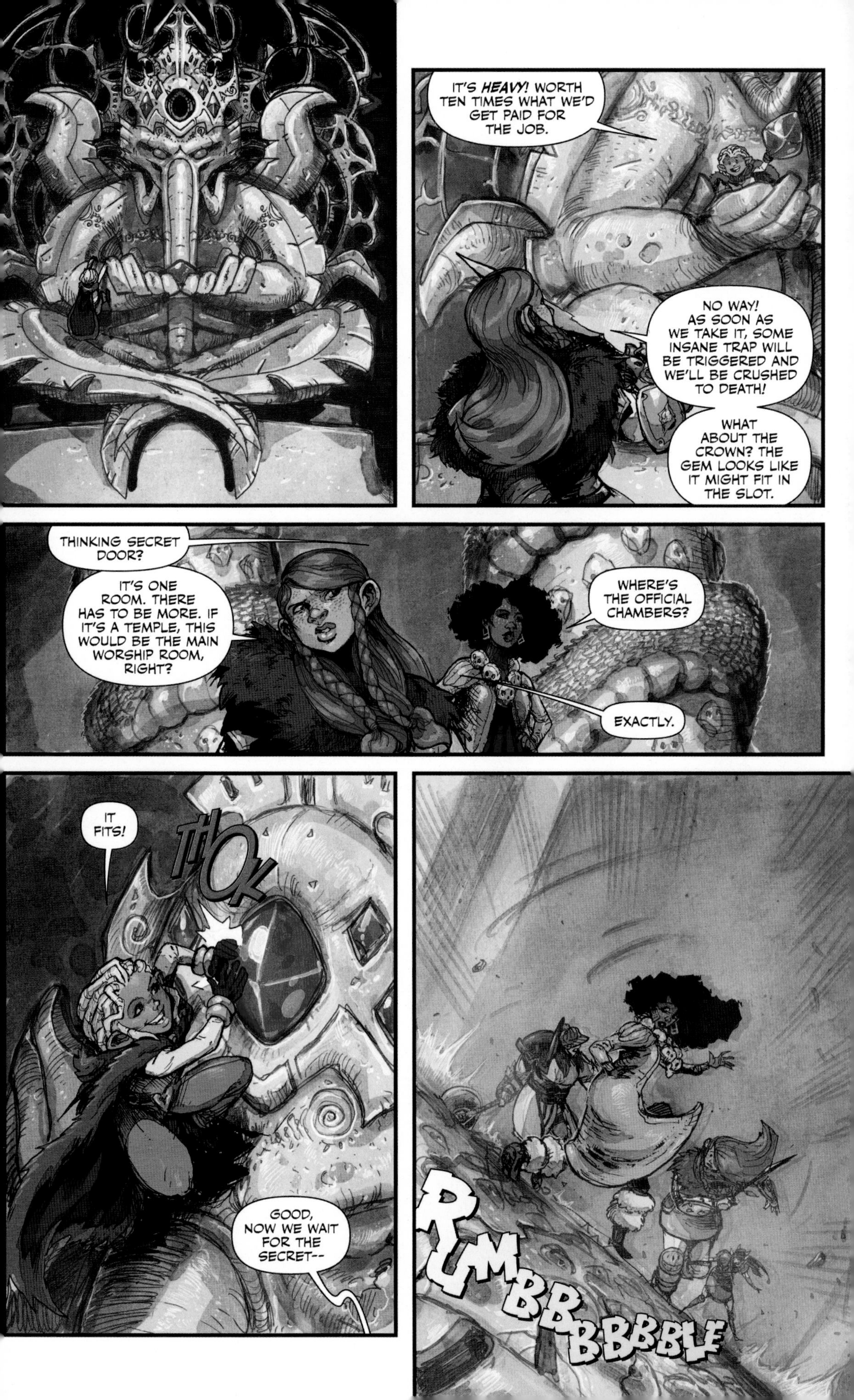
IT'S *HEAVY!* WORTH TEN TIMES WHAT WE'D GET PAID FOR THE JOB.
NO WAY! AS SOON AS WE TAKE IT, SOME INSANE TRAP WILL BE TRIGGERED AND WE'LL BE CRUSHED TO DEATH!
WHAT ABOUT THE CROWN? THE GEM LOOKS LIKE IT MIGHT FIT IN THE SLOT.
THINKING SECRET DOOR?
IT'S ONE ROOM. THERE HAS TO BE MORE. IF IT'S A TEMPLE, THIS WOULD BE THE MAIN WORSHIP ROOM, RIGHT?
WHERE'S THE OFFICIAL CHAMBERS?
EXACTLY.
IT FITS!
THOK
GOOD, NOW WE WAIT FOR THE SECRET--
RUMBBBBBBLE

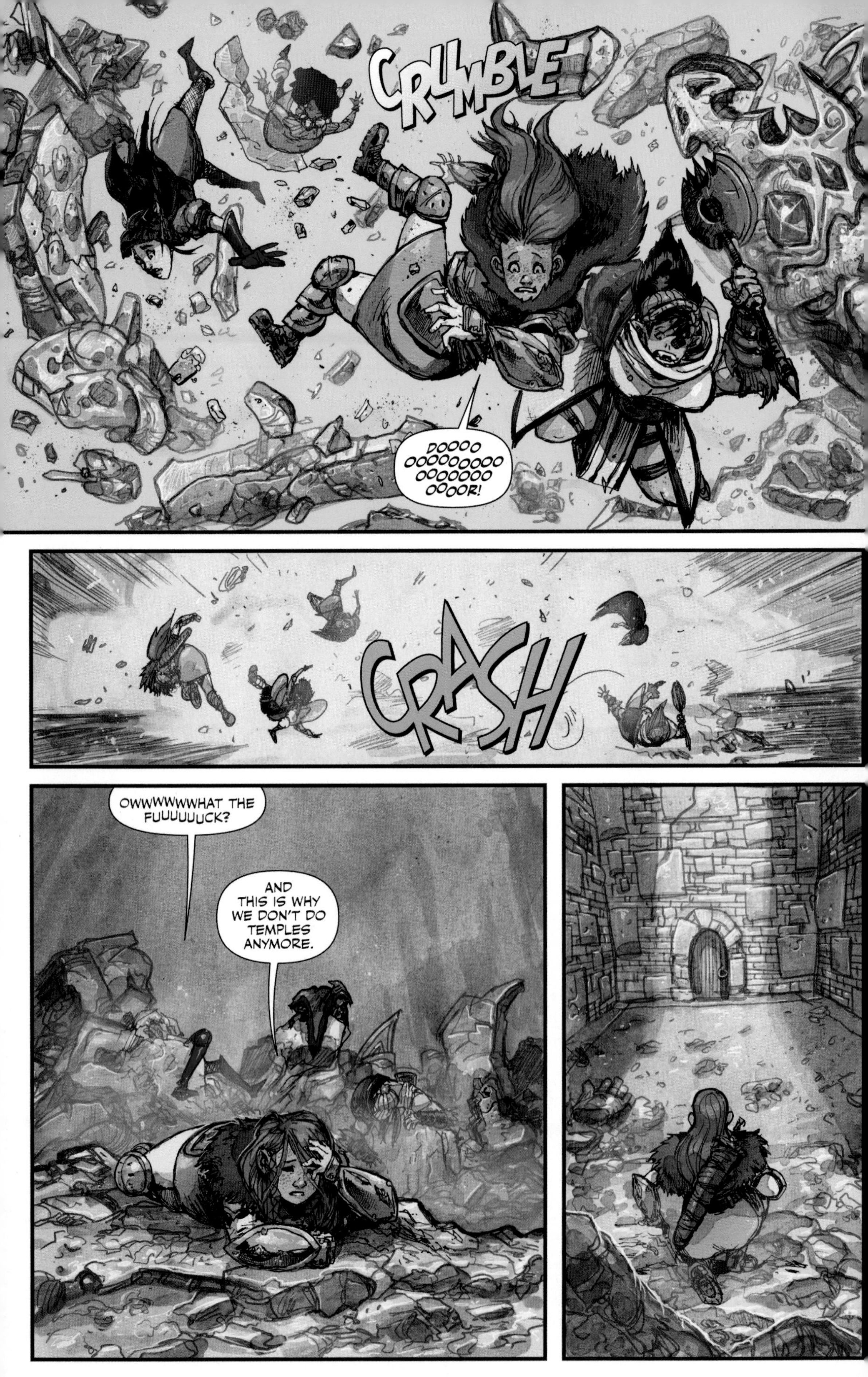
CRUMBLE
DOOOO OOOOOOOOO OOOOOOO OOOOR!
CRASH
OWWWWWWHAT THE FUUUUUUCK?
AND THIS IS WHY WE DON'T DO TEMPLES ANYMORE.

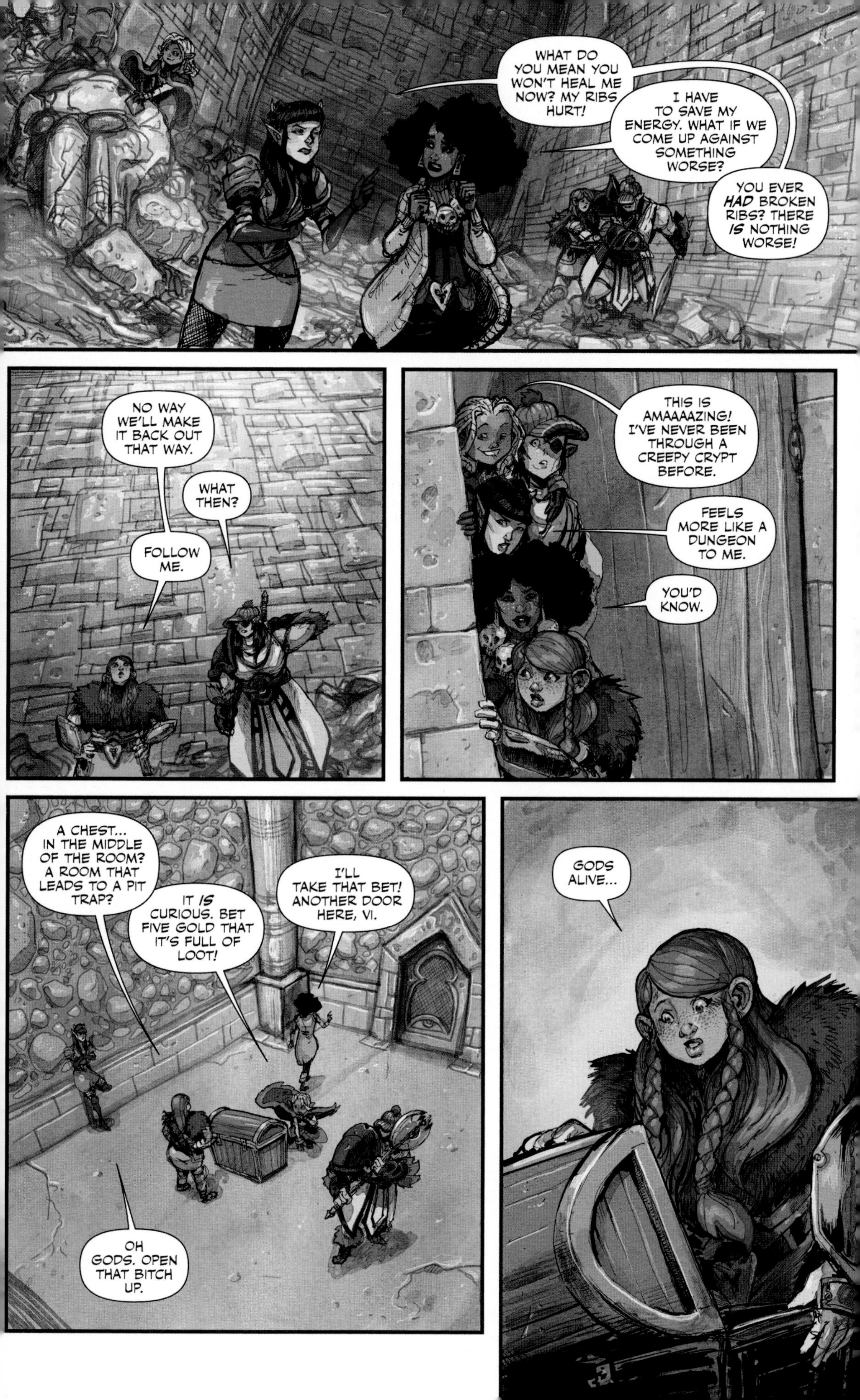
WHAT DO YOU MEAN YOU WON'T HEAL ME NOW? MY RIBS HURT!
I HAVE TO SAVE MY ENERGY. WHAT IF WE COME UP AGAINST SOMETHING WORSE?
YOU EVER *HAD* BROKEN RIBS? THERE *IS* NOTHING WORSE!
NO WAY WE'LL MAKE IT BACK OUT THAT WAY.
WHAT THEN?
FOLLOW ME.
THIS IS AMAAAAZING! I'VE NEVER BEEN THROUGH A CREEPY CRYPT BEFORE.
FEELS MORE LIKE A DUNGEON TO ME.
YOU'D KNOW.
A CHEST... IN THE MIDDLE OF THE ROOM? A ROOM THAT LEADS TO A PIT TRAP?
IT *IS* CURIOUS. BET FIVE GOLD THAT IT'S FULL OF LOOT!
I'LL TAKE THAT BET! ANOTHER DOOR HERE, VI.
OH GODS. OPEN THAT BITCH UP.
GODS ALIVE...

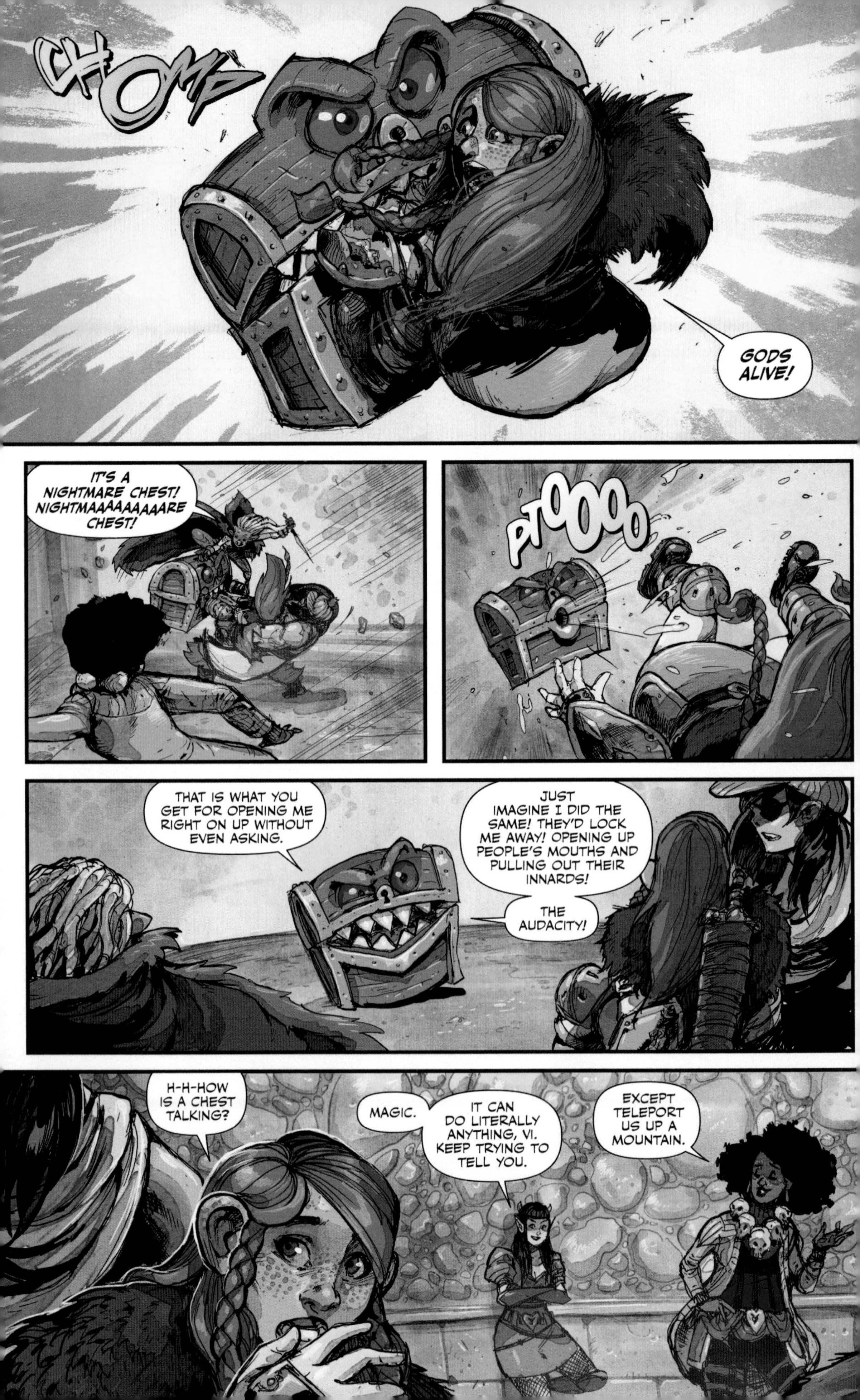
CHOMP
GODS ALIVE!
IT'S A NIGHTMARE CHEST! NIGHTMAAAAAAAAARE CHEST!
PTOOOO
THAT IS WHAT YOU GET FOR OPENING ME RIGHT ON UP WITHOUT EVEN ASKING.
JUST IMAGINE I DID THE SAME! THEY'D LOCK ME AWAY! OPENING UP PEOPLE'S MOUTHS AND PULLING OUT THEIR INNARDS!
THE AUDACITY!
H-H-HOW IS A CHEST TALKING?
MAGIC.
IT CAN DO LITERALLY ANYTHING, VI. KEEP TRYING TO TELL YOU.
EXCEPT TELEPORT US UP A MOUNTAIN.

LOOK, UM... CHEST--

MARCY.

OK, SURE. MARCY. WE DIDN'T KNOW--

I DID.

BESIDES HANNAH, WE DIDN'T KNOW. THIS IS ALL VERY NEW TO US. AND, WE'VE JUST FALLEN DOWN A HOLE, I IMAGINE MOST OF US HAVE CONCUSSIONS...

IT'S BEEN A LONG DAY.

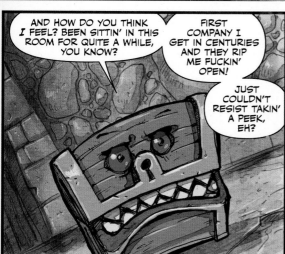

AND HOW DO YOU THINK *I* FEEL? BEEN SITTIN' IN THIS ROOM FOR QUITE A WHILE, YOU KNOW?

FIRST COMPANY I GET IN CENTURIES AND THEY RIP ME FUCKIN' OPEN!

JUST COULDN'T RESIST TAKIN' A PEEK, EH?

I APOLOGIZE. TRULY. SEE, PEOPLE LIKE ME...WHEN WE SEE A CHEST, WE OPEN IT. IT'S THE SORT OF THING FILLED WITH TREASURE...OR RELICS, OR...

...I DIDN'T EXPECT ONE TO EVER BE ALIVE.

CHEST? I'M NOT A CHEST! I JUST LOOK LIKE ONE!

O-OK.

IT HARDLY MATTERS. I'M ONLY HERE TO SEND YOU ON YOUR WAY WITH THE FIRST PIECE, ANYWAY.

MEET INTERESTING PEOPLE. LAID BACK ATMOSPHERE. QUIET LOCATION. LONG TERM EMPLOYMENT.

SOUNDED LIKE A DREAM JOB. IMAGINE MY SURPRISE.

WHAT IS IT, MARCY?

THE *SILVER CYLINDER.* THE FIRST OF THREE PIECES THAT COMBINE INTO A SINGLE POWERFUL ARTIFACT. IT IS THE ONLY WAY TO ESCAPE THIS PLACE.

THROUGH EACH DOOR YOU WILL FACE AN IMMENSE CHALLENGE, AND SHOULD YOU ACHIEVE VICTORY ANOTHER PIECE SHALL BE AWARDED.

WHAT IF WE FAIL?

FUCKED IF I KNOW.

WE CAN TAKE YOU WITH US, MARCY. YOU DON'T NEED TO BE ALONE DOWN HERE, ANYMORE.

SURELY YOU'VE SERVED--

YOU'RE SWEET, KID. REAL FUCKIN' SWEET. BUT, I SIGNED A CONTRACT.

SHHHHHHH. JUST GO.

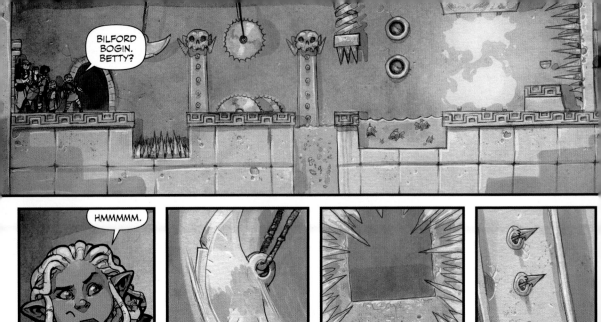

BILFORD BOGIN. BETTY?

HMMMMM.

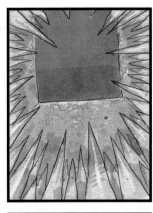

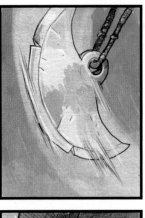

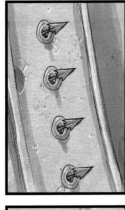

GOT IT. OKAY, HERE WE GO.

HANNAH, CAN YOU MAGIC FLOAT THAT BITCH OVER HERE?

DONE.

VMMMMM

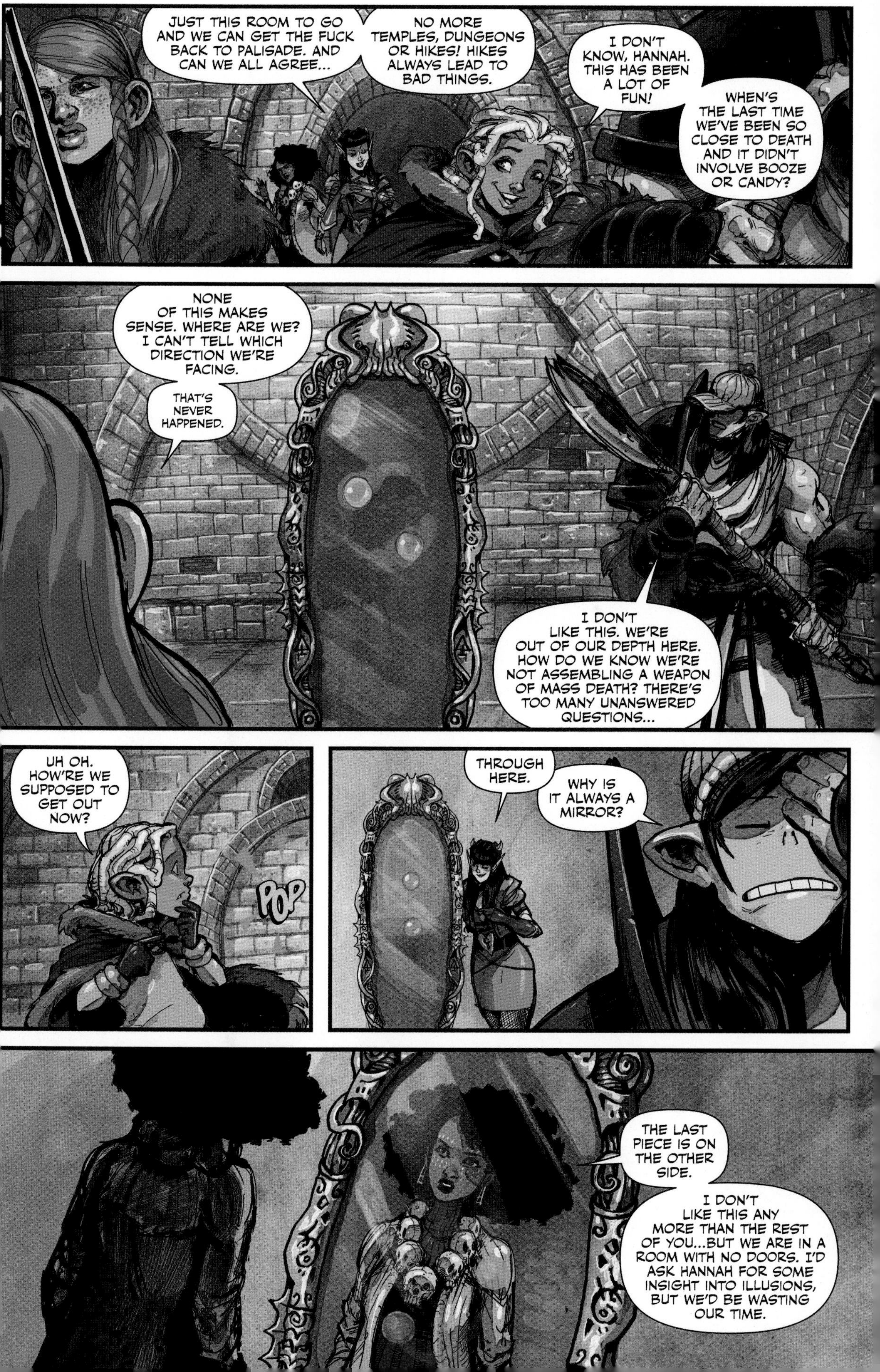
JUST THIS ROOM TO GO AND WE CAN GET THE FUCK BACK TO PALISADE. AND CAN WE ALL AGREE...
NO MORE TEMPLES, DUNGEONS OR HIKES! HIKES ALWAYS LEAD TO BAD THINGS.
I DON'T KNOW, HANNAH. THIS HAS BEEN A LOT OF FUN!
WHEN'S THE LAST TIME WE'VE BEEN SO CLOSE TO DEATH AND IT DIDN'T INVOLVE BOOZE OR CANDY?
NONE OF THIS MAKES SENSE. WHERE ARE WE? I CAN'T TELL WHICH DIRECTION WE'RE FACING.
THAT'S NEVER HAPPENED.
I DON'T LIKE THIS. WE'RE OUT OF OUR DEPTH HERE. HOW DO WE KNOW WE'RE NOT ASSEMBLING A WEAPON OF MASS DEATH? THERE'S TOO MANY UNANSWERED QUESTIONS...
UH OH. HOW'RE WE SUPPOSED TO GET OUT NOW?
POP
THROUGH HERE.
WHY IS IT ALWAYS A MIRROR?
THE LAST PIECE IS ON THE OTHER SIDE.
I DON'T LIKE THIS ANY MORE THAN THE REST OF YOU...BUT WE ARE IN A ROOM WITH NO DOORS. I'D ASK HANNAH FOR SOME INSIGHT INTO ILLUSIONS, BUT WE'D BE WASTING OUR TIME.

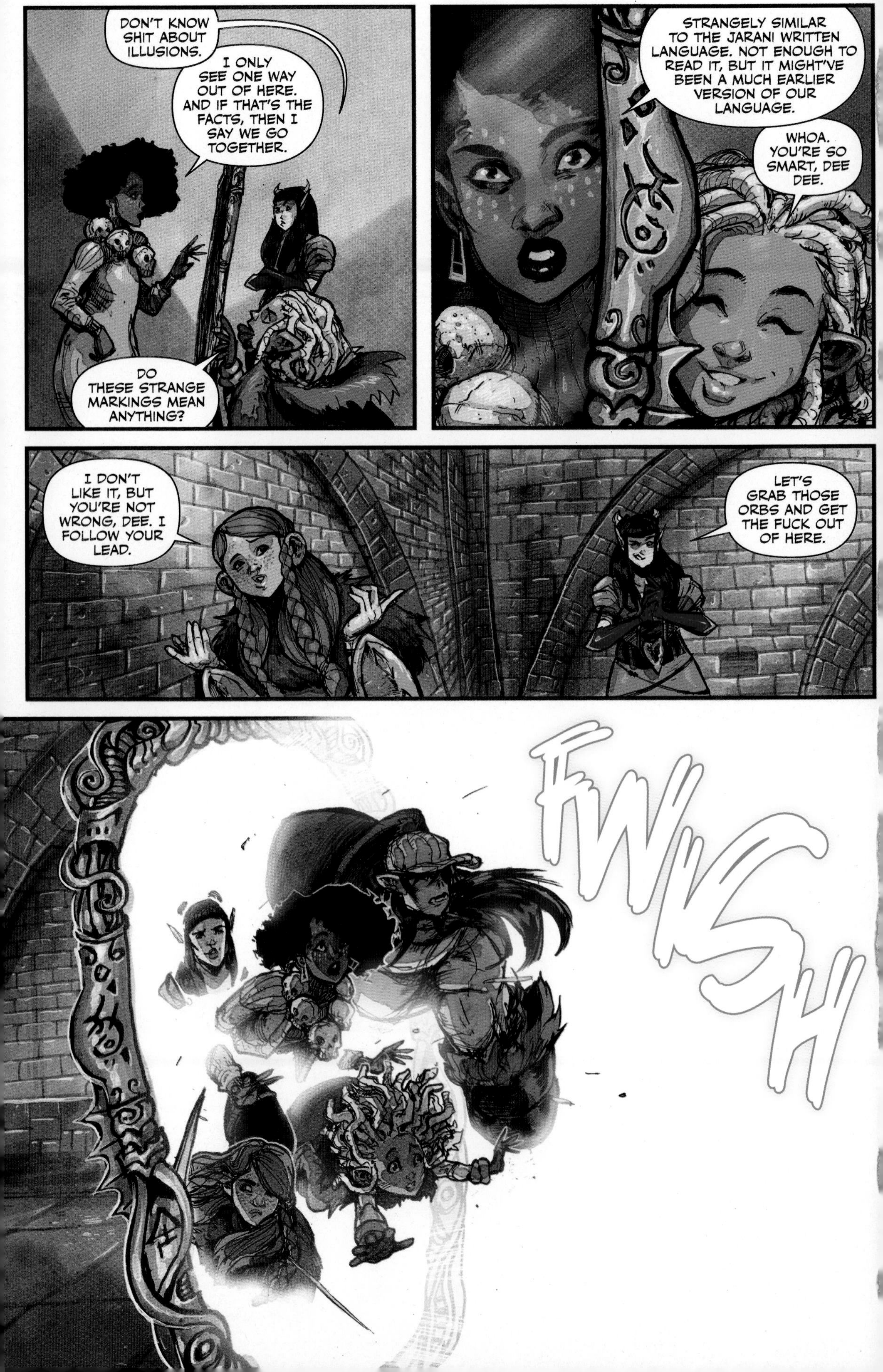
DON'T KNOW SHIT ABOUT ILLUSIONS.
I ONLY SEE ONE WAY OUT OF HERE. AND IF THAT'S THE FACTS, THEN I SAY WE GO TOGETHER.
DO THESE STRANGE MARKINGS MEAN ANYTHING?
STRANGELY SIMILAR TO THE JARANI WRITTEN LANGUAGE. NOT ENOUGH TO READ IT, BUT IT MIGHT'VE BEEN A MUCH EARLIER VERSION OF OUR LANGUAGE.
WHOA. YOU'RE SO SMART, DEE DEE.
I DON'T LIKE IT, BUT YOU'RE NOT WRONG, DEE. I FOLLOW YOUR LEAD.
LET'S GRAB THOSE ORBS AND GET THE FUCK OUT OF HERE.
FWISH

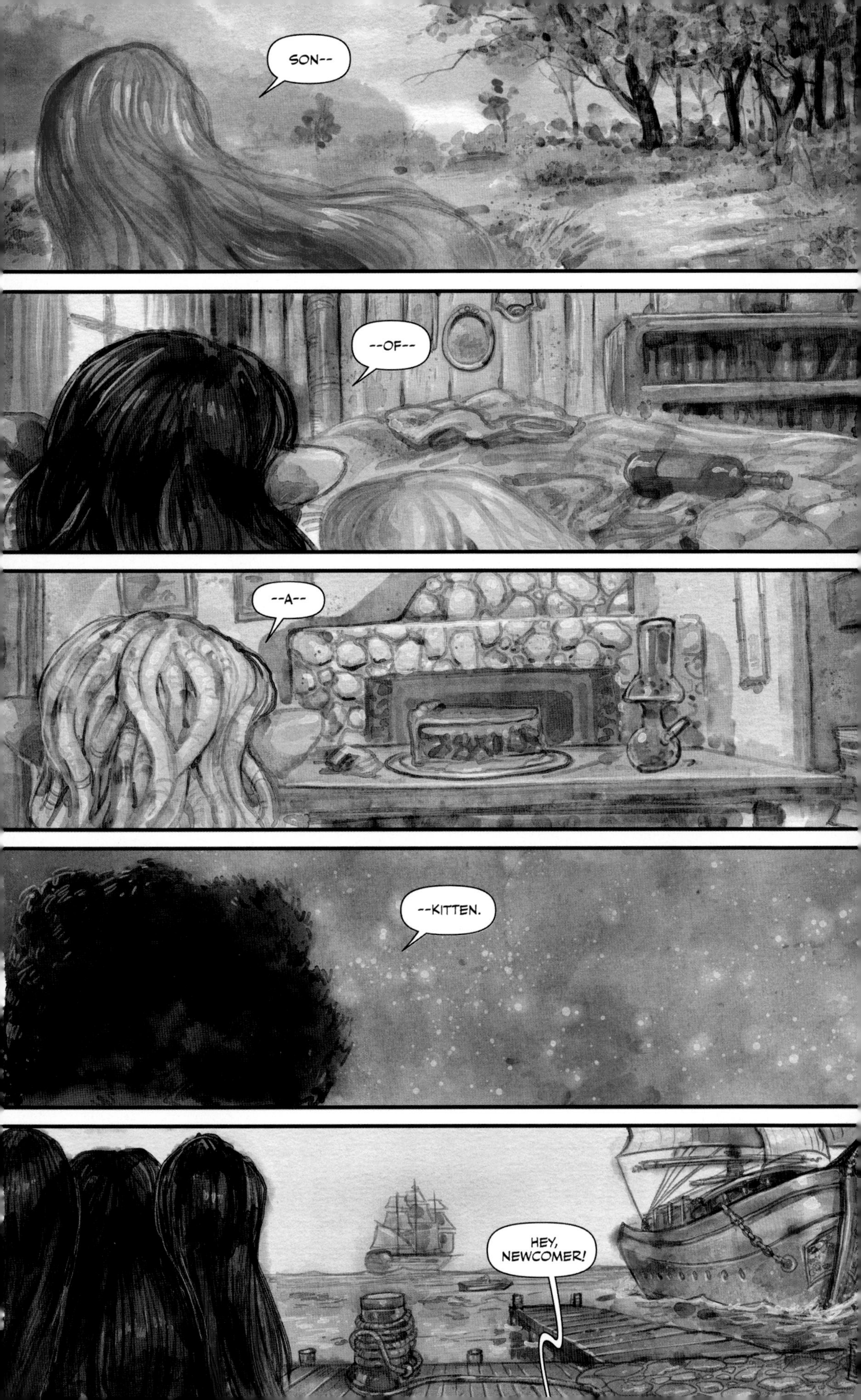
SON--
--OF--
--A--
--KITTEN.
HEY, NEWCOMER!

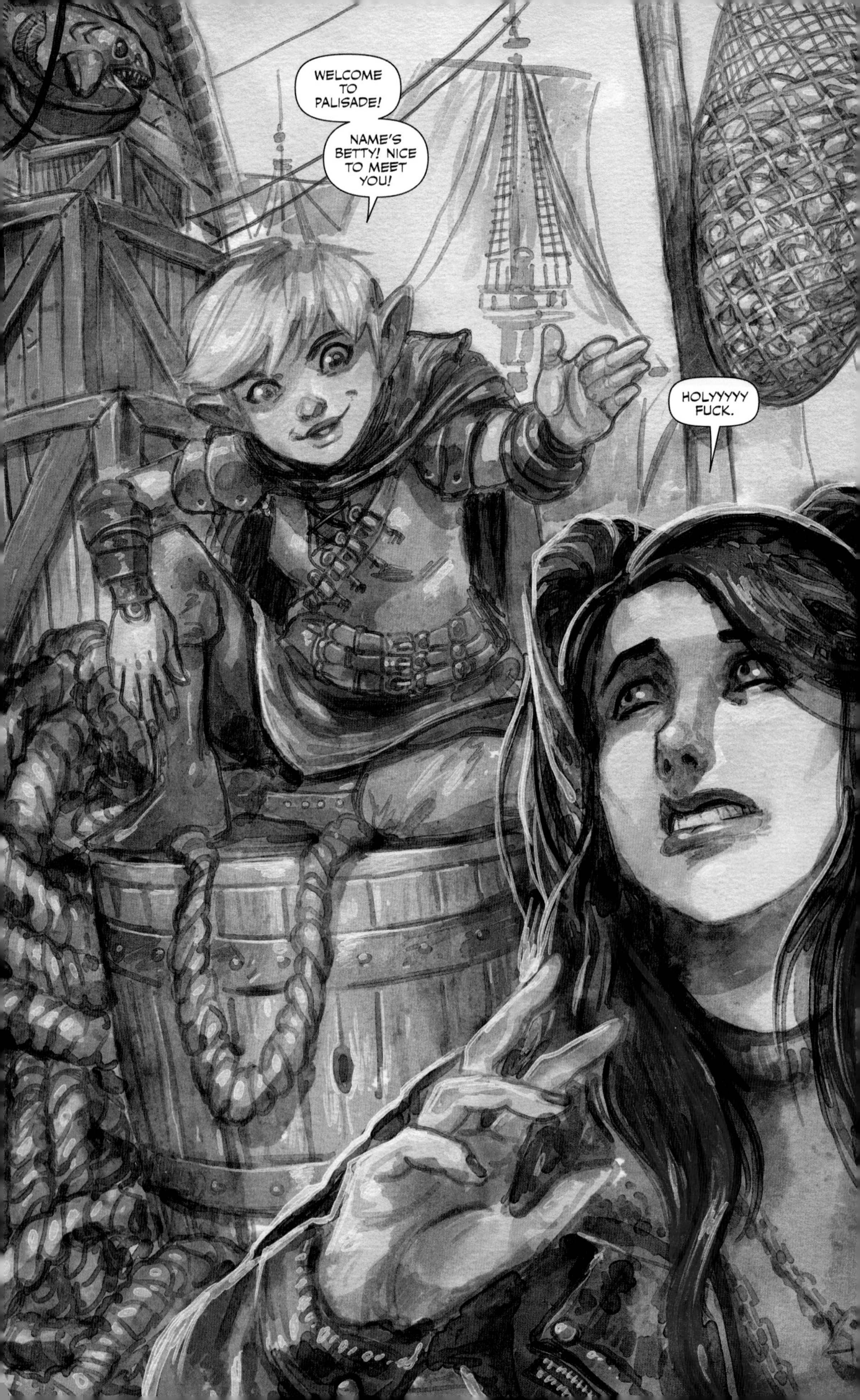
WELCOME TO PALISADE!
NAME'S BETTY! NICE TO MEET YOU!
HOLYYYYY FUCK.

CHAPTER FIVE

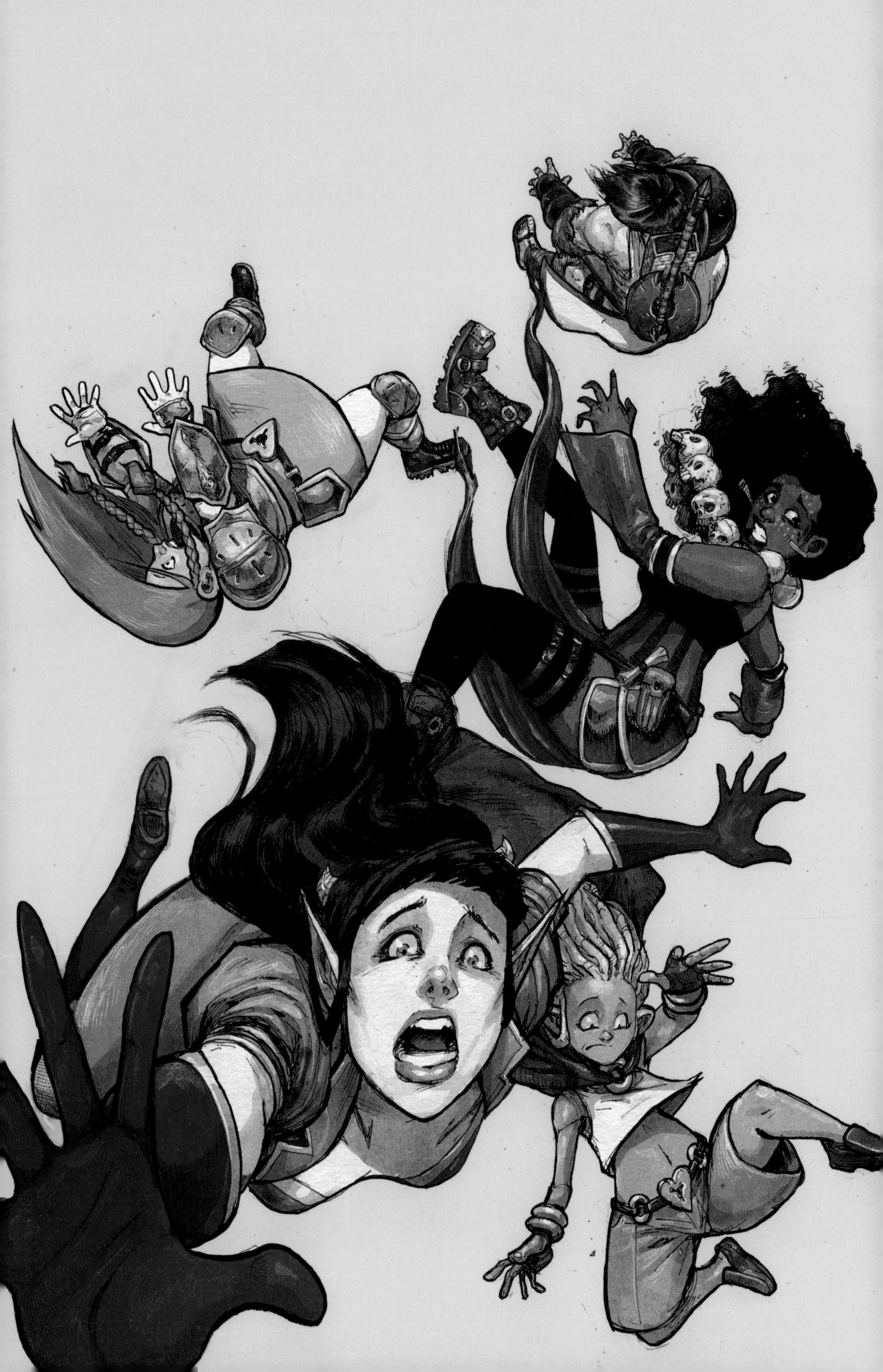

Issue #5 cover B

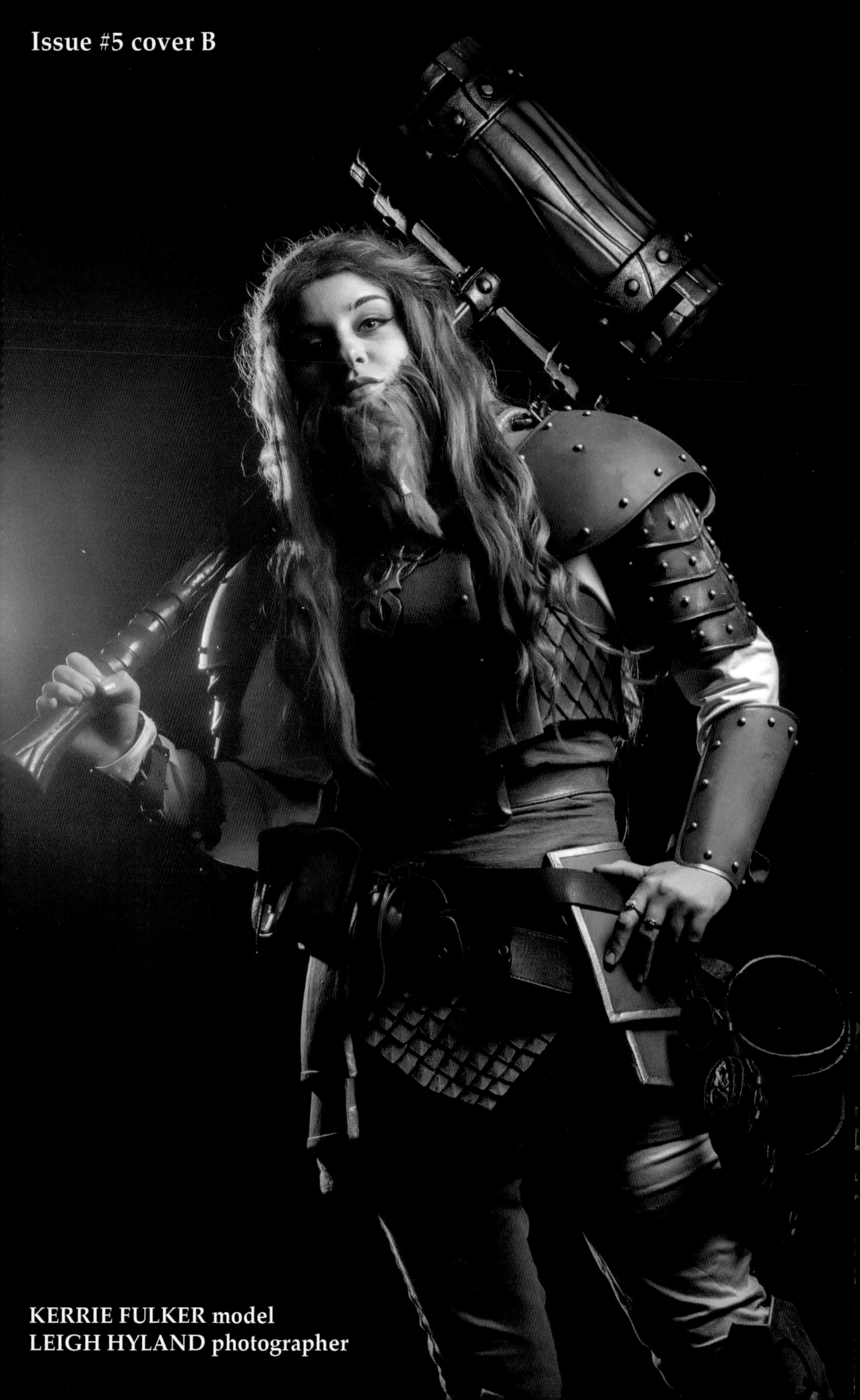

KERRIE FULKER model
LEIGH HYLAND photographer

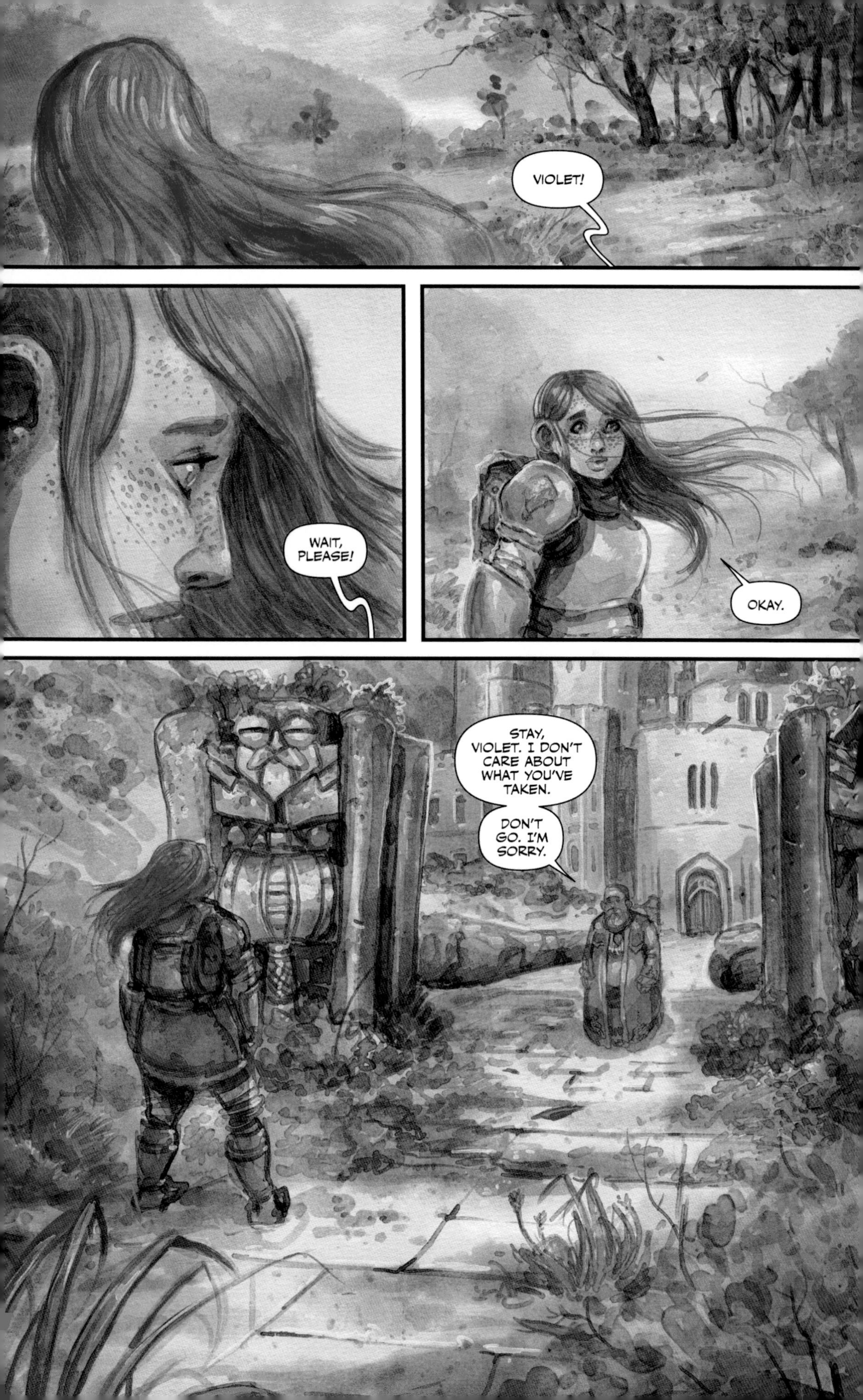
VIOLET!
WAIT, PLEASE!
OKAY.
STAY, VIOLET. I DON'T CARE ABOUT WHAT YOU'VE TAKEN.
DON'T GO. I'M SORRY.

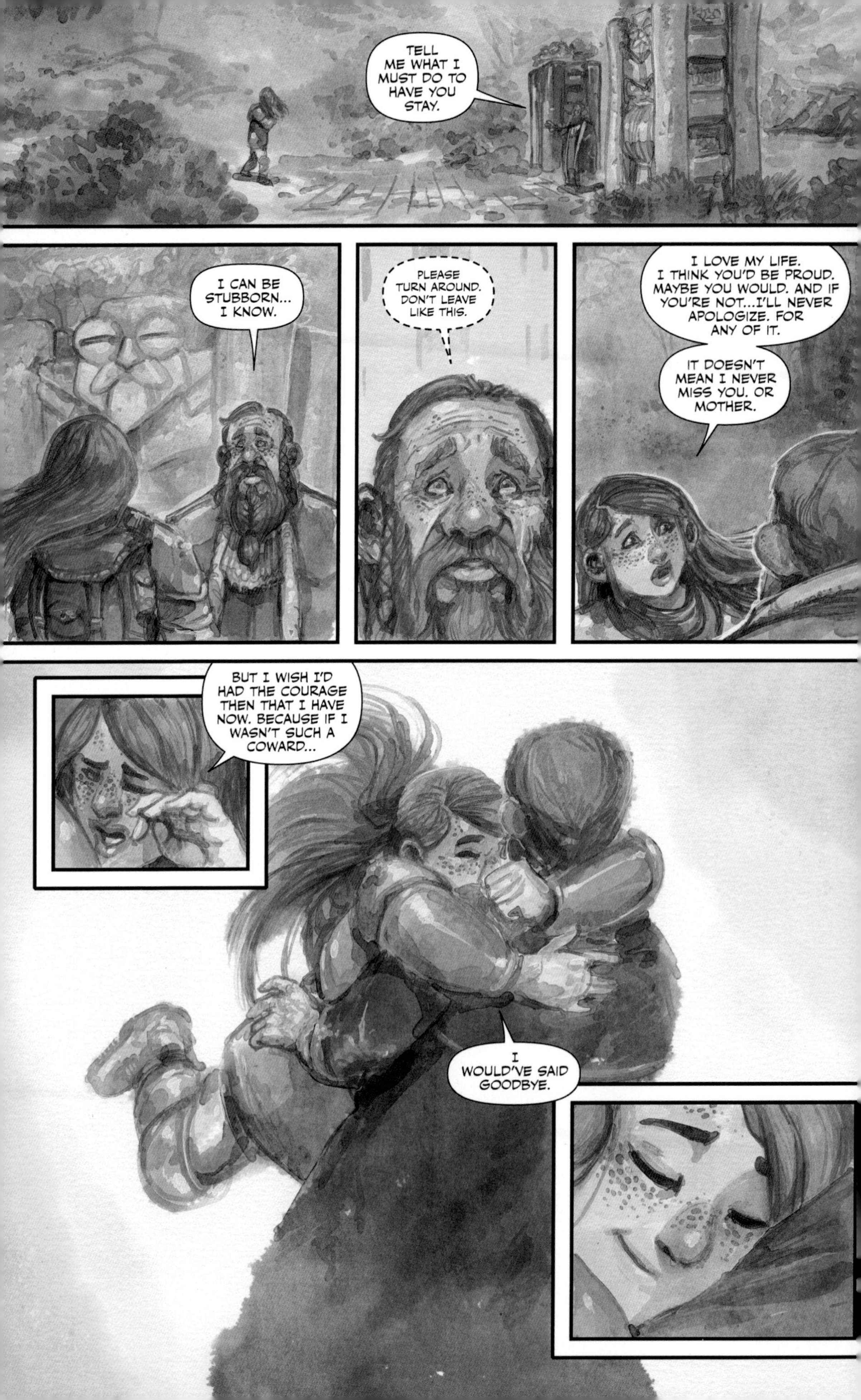
TELL ME WHAT I MUST DO TO HAVE YOU STAY.
I CAN BE STUBBORN... I KNOW.
PLEASE TURN AROUND. DON'T LEAVE LIKE THIS.
I LOVE MY LIFE. I THINK YOU'D BE PROUD. MAYBE YOU WOULD. AND IF YOU'RE NOT...I'LL NEVER APOLOGIZE. FOR ANY OF IT.
IT DOESN'T MEAN I NEVER MISS YOU. OR MOTHER.
BUT I WISH I'D HAD THE COURAGE THEN THAT I HAVE NOW. BECAUSE IF I WASN'T SUCH A COWARD...
I WOULD'VE SAID GOODBYE.

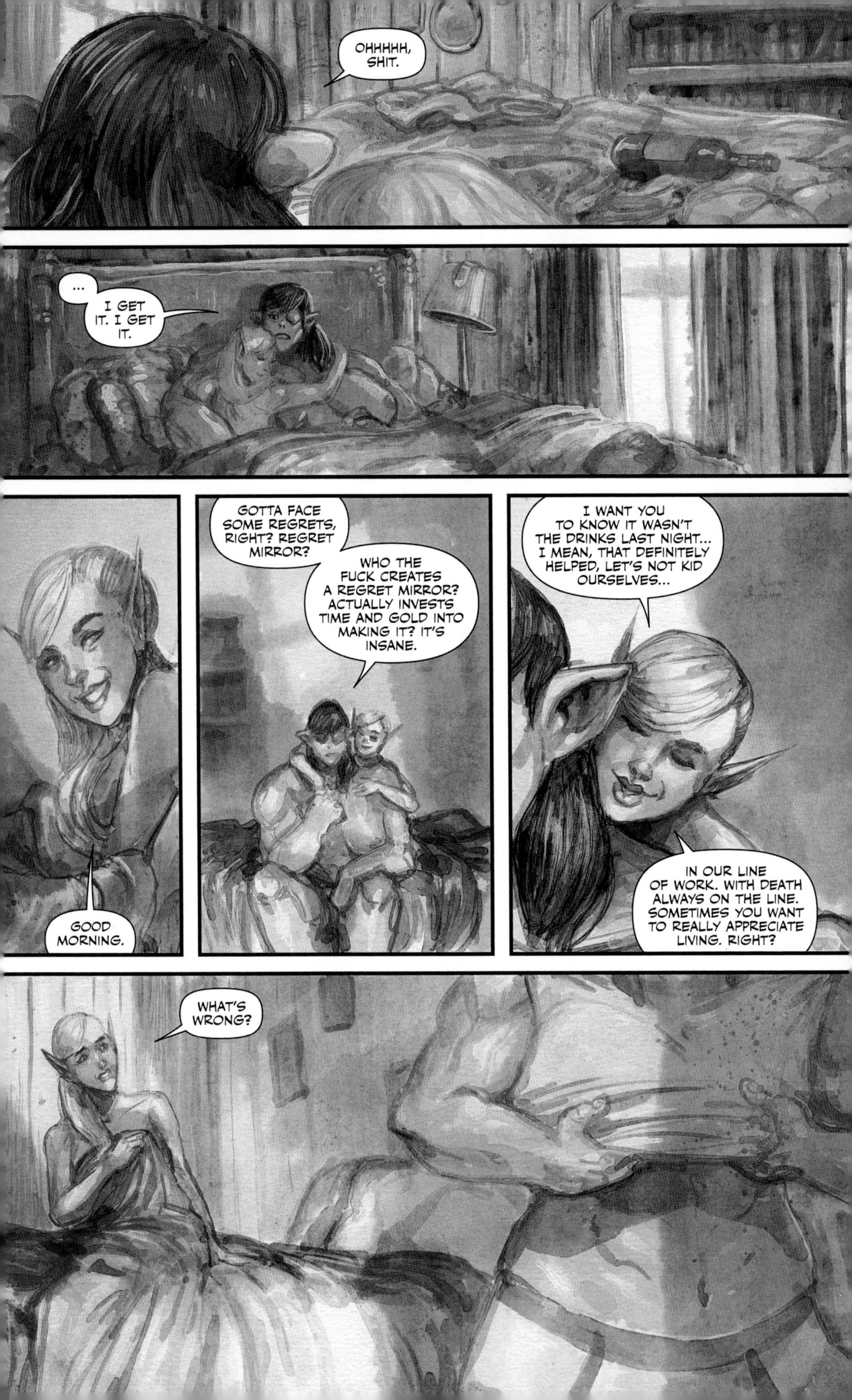
OHHHHH, SHIT.
... I GET IT. I GET IT.
GOOD MORNING.
GOTTA FACE SOME REGRETS, RIGHT? REGRET MIRROR?
WHO THE FUCK CREATES A REGRET MIRROR? ACTUALLY INVESTS TIME AND GOLD INTO MAKING IT? IT'S INSANE.
I WANT YOU TO KNOW IT WASN'T THE DRINKS LAST NIGHT... I MEAN, THAT DEFINITELY HELPED, LET'S NOT KID OURSELVES...
IN OUR LINE OF WORK. WITH DEATH ALWAYS ON THE LINE. SOMETIMES YOU WANT TO REALLY APPRECIATE LIVING. RIGHT?
WHAT'S WRONG?

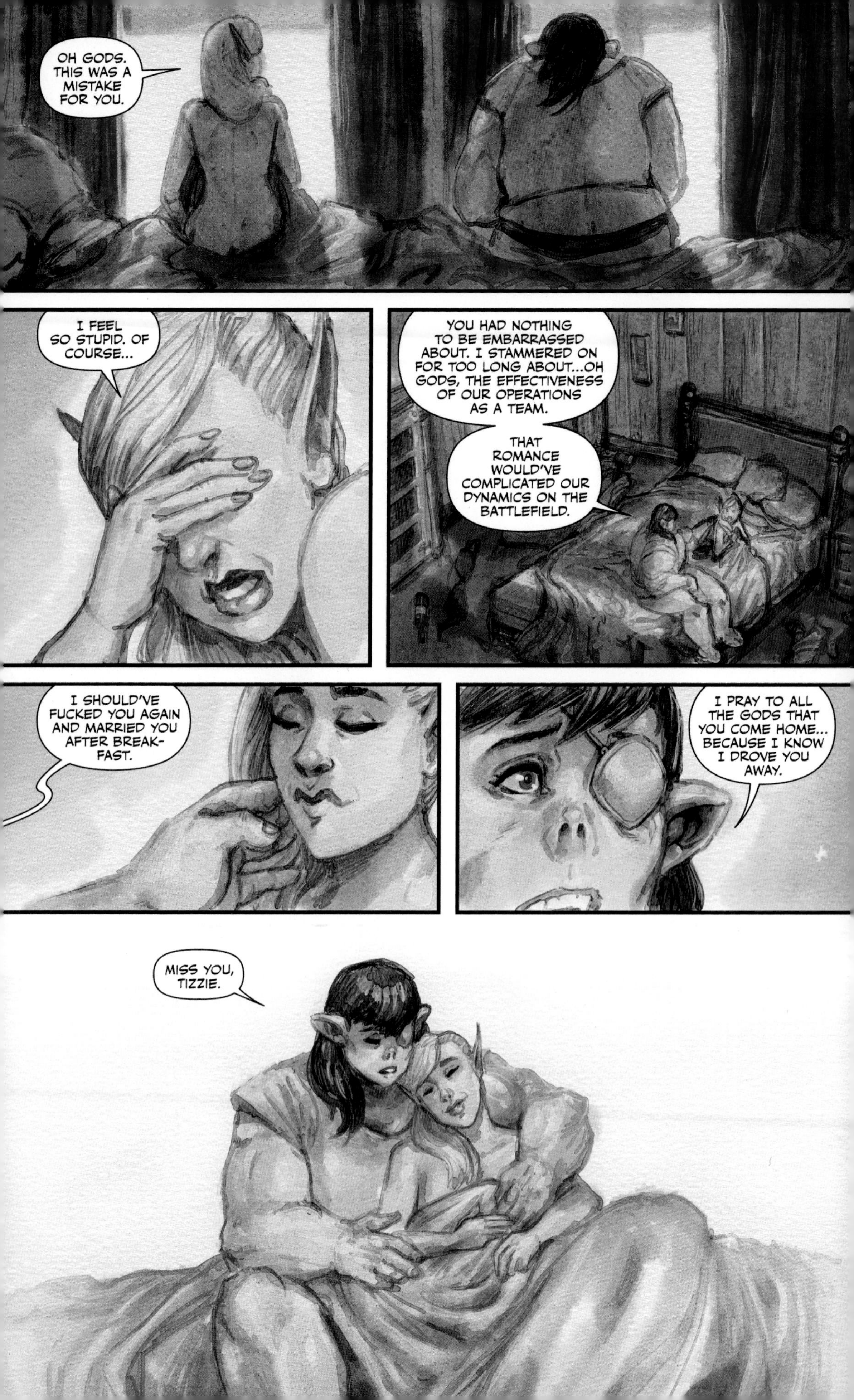
OH GODS. THIS WAS A MISTAKE FOR YOU.
I FEEL SO STUPID. OF COURSE...
YOU HAD NOTHING TO BE EMBARRASSED ABOUT. I STAMMERED ON FOR TOO LONG ABOUT...OH GODS, THE EFFECTIVENESS OF OUR OPERATIONS AS A TEAM.
THAT ROMANCE WOULD'VE COMPLICATED OUR DYNAMICS ON THE BATTLEFIELD.
I SHOULD'VE FUCKED YOU AGAIN AND MARRIED YOU AFTER BREAK-FAST.
I PRAY TO ALL THE GODS THAT YOU COME HOME... BECAUSE I KNOW I DROVE YOU AWAY.
MISS YOU, TIZZIE.

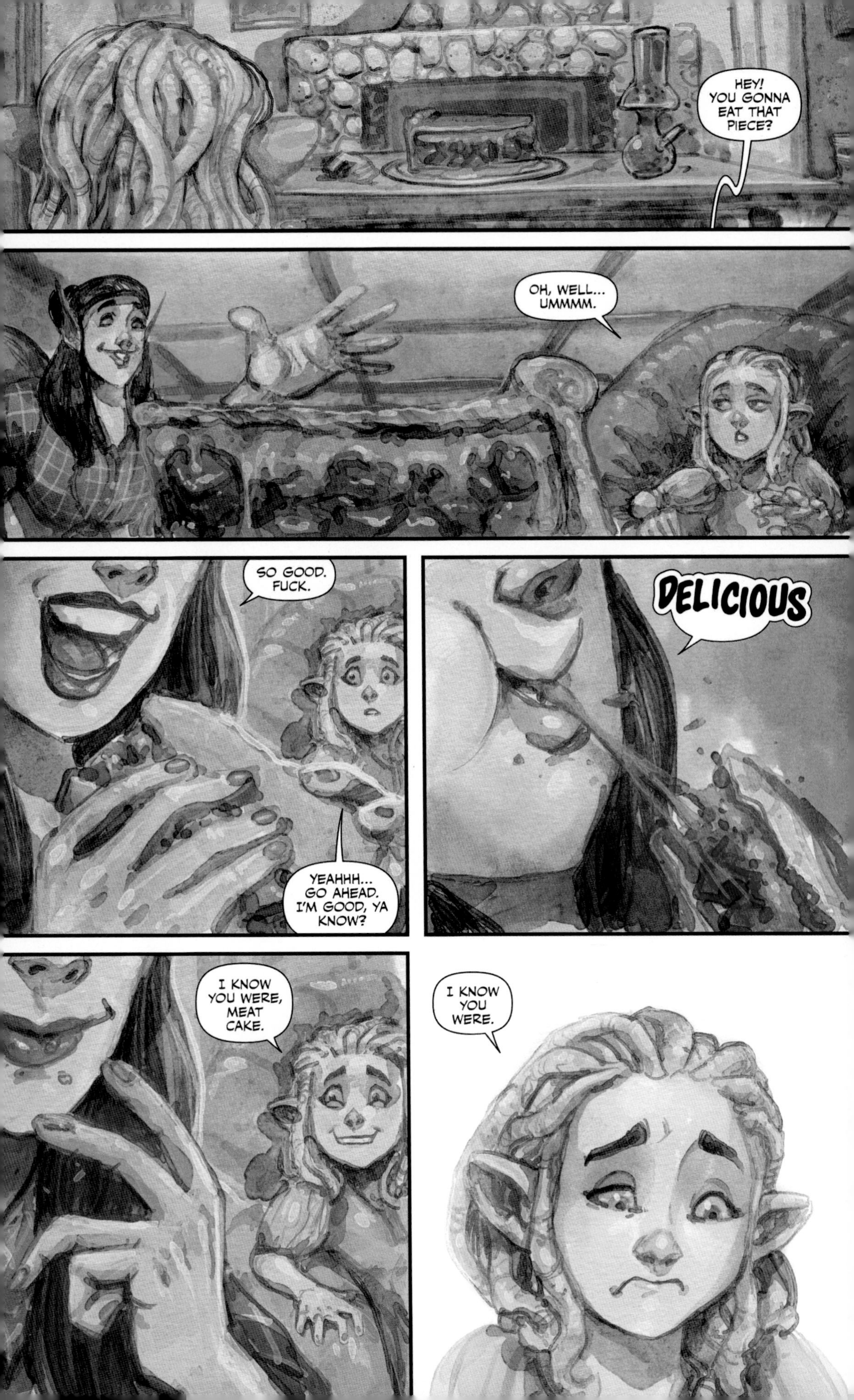
HEY! YOU GONNA EAT THAT PIECE?
OH, WELL... UMMMM.
SO GOOD. FUCK.
YEAHHH... GO AHEAD. I'M GOOD, YA KNOW?
DELICIOUS
I KNOW YOU WERE, MEAT CAKE.
I KNOW YOU WERE.

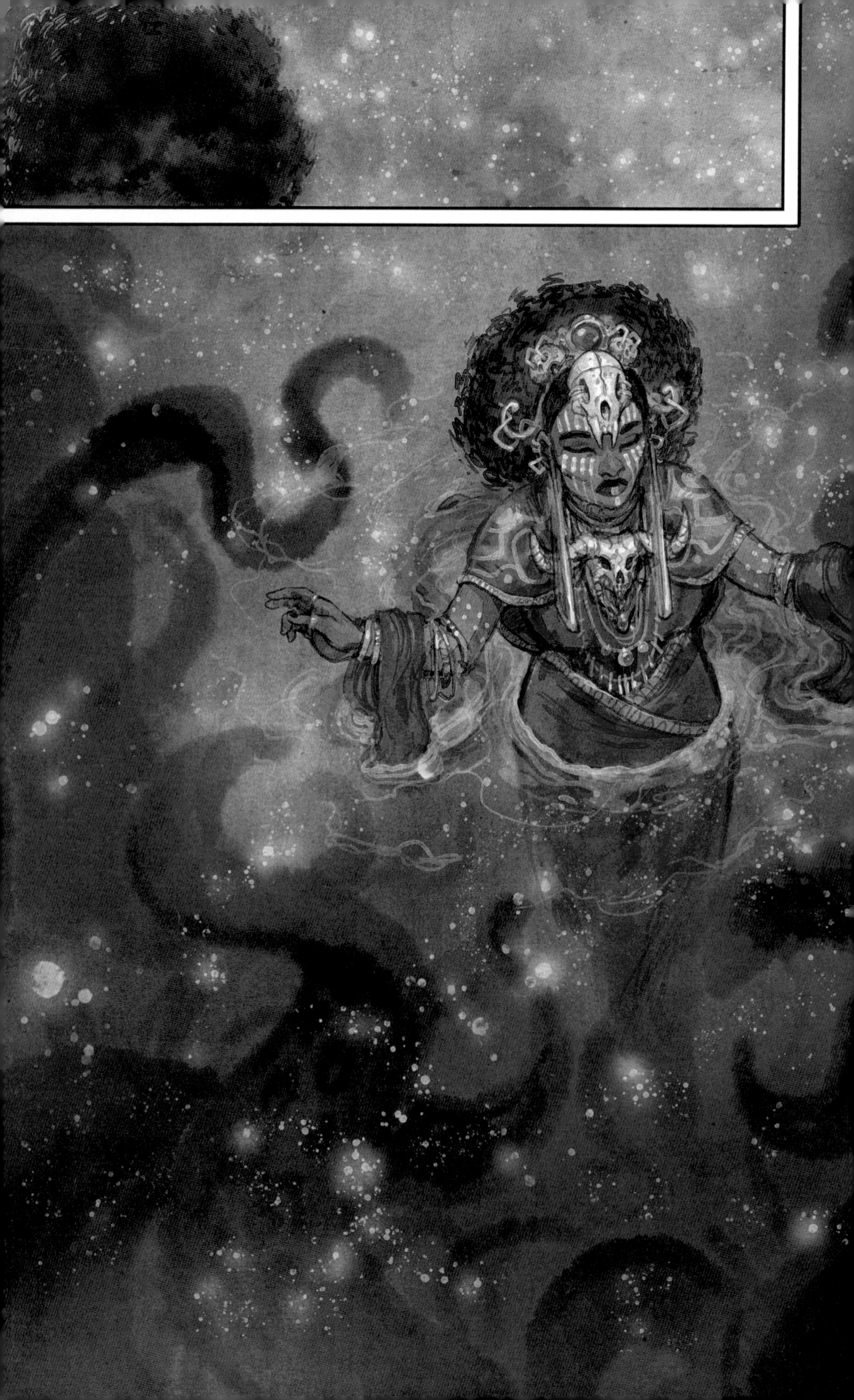

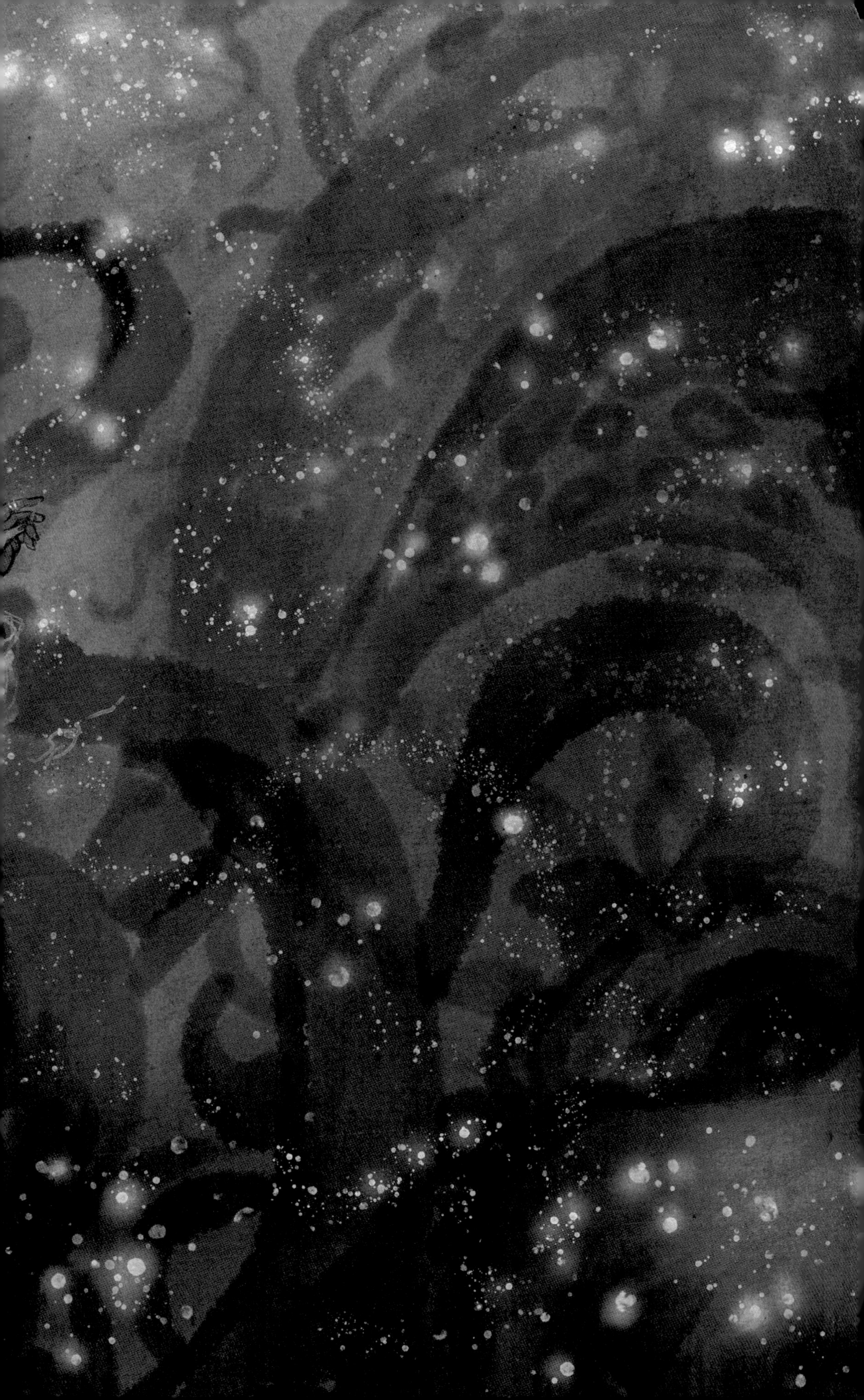

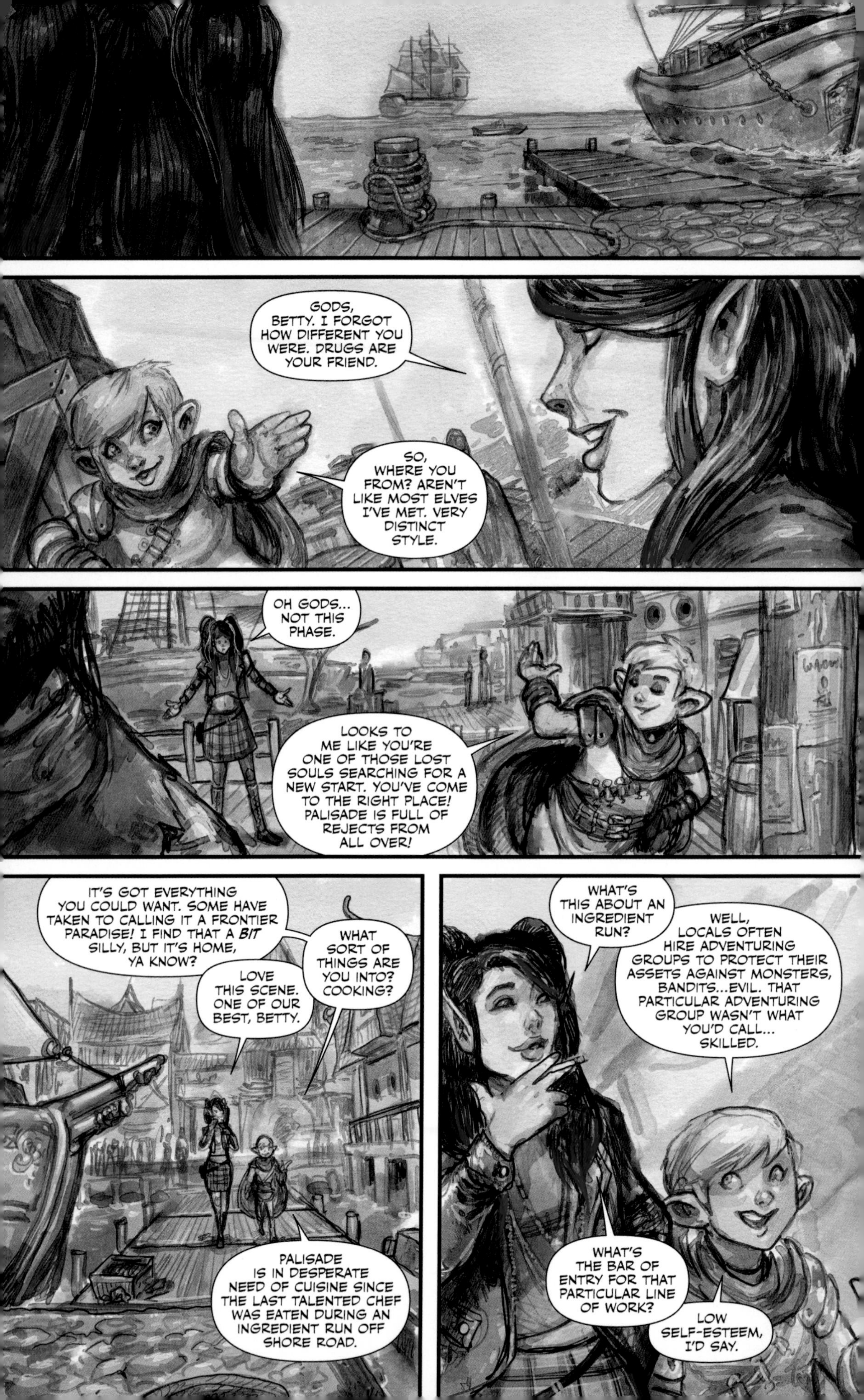
GODS, BETTY. I FORGOT HOW DIFFERENT YOU WERE. DRUGS ARE YOUR FRIEND.
SO, WHERE YOU FROM? AREN'T LIKE MOST ELVES I'VE MET. VERY DISTINCT STYLE.
OH GODS... NOT THIS PHASE.
LOOKS TO ME LIKE YOU'RE ONE OF THOSE LOST SOULS SEARCHING FOR A NEW START. YOU'VE COME TO THE RIGHT PLACE! PALISADE IS FULL OF REJECTS FROM ALL OVER!
IT'S GOT EVERYTHING YOU COULD WANT. SOME HAVE TAKEN TO CALLING IT A FRONTIER PARADISE! I FIND THAT A *BIT* SILLY, BUT IT'S HOME, YA KNOW?
LOVE THIS SCENE. ONE OF OUR BEST, BETTY.
WHAT SORT OF THINGS ARE YOU INTO? COOKING?
PALISADE IS IN DESPERATE NEED OF CUISINE SINCE THE LAST TALENTED CHEF WAS EATEN DURING AN INGREDIENT RUN OFF SHORE ROAD.
WHAT'S THIS ABOUT AN INGREDIENT RUN?
WELL, LOCALS OFTEN HIRE ADVENTURING GROUPS TO PROTECT THEIR ASSETS AGAINST MONSTERS, BANDITS...EVIL. THAT PARTICULAR ADVENTURING GROUP WASN'T WHAT YOU'D CALL... SKILLED.
WHAT'S THE BAR OF ENTRY FOR THAT PARTICULAR LINE OF WORK?
LOW SELF-ESTEEM, I'D SAY.

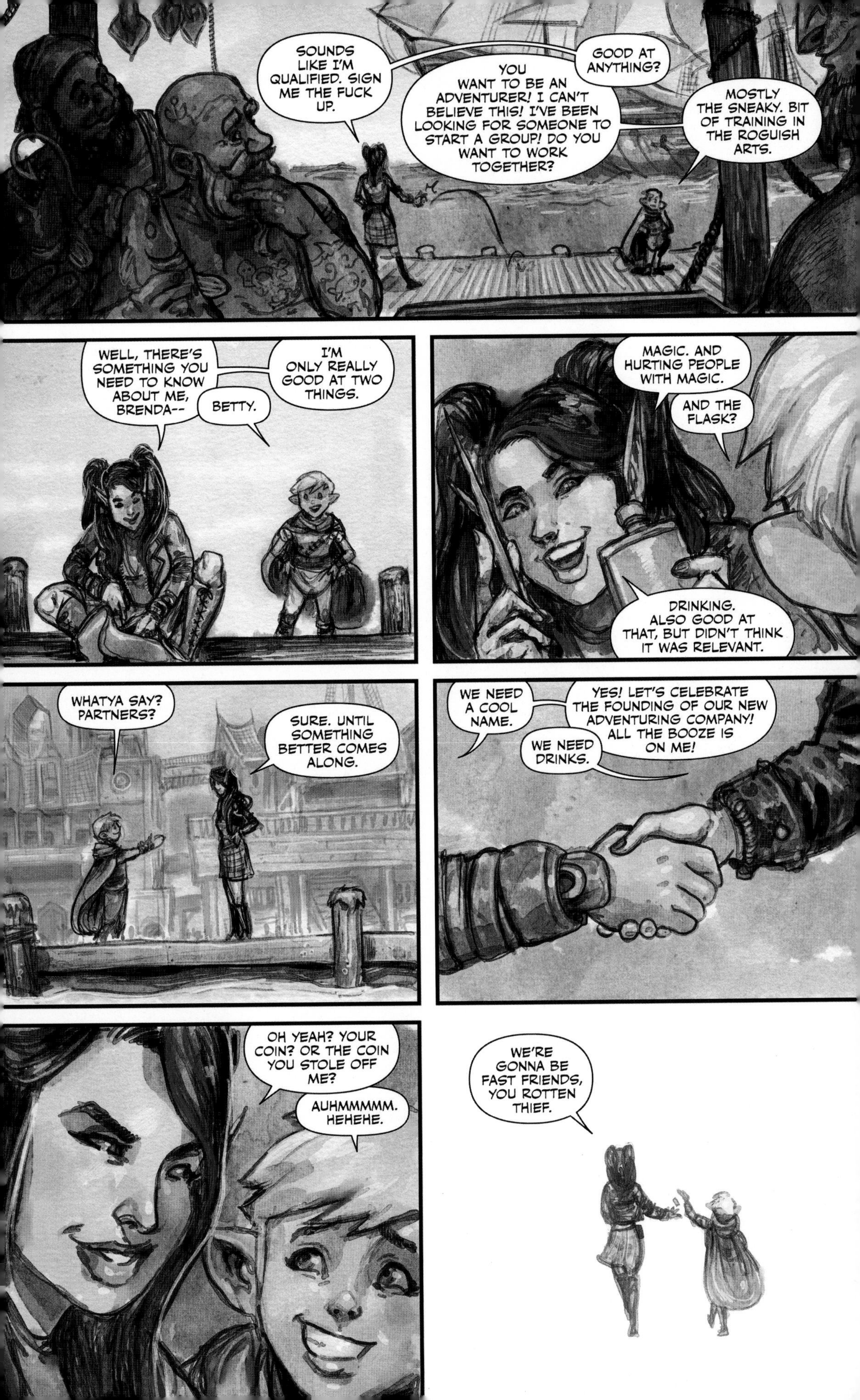
SOUNDS LIKE I'M QUALIFIED. SIGN ME THE FUCK UP.
YOU WANT TO BE AN ADVENTURER! I CAN'T BELIEVE THIS! I'VE BEEN LOOKING FOR SOMEONE TO START A GROUP! DO YOU WANT TO WORK TOGETHER?
GOOD AT ANYTHING?
MOSTLY THE SNEAKY. BIT OF TRAINING IN THE ROGUISH ARTS.
WELL, THERE'S SOMETHING YOU NEED TO KNOW ABOUT ME, BRENDA--
BETTY.
I'M ONLY REALLY GOOD AT TWO THINGS.
MAGIC. AND HURTING PEOPLE WITH MAGIC.
AND THE FLASK?
DRINKING. ALSO GOOD AT THAT, BUT DIDN'T THINK IT WAS RELEVANT.
WHATYA SAY? PARTNERS?
SURE. UNTIL SOMETHING BETTER COMES ALONG.
WE NEED A COOL NAME.
YES! LET'S CELEBRATE THE FOUNDING OF OUR NEW ADVENTURING COMPANY! ALL THE BOOZE IS ON ME!
WE NEED DRINKS.
OH YEAH? YOUR COIN? OR THE COIN YOU STOLE OFF ME?
AUHMMMMM. HEHEHE.
WE'RE GONNA BE FAST FRIENDS, YOU ROTTEN THIEF.

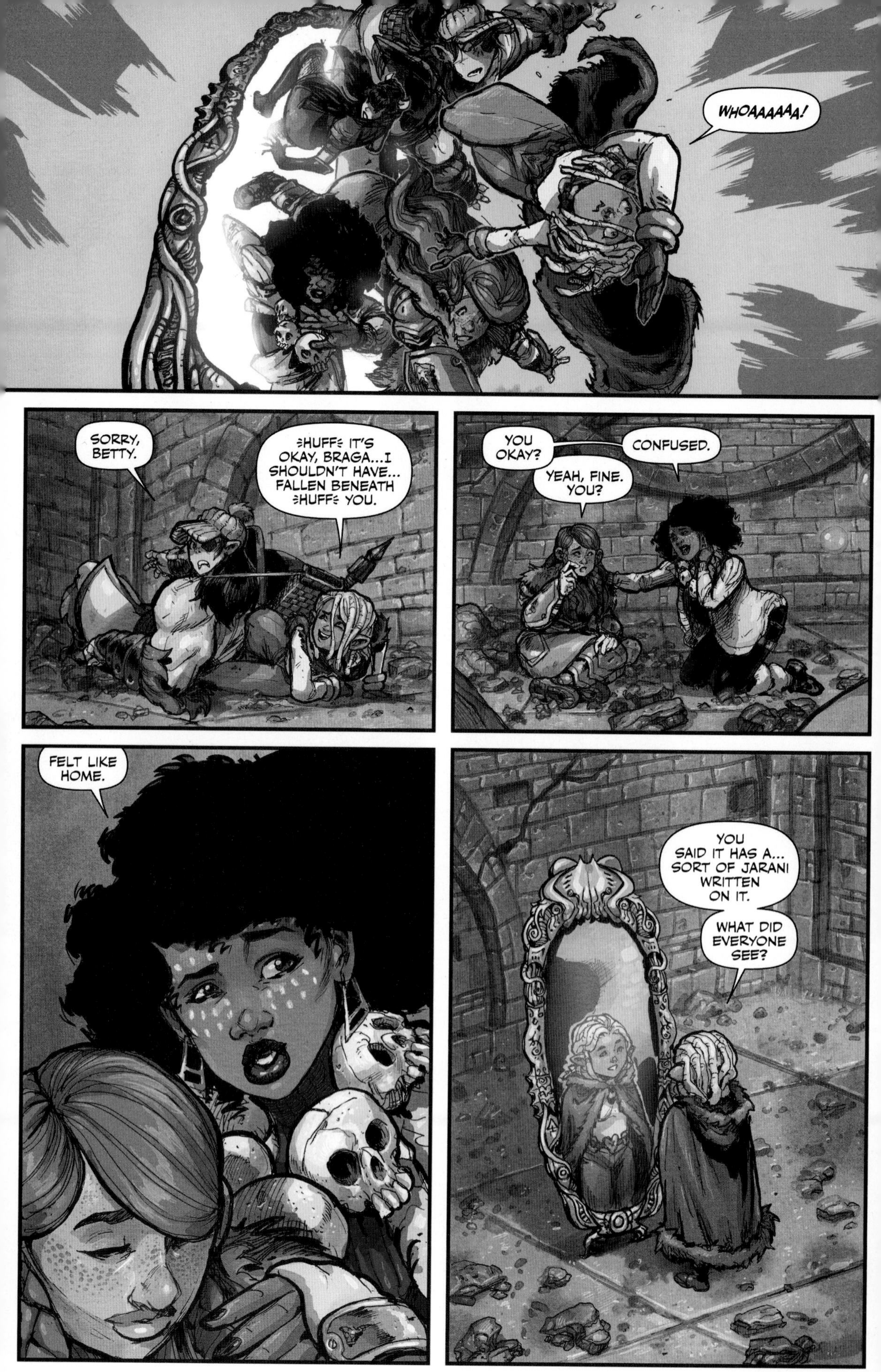
WHOAAAAAA!
SORRY, BETTY.
=HUFF= IT'S OKAY, BRAGA...I SHOULDN'T HAVE... FALLEN BENEATH =HUFF= YOU.
YOU OKAY?
CONFUSED.
YEAH, FINE. YOU?
FELT LIKE HOME.
YOU SAID IT HAS A... SORT OF JARANI WRITTEN ON IT.
WHAT DID EVERYONE SEE?

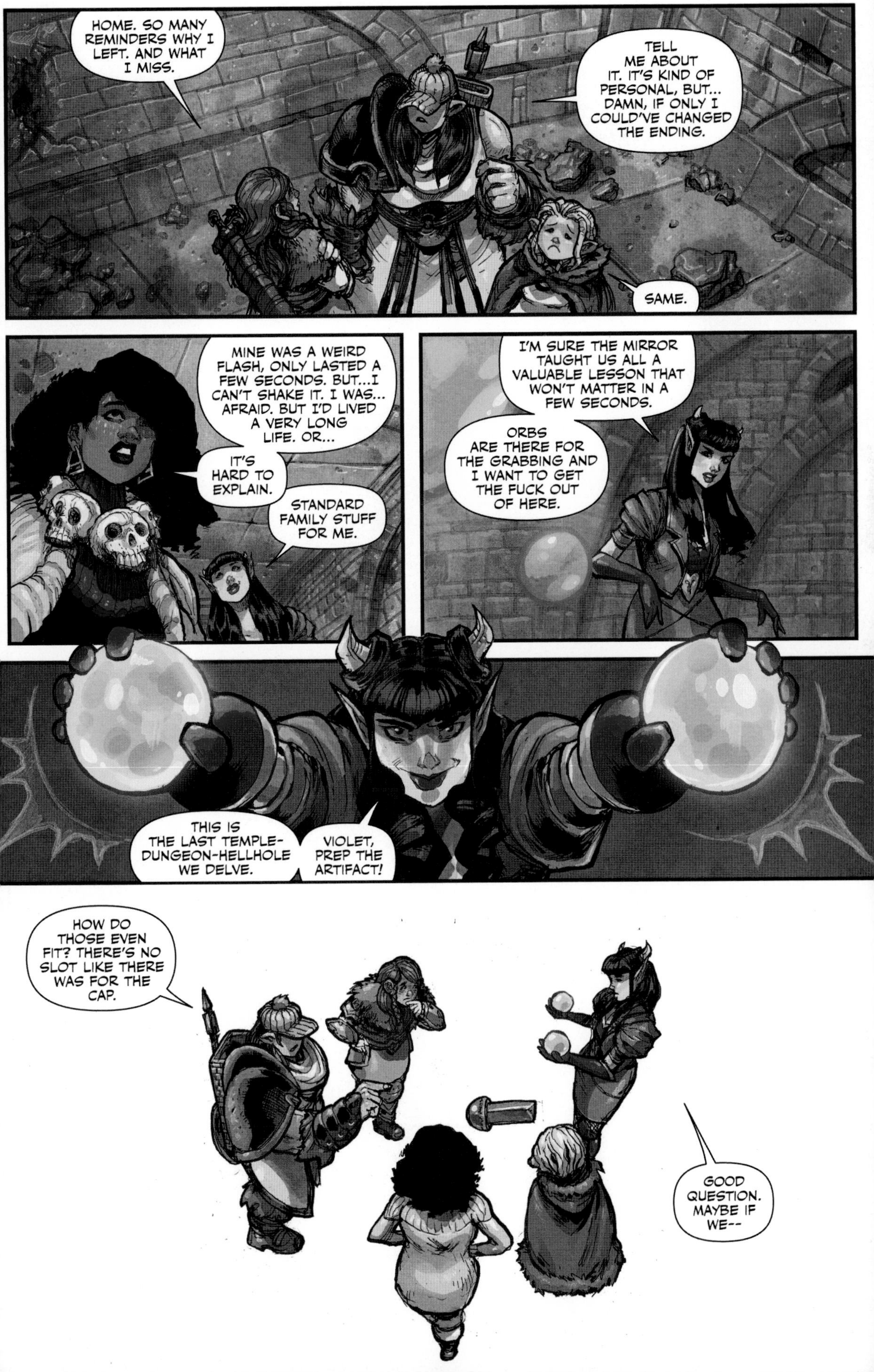
HOME. SO MANY REMINDERS WHY I LEFT. AND WHAT I MISS.
TELL ME ABOUT IT. IT'S KIND OF PERSONAL, BUT... DAMN, IF ONLY I COULD'VE CHANGED THE ENDING.
SAME.
MINE WAS A WEIRD FLASH, ONLY LASTED A FEW SECONDS. BUT...I CAN'T SHAKE IT. I WAS... AFRAID. BUT I'D LIVED A VERY LONG LIFE. OR...
IT'S HARD TO EXPLAIN.
STANDARD FAMILY STUFF FOR ME.
I'M SURE THE MIRROR TAUGHT US ALL A VALUABLE LESSON THAT WON'T MATTER IN A FEW SECONDS.
ORBS ARE THERE FOR THE GRABBING AND I WANT TO GET THE FUCK OUT OF HERE.
THIS IS THE LAST TEMPLE-DUNGEON-HELLHOLE WE DELVE.
VIOLET, PREP THE ARTIFACT!
HOW DO THOSE EVEN FIT? THERE'S NO SLOT LIKE THERE WAS FOR THE CAP.
GOOD QUESTION. MAYBE IF WE--

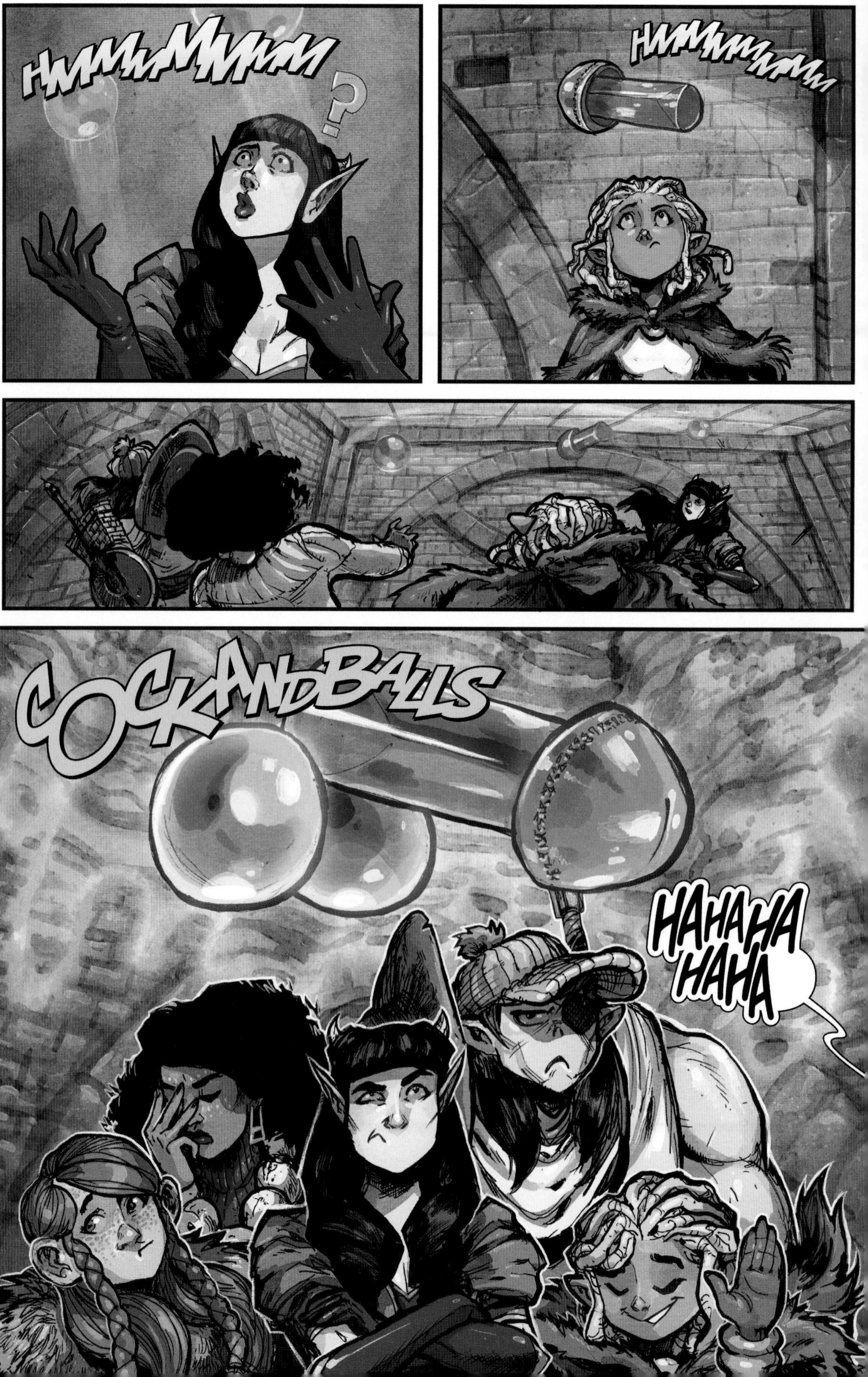

HMMMMMMM
?
HMMMMMMMM
COCKANDBALLS
HAHAHA
HAHA

WONDERFUL! WHAT A THRILLING ADVENTURE! I HAVE BEEN THOROUGHLY ENTERTAINED!

YOU HAVE MY DEEPEST THANKS FOR DISPELLING THIS AGONIZING STREAK OF BOREDOM.

COMEDY, ACTION... DRAMA!

EVEN A FEW TEARS, GOOD FOR THE SOUL. MY SOUL. YOURS. DELICIOUS TEARS.

OH, THESE MARVELOUS EMOTIONS! I'VE LONGED FOR EVEN A SMALL EMBER TO IGNITE THE FIRES OF FEELING. AND, BY YOUR SUFFERING...NAY, YOUR *BRAVERY*, I HAVE BECOME AN INFERNO!

IF THERE'S ANYTHING I'VE LEARNED FROM ADVENTURING...KILL 'EM WHILE THEY'RE PONTIFICATING.

HEY, WE DON'T EVEN KNOW IF THE FISH PERSON IS EVIL. HE DOESN'T LOOK EVIL.

THEY RARELY DO.

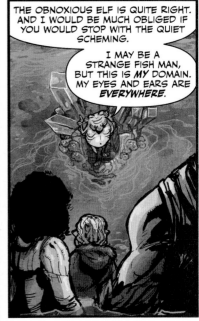

THE OBNOXIOUS ELF IS QUITE RIGHT. AND I WOULD BE MUCH OBLIGED IF YOU WOULD STOP WITH THE QUIET SCHEMING.

I MAY BE A STRANGE FISH MAN, BUT THIS IS *MY* DOMAIN. MY EYES AND EARS ARE *EVERYWHERE*.

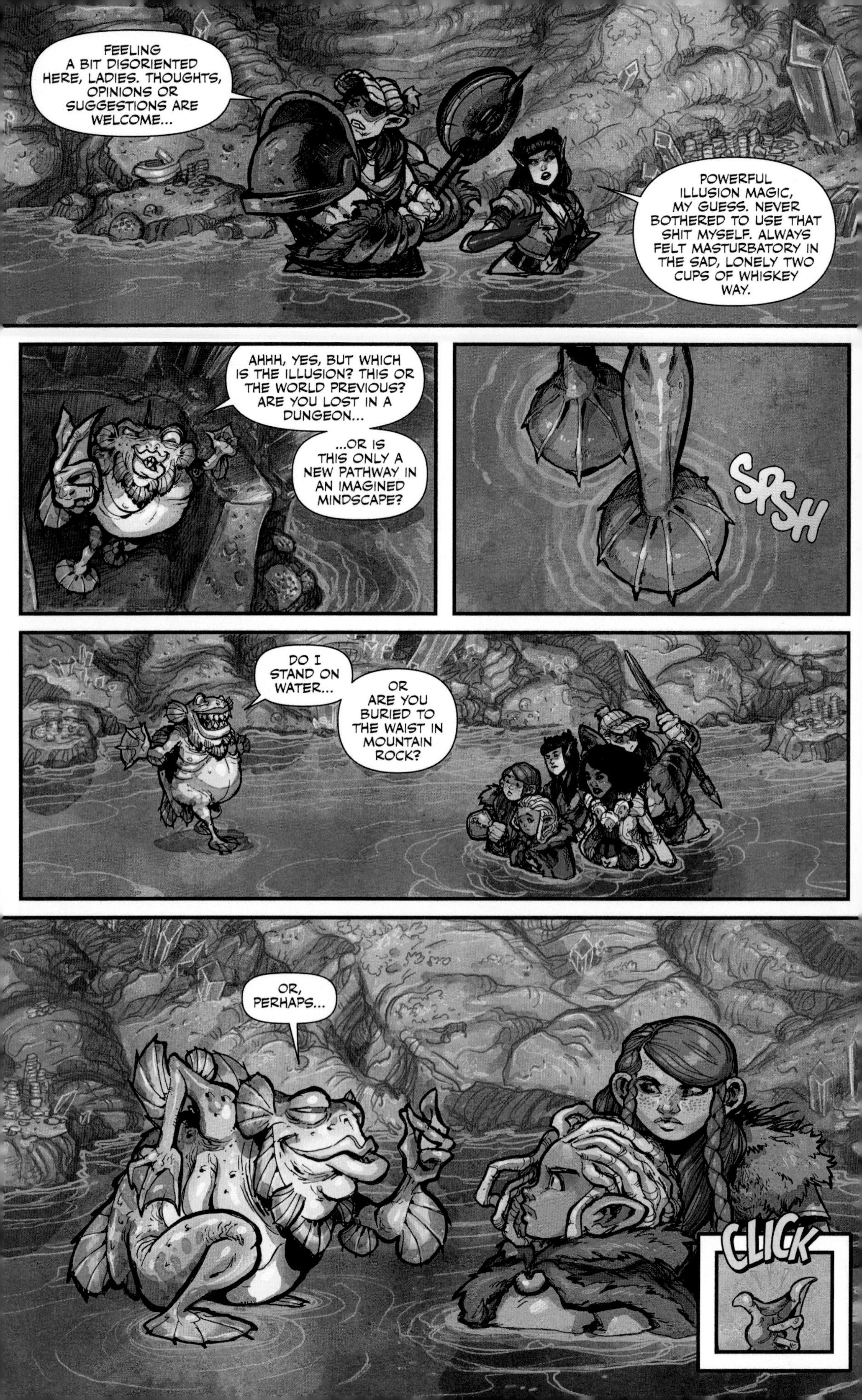
FEELING A BIT DISORIENTED HERE, LADIES. THOUGHTS, OPINIONS OR SUGGESTIONS ARE WELCOME...
POWERFUL ILLUSION MAGIC, MY GUESS. NEVER BOTHERED TO USE THAT SHIT MYSELF. ALWAYS FELT MASTURBATORY IN THE SAD, LONELY TWO CUPS OF WHISKEY WAY.
AHHH, YES, BUT WHICH IS THE ILLUSION? THIS OR THE WORLD PREVIOUS? ARE YOU LOST IN A DUNGEON...
...OR IS THIS ONLY A NEW PATHWAY IN AN IMAGINED MINDSCAPE?
SPSH
DO I STAND ON WATER...
OR ARE YOU BURIED TO THE WAIST IN MOUNTAIN ROCK?
OR, PERHAPS...
CLICK

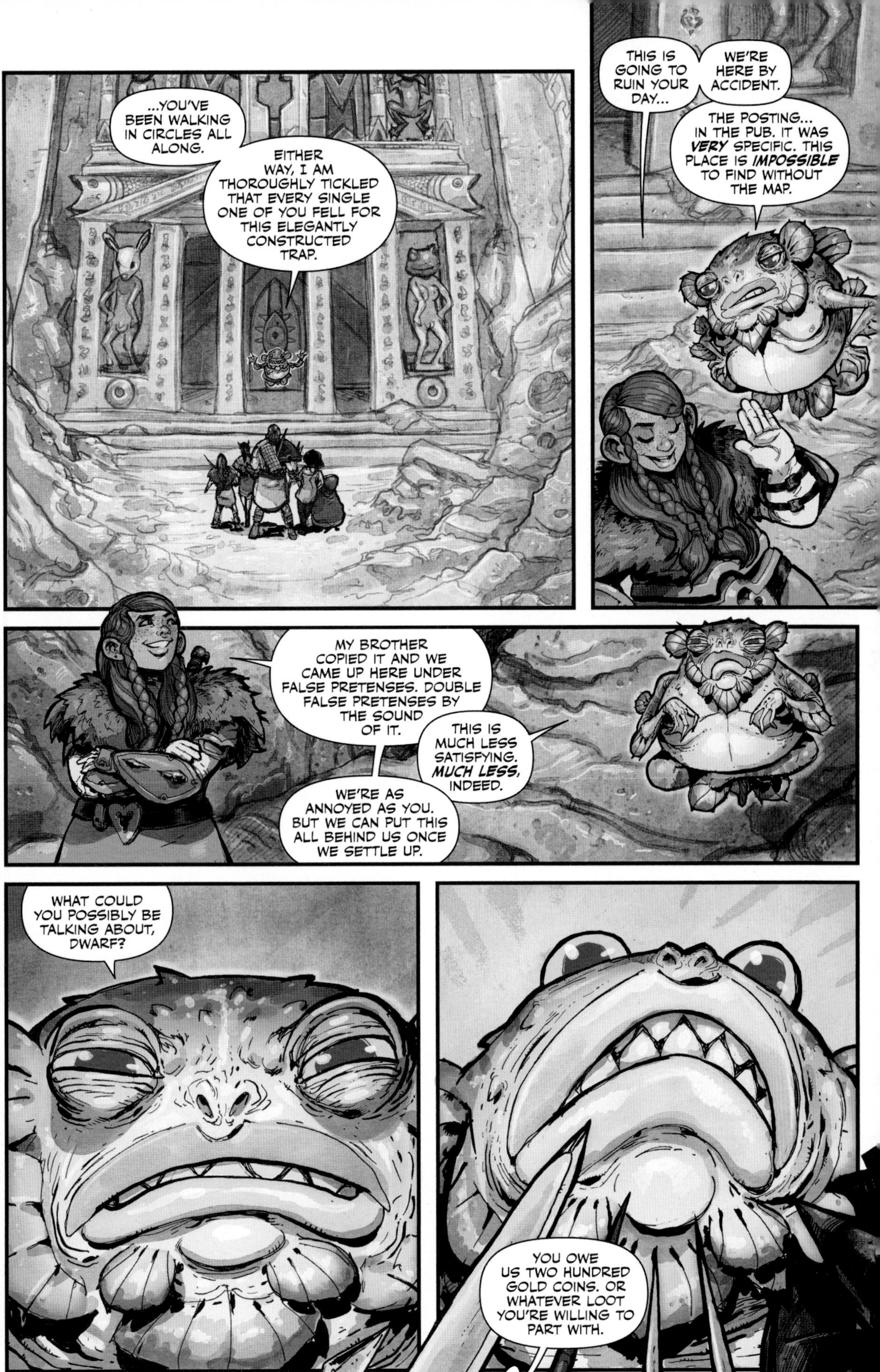
...YOU'VE BEEN WALKING IN CIRCLES ALL ALONG.
EITHER WAY, I AM THOROUGHLY TICKLED THAT EVERY SINGLE ONE OF YOU FELL FOR THIS ELEGANTLY CONSTRUCTED TRAP.
THIS IS GOING TO RUIN YOUR DAY...
WE'RE HERE BY ACCIDENT.
THE POSTING... IN THE PUB. IT WAS *VERY* SPECIFIC. THIS PLACE IS *IMPOSSIBLE* TO FIND WITHOUT THE MAP.
MY BROTHER COPIED IT AND WE CAME UP HERE UNDER FALSE PRETENSES. DOUBLE FALSE PRETENSES BY THE SOUND OF IT.
THIS IS MUCH LESS SATISFYING. *MUCH LESS*, INDEED.
WE'RE AS ANNOYED AS YOU. BUT WE CAN PUT THIS ALL BEHIND US ONCE WE SETTLE UP.
WHAT COULD YOU POSSIBLY BE TALKING ABOUT, DWARF?
YOU OWE US TWO HUNDRED GOLD COINS. OR WHATEVER LOOT YOU'RE WILLING TO PART WITH.

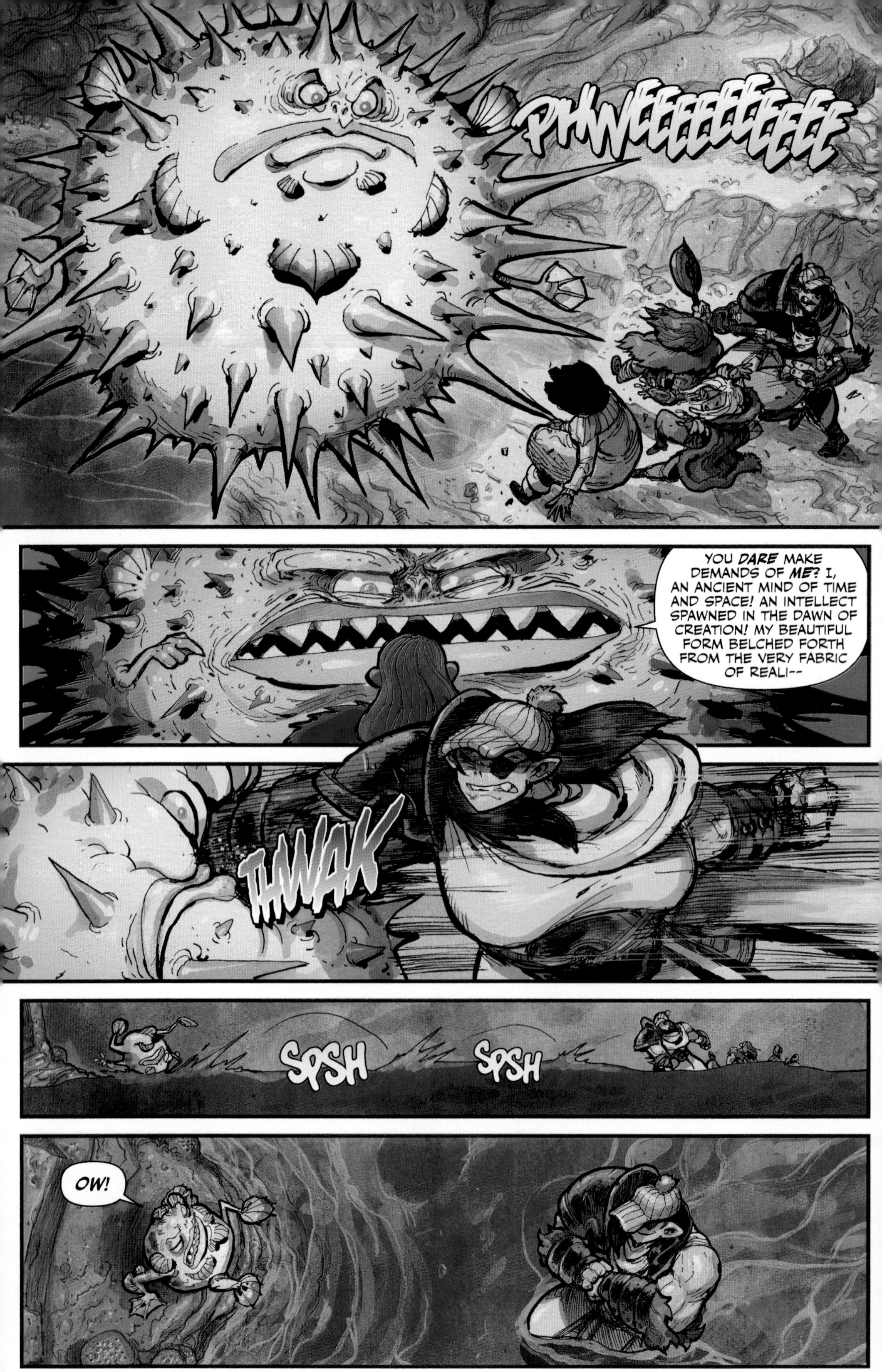
PHWEEEEEEEEEE
YOU *DARE* MAKE DEMANDS OF *ME*? I, AN ANCIENT MIND OF TIME AND SPACE! AN INTELLECT SPAWNED IN THE DAWN OF CREATION! MY BEAUTIFUL FORM BELCHED FORTH FROM THE VERY FABRIC OF REALI--
THWAK
SPSH
SPSH
OW!

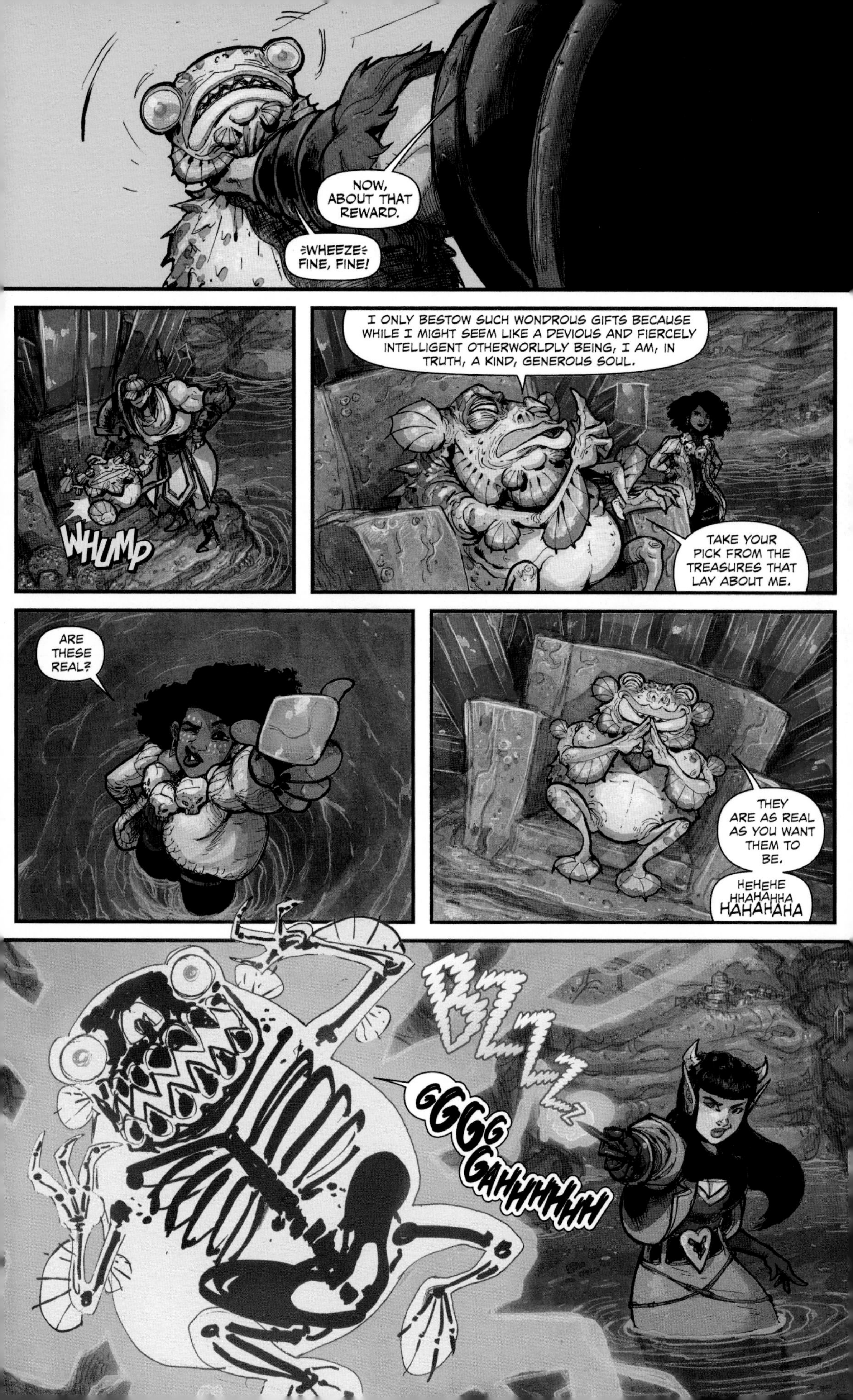
NOW, ABOUT THAT REWARD.
≡WHEEZE≡ FINE, FINE!
WHUMP
I ONLY BESTOW SUCH WONDROUS GIFTS BECAUSE WHILE I MIGHT SEEM LIKE A DEVIOUS AND FIERCELY INTELLIGENT OTHERWORLDLY BEING, I AM, IN TRUTH, A KIND, GENEROUS SOUL.
TAKE YOUR PICK FROM THE TREASURES THAT LAY ABOUT ME.
ARE THESE REAL?
THEY ARE AS REAL AS YOU WANT THEM TO BE.
HEHEHE HHAHAHHA HAHAHAHA
BZZZZ
GGGG GAHHHHHH

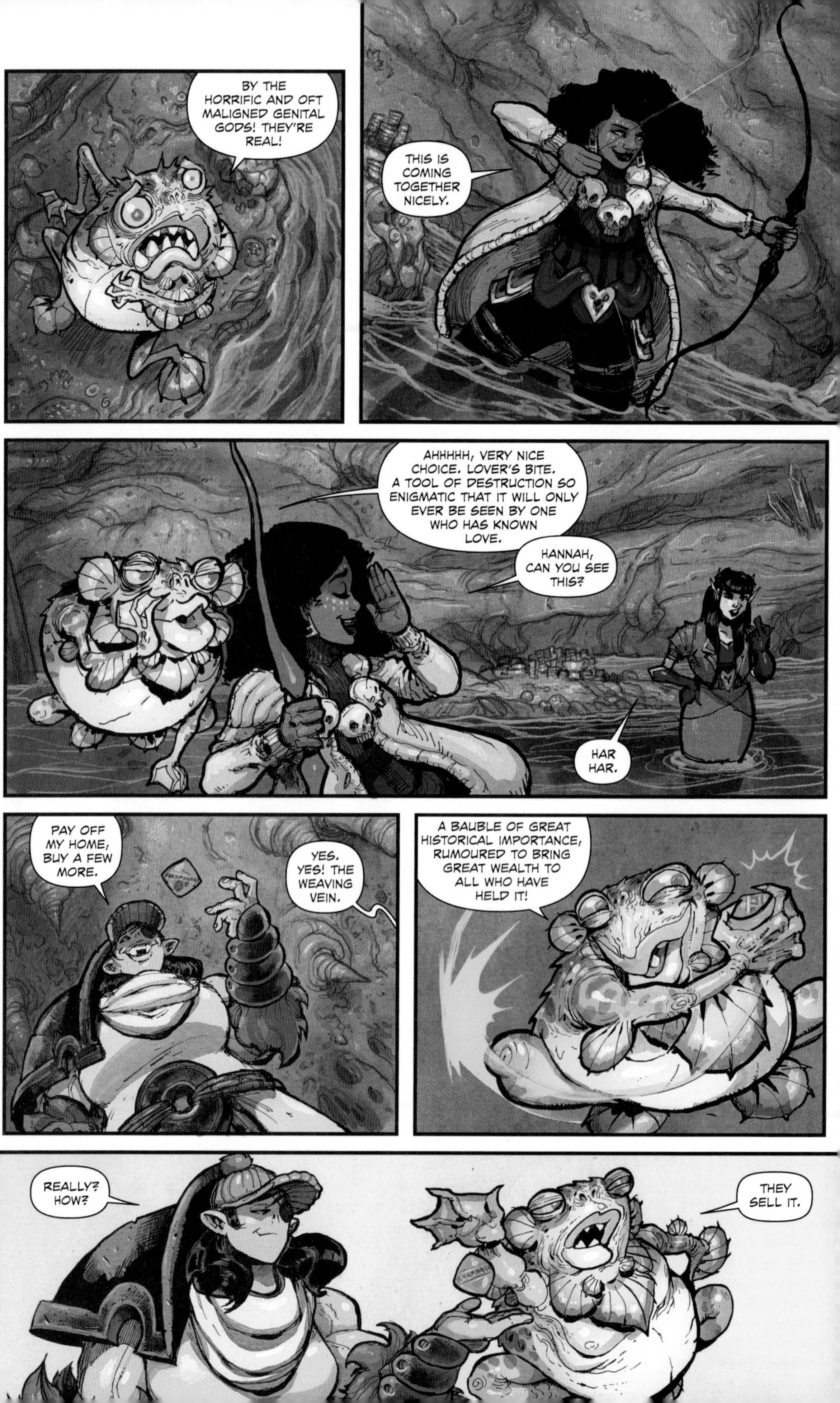
BY THE HORRIFIC AND OFT MALIGNED GENITAL GODS! THEY'RE REAL!
THIS IS COMING TOGETHER NICELY.
AHHHHH, VERY NICE CHOICE. LOVER'S BITE. A TOOL OF DESTRUCTION SO ENIGMATIC THAT IT WILL ONLY EVER BE SEEN BY ONE WHO HAS KNOWN LOVE.
HANNAH, CAN YOU SEE THIS?
HAR HAR.
PAY OFF MY HOME, BUY A FEW MORE.
YES. YES! THE WEAVING VEIN.
A BAUBLE OF GREAT HISTORICAL IMPORTANCE, RUMOURED TO BRING GREAT WEALTH TO ALL WHO HAVE HELD IT!
REALLY? HOW?
THEY SELL IT.

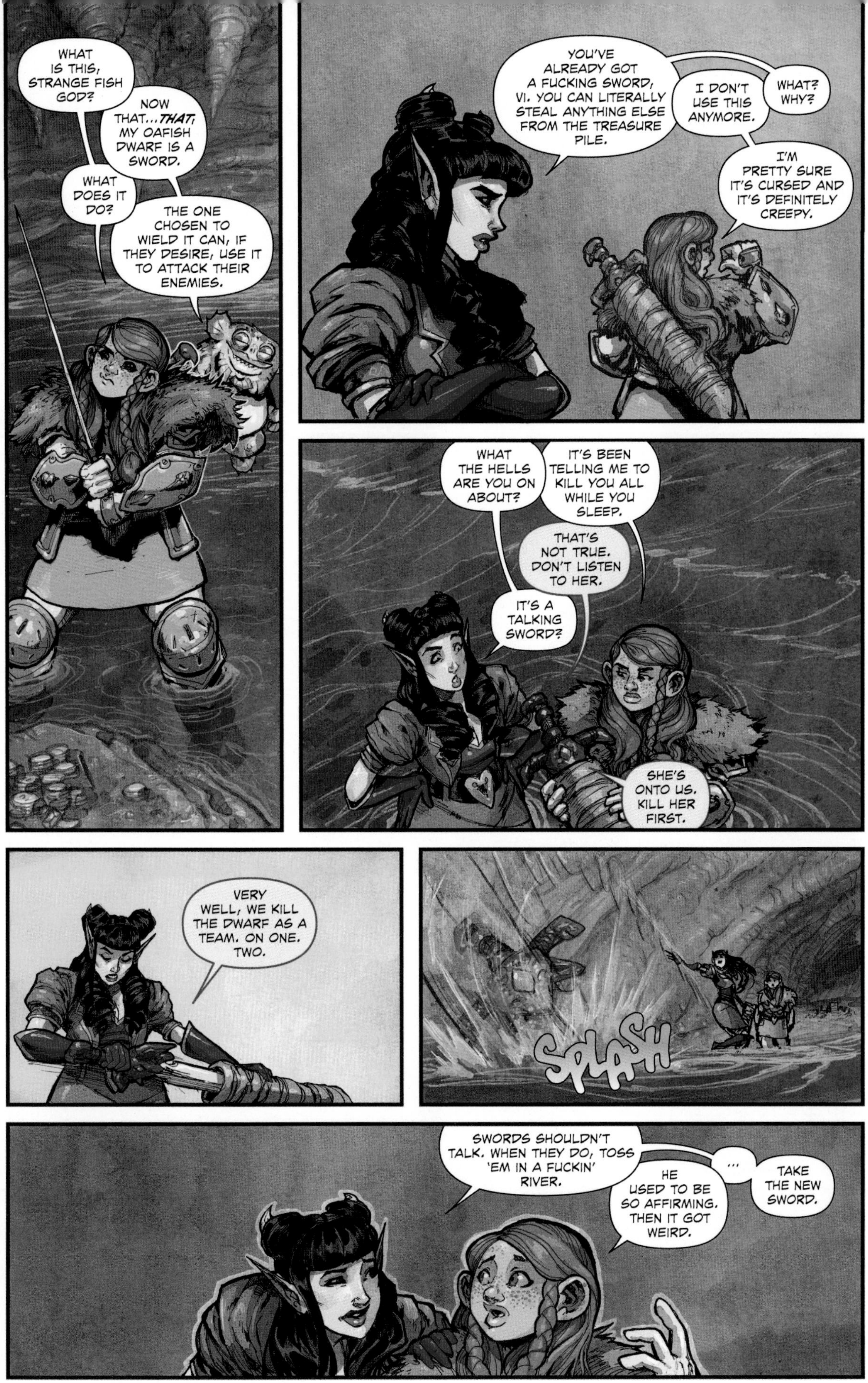
WHAT IS THIS, STRANGE FISH GOD?
NOW THAT... *THAT*, MY OAFISH DWARF IS A SWORD.
WHAT DOES IT DO?
THE ONE CHOSEN TO WIELD IT CAN, IF THEY DESIRE, USE IT TO ATTACK THEIR ENEMIES.
YOU'VE ALREADY GOT A FUCKING SWORD, VI. YOU CAN LITERALLY STEAL ANYTHING ELSE FROM THE TREASURE PILE.
I DON'T USE THIS ANYMORE.
WHAT? WHY?
I'M PRETTY SURE IT'S CURSED AND IT'S DEFINITELY CREEPY.
WHAT THE HELLS ARE YOU ON ABOUT?
IT'S BEEN TELLING ME TO KILL YOU ALL WHILE YOU SLEEP.
THAT'S NOT TRUE. DON'T LISTEN TO HER.
IT'S A TALKING SWORD?
SHE'S ONTO US. KILL HER FIRST.
VERY WELL, WE KILL THE DWARF AS A TEAM. ON ONE. TWO.
SPLASH
SWORDS SHOULDN'T TALK. WHEN THEY DO, TOSS 'EM IN A FUCKIN' RIVER.
HE USED TO BE SO AFFIRMING. THEN IT GOT WEIRD.
...
TAKE THE NEW SWORD.

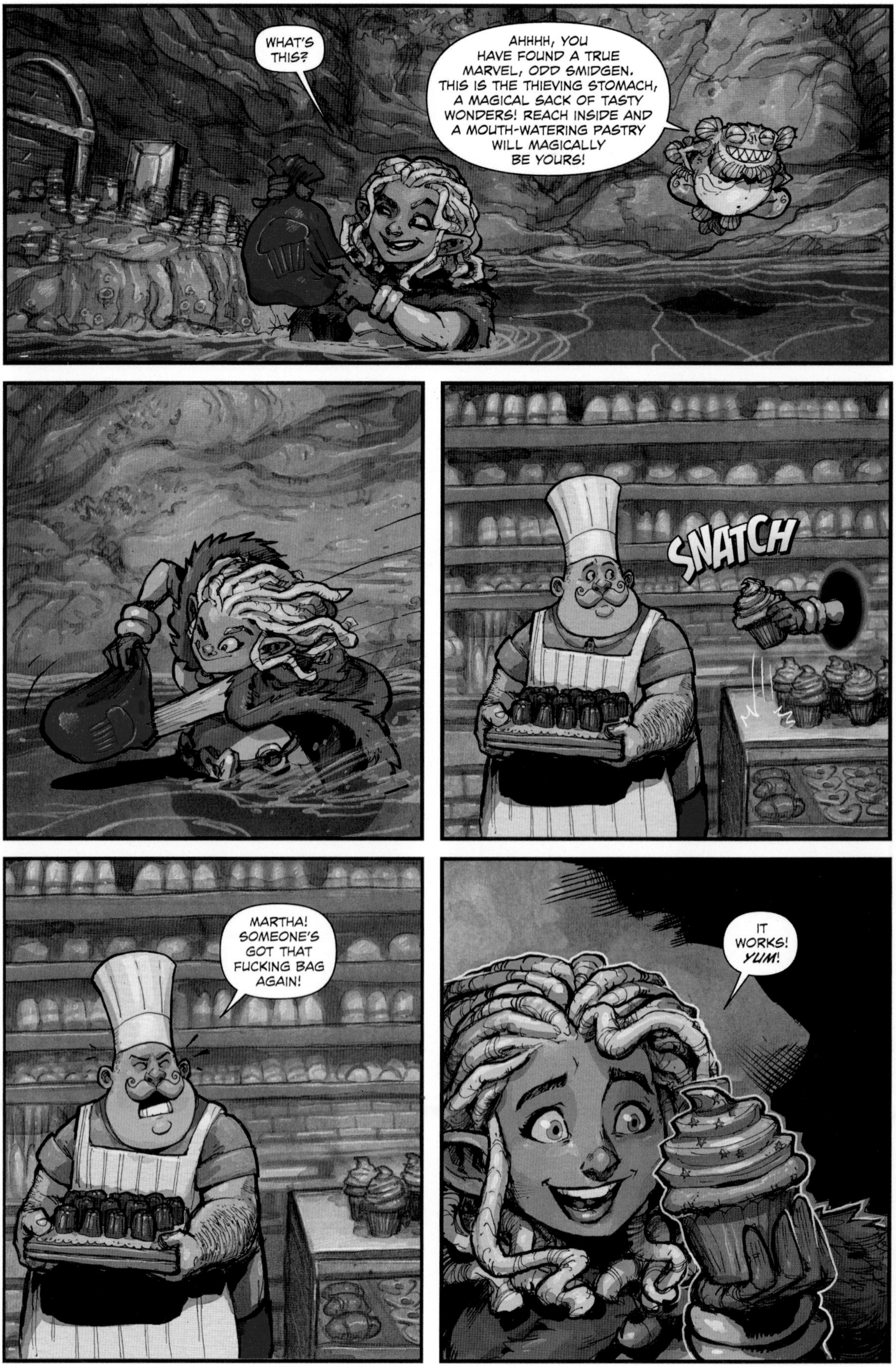
WHAT'S THIS?
AHHHH, YOU HAVE FOUND A TRUE MARVEL, ODD SMIDGEN. THIS IS THE THIEVING STOMACH, A MAGICAL SACK OF TASTY WONDERS! REACH INSIDE AND A MOUTH-WATERING PASTRY WILL MAGICALLY BE YOURS!
SNATCH
MARTHA! SOMEONE'S GOT THAT FUCKING BAG AGAIN!
IT WORKS! YUM!

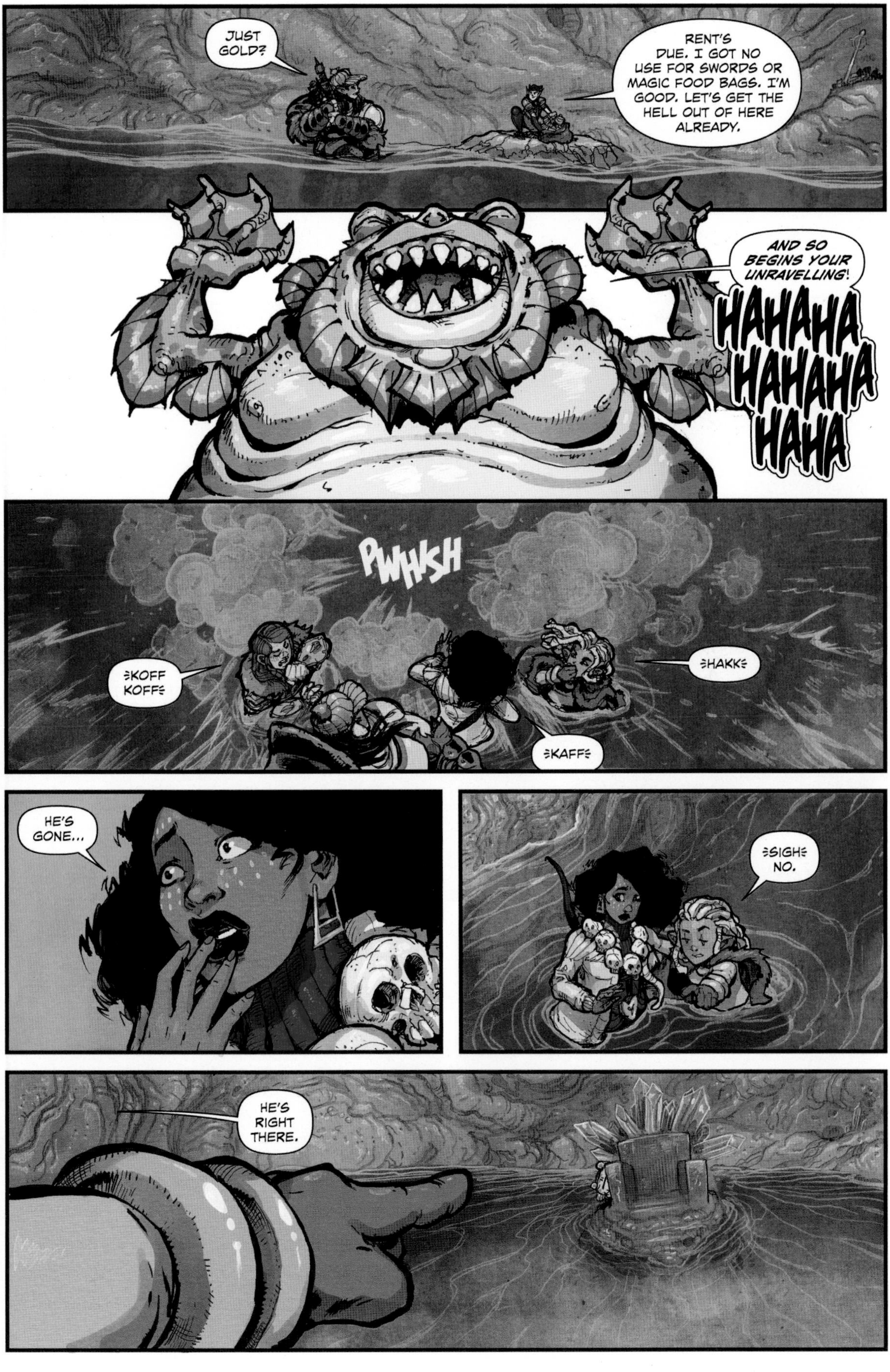
JUST GOLD?
RENT'S DUE. I GOT NO USE FOR SWORDS OR MAGIC FOOD BAGS. I'M GOOD. LET'S GET THE HELL OUT OF HERE ALREADY.
AND SO BEGINS YOUR UNRAVELLING!
HAHAHA HAHAHA HAHA
PWHSH
KOFF KOFF
HAKK
KAFF
HE'S GONE...
SIGH NO.
HE'S RIGHT THERE.

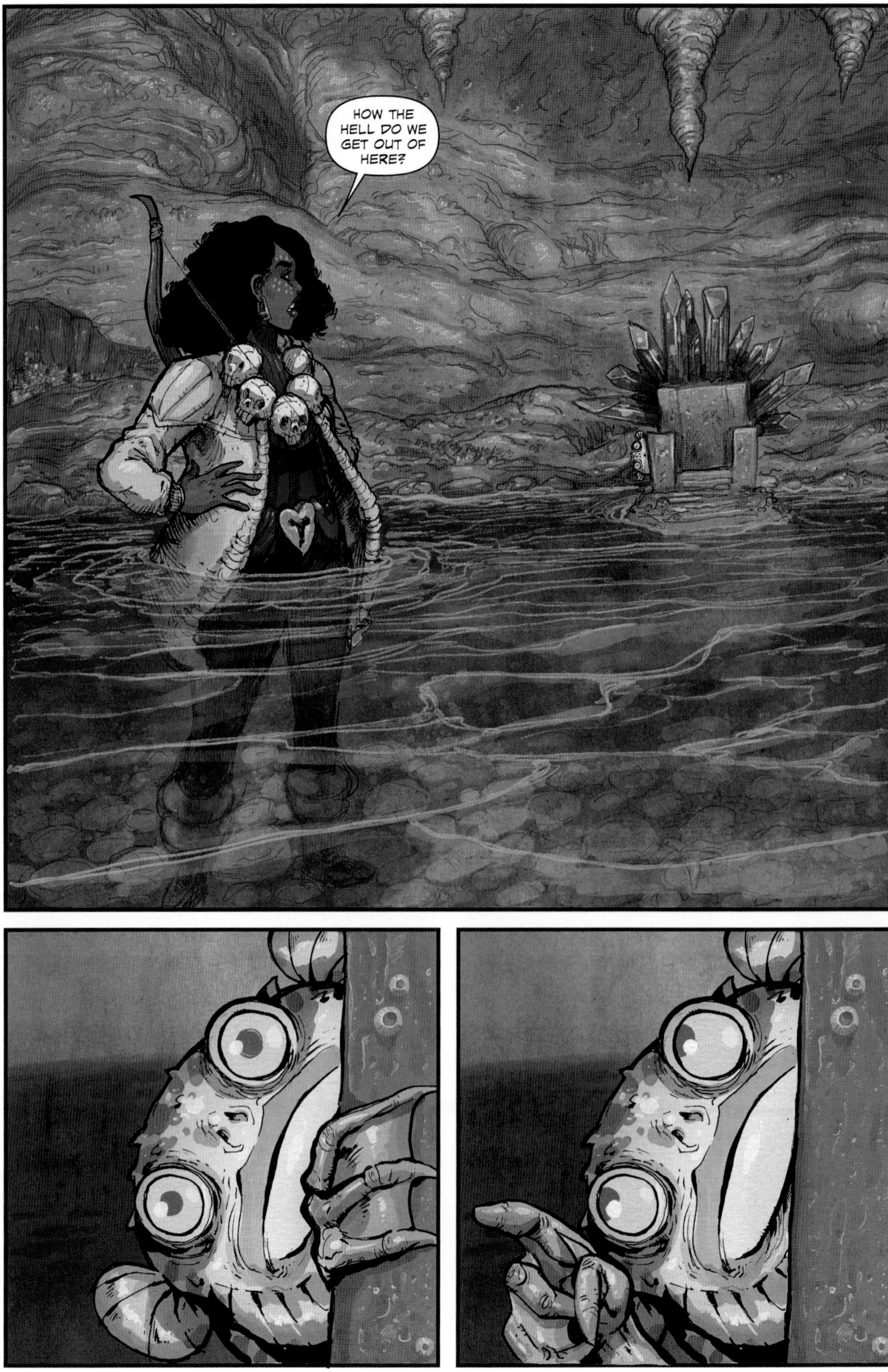
HOW THE HELL DO WE GET OUT OF HERE?

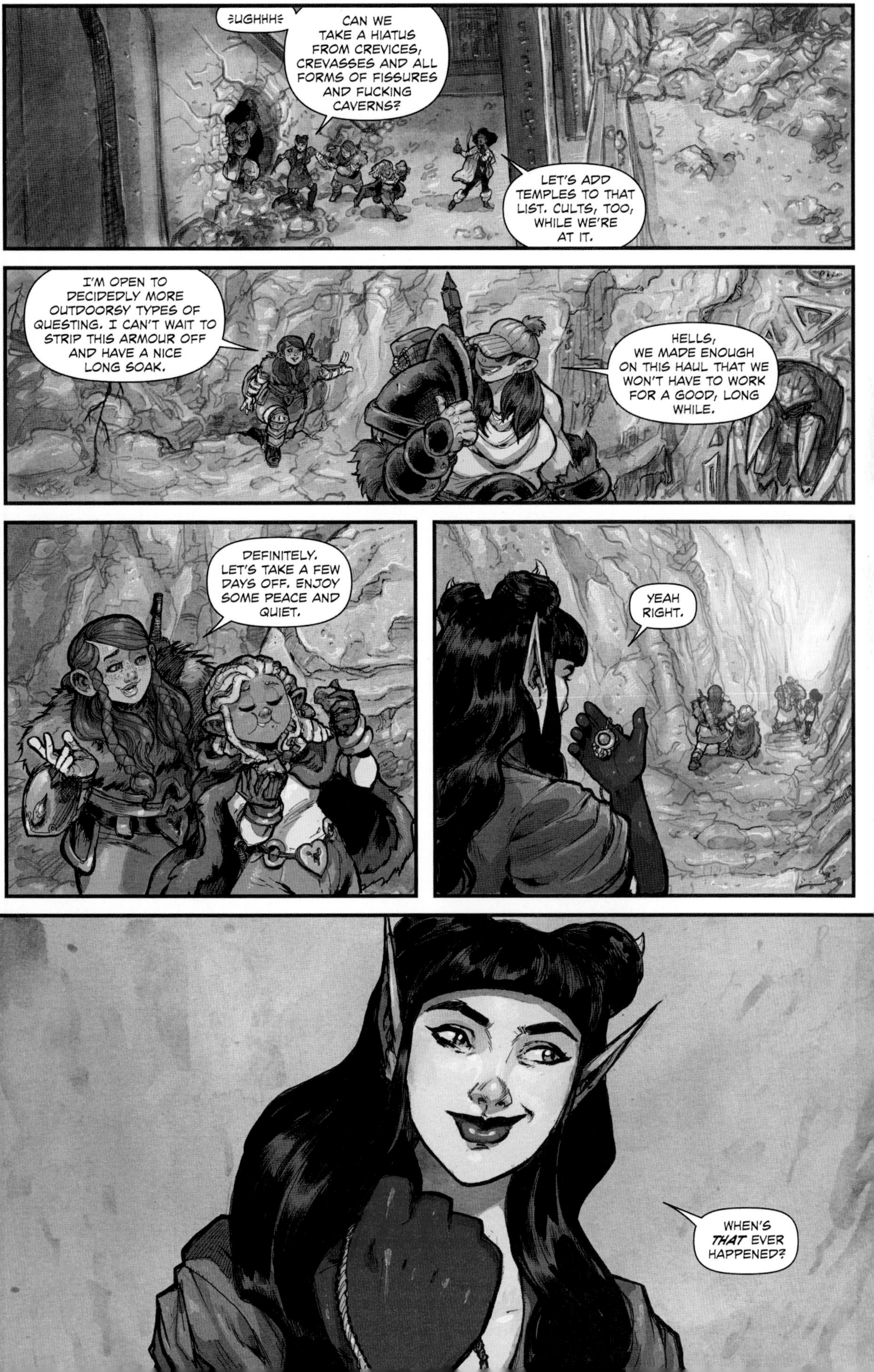

ƎUGHHHƎ
CAN WE TAKE A HIATUS FROM CREVICES, CREVASSES AND ALL FORMS OF FISSURES AND FUCKING CAVERNS?
LET'S ADD TEMPLES TO THAT LIST. CULTS, TOO, WHILE WE'RE AT IT.
I'M OPEN TO DECIDEDLY MORE OUTDOORSY TYPES OF QUESTING. I CAN'T WAIT TO STRIP THIS ARMOUR OFF AND HAVE A NICE LONG SOAK.
HELLS, WE MADE ENOUGH ON THIS HAUL THAT WE WON'T HAVE TO WORK FOR A GOOD, LONG WHILE.
DEFINITELY. LET'S TAKE A FEW DAYS OFF. ENJOY SOME PEACE AND QUIET.
YEAH RIGHT.
WHEN'S *THAT* EVER HAPPENED?

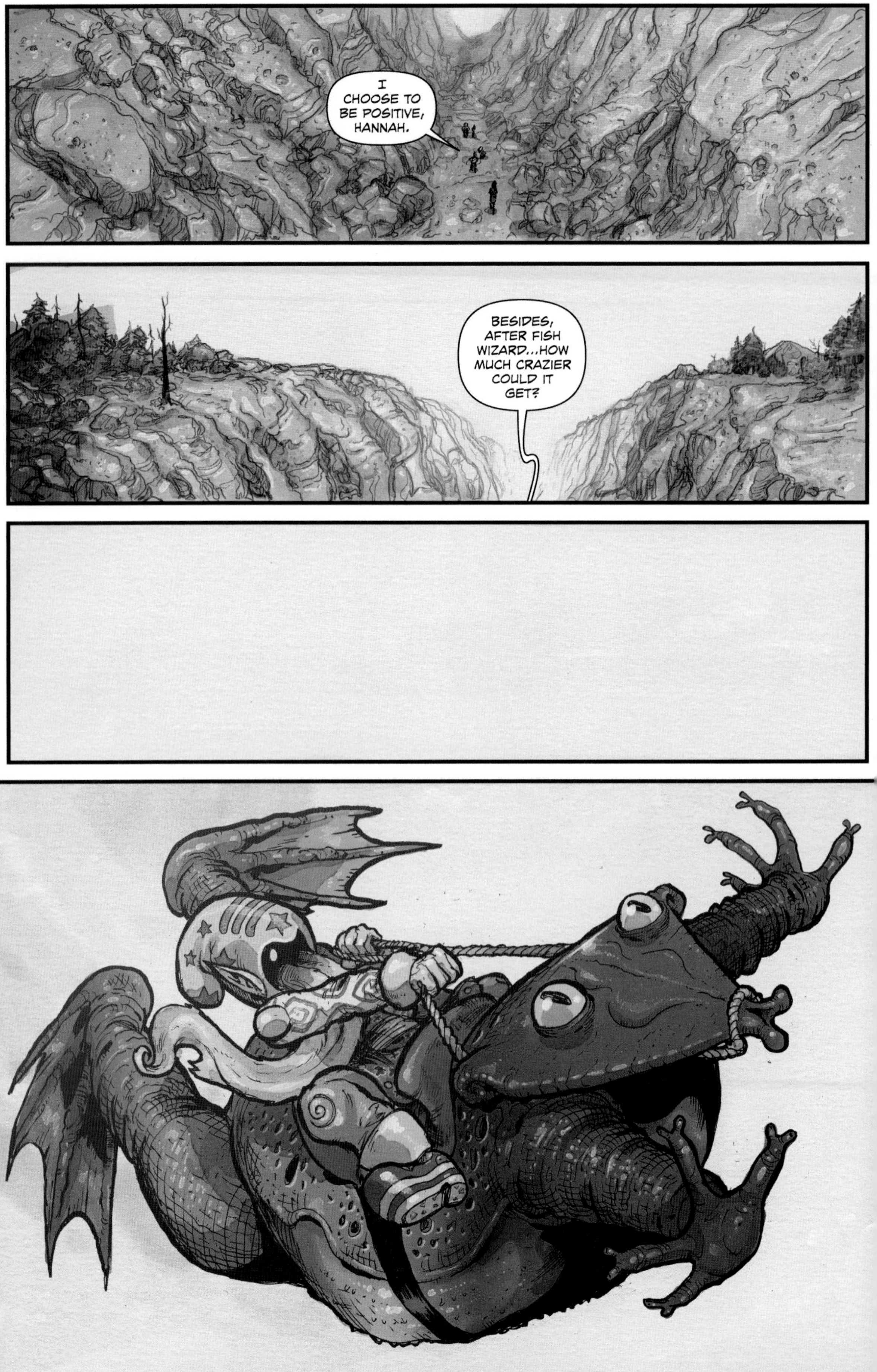
I CHOOSE TO BE POSITIVE, HANNAH.
BESIDES, AFTER FISH WIZARD...HOW MUCH CRAZIER COULD IT GET?

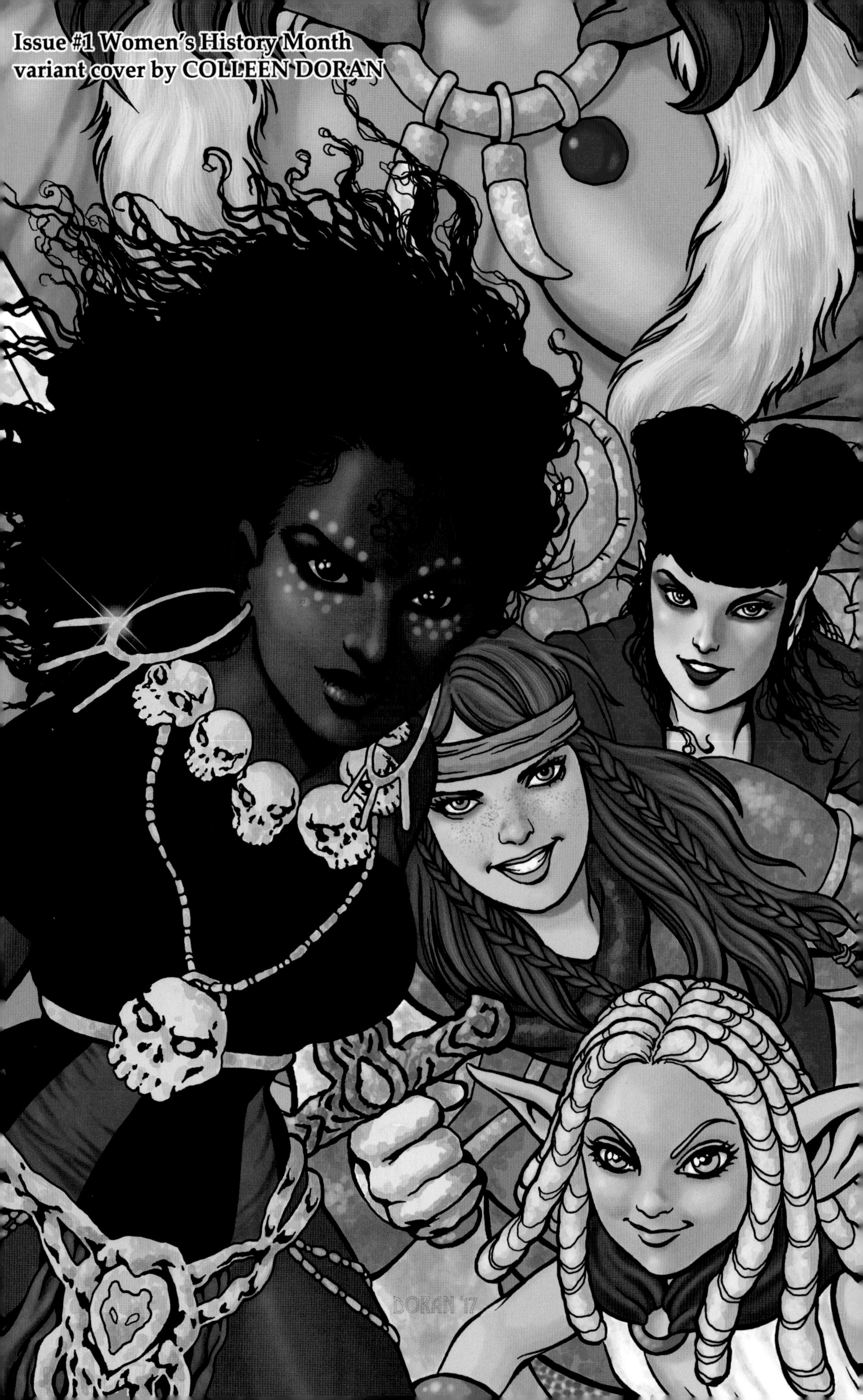
DORAN '17

Issue #1 Women's History Month
variant cover by COLLEEN DORAN

Issue #4 Images of Tomorrow variant cover
by JIM VALENTINO and CHANCE WOLF

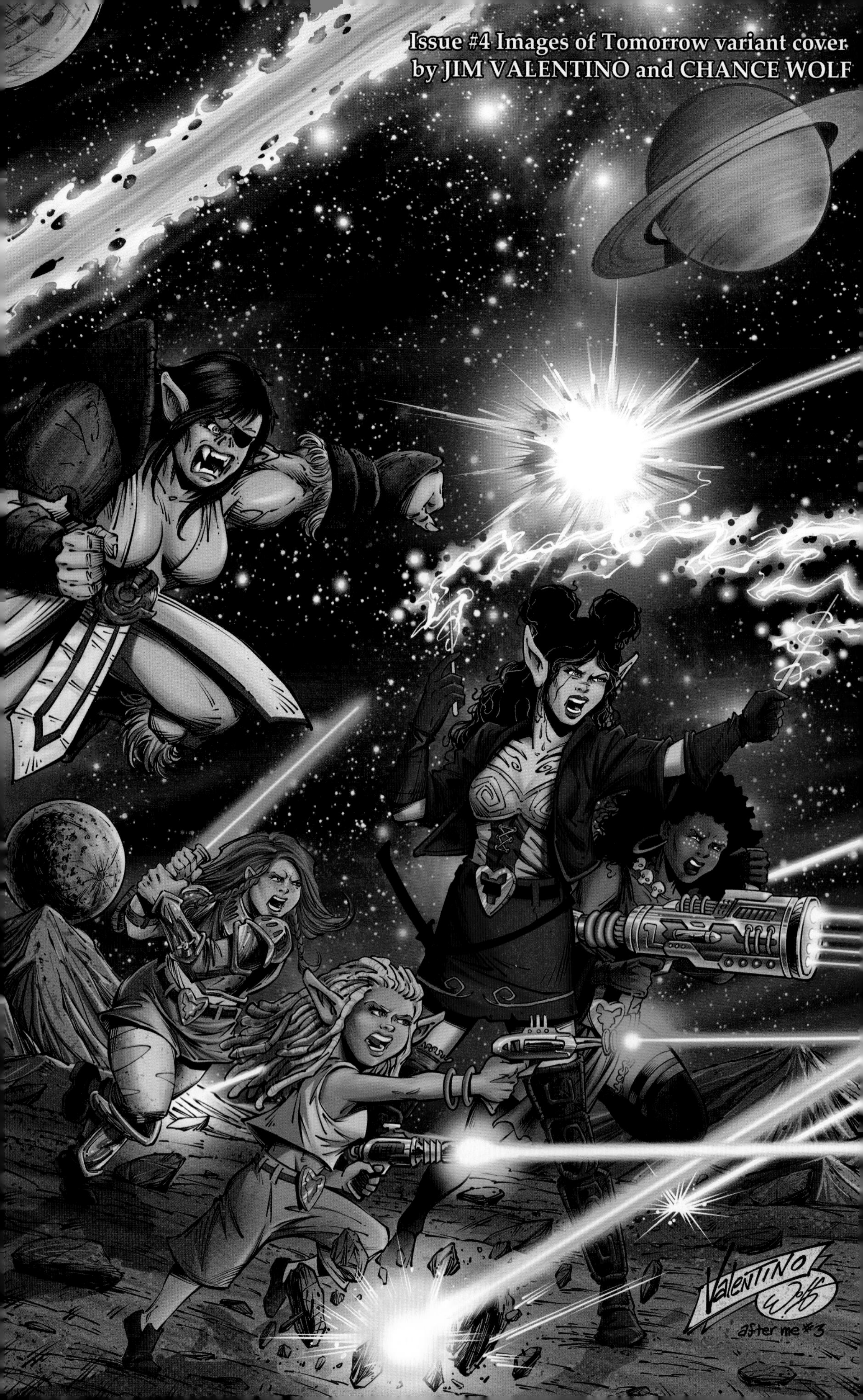
Valentino
after me #3

Issue # 5 cover/back cover C

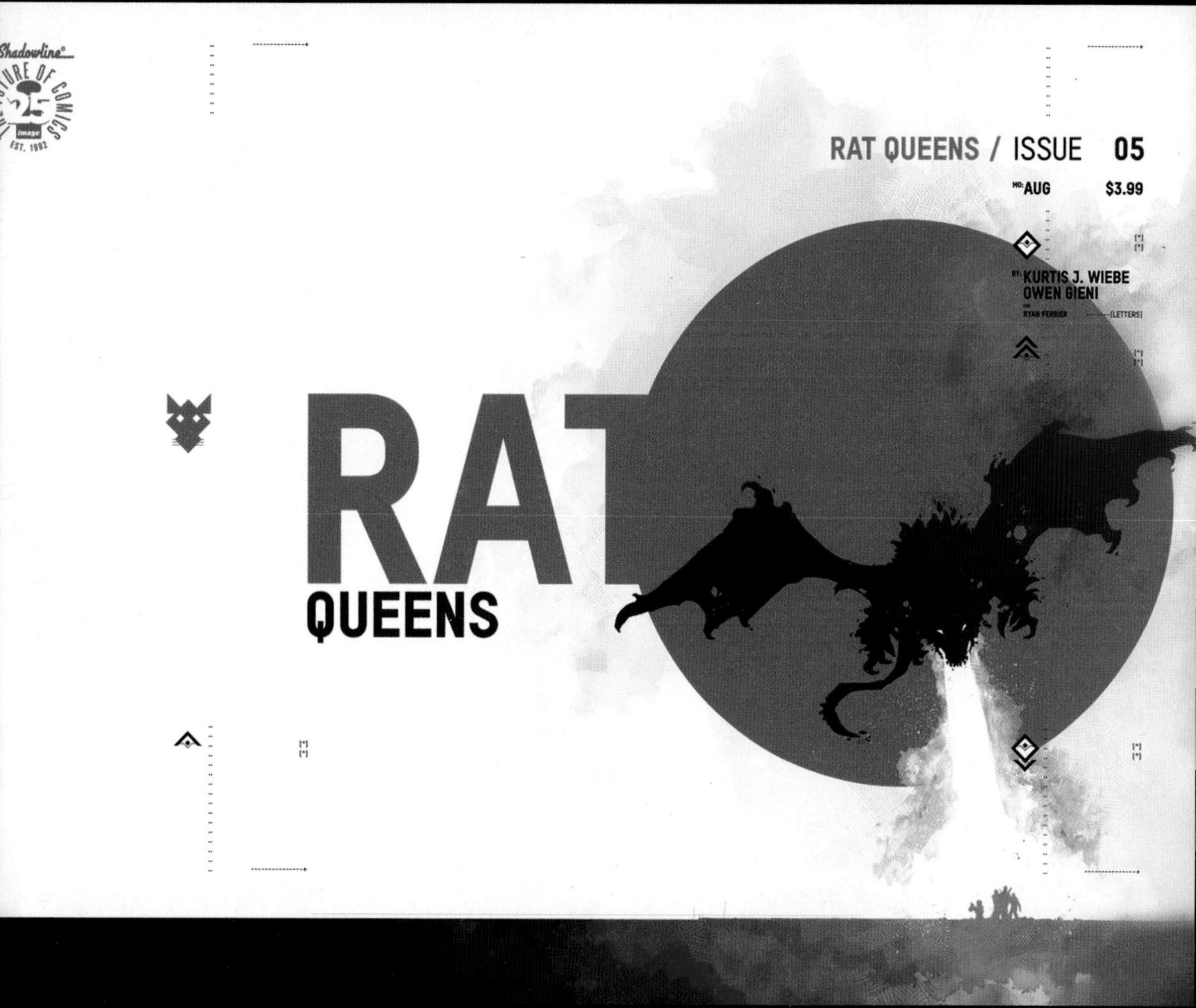
Shadowline
RAT QUEENS / ISSUE 05
AUG $3.99
KURTIS J. WIEBE
OWEN GIENI
RYAN FERRIER [LETTERS]
RAT
QUEENS

by JONATHAN HICKMAN

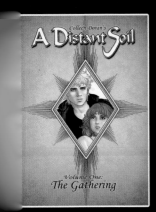

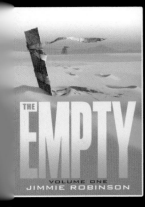